MOONL1T MERCURY
EVOLUT1ON OF SEOUL

LARA HAUGHTON

DEDICATION

To all those who doubted me… You were wrong.

QUICK THANK YOU!

I'd like to thank all the people who participated in helping my dreams come true. You all were more than amazing and I am extremely grateful for all the time, work and dedication you put into creating my first novel. I am looking forward to growing and succeeding with my Moonlit Mercury team! You all are the best!

Editor:
Andre Rios
Email for Business Inquires: PolarisAR@gmail.com

Front Cover Design:
Shawna Beck
Website: www.shawnabeck.com
Facebook: www.facebook.com/shawnabeckphotography
Instagram: @shawnabeckphoto

Back Cover/Graphic Designers:
Rachel Ellinor:
Facebook: www.facebook.com/rachel.ellinor

Tina Contreras
Facebook: www.facebook.com/tina.contreras.98

Contents

Acknowledgements i

BEST BEHAVIOR

The night was young and it was even colder than the night before. Outdoors, snow flooded the city of New York, creating thick white blankets over the streets and trees. The members of the Death Dealer Alliance Guild, also known as the DDAG, were readying themselves for an action-packed evening. Jason stood beside his best friend and comrade, Ariel, who kept a solemn expression on her pale face. She anticipated that night more than her fellow Death Dealers. She craved nothing more than having Alexander Cyclamen's head on a spike. The only thing glued in her mind was to rip off Cyclamen's flesh while his blood dripped in between her long fingers.

The assassins in Faction Divide were scattered all over the locker room in District North America's DDAG headquarters. They began to arm themselves with their choice of weaponry: some members enjoyed the adrenaline of a firearm: a glock, machine gun, semi-automatic rifle–whereas others preferred the silent approach of a crossbow or longsword. As for one solider, Ariel, she enjoyed the subtlety of a single dagger, which was given the name of Mercury, after its core element. An older man, who lived alone in the Outerwoods—the "forgotten" regions of the New World—took it upon himself to craft the dagger with the most lethal substance imaginable: moonlit mercury. It took more than a few months to craft, yet Ariel waited patiently for her request: it was worth it. The beautiful solid silver creation with an emerald quillion fit perfectly in her petite hand. Due to its lightness, Ariel could move so quickly and swiftly, her body never made a peep.

Each member of the DDAG wore the traditional uniform: they were covered in black from head to toe. They had the option of either a long sleeve or short sleeve cotton shirt, cargo pants with pockets designated to carry extra items—a flashlight and a 3-D map that included a compass—and combat boots. Occasionally, a Death Dealer would add a black cap or mouthpiece.

With confidence, Jason looked over his guild proudly with his wide and alert, light-brown eyes. The night always began with the captain of the guild pumping his troops by asking, "Are we ready to serve justice?" to which they all shouted, "Yes sir!" proudly in unison. Even on cold and gloomy nights, the Death Dealers were ready to complete their quest for the DDAG and rid the New World of the evil lurking about—one terrorist at a time. Finally, Captain Jason Lilly ordered the guild to move out. A dozen men and women hurried to their feet and hustled outside. There were two white vans parked out front. The Death Dealers split themselves up, jumped inside and drove away to the mission site.

Approximately ten minutes later, they reached the destination but parked a mile away from the target location. The assassins dismounted from the vehicles and skulked along the ghost streets. None of them spoke. They moved quietly and kept an eye out for anything suspicious.

The streets were lifeless. Only streetlamps had some soul left in their jagged poles that dimly lit the ground beneath them. Moss devoured Earth's antiques and random sprigs of grass and weeds were gaining height above the cracked pavements.

Five centuries ago, the world was filled with more than seven billion people. However, Earth—as it was once called—was dying: pollution, destruction of nature, widespread diseases, animal slaughters, and so many other significant events were killing Earth and all the gifts Mother Nature bared.

Now, only 200 million people remained and most animals are extinct. Due to fewer destructive humans, slowly Mother Nature had been reclaiming her throne in a New World. Some countries, like Malaysia, had come alive again in layers of green: trees, vines, grass, leaves, flowers….Whereas in Iceland, water had risen and consumed every ounce of its island country. Water levels drowned everything within the span of a century. Events similar to these, and some more tragic, took over what was once people's homes, forcing them out of the comfort of their country and having to move to different regions of the world.

Ariel's natural violet eyes glistened in the bright light of the full moon and her velvet red hair danced lightly on her back as she sashayed. The beautiful Death Dealer loved snow. It brought back fond memories of her childhood. Each time the world was covered in white, her delicate mouth would curve in happiness.

Jason investigated the darkness, being cautious of the silence around him.

"Wait," Captain Lilly whispered to his league of assassins. They halted.

Up ahead, trees created a pathway to an abandoned ballroom, once called the Golden Throne Room. Maybe it was gorgeous once, but ever since the rise of the Black Plague II Infections, it was just another abandoned object and a hideout for mobsters. Unfortunately, this was common for vacant buildings in the New World. The architecture of the property resembled the French style of Paris during the 1950's B.P. (Before Plague). Each twelve-foot section had a panel of windows with random tiles broken and others boarded up. Surprisingly, the electricity remained strong. To the east, an empty balcony with one table and two rusted chairs was engrossed in a thick fog from the heavy snow.

Jason listened closely for any murmurs within the empty vacant point. He turned around, looking back at his guild. With both arms stretched out and his hands up, he bent his elbows in. Like a colony of hungry bats, the Death Dealers flew into the pine trees that paved the way to the tired old building, landing on the strong branches and hiding themselves in between the long pine needles.

Ariel tapped Jason on the shoulder. "There is a possible entrance to the west. Part of the roof is broken," she whispered.

Jason grabbed his infrared binoculars from his pouch and examined the possibility. In the north part of the building was the dance hall, and there sat Alexander Cyclamen himself, along with his gang of sick and twisted merry men. They were drinking and gambling the night away while the rest of humanity locked themselves in their homes, fearing the night, for it had become an enemy.

Jason counted three lookouts: the first was a yawning fat man guarding the back exit. A tall, thin man was smoking a cigarette at the entryway and the third teetered his way to the balcony like an untalented dancing piece of spaghetti. He sat himself down, plopped his long feet on top of the table, and cheerfully sang to himself.

"Looks like his security is short; there's one at the entrance, one at the exit, then there's a drunkard at the balcony. Easy enough." Jason returned his binoculars to his pouch. "We enter through the roof. Move out."

The Death Dealers sprung themselves from the branches, flew through the cold air, light as feathers, and quietly landed on their feet on the rooftop. They cat-walked across, gliding on their toes, making their way inside a conference room.

Inside was not much warmer. The snow crept its way indoors, hugging every worn-out piece of furniture. The entire room was full of debris and had the scent of piss.

Ariel noticed a fireplace behind her with a golden vine design framing it. She placed the face of her palm on top of the mantle and gently caressed her hand straight across. Historical architecture amused her. More like, she had an obsession with it. There were so many different styles, colors, materials and unknown histories within each building design. If walls could speak, she'd ask them to tell her their history and share stories about the people who walked in and out of the rooms. Ariel's mind began to contemplate how many people had possibly stood in front of that fireplace throughout its existence, carrying either a delightful or sorrowful conversation. Hundreds? Thousands? A million, maybe? What stories were exchanged over a lit fireplace?

"Let's move," Jason commanded.

Ariel marched up to her captain. "Alexander is mine." She about-faced to dart away. Despite her tiny figure, she was the fastest assassin of her guild and unbelievably strong, especially after taking Vitality: a magic pill with the intention to level up a Death Dealer's strength, speed, and excogitation. It was also known as the adrenaline pill.

Jason gripped Ariel's arm, refusing her demand. "No," he made clear. "You will stick with me and the others. Do you understand?"

Ariel rolled her eyes, annoyed at his authority. Desperately, she wanted to escape from his grasp. She fought to retrieve her arm back but this led Jason to tug her harder, bringing her close. "When we catch Alexander, I promise he's yours. Do what you will with him."

Ariel looked away. She hated negotiating.

"Look at me," Jason hissed. Ariel grunted, forcing herself to obey. "Until then, do not disappear from the group to try to find Cyclamen by yourself. I'm going to ask you again: Do you understand?" She wanted to leave. Turn invisible and do as she pleased. However, she had to comply with his demands. No question about it. Finally, she nodded. "Good," Jason said, satisfied. "Follow the team."

Son of a bitch! Ariel cursed to herself. She never tolerated orders. Jason often admonished her for her rebellious mischief, warning her to be careful, yet she never listened. There were too many expectations that came with being an assassin for the DDAG. With regret, Ariel knew what had to be done. Sergeant Kurtis Lotus of Faction Divide had not been fond of Ariel for quite some time. Being on her best behavior was vital to getting back under his good graces—her career as an official Death Dealer depended on it.

Lotus disliked the brashness of Ariel's character. Taking orders was a flaw, yet speaking without thinking and doing without thinking were—what she called—her strong points.

At the DDAG headquarters, many cases submitted were auto-denied. Ariel found this to be unfair. Whole-heartedly, she believed in justice and fending for the weak. Countlessly, she'd sneak her way into the DDAG's system to steal confidential files. As she read over them, she'd pick cases with solid evidence and take on side missions without consent from Jason, her sergeant, the king and queen of the New World, and even the royal cabinet.

Lotus caught Ariel during her last rebel. If it weren't for Jason's strong defense, possibly Ariel would've been removed of all titles; worse, there would've been immediate discharge from all affiliations within the Death Dealer Alliance Guild.

Ariel must behave. Otherwise, she'd have to say bye-bye to the DDAG.

"Zaire," Jason called out.

"Sir?" he answered.

"Get the man at the exit. Seraphina?" Jason's second-in-command. She remained at first position: attention. She stood tall, fists closed, and her eyes met with those of her superior. "Your target is at the entrance. Make it quick and effortless." She bowed at the waist, then blended in with the darkness. "Bodhi?"

"Already on it," he assured. He stormed ahead, never looking back.

Seraphina moved in the dark gracefully as though she were born in it. She kept close to the wall, feeling every crevice against her lean back. With her head held high, she kept focused and aware. The brown in her eyes was so dark, they almost blended in with the night. The color was so rich, most people confused them with black, like the ebony of her long and perfectly straight hair.

As Seraphina grew closer to her target, sounds of him inhaling a cigarette echoed down the hallway. Remembering the files she read last night, she realized who she was gazing upon: Jude, commonly known as Jay in the streets. One of many men in Alexander's gang.

"There are so many reasons why I shouldn't be the lookout, Alexander." Seraphina watched carefully in the shadows as Jay went on to tell a pathetic tale of heated heartache. "No. You just do what I tell you!" he mocked loudly, whirling his hands around. "I should have told him, 'Fuck you, you ugly, scarred, overly-tanned motherfucker!'" He threw a middle finger up in the air and snorted to himself. "Yeah, right. Then my ass would've gotten shot or I would've been chopped up into a million pieces."

Seraphina took a gander at the front desk. Soundlessly, she slid her way behind the counter.

There was a soft *crash* that grabbed Jay's attention. "Hello?" he called out. No one answered except the repeated echo of his dry voice. He whipped out another cigarette. With pure talent, a match was lit in between his thumb and pointer-finger. *Puff. Puff.* He twirled it around until the flame turned into smoke, then tossed it aside.

"Whatever," Jay groaned. He shut his eyes and began rubbing his scrunched forehead. *Great, here comes another headache*, he thought.

CRASH!

"What the fuck?" Jay squealed.

It sounded like a chair being thrown across the room.

"Who's there?" Jay's muscles tightened. Quickly, he took out his handgun from his blazer and spun on his heels, preparing himself to shoot at what was lurking about. For a moment, he froze his frigid lanky body, listening for any peculiar sounds. He put out his cigarette by grinding it under his oxford shoe.

There was no one to be seen, however, a sixth-sense told Jay he was not alone. He decided to search the area thoroughly. Maybe an alley cat had found its way inside. Still, something was off. He wanted to lure whatever IT was, out.

"I know someone's here," Jay yelled. "Don't think I won't shoot ya!" He moved cautiously, keeping light on his toes. He searched around broken crates. Nothing. Underneath a coffee table. Nothing. The hallway, key room, a random closet. Nothing.

"Shit," Jay muttered. "I guess I am hearing things." He returned the gun to its holster and walked back to his original post.

"If only I could see things. Like a woman with huge tits wanting my nuts," Jay laughed. His imagination inclined to a robust ginger kneeling to him, and she had a firm ass and pouty lips. "Even if it were a ghost, I'd be okay with that. Of course, it'd be better if it were a real woman." His penis hardened. "Hmph…," he groaned, adjusting himself. "I need to get laid." He reached for his cigarette box, ready to light another.

"How about you get slaughtered by a woman, instead?" Seraphina whispered in Jay's ear.

Seraphina's warm breath and surprise visit made the hair on Jay's neck stand up. Before he could react, Seraphina already had her hand cuffing his balls. She squeezed them tight, turning his peach complexion to a reddish-orange. The pain was so tremendous, it was impossible to move, let alone think. He was frightened and frozen in her grasp. The fiercer she gripped, the more his breath shortened.

Seraphina pulled out a longsword behind her. The metal sounded so clean as it slid out of its scabbard. She dug her nails deep into his scrotum, yearning for him to bleed.

With its sharp tip, Seraphina placed the longsword under his ear. *No!* Jay thought. *Fuck this!* He lunged back, hoping to pry himself away from Seraphina.

"Oh, no, you don't," Seraphina chuckled. With one clean swipe, the edge of the sword slit its way across his rugged throat. Seraphina held Jay's forehead back as soon his body began to jitter. He gurgled out pints of blood and it flowed down like a rapid waterfall. The wet red paint covered his chest, his ribs, then made its way down to Seraphina's petite fingers, covering them like a warm liquid glove.

Seraphina enjoyed the way Jay's body spasmed against her chest. It meant his life would soon end. She grabbed Jay's hair, pulled his head all the way back and with great power, she raised her sword high then swung it straight down.

HI-YAH!!! A slice later, Jay's head detached from his body. Seraphina released his bottom half, allowing it to plummet messily on the floor.

Seraphina's face was covered in Jay's blood like war paint. She embraced her kill as she brought his head up to meet her gaze. "Strange," she snickered. "You were actually cute." She dropped his head like a sack of potatoes, placed her foot on his cheek, then kicked it across the room.

A red river streamed over the floor and the bottom of Seraphina's boots. She walked over to the headless body and decided it was time for cleanup. Seraphina removed the bloodstains from her longsword on each side, using Jay's blazer as a cloth. Proudly, she smiled as most of the enemy's red ooze disappeared. "Clean-up. Not bad."

Meanwhile, Zaire was on the prowl. He bolted his way to the exit door but moved quietly, allowing nothing to get in his way. His wavy, medium-length hair floated behind him in midair. He was moving so fast, he hadn't noticed he arrived in a chapel—possibly once meant for weddings or special ceremonies. He observed the area while putting on fingerless gloves, originally placed in his back pocket for easy access.

Angel statues decorated the altar but they were mostly broken. One of them had their wings chopped off and another had only a single eye. Staring upon child-like statues made Zaire feel uncomfortable. He felt as though they were trying to invade his soul: capture the innocence he had left. He didn't stare at them for long. He only glanced over, then continued to pass on by.

Suddenly, a cold wind crept its way inside, making Zaire shiver, but then he heard a deep voice mumbling from behind the walls.

Zaire snuck over to one of the windows, keeping low. When he peeked over, a fat man named Todd was moronically badgering at his cell phone. Apparently, he was angry at it for not having signal. Zaire had to get outside. But how? He looked up. *Bingo!* Then quickly, formulated a plan.

"I hate coming over here, man," Todd whined. "I get no fucking service!" In between his chubby palms, he slammed it continuously, certain this would bang it back into shape. "Come on, you stupid piece of shit!"

Boom! The sound was coming from the parking lot. "Huh?" Todd wobbled his way to the corner of the building. A pack of crows fluttered and cawed overhead, making him flinch and jump around. Shimmering black feathers landed on his sweaty bald head. He brushed the feathers off him, practically fighting with himself. "I thought crows were extinct. You oughtta be. Worthless animals!"

Todd felt a vibration under his overgrown hand. It was a text notification. Surprisingly, he managed to find decent reception. Joy smeared his soggy face. His spirit lifted. "Hell yes!" he rejoiced. "Now, I won't be so damn bored."

A whistle came from above. *Whoo-whoo-wooy-whoo-whoo.*

Todd shot up. "What the fuck?"

Zaire was perched on the frame of a broken window. Quickly, he leaped and glided down, piercing through the air like a golden eagle anticipating its prey.

In seconds, Zaire's forequarters stomped on top of Todd's shoulders, pinning both of them to the wet, cold cement. The impact sent Todd's phone flying across the pavement to lose itself in a hill of snow.

Zaire erected himself from the ground. At turbo speed, he returned on top of Todd, forcing all of his weight on him. He bent his knees and plunged them deep into Todd's ribs. Not only was this painful, it burned. Zaire's hands hugged around the fat man's neck. Todd would have screamed if he could, but he was losing air. Todd squirmed like a helpless child, determined to get the ponytail man off him: he kicked and smacked Jay's arms but not once did the assassin flinch.

All Zaire needed was a second to knock Todd out. To the left was a broken cement block. Immediately, he gravitated toward it, picked it up, and jabbed it hard on the side of Todd's face, knocking him unconscious.

As the bald man was temporarily dead, Zaire stood up and placed his feet on either side of his neck. He reached over his shoulder and took out his lucky crossbow. With one eye shut, he aimed the weapon behind Todd's thick head. As he pulled the string back, he took a short breath, then pulled the trigger. The steel-pointed arrow slayed its way behind Todd's head and connected to his right eye.

After a sneer, Zaire flipped the fresh corpse around. Suddenly, he noticed some markings across the terrorist's chest. Zaire lowered Todd's green shirt and noticed it was a beautiful portrait tattoo of a little girl with curly hair. His daughter, maybe? For a moment, he wondered if he had just ended the life of a father. He too had a baby girl, named Reese. A daughter does not deserve a life without a father. However, it was times like these he had to remind himself it was all part of the job. The DDAG does not tolerate the New World's enemies, even if he or she were to have a family.

Bodhi sat back for a while and viewed the drunken man, Derek, from a distance. He continued singing to himself after finishing a cheap bottle of liquor. The song was personally written by Derek, it seemed. The verses were unorthodox with no rhythm. A beautiful woman named Patty—who apparently aroused him very much—was consistently mentioned. This mysterious "Patty" lacked interest. Because of this, Derek sang about not only raping her but killing her.

Bodhi took into account, the lights that flickered in the room and he knew this could be an advantage. The room itself was small and tough to navigate, but Bodhi blended in by scrunching his body into any tight and darkened area.

Derek walked over to the railing of the balcony, pulled out his wanker and took a long piss. He snorted, "You like that, Patty? You beautiful bitch."

Who is Patty? Bodhi wondered. *Why is she so important to him?* He hoped that whomever she was, she was safe.

"I can't wait to see that cunt again," Derek laughed. "That girl don't know what's about to hit her." He grabbed his machine gun without realizing his small penis still flopped outside his grey trousers.

Once Derek stepped foot back inside the room, there was a *woosh!* Suddenly, Derek's eyes became severely irritated. He clawed at his face, hoping to scratch the burning itch away. It felt like a pile of hot sand had blown right into his corneas.

"What the hell?!" Derek screamed, still pawing away. "Why? What?" he screeched, slurring his words. "Fuck! I…I can't see!" He trembled his way over to a footstool that got in his way. *Oomph!* He tripped and his machine gun made a getaway. "Shit!" He outstretched his hands on top of the dirty carpet, hoping to feel his way around the room to retrieve his weapon back. He felt pieces of wood—that could easily blister his rough fingers—and sheets of dirty old paper with meaningless nonsense printed on them. Goosebumps dotted his arms. "What is happening?" he asked himself with raging tears falling from his sockets. "I can't see!"

"Can you see me now?!" Bodhi menaced. He hovered over Derek wearing a white barakoa mask called Fantasia. It created any image a Death Dealer wanted to bestow upon their victim once magical dust (Elixia) made its way inside their body.

Derek had been drugged; Bodhi's game began.

Derek squinted up at the masked figure. "Patty?" He did a double-blink. His vision may have been blurry but he could recognize the woman of his dreams—tall, blonde hair and green eyes—anytime, anywhere.

Derek—still glued to the floor—drooled over the wonderment, dressed in racy white lingerie that adorned her curvy body and matching stockings holstered her thick legs while red pumps hugged her feet. Patty squeezed her voluptuous breasts as she curled her plump lips. *Mmm…,* she moaned. "I always knew you wanted me."

Derek was insanely titillated. "That's all I ever wanted, baby. I can't believe you're actually here," he squealed as his dick hardened.

Patty gave Derek a winsome smile. She pulled up a chair and asked him to sit. Patty kept an eye on him as her straps delicately dropped from her shoulders. Sweet nothings escaped her lips as she lap-danced all over his happy place. She thrust her body forward, shoving her pushed-up breasts in Derek's wretched face. Happily, he buried himself in between them, stretching his tongue down to her nipples. He couldn't get enough. She was everything he ever wanted. The alcohol and Elixia ran wild within him. It rewarded him with courage and a delusion to approvingly frisk her. He wanted to bend her over the nearest table and shove himself inside her wet pussy.

Derek was about to frisk his way underneath Patty's corset until she randomly spun away. "Where the fuck are you going?" he barked.

"Just wait," Patty gushed. She skipped over to a drawer.

"Get the hell back here!" Derek demanded, squeezing his hard cock.

"Coming," Patty sang. She strode back with both hands behind her back as her hips swayed gracefully. Derek was anxious for the next scene in this surreal moment. A million fantasies flooded his mind. She stopped to examine Derek closely.

Derek's hormones raged and he could no longer wait to eat her juicy snatch and fuck the shit out of her.

Derek sprinted for a kiss. He was so close to her, he could already taste her peach lip gloss.

However, something cock-blocked him. A sudden pain radiated from Derek's gut.

Uh...uh..., Derek quivered. He nervously looked down. *Aaahhh!!!* A knife was plunged straight through him.

Patty sparked with delight. She pulled him closer, jabbing the blunt knife deeper and deeper until she could feel the metal sawing his skeleton. Gently, she massaged her fingers through his messy hair. She cuddled up next to his ear and softly she asked, "Do you want me now?" Her mouth watered at the sound of Derek dying. She licked the side of his face.

Ugh!!! Derek cried. He tried to pull out the blade, but Patty was unexpectedly stronger than him. Eventually, blood gushed out of his mouth like raging vomit. It poured over her blonde hair and barely missed the tip of her small nose. *Purrr....* She felt sensational. She threw a free arm over his shoulders and hugged him tight.

"Pity." With full force, Patty twisted the knife and struck one final blow. The knife's tip bled once it sky rocketed out from his back.

Bodhi removed the mask and observed Derek's jerking body. Carefully, he retracted the knife and allowed Derek to fall on his own. The body still flinched as it crumbled to the floor.

Bodhi stormed off, refusing to stay a second longer.

Meanwhile, Jason, Zaire, Ariel and the rest of the DDAG team were minutes away from the main event in the dance hall. With all crony watchmen out of the way, they now had a clear advantage over the ballroom.

Ariel reached into the pocket of her trench coat and pulled out Mercury. She couldn't help but grin every time she saw her.

"We shall have a grand entrance in no time," Seraphina called out, catching up with the group.

"How do you suppose we do that?" Ariel asked, both curious and anxious as she tossed Mercury in her hand. That son-of-a-bitch, Cyclamen, was only a few feet away and she could practically smell his migraine-inducing cologne and expensive cigars. Her entire body charged with adrenaline. Alexander Cyclamen's death was going to be the night's sweetest gift.

"They're all in one room. It's an easy finish." Seraphina moved with purpose as she looked over Faction Divide. "My suggestion? Instead of escorting ourselves through the door, let's surprise them with The Avalanche. It's never been done, but if any DDAG faction can execute this effectively, it's us." She smirked to her captain. "What do you think, boss?"

Jason was sold. "I say your plan should be more than sufficient. In fact, it's perfect. This old piece of rubble is bound to collapse any day now. We will go big." He loaded his shot gun with four barrel rounds. "Assassins!" he called out. Loud and proud.

No, Ariel thought. *We cannot follow through with this plan.* She knew she shouldn't argue, but….

"Ready?" Jason looked around for Bodhi. He had yet to return. *He'll catch up.* There's no need to slow down. "Line u—"

"Hey!" Ariel interrupted. "You do realize this plan could demolish the entire building, right? The ballroom is already fucked in its own right. We shouldn't add to the destruction, not just for the building's sake but for ours." She emphasized her words through genuine fear in her violet eyes. She knocked on the walls. They were thin and hollow. "With any more force on these walls, the entire place could collapse. We all may get seriously hurt, if not killed! The structure is not strong anymore. It's fragile."

Jason stampeded away, embarrassed by his own best friend. This was not the time for Ariel to enforce what she felt was right. "We will move forward with The Avalanche," Jason finalized. Ariel filled him with indignation.

Jason instructed the assassins to line up against a wall. Soon, they'd fight through it and surprise Alexander Cyclamen and his men on the other side.

The group was lining up when Jason tapped Ariel's arm with the barrel of his shotgun. She looked at him and bit her tongue, refraining from saying anything remotely stubborn or defensive. "Usually, I don't mind hearing what you have to say, but do not, under any circumstance, question my authority in front of others again. Remember, you're on probation." She kept her mouth shut. Partly, she did not believe a word Jason was saying, but there was a small part of her that was fearful. At any moment, she could jeopardize her entire future. She looked him in the eye but instead of spatting her sarcastic remarks as she was known to do, she bowed, mockingly.

"Ariel," Jason hissed. "Don't test me."

"Fine," Ariel grunted, scampering away. Ariel got in line. Nine pairs of eyes were daunting her, making her feel uneasy. She ignored them and pretended not to mind their judgmental expressions.

A shadow was trudging down the hallway. Ariel noticed it was Bodhi slouched over with loose hands. "Hey!" She waved, trying to grab his attention.

"Hey," Bodhi sighed, completely oblivious to Ariel's gesture. Physically, he stood among allies—he was a fellow Death Dealer ready to fight for the good people of the New World. Mentally, he was distant. Ariel knew something was eating at him like maggots on flesh.

"Eyes and mind here, buddy." Ariel tried to make him laugh but he was absentmindedly gaping at the floor.

Ariel noticed his fingers moving as if they were being electrocuted. This was a well-known sign of Vitality beginning to wear off. She held his hand. Bodhi forgot where he was. He looked at her and shook his head, forcing himself back to reality.

"Are you alright?" Ariel asked.

"Yeah," Bodhi said, retrieving his hand back. The after-effects of Vitality are embarrassing. It begins with a pounding, uncontrollable migraine then blistering twitches in the fingers and feet. Temporarily, this makes a Death Dealer weak. Taking Vitality at the proper time is crucial. If taken too early, someone may wind up dead.

"I'm okay," Bodhi smiled as he quickly popped back an adrenalin pill.

Static radioed through the assassins' ear pieces. "Death Dealers, we're about to execute." Jason's voice came in clearly. "Be ready on three."

Here we go, Ariel thought, still hating the chosen plan. Twelve members of the DDAG were aligned with weapons set aside momentarily. The only instrument they needed was the strength in their hands fueled with Vitality.

Seraphina sneered at Ariel. "I find it ridiculous that you question the captain, even though you're under probation, need I remind you," to which Ariel rolled her purple eyes.

"Yes, and sometimes I find it ridiculous how you secretly want Jason's role as captain," Ariel fired back. "Most people are oblivious to it. As for me, well, I'm not that stupid."

Seraphina guffawed at Ariel's inappropriate theory. "I don't want to be captain. I'm just that good."

"Three…," Jason began the countdown.

"If you say so," Ariel huffed.

"Two…."

I'm coming for you, Alexander.

"One...."

Together, the deadly assassins began tearing their way through the walls. The drywall rained all over them, but that didn't stop them. They punched left and right, breaking the wooden barriers that got in their way. Together, they were a team: a faction that overshadowed the other six in the New World. They were the best. They were number one. That night, they were going to prove it once again.

Five minutes earlier....

"Give me another drink, will ya?" Alexander asked one of his noble henchmen. The loyal man, with a smooth, clean face and dark hair, hurried over to the bar. "This time, get me a whiskey," he yelled.

Cyclamen never failed to style up in a white suit more dazzling and sterile than the falling snow outside. Usually, there was much to discuss with his men but that night, he wanted to enjoy the simplicities of life: hard drinks, expensive cigars and winning money on Blackjack.

Roger, known as Alexander's pet, came rushing to his boss' side. A nervous tick poked his nerves.

"Sir," Roger began. "I feel we may have a problem."

"What makes you think I want to hear you talk?" Alexander muffled. He was anticipating the next round of 21. A newly poured, dry whiskey was handed to him. He downed it in one quick gulp, then barked for another.

"I was just hoping that maybe we can send more men to hunt around the place. My instincts are telling me a surprise is coming."

"SHUT UP!!" Alexander screamed, making Roger jolt. Roger removed his glasses and his stout hands shook timidly as he cleaned the lenses with the tail of his dirty shirt. "Let me enjoy the night, for fuck's sake."

"Ye-...Yes sir," Roger muttered.

A noise was coming from the walls. *Tap, tap, tap*.... The sound was barely noticeable, especially when the ballroom was filled with loud banter, shuffling cards, and shaken ice. Roger slid his glasses back on, as if they would somehow help him hear better. No one else seemed to notice the questionable sounds from yonder. Everyone was carrying on with the night, hardly bothered. Sweat showered underneath his armpits and back.

Tap, tap, tap.... The strange beatings behind the walls escalated and began to reverberate. Roger noticed Cyclamen stood up as he started to grow suspicious of the rumbling walls. The former bustle from the rowdy men was reduced to confused whispers.

Cyclamen ordered his men to pull out their weapons.

Suddenly, the walls exploded. *BOOM!!!* The entire ballroom violently shook. Chandeliers rattled and fell out of place. The extravagant mirrors on the walls fumbled to the ground with a clash. The walls were being slaughtered by mysterious fists plowing their way from the other side.

"What the fuck is going on here?" Alexander roared.

BAM!!! Out popped a team of Death Dealers with supersonic strength. They completed their journey through the wall and now, the real fight began.

The assassins wasted no time in the heat of battle. Once they reached the dance floor, they mushed.

Bullets and arrows began whizzing all over the room.

Zaire aimed his crossbow at two men in a line who were coming at him. Quickly, he pulled back his arrow then fired away. The men clung together at the eye. *Woosh!* They jetted in the air and not a moment too soon, they met their fate at the end of a broken piece of rubble.

There was a scream. *Aaahhh!!!* It grasped Zaire's attention. A man with a steel bat was charging for him. Zaire knew the man was ready to swing at his head.

"Too easy," Zaire sang to himself. "Come to papa."

Unknowingly, the terrorist was falling into a trap.

"Almost there," Zaire whispered as he prepared another arrow. He drew the string back and the ammo clinked into place. Zaire situated the crossbow above and just to the inside of his arm pit. Patiently, he waited.

The target gritted his yellow teeth and swung with all his might. *Aaahhh!!!* He was quick, but not quick enough.

POW! The arrow shot through the man's brain. The bat sprung from the terrorist's grip as his body jerked to the ground.

"Good boy," Zaire chuckled.

More than fifteen of Alexander's men were fired up and ready to murder some Death Dealer scum—or try their hardest to.

Seraphina noticed two men falling behind the group. Others were close enough to seize her, but Seraphina flipped way, way up, high above the rest, over the gang of terrorists.

Once Seraphina reacquainted with the floor, she surprised the two sloth men, freezing them in their tracks: exactly what she wanted. She brought her longsword to her chest then executed a perfect pirouette. As her petite body spun, the men were too busy questioning whether they should fight.

"Run, you idiot!" one of them bellowed.

Before they could escape, Seraphina performed a double pirouette and her longsword began to slice its way through their bodies. *Argh! Aaahhh!!!* The men cried. The sword slashed at their face then their neck. *Ugh....* Seraphina continued spinning until the blade extended to their waists. Once the air whistled, Seraphina ended her ballerina performance and overlooked an audience of skin, bone, blood, organs, and fingers. Nothing was left of them except hips, legs and immobile feet. Seraphina smiled, then stammered off for the next target

Short and stumpy Roger was desperate to hide from the calamity until...*CREAK!* The central chandelier was shot down from the ceiling. It was coming for Roger at great speed. He had to get out of the way. With his stubby legs, he leaped as far as could. *CRASH!!!* The large piece of glass crashed below, shattering into a million pieces. Luckily, for Roger, he escaped just in time. He screamed as he hit the floor. "Argh! I told him, I fucking told him!" Roger cried. He moved his face to one side to catch some air. *Cough.* He was about to get back on his feet but there were a pair of leather boots right in his face. "Huh?"

OUCH!!! Roger's face got kicked in. "Shit!"

Bodhi pounded a fist into Roger's glasses. *SMASH!* The lenses cracked into tiny shards then exploded into his eyes. "ARGH!!!" His vision was now a blur of red and orange tones.

"Let me go," Roger begged and pleaded. "Please, let me go!"

Seraphina pulled out her almighty sword. Bodhi stepped aside and courteously offered her the final blow.

"Don't mind if I do," Seraphina squealed. She sauntered over to the fat boy with her weapon scuffing along the floor.

"I'm just the messenger. I do it for the money. Not to hurt anyone," Roger sobbed. Sadly, for him, neither Bodhi nor Seraphina were the forgiving type.

"Wrong! You're part of the problem," Seraphina sassed. With a formal practice move, she swung fiercely. *Hi-yah!* Mid-scream, the sword spliced its way through his fat head. A disgusting gushing sound came after Cyclamen's pet's face split in half. Seraphina brought her sword over her shoulder and stared at the dead man, feeling quite pleased.

"That was easy," Bodhi said, impressed.

Seraphina smiled. "Yes. Now, if you would only let me train you in sword fighting—"

Bodhi decided it was time to leave and move on to the next fight. "No, thank you! Got more terrorists to fry!"

"That boy needs to grow some balls," Seraphina said to herself.

Jason was having a party of his own. He fought flawlessly, making him a worthy DDAG captain. He rightfully led the best faction in all seven districts. It was headshot after headshot. No one could even come close to him. A man darted to Jason's left. A bullet kissed his forehead. Another attempted to jump over him. Jason grabbed his legs, pile drove him to the ground then blasted a round right through his skull.

"Fuck you!" a random man shouted. He noticed Jason was about to reload. That might have given the scoundrel enough time to murder the captain of Faction Divide.

The man sprinted his way to Jason with his machine gun firing. *Bam, bam, bam!*

Jason sprinted to hide behind a fallen table. He could feel the man's bullets almost striking his back. Once he jumped behind the fragile piece of furniture, he hurried to finish reloading. He took a quick peek and noticed the man was not giving up. Jason picked up a heavy block of rubble and pitched it at the man's legs.

"Fuck!" As the man fell, he was unintentionally shooting a crown of bullets over his head.

Jason rushed over to him and smacked his gun out of sight. He forced the pitiful man up. Instead of a bullet finish, he pulled out a pocket knife underneath his pant leg, placed it in between his fingers and began jabbing his life away. *Augh! Ah! Argh!* The man croaked as Jason stabbed his shoulders, arms, breasts, neck, anywhere his heart desired.

Finally, the terrorist's mouth was overloaded with blood. The match was almost complete. Now, it was time for the knockout.

Jason let out a hungry roar, *Yaaah!* With full force, he swung up. An uppercut later, the man was finished by a knife hooked through his chin.

Jason eyed the dead man, whose blood was now smeared all over his dark skin. "Punk-ass bitch!"

Meanwhile, Ariel was combing the room for Cyclamen. Taking her off-guard, a man plunged at her. Luckily, she rolled back in time and elongated the distance between them.

"Let's go," Ariel encouraged. As he flew through the air, she reached out and grabbed him by the neck. She held him like a tired old ragdoll she refused to play with any longer. His feet were dangling, nowhere near touching the floor. "Where's Alexander?"

"Go to Malum," he coughed.

"Ariel!" a voice called out. She turned in the voice's direction. "Alexander Cyclamen," Ariel said, darkly. "There you are."

"My sweet, sweet, baby girl," Cyclamen cooed.

Ariel looked back at the worthless human that remained in her clutch. "I don't have time for you." With just her fingers, Ariel singly squeezed his neck. *Crunch!* Once his bones cracked, he was finished. She tossed him away with the same respect as a garbage bag.

"Don't wake me if this is a dream," Cyclamen spoke with an effusive charm. His cologne suffocated Ariel's nostrils. She always hated his foul scent. From his coat pocket, he pulled out his favorite cigar: a brand named Hoji from District South America.

Ariel didn't realize the war around her was coming to a close. She was sidetracked by Cyclamen's wretched appearance. Only a few of Alexander's men managed to survive this long. It wouldn't be much longer until his whole chain of comrades was obliterated.

"Jason," Cyclamen called out. Ariel was unaware Jason had crept up behind her. "Nice to see you here."

"Likewise," Jason scorned.

After taking a big hit from his cigar, Cyclamen asked, "How about you and I talk about this, huh? Man-to-man? Over a drink?"

"We don't work with terrorists," Ariel interrupted. Her violet eyes narrowed and her body tightened as the hatred for him swelled. She was near to losing focus and mauling him right then and there.

"Steady," Jason murmured to Ariel. "Remain calm."

"Listen to him, Ariel," Alexander carried on. "We wouldn't want you to do anything rash." The guild began circling around Cyclamen in a linked formation, eliminating any prospect of escape.

Ariel's tension boiled. She wanted him annihilated. He didn't deserve to live.

"Why don't you just take me in? I have so much information to give you," Cyclamen tried to persuade.

"LIAR!!!" Ariel roared.

"I have some knowledge about the uprising of the Black Plague II Infections. You really want to off me?" Cyclamen asked, overlooking the assassin herd. "Go ahead, then. Don't be upset with me when you all realize how completely unprepared you are for the New World War."

"What are you talking about?" Jason asked with arms crossed.

"Don't listen to him," Ariel urged, tightening her grip on Mercury.

"Shh!" Jason snarled. "What New World War?"

Alexander chuckled and took a long hit of Hoji. "I will only tell you if you let me live. Consider that negotiation."

"Give me a clue and I'll consider it," Jason vowed.

Ariel didn't want to believe her ears. Jason had promised Alexander to her. Now, there might be a slim chance of him surviving, all because he was lying about a New World War? *This is bullshit*, Ariel screamed in her head. *Complete bullshit!*

"Sure," Cyclamen began. "It all began in District Asia in the city of Seoul, Korea."

Ariel was fumed. Seoul, Korea was her birthplace. However, it had become a ghost town. Only a few hundred people stayed behind, living in the Outerwoods of the city.

"Why Seoul? That doesn't make any sense," Ariel muddled.

"You asked for a clue. I gave you one," Cyclamen reminded her. "If you want to know more, please escort me to the DDAG headquarters, where we can sit down and get to know each other a little better."

"You know he is lying," Ariel barked to Jason. "Don't listen to him! Let me kill him!"

Jason frowned at his best friend and hated what he was about to do. "Ariel—"

"Don't you fucking tell me no!" Ariel yelled, defiantly. "You promised me."

"I know," Jason admitted. "But I can't let you have him yet. He could be leading us to something big. For all we know, he could be on the verge of outing several terrorist groups. This could help us eliminate them."

Ah! Ariel punched a glass sitting on a table beside her.

"Someone's feisty," Alexander said.

"Shut your maggot-pie mouth, Cyclamen! Jason, you promised me!!" Ariel persisted.

"You also promised to not question my authority again!" Jason argued back.

Ariel glared at Cyclamen standing in a brood posture. He was right there: only a few feet away! "I didn't promise a thing!"

"Ariel!" Jason cried out, trying to stop her. "No!!"

Ariel shoved Jason out of the way. With her powerful legs, she sprung forward and toppled over Alexander's chest. He nosedived to the floor. Ariel upturned his body and climbed over him. The silver in Mercury's body shined in the moonlight as Ariel aimed her at Cyclamen's neck.

"Do it," Cyclamen coaxed as he was losing himself in Ariel's violet irises. Despite her violent affection, he enjoyed the beautiful assassin hovering him. Ariel targeted his throat, pointing the tip at his peeping Adam's apple. "Come on," he insisted. "I want you to."

Click!

"But I'd advise you to hurry," Cyclamen grinned.

"What was that?" Jason quickly began looking over the room.

"Oh, nothing," Cyclamen chanted. "Only an explosive gift for my little red head."

Jason noticed Cyclamen's hand inside his pocket. He was holding something.

It's a bomb! "Divide!" Jason screamed. "Get outside, NOW!"

Angrily, Ariel pounced back to her feet, leaving Cyclamen behind.

"Move, move, move!" Jason shouted. "Hurry up!!"

Ariel didn't look back.

The Death Dealers raced for the exit and back to the white vans.

Ariel was almost at the door. Who knew how long they had to escape. There was no time to figure it out.

Ariel sprinted, fearing for her life. Once she stepped outside, she jumped.

BOOM!!! The bomb exploded and the impact tossed Ariel in the air like a newborn babe. As soon as her body hit the street, she covered her head, protecting herself from any flying objects. The eruption of the collapsing building sounded like an active volcano. She knew the building was going to be destroyed, but not by Cyclamen. The Avalanche abused the building but the bomb murdered it.

Ariel thought the nightmare was over, but there was one final blow: *BOOM!!!*

Ariel slowly uncovered herself, afraid to look at the results. The building was now one with the ground and clouds of smoke fogged the air.

Ariel sat up, saddened at the sight of the newly-destroyed structure. She held her legs close to her chest. The night was filled with broken promises and horrific conclusions. Another ancient building was destroyed and yet another piece of Earth was gone forever. This time, the good guys had a part in it. Instead of racing back to meet the others, she took a moment to say goodbye to the beauty that was killed.

Alexander Cyclamen was dead—not by her hands, but dead. She felt there was no true justice served. Still, he was now a corpse no one would miss. But one question did pop in her mind: Why did he say a New World War was happening in Seoul, Korea, her hometown? He had to be lying. She was sure of it. However, Jason may be right. Alexander might be telling the truth. Either way, she was going to find out.

HOME

A riel got up from the cold, wet snow and wiped the remains off her backside. She gazed over at the now-destroyed ballroom, furious at its destruction and saddened by its history—lost before she could come to know it. Jason and the others were waiting for her back at the vans. Partially, she wanted to remain at the scene alone to ponder the endless possibilities of what may have happened within its once-golden walls. However, she had to go. It was time to leave and head back to headquarters. At least Alexander Cyclamen was no more. Even though his death was not fulfilled by her own hands, the New World had one less evil being to worry about.

Ariel headed back to meet with her guild. On the way, a subtle glow peeked underneath a pile of snow. Using Mercury, she scraped away the white, pressed pigments, exposing a vibrating cell phone. The screen showed no name but instead, a private number was calling. A sixth sense kicked in, convincing Ariel to keep it close. She grabbed the phone and with the face of her thumb, shut the device and slid it inside the side pocket of her cargo pants.

"Is everyone here?" Jason asked, looking over his team as they loaded up in the two vehicles. One-by-one, he counted heads. *Where's Ariel?* he wondered, beginning to worry.

Then a familiar voice called out, "Hey!"

To Jason's relief, it was his best friend, Ariel Rose, walking up to him, still alive, her heart still beating. At that moment, he wanted to spread his arms open and grasp her with a firm hug.

"I told you The Avalanche was a terrible idea!" Ariel grunted. "Then Cyclamen surprises us with a bomb? What the fuck!"

All hopes of enjoying momentous gratitude dispersed into thin air.

"You...." Ariel paused. "Why do I get the feeling I am being watched?" she asked Jason. After biting her bottom lip, she scoped the area and noticed a field of eyes antagonizing her, making her feel uneasy.

Confused, Ariel huffed, "What?" Nervously, she pulled her long hair back into a ponytail, feigning cool detachment in the midst of pressing anxiety. *Why is everyone looking at me?*

Jason sighed deeply and placed his hand over his best friend's shoulder, silently praying she wouldn't overreact. However, Ariel could feel tension oozing from him, making her even more anxious. "It doesn't matter," he finally spoke. "I'm glad you're okay." He looked over his team. "Let's go home."

Ariel pried Jason's hand away. Suddenly, a flame of intolerable pain fired inside her skull. The aftereffects of Vitality commenced. The migraine felt like little demons were pounding nails along her forehead, all the way down to the teeth and gums. Almost immediately, the second effect came into play. Ariel fought to pull her hand up with convulsing fingers to massage her forehead.

With enough strength, Ariel could mostly ignore the pain. She glared at Jason, knowing something questionable was happening. Something important. Maybe, without realizing, she messed up. That's what usually happened.

Was it the uncontrollable anger she let out during her spontaneous attack on Alexander Cyclamen? It had to be.

"Bullshit, buddy," Ariel groaned, still suffering a god-awful headache, but fighting her way through. "I'm sorry for not listening, but Cyclamen was originally promised to me."

"I'm not angry with you," Jason promised her. "You and I are fine. Try not to turn this into a dramatic episode. The last thing you and I need is more unwanted stress."

Jason's words would be comforting if they were believable. Ariel sensed dishonesty escaping his lips. However, she'd rather not continue to argue during the brutally painful aftereffects of Vitality. It was difficult enough to deal with.

"What a night, huh?" Jason asked, switching topics to lighten the mood. "I killed so many terrorists tonight. It was great."

"Good for you," Ariel mocked. Her attention still lingered onto the throbbing pain across her forehead.

"Daaaaaamn right!" Jason boasted. "That's what happens when you're the captain of the best faction in all of the New World, baby!"

This made Ariel laugh—barely. Jason had always been Ariel's balance. He kept her sane, even during her darkest times. Ariel was often called serious, stubborn, and wild. Jason, on the other hand, enjoyed being surrounded by people and his soul was carefree. During DDAG hours, Jason was a hardcore professional, but outside, he was the complete opposite—himself. Ariel admired his flamboyancy but she didn't envy it. Truly, she accepted who she was and loved it.

Eventually, Ariel shrugged and her mind transitioned to something special. Back in her one-bedroom apartment, a lovely bottle of dry wine was sitting on her dining room table. She had been saving it for a worthy, celebratory kill and tonight she couldn't wait to indulge. Cyclamen's death was as good an excuse as any to take in the flavors of aged apricots and vanilla and pairing it with some almond cheese mixed with habanero bits. *Good riddance, Alexander Cyclamen. You will not be missed.*

"Ready to go?" Jason asked.

Ariel nodded. She placed one foot inside the van, but then, as the wind changed pace, a sudden ruffling noise came from the empty streets behind her. Curious, she gazed over her shoulder before settling down. After the bombing of the Golden Throne Room, a thick layer of fog smoked up the cold air, still fumigating the surface.

Slowly, two black figures were approaching.

Jason noticed who was coming forward. "Hey, get in the van, okay?" he begged Ariel.

"No!" Ariel snapped. "Why?" Quickly, she reversed back onto the snowy ground. *Who's that?* she asked herself. Jason wouldn't be pushing her away if it were two Death Dealers. After all, what's to fear when it comes to allies? So, who exactly was there?

The two dark figures began to emerge from the fog and the moonlight shined over their faces, exposing their identities.

Oh, hell no! Ariel screamed inside her head as she curled her hands into firm fists. The muscles in her ribs tensed up and the beating of her heart flurried like a ferocious hurricane. Before her stood the man she loathed most. A man whom, among anyone in all of the New World, she despised passionately; Alexander Cyclamen. Seraphina had him handcuffed under her brute grip. So much for celebration tonight. The dry wine must remain unopened for another time.

Through hammering pain, Ariel spoke with clenched teeth. "How…what?" She turned to Jason who looked away. She closed her eyes and thought, *He's dead!* Out loud, she counted to three, then slowly reopened her eyes, hoping within a single blink the sight of that asshole would disappear. Unfortunately, this was reality and he stood there smiling his insane smile. Ariel could taste the stench that lingered off his cheap cologne, making her want to vomit.

"Why is he here?!" Ariel paused. "Wait…How is he here?"

Instead of waiting for an answer, Ariel reached over for Mercury to plunge its quillon into Cyclamen's square jaw. Jason realized Ariel was about to attack.

Before Ariel could smash his face in, someone blocked her way. Jason ran in between the two enemies and gripped Ariel's wrists. He held her back with all his might, even through her gallant battle of demanding release. Due to the lack of Vitality in her bloodstream, her captain's strength overpowered hers.

Ariel felt her boots grinding across the dirty pavement as Jason was pushing her back. "Hey, hey, hey!" Jason yelled, eventually pinning Ariel against a broken fence.

"How the fuck did he escape?!" Ariel screamed. "That homicidal bitch was in my hands for a second. A second!! The next thing I know the building starts to collapse because of that ugly bastard over there! Also, you agreed to Seraphina's idiotic plan to wreck our way through the damn walls. We helped kill a historic structure instead of our target inside!!"

Grrr…. Jason slammed his eyes shut, mentally forcing himself to relax. "First of all, calm your ass down. Second, we did not destroy anything that wasn't already falling apart," he persisted. "Cyclamen tore the place apart, not us!"

Jason's voice grew louder. "We went through the walls but we did not demolish its core foundation." Evidently, he freed her from his human chains that caused redness to circulate her wrists

"You know what I mean!" Ariel sassed. She rubbed her arms, hoping to release the mild discomfort. "How did he get out?" she asked, demanding answers. "I left him there. The possibility of him surviving had to be slim-to-none. Seriously, how did that happen?!"

"Sir," Seraphina interrupted, capturing Jason's attention. "What would you like me to do with Cyclamen?"

Ariel revolted. "Why are you asking him, you twat?! Alexander Cyclamen is mine!"

Unamused, Seraphina ignored the cheap name-calling and ventured back to her conversation with her captain. "Sir? Would you like me to sit him inside the van? Anywhere in particular?"

Ariel parted her lips but Jason leaned in and covered her mouth with his gloved hand. He begged for her to calm down. She rolled her eyes, hating that she had to listen.

Jason requested that Seraphina take Cyclamen inside the first van. "Make sure his hands remain cuffed behind his back."

Seraphina was almost free from the drama until Ariel jumped in again. "You're bringing that asshole back to headquarters? Really?!"

"Come on, my beauty," Alexander chanted, trying to be charming. "You know you can't be away from me for too long. It'll drive you crazy." He sealed his statement with an air kiss.

"Fuck you!" Ariel blurted, gifting him with a long middle finger in return.

Jason huffed. "Get him out of here." Seraphina grabbed Cyclamen by the hands and neck and maneuvered him out of sight.

"I will explain everything if you stay cool-headed, alright?" This was not just for Ariel's sake, but for his.

"Explain what?" Ariel eyed the night sky, trying to find peace with nature's art above her. The stars twinkled happily throughout the Lord of Life's universe. They surrounded a full and bright moon hanging low in the dark. She hugged herself, trying to remain calm. Happy thoughts trickled in: rubies, her aunt Faith, and Neuschwanstein Castle. She'd never seen the castle's glory personally, but through photos and various paintings. She dreamt to gaze upon its beauty one day. That's if it survived in the New World. She hoped it didn't die with Earth.

Jason was about to admit what he had done. He convinced himself it was for the best, even though guilt seized his heart. He stepped back to view Ariel from a distance.

"I had Seraphina save Cyclamen."

Ariel turned around with her purple eyes blaring. "You. Did. What?" She hoped she had a case of swimmer's ear.

Jason hated upsetting his best friend, but his duty as captain was to do the right thing. "There was no way around it, Ariel. We had to get him out. Once you left Cyclamen, I noticed Seraphina was closest to him. I yelled for her to get him out alive. I have questions for him. Many questions. He only mentioned Seoul because his life depended on it. If he had the chance to escape, we never would've known about this New World War."

Ariel chuckled angrily and looked beyond the pine trees. Nothing remained but the crumbs of the Golden Throne Room and everlasting smoke. She glared back at Jason.

"Alexander Cyclamen is a lying piece of shit," Ariel spat. "You, of all people, should know that. There is nothing in Korea anymore." She paced back and forth, viciously kicking snow with the toe of her boots. "There's no one except the Rural Outsiders, who don't even live in Seoul. They live in the Outerwoods. Seoul has no food. No water. That city has nothing to offer to anyone, anymore. This "war" will never happen. Why? Because it's not real. He only mentioned our hometown to get a reaction out of us. It didn't work on me, but obviously, it worked on you, Captain."

Jason's irritation ballooned up, and he was about ready to pop.

"Ugh! Okay. Most of the time, you're right," Jason admitted. "I fully trust your judgement, especially when it deals with terrorists. You do have the best perspective out of everyone in our DDAG team."

"Thank you!"

"But… This time you're wrong, buttercup." Jason booped her nose.

When it came to Cyclamen, it was difficult to convince Ariel his life was worth saving. She needed copious details.

"Give me a good explanation as to why you believe a scumbag over your best friend of ten years." Ariel lifted her right eye, crossed her arms and tapped her foot as she waited for an answer.

Here goes nothing, Jason thought. "About three months ago, our DDAG headquarters started receiving many calls and letters from the Rural Tribes in District Asia about suspicious activity happening in Seoul. Not much information has been given at this time, but Sergeant Lotus has arranged a private meeting tomorrow afternoon to discuss—in depth—what we know so far. This may be the biggest and most complex mission to date."

Finally, the nagging head torture completely dissipated. Ariel felt well again. The pain was no longer an issue.

Wait.... Ariel didn't realize what Jason had said until now.

"Mission?" Ariel was confused and peeved. "I never received an email or phone call about this meeting."

"Ummm....About that," Jason muttered, nervously cracking his knuckles.

Ariel had no tolerance for jokes or beating-around-the-bush. Jason cleared his throat. "That's because...." He trailed off, regretting what he was about to admit. "You're— Well— you're not coming to the meeting...or to Seoul." When Ariel was angry, she had a certain *look*. This *look* made people edgy and currently Jason felt like a convict in a visual prison under her glaring eyes, which dug deep into his soul. He tried to ignore her evil stare by looking out at the empty streets: a blackened abyss.

Jason remembered storming into Lotus' office, angry at the fine print written at the bottom of the letter. He, along with all the DDAG members of Faction Divide, had to swear to not mention the meeting or the case to Ariel Rose.

For hours, Jason fought, insisting that his sergeant was making a terrible mistake. Sadly, Lotus was adamant with his decision. Unfortunately, Jason had lost the argument. He knew somehow, Ariel would find out about the case before the first official meeting. There was no point in hiding it from her any longer.

"Sergeant Lotus was clear about not wanting you involved with this case due to the emotional attachment you have to the city. Plus, he mentioned your probation. I cannot argue with that. I'm sorry, Ariel, but you need to stay behind.

Lotus even brought it to the attention of the king and queen's cabinet and they gave him approval. You will train novice Death Dealers and tend to local cases only. Professional Death Dealers from other factions will be notified if you need any help."

Novice Death Dealers? Ariel cringed at the sound of *novice*. She was superior to them. Why should she get stuck with a bunch of trainees?

"Explain this," Ariel began. "While you all left me behind, what were you going to tell me when I asked why is everyone gone? Hmm?"

Jason hadn't thought about that, really. His focus leaned more toward getting her to Seoul, not leaving her on the sidelines.

"Honestly, I don't know. I guess Sergeant Lotus would've made something up."

Ariel pressed on the back of her teeth with her tongue while clenching her hands around her arms. "Do you trust me to babysit a bunch of newbies? I mean, really?"

Jason nodded. "Actually, I do. I know you would not let anyone get hurt on your watch. It's time for you to step up and take leadership for once."

"Leadership...," Ariel muttered to herself. "How overrated."

Jason smirked, hoping she'd tone down the aggression.

"Fine!" Ariel spat. *Newbies, though? Really?* "But why do I have to sit back and watch you all portal away to Seoul? You were born and raised in the same city I was. You're not that much different from me. Why not also hold you back?"

That last question stung. Jason handled himself maturely by not screaming at Ariel for her brazen attitude. Her accusation was beyond uncalled-for. He walked up to her and looked her dead in the eye. Only a breath was in between them.

"You and I are distinctly different," Jason said. "Since I am captain for Faction Divide, unlike you, I don't allow anything personal get in my way. However, I have fought—with my title on the line—for you. Yet, you continue to involve yourself in petty bullshit. I refuse to have my best friend terminated from my guild due to her embryonic decisions, especially when she is a great assassin."

Ariel was always caught off guard when Jason spoke with such brutal honesty—he rarely did.

Jason continued. "Also, you know why it'd be difficult for you to come along. Don't make me say it."

Her past. Ariel hated talking about it. Most of her childhood was shattered memories and she did not enjoy revisiting them. She backed away from Jason, refusing to argue any further.

"Either way, this should've been brought to my attention." Ariel took a breath and lowered her voice. "I am a Death Dealer and a damn good one at that. I may not be the best at following orders, and I know I'm being watched, but I should still be in the loop. It's only fair."

Jason thought back to his fiasco with Sergeant Lotus: "Sergeant, this is ridiculous. I know she can be reckless, but she's just as important to this guild as any of the others."

"My decision has been made, Captain Lilly. I don't want to hear anymore, about it." And those were the sergeant's final words.

Jason sighed at Ariel. "I know. Not being able to tell you anything is tough. I hate it. But I have fought for you, endless times. Over and over, I have saved your ass from being terminated from the DDAG. You're welcome." Ariel propped her hands on her hips and gave him a look that told him he'd better get to the damn point. "Believe me when I say, trying to convince Lotus to bring you on the mission was like pulling teeth."

Ariel was clueless to how hard Jason had fought for her against Sergeant Lotus. If only she had been there to see.

"He focused on what he felt was the right thing to do for the case. He cares about you. I know he does. But it's too risky for you to join us, especially with your rebellious nature. This case is paramount. Otherwise, he would never have banned you. I understand his decision to not include you." This was half-true. Jason understood to a certain extent. "But what you need to realize is what Lotus says, goes. Plain and simple. Don't expect me to try arguing with him again. He's had enough."

No words could formulate to make sense out of this mess. Ariel felt bad. Jason had defended her countless times. Unintentionally, she had gotten used to doing what she pleased with zero concern for the consequences. No matter how atrocious or common her acts of rebellion were, her captain, head knight, best friend and companion would be there to protect her against all evil. Jason kept her safe from termination and she remained in the Death Dealer Alliance Guild because of him.

Ariel's life as a Death Dealer meant more than killing the bad guy. Being an official assassin granted her a form of empowerment. Protecting those who couldn't fend for themselves made Ariel feel like a superhero.

Jason and Ariel grew silent and only exchanged vain stares. Clearly, Jason was right, but Ariel's gut was begging her to go to Seoul.

Ariel's anxiety revved up, and her thoughts redoubled. *What could be happening in my hometown? Cyclamen is lying to you. What does "New World War" even mean? Is*

Cyclamen lying? He has to be. What if he isn't? Seoul has to be just another ghost town by now.

Suddenly, a low but creepy voice whispered, *You must venture to Seoul!*

Ariel's face crinkled up as she looked around curiously, but only Jason was in view. He bobbed his head, hoping she'd hurry back to the vans.

The voice crept back, *Go to Seoul! Go to Seoul!*

"Alright!" Ariel screamed. "Shut up!"

"Woah!" Jason jerked. "Stop being hot-and-cold with me. I've done all I can for you, dammit!"

Ariel was unaware she was thinking out loud. That voice: where did it come from?

Seoul....

Ariel huffed. "Let's go home."

No expression alluded on her pale face when Jason tried to figure out how she was feeling. Even her body language was monotonic.

"I'm good. I'm fine," Ariel rambled. "Can we go, now?"

Quickly, Ariel stormed into the getaway car, forgetting Alexander Cyclamen was a passenger on board. They eyed one another when she hopped inside. Her nosed flared as she passed Cyclamen and his grotesque stench.

An empty seat was up for grabs in the back, far from Cyclamen and Seraphina. Ariel hurried over and immediately pounced on the firm cushion. As she plopped her legs on the seat, she shut her eyes and tried to concentrate on her breathing instead of the catastrophic collage trapped in her mind. The mixture of scatter-brained questions whipped wildly in her brain: *Why did Sergeant Lotus single me out? I have to go to Seoul. But I can't. Should I talk to Lotus myself?*

"How are you doing, Little Velvet?" Zaire asked, pulling her out of messy thoughts. Little Velvet was the first nickname Ariel had ever been given. It began when both she and Zaire trained at the DDAG academy in District Europe, in the city of London. With most of Ariel's first encounters, people immediately fell in love with her hair and kittenish violet eyes. Many refused to believe the rich velvet color was natural and not artificial, especially when both of her parents had dark brown locks. At first, Ariel thought nicknames were childish, yet over time, she learned to embrace the adorable name with its personable attachment.

"I'm doing alright, Mr. Iris," Ariel groaned as she stretched her back. Her spine popped in two places, giving her a mild satisfaction. *Oh yeah!* "How's the wife and daughter?"

Zaire had a dashing smile that lit up a room. "They're still alive and well." He pictured his princess, Reese, with her angelic smile that brought joy to even the most cruel person. Zaire loved watching her play as her curly brown hair bounced on her tiny shoulders. Her laugh was what he adored most. When his little princess was happy, nothing else mattered.

"You should relax," Zaire suggested. "Rub off the negativity you constantly carry."

This made Ariel laugh because it was true. Zaire—although handsome—was incredibly sweet. He had to be one of the most caring people in all of the New World. His wife was a lucky woman.

"Relax," Zaire repeated. He gently massaged her sore legs as he hummed softly.

Slowly, Ariel began to drift away. A cold breeze made its way inside the sheltered vehicle, making Ariel shiver. She turned on her side, brushing up against the cushion for some warmth. After inhaling the cold wind, she released it. A moment later, she was fast asleep.

Bang, bang, bang!!! "Wake up, doll face," Seraphina bellowed with malicious pleasure. She rocked Ariel's body side-to-side. Ariel was scared awake. *Aahh!* Seraphina jumped back. Ariel slept the entire way back to headquarters. *I felt like I slept for hours.*

"Get up," Seraphina barked as she chewed her mint blue gum obnoxiously loud. One of Ariel's pet peeves was loud chewing, but more so, loud popping. Seraphina brushed her thick, raven-colored hair to her right side. On her left, Seraphina never failed to add two fishtail braids, randomly placed behind her ear.

"I'm awake, you shit-mouth asshole," Ariel groaned in a raspy tone as she rubbed her heavy eyes.

Seraphina moaned, "Oh…," then followed with a sarcastic, "Talk dirty to me, baby."

"Shut up!" Ariel noticed it was only her and Seraphina remaining in the van. *Wait….*

"Where's—"

"Jason?" Seraphina interrupted. "Inside doing captain-y duties most likely. Cyclamen? Also, inside. He's being taken to the sergeant for questioning, then he's a prisoner for the rest of his life."

Ariel was still groggy from the drive.

Seraphina was now bored. "Alright. Well, get out of your sweaty clothes and get your tired ass home."

"I like it better when you don't talk," Ariel added.

"Yup," Seraphina smacked, hopping out of the van. "So do many of my lovers." Before disappearing into the gothic castle straight ahead, she let out one last roaring *pop!*

"Bitch!" Ariel whispered. Finally, she had enough consciousness to walk, but her body was scorching.

"Fuck." Sweat drenched her chest and arms like a heated, moist washcloth. She rolled up her sleeves, hoping to cool down.

Ariel got up and headed inside the castle straight ahead, known as the Death Dealer Alliance Guild Headquarters, Faction Divide.

Four thick, grey stone walls encircled the headquarters. As you enter, it's hard to ignore how majestic the place was designed. Golden chandeliers guided your way through every hallway. The largest chandelier, inlaid with diamonds, hung inside the fanciful banquet hall. On the walls, paintings were the most venerated features. Many of them had been saved during Earth's fall and was brought back to life during the early years of the New World through the hard work of a professional art restorer. It would take days to view the castle in its entirety. Even then, one wouldn't truly have been able to see it all.

Each painting shared a mysterious story. One of Ariel's favorites featured a beautiful, ivory-skinned woman with a blue headdress atop a black canvas. A gold scarf layered over the blue headdress and casually, loosely draped behind her head, barely missing her back. It seemed that either a golden robe or dress with a white collar embellished her body. She was positioned in such a way you felt her bulging, nut-brown eyes following you. There was also a single pearl painted on her left earlobe. Sadly, its original title and artist's name had been lost. It was renamed, *Pearl.*

Not much of Earth's history—before the Black Plague II Infections—was known. In modern times, most artists created their interpretations of Earth through various styles of paintings and pictures. Archeologists had found strange objects that clued about life before the plague. For instance, a man found a circular, spinning box that, once he figured out how to work it, displayed moving images of people interacting with each other through scripts that must had been pre-written. Archeologists believed this was a form of entertainment called "movies."

Ancient linguists were responsible for translating documents. Supposedly, there used to be hundreds—if not thousands—of different languages spoken all over Earth. Today, the only official language was English and had been for over 500 years.

Ariel studied some ancient languages during her years at the DDAG academy, including Portuguese, Italian and Arabic. If it weren't for historical architecture, her passion would be language. She wished she lived in a time where there was diversity of the tongue. Imagine people conversing in other languages. How fantastic that must've been.

As Ariel trailed for the locker rooms, Mason was creeping up behind her. He was a short man with an ill-temper who believed himself to be a god with men and women. His spiky hair was now drenched over his smug face after wearing a cap during the mission. He slacked down to orange basketball shorts and a white tee that was too tight for his husky figure. His nipples poked out disgustingly as if the temperature were below zero.

Ariel noticed the dwarf man approaching. She tried to pick up the pace but it was too late. His stubby legs caught up with her. Due to his short stature, Mason had to look up to her.

"So, I overheard you didn't know about our private meeting with Sergeant Lotus tomorrow? Sucks, don't it?"

You and everyone else in this damn guild, Ariel thought. She wanted to punch Mason in his pedophile-looking face but held back. The extra pointy eyebrows were what did it. They were unnatural for a man, in Ariel's opinion. For some reason, overly arched eyebrows screamed pedophilia.

"I bet it sucks more that your perfect boyfriend, Captain Lilly, didn't do a damn thing to get you an invitation." Ariel froze. "Ouch!" Manson laughed. "Does it sting?"

Ariel eyed him with intensity. "I was hoping you'd understand the definition of 'shut-the-hell-up' by now. Yet, you're still at the maturity level of someone who graduated level one."

In the New World, there were seven levels of beginner school. Children started beginner school at the age of five. Each level was two years long. Teachers taught a wide range of topics, including grammar, writing, introduction to technology, New World History, and nutritional health. After level seven, young graduates were given three options: to continue education and become a member of various high-advanced jobs such as a doctor, farmer or teacher. There was also an Opt-Out Option: Men and women could choose to discontinue their education and take on small jobs. Then there was the least popular option: To become affiliated with the Death Dealer Alliance Guild in a variety of fields. The DDAG offered careers like administrative assistant, DDAG informant, accounting, payroll, and much, much, more.

"What? Are you pissed off that I call you and Jason out?" Mason licked his chapped lips. "When are you two going to admit you're fucking, huh?"

Ariel's patience was lacking. Hell, it was becoming shorter than Mason.

"Well?" Mason continued with a mocking tone. "I mean, why else would he keep your ass around? I bet that pussy of yours is tight, warm, and delicious."

Ariel yanked out Mercury from her sheath. With a tight clutch, she gripped the edge of the blade, turned it around and smashed it against Mason's bulging eye.

Argh! Mason howled, losing balance.

Ariel grabbed the collar of his shirt and pulled him in close. The warmth of her breath fogged his t-zone.

"You spread one more rumor about Jason and me and I will rip out your soul. I swear to the Lord of Life I will grip you by your neck and dangle you in the air. Before you know it, I will gruesomely pull out your trachea along with your jaw and tongue then happily display it to the world as your blood spills all over my hands. I will bathe in your blood and even light candles around me to make the night romantic. Once I bathe in your blood water, I will happily sip some fucking wine and replay the event in my head over and over again. Now, fuck off." She shoved Mason back as far as her strength would allow. He messily caught himself on a side table.

Ariel twirled Mercury around her finger and returned it to her sheath. Quickly, she stormed out of the area, leaving Mason behind to cry.

After a quick shower, Ariel slid into comfy jeans and a plum-colored turtleneck. She headed outside to the middle bailey where her car was parked toward the exit gate. She threw her backpack inside the trunk, but before sitting down, she took in the view of her faction.

The castle stood radiantly below the ebony sky. It was inspired by a castle called Corvin that once stood in Transylvania, Romania, in District Europe. Unfortunately, Transylvania was now a region lost under the sea.

The gothic architecture was more than beautiful; Ariel thought it was perfect. On top of the tallest orange pinnacles waved the official DDAG flags with the symbol etched in: a longsword wrapped in a bold green vine, slashed down the middle of an OMEGA sign. Its borders were two C-shaped olive branches.

To the west was a guardhouse tower strictly for Death Dealers. It had two locker rooms, a weaponry vault, a gym and a customized library. A backup weaponry vault was built in the arsenal tower, northeast of the castle's layout. Also, an underground prison was built three levels below the tower for any terrorists lucky enough to survive after crimes they had committed.

The chapel was where the sergeant—in this case, Sergeant Kurtis Lotus—resided each and every day. There he made daily phone calls and tended to other bossily duties. Many important DDAG meetings were held downstairs in the chapel in a large conference room. Inside was a white, rectangular table and golden chairs with red cushions. Up front was the projector where Jason regularly projected pictures of evidence, suspects, or notes.

There was also a watchtower overseen by two snipers. Snipers were volunteers and the position was alternated monthly. When sniping, taking outfield missions was forbidden.

The forebuilding held the fancy banquet hall for celebrations or masquerades and there were many of them.

The last and most important part of the palace was the large and extravagant keep in between the lower and middle bailey. In the keep sat the king and queen of the New World. Repetitive discussion over the dos and don'ts of the New World happened at Faction Divide. Each and every executive decision regarding the lives of two-hundred million people in a single, worldwide democracy passed in that keep. This was special and very important to all assassins who ever had the privilege of working in District North America. Even Ariel loved having her king and queen close to her. Their names: King Sebastian Peony and Queen Kora Amaryllis.

Ariel failed to realize the time. It was almost four in the morning. She charged up her tiny, four-door, metallic-black car. Once it gained strength, she drove home.

Ariel threw herself on the bed and enjoyed a cup of warm apple cider with cinnamon sticks. Next to her was a small bowl of her favorite snack: rubies. This sweet treat was made up of cherries covered in a honey coat and baked long enough to have a small crunch in every bite.

Ariel brought out the cell phone she found outside the broken ballroom. Luckily, when she turned it on, no pin or password was required for accessing the device.

"So much for security," Ariel muttered as she munched on a handful of rubies.

First thing's first, Ariel skimmed through texts. There were only four contacts and the majority of the messages were received from a woman named Gwen. She had to be someone very special. Their conversations were raunchy. The other contacts sent bland but straight-forward messages. Some of them contained only a single word. *Could this be code for a secret hideout? Illegal laboratories for reviving the Black Plague II virus? How about illegal weapon exchanges hidden in underground markets?*

Moving on, but keeping those questions in mind, Ariel browsed the call log's history. Many phone calls were incoming, but none outgoing. Strange.

There was no email address, so scratch emails. A calendar was set but no events were created. Overall the phone seemed useless. There was nothing to go on. But then, Ariel opened the notepad and noticed a memo titled, *Evolution Begins in Seoul.* Ariel opened it, but nothing else was typed.

"What the hell?" Ariel asked herself. Her first instinct was to reach Jason. She dialed his number, but after one ring she hung up then threw her phone to the opposite side of the bed.

After downing the remains of her warm drink and inhaling the rest of her delicious rubies, Ariel turned off the lights and threw the covers over her head.

"Don't call him," Ariel told herself. "Just let it go." She exasperated and grabbed the phone again, sliding it under the covers with her. She pulled up Jason's contact information and was close to hitting the green phone icon.

This is important. He has to know. Plus, I need advice on whether I should keep the phone or toss it. Ariel continued to eye the screen as if she could telepathically dial her best friend. The anxiety within her kicked in.

I'm not going to Seoul but I may have a lead. What if I upset Jason even more? Does he even want to speak to me right now? He's probably asleep. Would he be asleep? She paused, trying to take her thoughts down a notch. *It is a memo that may or may not lead to something important. Argh! I don't know what to do....*

Eventually, Ariel decided against calling Jason. It was probably for the best. Maybe in the morning she could speak to him.

Ariel set her alarm to ring at ten. She wanted to make sure she'd get a decent night's sleep. After getting comfortable, she chanted a simple sleeping spell:

On this night I look upon thee
Lord of Life, bless me
With the power to close my eyes
From now until the next sunrise

Instantly, Ariel's eyes shut and she began to dream.

The night continued to fill the world with snow and the moonlight was shining sweetly. It overlooked the innocents of the New World, making them feel protected in their beds from the evil that hid in the outer darkness. When the moon was out, people felt safe. And tonight, it shined bright until the morning sky.

EVOLUTION HAS BEGUN

First thing in the morning, Jason knocked on Sergeant Lotus' office door. Kurtis swiftly offered him entry.

The sergeant sat on a huge, red, cushioned chair, signing away through a messy pile of papers. Never being the type to break habit, he was adorned with a blood-red collared shirt—steamed-to-perfection—and black slacks. Always, he wore his shiny golden trapezoid belt buckle that boasted wealth and professionalism. To top off his business attire, he always dressed his feet in the best onyx oxfords. They were cleaned once a week, every week with a specialized polish to keep them prime.

"Yes?" the sergeant asked Jason, barely glancing his bright blue eyes at him. His white skin seemed to have lost pigmentation that winter but the tanned-colored freckles around his nose and cheeks were more visible. Rarely, Kurtis visited the outdoors. Usually, he remained cooped up in the chapel, going over miles of paperwork or having important meetings with the royal cabinet or the king and queen of the New World.

Jason stood at attention, never failing to show manners. He bowed. "Good morning, sir," Jason greeted.

Kurtis huffed under his breath, "Yes." He jumbled through the pile of rubble messily scattered all over his desk. As he was autographing a clearance form, he stopped at his first name. A strange and questionable feeling came over him. He bit the inside of his mouth and looked up at Jason. After working with Captain Lilly for over five years, Kurtis knew the signs for when he was about to get upset with Jason. The sun shined bright in the crisp morning air, meaning Sergeant Lotus would be distracted with paperwork: it was the perfect opportunity to make a request while the sergeant was distracted with important DDAG matters.

Sergeant Lotus proceeded with caution. "It is a good morning. Now, I'd love to keep it that way."

Here it goes, Jason thought. *Work your magic.*

"It's about Ariel." Jason rushed his words but remained at attention with a keen stare.

Sergeant Lotus loathed hearing Ariel's name. Often, she caused confrontation in the workplace. Her rebellious antics and insubordination made Sergeant Lotus lose much respect for the Death Dealer. Whenever Jason slipped out Ariel's name, Lotus' body would tense.

It was safe to assume Sergeant Lotus hated the fiery assassin. On the contrary, he cared for her very, very much. However, keeping her in Faction Divide felt like another job entirely—a position he never applied for.

Kurtis ran his stubby fingers through his smooth blonde hair.

"Captain Lilly, if this is about the meeting happening within the next…"—he checked his watch—"…three hours—as I assume it is—obviously, you've brought this to her attention—you can forget about it. She is not—will not—be in any way a part of the mission in Seoul, Korea. Ms. Rose will remain here until further notice. I'd advise you to drop this whole ordeal entirely and go back to keeping your mouth shut."

Jason hesitated before continuing with his plea. Ariel could be a key to something big. He had to convince his almighty sergeant of her importance. "Actually, it's not about the Seoul case. Sir...."

"Oh?" Kurtis found Jason's statement bizarre. Why bring Ariel up at all, if she had nothing to do with the case? She couldn't possibly be any help. Still, he lacked any expression of interest.

Jason cleared his throat. "I wanted to know if I am able to bring Ariel along with me to interrogate Cyclamen."

Curtis snorted and responded without a second thought. "No."

Immediately, Jason fought with a minor yet effective defense. "Sir, if I may, I'd like to persuade you to change your mind. I have good reason for bringing this to your attention."

"You may not," Kurtis sneered coldly. He stapled a few papers together and slid them inside a folder labeled, "Confidential."

Jason didn't quit, but only fought harder. "I apologize, but I'd appreciate a chance to explain," Jason pleaded, positioning his hands in a prayer stance. Last night he lost sleep. The late hours were spent brewing up a plan to make Alexander Cyclamen talk. The most plausible solution was to have Ariel in that room.

Kurtis peered up at Jason with intimidating, icy blue eyes. He hoped the captain would escort himself out—however, Jason would not budge. Instead, he requested permission to sit.

"You'll be able to sit once you drop the idea of Ariel being included with this case." Kurtis fixed the cufflinks on his sleeves.

"Sergeant Lotus, I highly respect your decision." Jason spoke with pure honesty. "You're right. I did in fact, briefly speak about the case to Ariel last night—without wanting to do so." He raised his voice on the last part for emphasis. "To my surprise, for once, she actually understood why she can't be a part of the mission. She cooperated and agreed to stay behind to train and take local cases in District North America." With that statement, he hoped Sergeant Lotus would be open for discussion.

"She's plotting something," Kurtis hypothesized. He walked over to his mini bar by the window and poured himself a glass of whiskey. With gentle movement, the liquor swirled around in its glass vessel while glistening among the sun's rays. He indulged in a small gulp of sweetened apple and wheat as it flowed down his throat, feeling smooth and clean. Outside his window was a beautiful garden full of trimmed bushes. The flowers had decayed due to the winter season but the soft look of snow made up for the loss of blooming blossoms. Like Ariel, Kurtis enjoyed the colder months, especially when snow fell.

"Never in all her career as a Death Dealer has she been understanding of anything, Captain Lilly," Kurtis snickered. That was mostly true. Even Jason could not deny that. "Especially, when the situation deals with herself." That was definitely true.

"Believe me," Jason agreed, if not pandering, "I understand that more than anyone. She did give me her word, though. With my life, I trust her to do the right thing." Jason gazed upon his almighty sergeant who had dedicated his entire life to the Death Dealer Alliance Guild.

Since his first year, Lotus had done a damn good job of wiping the scum of the New World. His name was even placed in history books. All of the New World knew Sergeant Lotus as the best DDAG captain to have ever existed. Jason admired his bravery and longed to be as great and courageous as the infamous Sergeant Kurtis Lotus.

Kurtis finished the contents of his glass. Jason remained standing but ached to sit.

"If it helps," Jason continued. "She didn't ask me to speak on her behalf. She doesn't even know I'm here, let alone what I am asking you. Instead, I'm personally requesting permission for her to be in the Interrogation Room with Cyclamen and me. He won't just talk to her, he'd be speaking the truth."

"What makes you think that?" Kurtis tested, somewhat interested. "When you brought him in last night, he barely made a peep."

Cha-ching! Jason felt his idea was about to hit the jackpot. Without further ado, he pointed out something most people were not-so aware of.

"Because, Sergeant, neither one of us is his priority. There's only one thing in the DDAG he cares about."

"Oh?"

Jason, felt a hurdle of butterflies tingle in his stomach. However, he had to contain himself.

"Ever since he first laid eyes on Ariel, he became disgustingly infatuated with her. Whether Ariel admits it or not, she too is obsessed with Cyclamen." Jason brightened up with confidence. However, Lotus was not yet impressed. "Okay…." His smile dropped. "Anyway, they cannot get enough of each other. It's kind of like a love-hate marriage. The main difference is this: Ariel despises Cyclamen with every ounce of her being. Whereas Cyclamen…well…his intentions are more of a sexual nature, if you know what I mean." Jason gave a wink. "If it weren't for her presence last night, he never would've mentioned Seoul in the first place. Guaranteed."

Jason pointed to the chair.

"Sit down!" Lotus barked.

Relieved, Jason jumped into the comfortable seat, exclaiming a brief "Thank you!" before continuing his theory.

"I believe if Ariel is in the Interrogation Room he'll open up. I may have to leave them alone, which I don't mind doing if it gets him talking. My only request is to keep an eye on them in the Observation Room in order to prevent any potential threats to either him or her. If they're alone for too long it may become chaotic."

Trying to understand how Sergeant Lotus felt was complicated. Over the years, he managed to perfect an expressionless semblance. He poured himself another glass and caressed the rim with a delicate touch.

"Sir, don't you think drinking at 9 a.m. is a little early? Especially, two glasses? Eleven should be the earliest time to start drinking." Jason proposed.

"Shut up," Lotus grunted.

"Sorry."

Jason's hands were clammy as he waited for an answer. His velvety brown skin littered with goosebumps the longer silence controlled the room. A forest of black hairs grew over his arms.

Finally, Lotus made a decision. "Five minutes."

Hell yeah! Jason wanted to get up and kiss both of his sergeant's fat cheeks but there were boundaries.

"That's all I'll allow. It must be done before the 12 o'clock meeting," Lotus persisted. "Now, get going."

Jason felt victorious. "Ten minutes," he declared.

"Five."

His confidence was merely hanging on. "Seven minutes?"

"Five."

Alas, his confidence fell. Jason had climbed up the high mountain but never made it to the top.

Jason groaned. "Deal."

"Before you go, I want to set some ground rules." Lotus threw back his second glass of whiskey.

"Of course!" Jason said.

"I want the interrogation recorded: from beginning to end," Kurtis instructed. "Also, I'd like to make something clear. Ariel will still be banned from any and all details pertaining to the Seoul, Korea case after this interrogation. If I hear anything from anyone suggesting that she knows even an ounce of what is happening out there, I will make sure the king and queen pull her out completely from our faction. If not them, I'll escalate it to the royal cabinet. Maybe I'll even have her terminated. Her entire career as a Death Dealer will be expunged. Do you understand?"

Jason answered with a strong "Yes."

"Good." Lotus slammed his glass on top of the counter. "Now, get out of my office."

Bodhi and Ariel were on the Training Grounds—located on the upper bailey—shooting a few rounds of bullets, then moved on to a few rounds of arrows. Generally, Bodhi didn't speak much. He was quite shy and timid. However, today he was practically nonexistent. Ariel tried to get him to talk but no luck. Eventually, Ariel suggested a friendly game of skill: a competition of who can land the most headshots at a target dummy on the opposite side of the field. Each of them would have twenty tries and whoever "killed" the most people, won.

"If I win," Ariel began, tapping his cheek with the faux feather arrow, "You have to tell me why you are acting like a grump-grump. If you win, then the next bar tab is on me."

Bodhi happily sealed the bet with a firm, "Deal!"

With gloved hands, Ariel reached for her bow that stood on the ground. Since her first year of Death Dealer training, she'd kept the wooden piece of art close to her. A beauty it was. Both ends spiraled outward as they held the string, and feathers were engraved from top to bottom as if they were floating against a soft wind. In the New World, feathers symbolized luck.

Ariel checked the bow's string. Perfect! It was nice and taut. She readied herself with perfect posture. She pulled it straight back, making sure the arrow's shaft was placed right over her chest. It was best for her to keep one eye open. Her aim was off with both eyes trying to focus. In her head, she counted to three—*1...2...3...!*—then released the arrow, making it spin like a propeller as it whistled in the wind. Round and round it flew. The arrow plunged straight into the practice dummy's head and threads of hay were frightened away.

Ariel felt amazing and sang, "Your turn," with a great big smile. Her pearly white teeth distracted Bodhi for a moment. Ariel rarely smiled, but when she did, it was contagious and people always smiled back.

"I don't want to play this game anymore," Bodhi groaned. He cupped his hands together and warmed them with his thick breath.

"Come on," Ariel moped, tugging at his shoulder. "Don't be a sore loser. I swear, I'm not that good. Zaire is much better than I am."

"He doesn't count! He's the best out of everybody. But I bet you're using one of your spells against me." Bodhi busted out laughing.

Ariel studied magic and spell chanting at the DDAG Academy in District Europe, however, she was terrible at it. She only mastered a few minor spells, so she still considered herself an amateur when it came to anything magical.

"Asshole!" Ariel playfully shoved Bodhi aside. "That was rude!"

"Hey, maybe you should go back to school and become an alchemist or a sorcerer." Bodhi couldn't help taking one final jab.

"Fuck off before I break your legs!" Ariel hissed with her empty threat. "Anyway, smart-ass, you're up."

Now, it was Bodhi's time to shine. He zipped up his brown coat and made sure his scarf was secured around his neck.

Bodhi took more time to prepare. During his profession as an assassin, he preferred his body as a weapon or Elixia. Whether they were single or double-handed armaments, none were his forte.

Finally, Bodhi let his first shot loose, even after some struggle. It echoed in the air as it lifted into the sky. Oddly, it spun once then fell flat. After moments of guessing where the arrow would hit, it landed on the dummy's arm but embarrassingly bounced off. Bodhi was mortified and wanted to run away.

"I need practice." Bodhi sighed as he scratched his head, creating a mess of his thick black hair.

"No argument here, shy boy," Ariel joked. "That's what you get for making fun of my clueless, spell-chanting ass."

"You're probably right," Bodhi agreed.

Ariel softly nudged his jaw.

Ow! Bodhi chuckled, lightly pushing Ariel away.

"Let's continue then, shall we?" Ariel grabbed another arrow from her quiver. "I'll even give you a few pointers as we move along."

There were less than a handful of people Bodhi looked up to. Ariel was one whom he highly admired. He never admitted it out loud, but he dreamt to have the equivalency of Ariel's strength, courage and I-don't-care attitude. Bodhi felt puny standing alongside her. However, thanks to the meaningful friendship she had given him over the last few years, she inspired him to be more independent and less fearful.

"Sure!" Bodhi cheered. "Who knows. Maybe there will be a turn of events and I will be the glorious surprise victor!"

Ariel gasped. "I wouldn't go that far, but bring it on."

Let the games begin.

After twenty rounds of fun, Ariel won by seventeen points. Bodhi was unsurprised by his failure, but his archery skills did improve, which he appreciated.

The assassins sat on some cemented bleachers and casually watched Death Dealers training their novices out on the Training Grounds.

Ariel was desperate to know what was upsetting her friend but she was terrible at consoling. To the best of her ability, she asked, "So, what was wrong with you last night?" *Great job Ariel!* she thought. *What a way to blurt it out like that.*

Bodhi shook his head, still averse to opening up. "Nothing. Just personal problems at home."

Lies. All lies. Ariel falsified belief and played along.

"Maybe there are," Ariel said. "I may not know a lot of things, but what I know is this. Whatever is happening at home is not the main problem. Something else is bothering you. Talk to me."

Bodhi parted his lips but instantaneously retracted them. *Ugh!!! Bodhi, work with me!* When people didn't cooperate, Ariel got...impeccably irritated. However, she cared for Bodhi and wanted to be his shoulder to cry on.

Ariel lowered her voice. "You trust me, right?"

Bodhi nodded his head. Ariel sensed the sadness lingering in his brown eyes.

"I'm very grateful that you trust me. I think you're one of three—maybe four—that do," Ariel laughed. "Have I done anything to break that trust?"

"No," Bodhi peeped.

"Good. Now, spit it out, comrade!" Ariel hoped gearing her annoyance in a playful way would help. She popped her knuckles before massaging his neck and shoulders.

Bodhi picked at his cuticles while contemplating if he should admit the incident with Derek bothered him.

Ariel waited as her hands made their way to Bodhi's back. As she applied pressure to his spine her violet eyes got distracted by what was on the field. She glued her gaze onto a Death Dealer novice she had never seen before. Her name was unknown, but one thing was for sure, she was absolutely gorgeous.

The novice's chocolate brown hair draped all the way down to her thighs. Her skin, though not anywhere near as pale as Ariel's, was a creamy, almond-like complexion. Her lips were coated in a mauve pink lipstick, making them all the more inviting. She was on the sword-fighting mat, practicing with wooden swords against a member of Ariel's guild—a man named James. Her long legs moved swiftly across the blue mat. When James struck, the young woman blocked each hit and counter-attacked with a defense move, causing James to lose balance. He was about to deliver a roundhouse kick to her face. Quickly, she swooped under his leg. He missed. James bent his elbow, aiming for her chin. Immediately, she slapped him with the side of her sword. Both James and Ariel were satisfied with her quick wit and masterful reflexes. Her technique was breathtaking. Even when she made the puniest mistake, she practiced over and over again. Ariel felt she was viewing herself as a novice, back when she trained in District Europe.

Ariel's mouth salivated as she continued to eye that incredible warrior woman. After a time of ongoing leering, Bodhi broke her concentration.

"Derek," Bodhi sighed. Ariel stopped massaging him and plopped to a seat in front of him.

"Derek?" Ariel asked, trying to put a face to the name.

"He was the man I killed last night," Bodhi began. "When I got to his location, he was singing. His voice was awful, but what bothered me was he kept mentioning a woman named Patty."

Ariel pawed at her ear. "And? What about Patty?"

Bodhi had to provide vivid details, unfortunately.

"It was the way he was talking—or singing—about her. It wasn't a love song but rather a hateful one. She turned him down and he was not happy."

"Great!" Ariel projected. "Fuck him."

"No, it's bad!" Bodhi huffed. "She rejected him. I'm assuming many times. This caused him to rape her…or think about raping her. I'm not sure. I don't know if this has happened yet or if he had some kind of disturbing fantasy, but he was way too excited about doing these terrible and inhumane things."

The menacing lyrics replayed in his head like an outdated music box: *I want to fuck you till you bleed. The deeper I go the more it will cause you to scream. I want you to be my one and only lady. I'll find a way for you to not keep me waiting.*

Ariel found no words to make the situation better. She had never been in a victimized position where a man tried to commit anything risqué without permission. The mature thing to do was be Bodhi's friend.

"I'm so sorry," Ariel said, genuinely. "There's nothing you can do about it now."

"I used Elixia on him," Bodhi mumbled, wiping his watery eyes with the brink of his sleeve. "Derek was so drunk. I took advantage of that. I made him believe Patty was in the room. I used a woman who may have been a victim of rape or could've been one! I made him envision her, erotically. She danced until I made him think she jabbed a knife straight through him." A mix of emotions blasted in his heart. "I should've just killed him without wearing a mask, or I could've easily used Alexander Cyclamen instead of Patty but instead I used her in a sexual and criminal way. I don't know who she is or what she looks like, but for some reason my gut is screaming at me to find her. Help her. Check up on her. I need to apologize for what Derek had done or what he could've done. I also need to apologize for my actions."

"Stop right there," Ariel interrupted, raising her hand for Bodhi to pause. "First of all, you have done nothing wrong." She held his hand. "You used the strongest weapon imaginable against Derek. I bet he had never been such a wuss in his entire life. Patty had the right to shove horror in that asshole's face before sending him off to live in the depths of Malum with the Lord of Darkness. Using her to your advantage was smart. Also, if you feel like you must check up on this girl Patty, then do it. Listen to your instincts to do the right thing. Fuck everything else."

Bodhi shook his head 'no.' After all, it was dishonorable for a Death Dealer to break DDAG law: go outside of the royal cabinet and the king and queen. The DDAG equaled life. There was nothing more important.

"I can't." Bodhi covered his face. "This would still be considered DDAG business since she's connected to a terrorist. A recently killed terrorist. Wouldn't that make the situation even worse? What if Sergeant Lotus found out?"

Ariel wrapped her arms around Bodhi to calm him. "He won't," Ariel assured. "Not if you don't let him."

"But you got caught." *Shit!* Bodhi hoped he didn't offend Ariel.

Ariel took a deep breath. It's true. She had gotten caught many times.

"I've been caught with more things than you can count, but that's because I'm careless when it comes to myself," Ariel admitted. "However, when it deals with someone I care about, I refuse to let anything bad happen to them. I won't allow it."

With his life, Bodhi trusted Ariel. He just lacked the amount of courage she carried.

"I'll think it over. If I decide to go through with it, who knows how long it'll take before I can figure out where Patty lives. Besides, there's some business I have to take care of first."

Ariel knew what he was referring to. "The Seoul case?" Bodhi's eyes widened. "Don't worry about it. Jason told me I'm not invited to Sergeant Lotus' party."

Bodhi felt terrible. Like Jason, he hated keeping Ariel out of DDAG business. "I'm sorry. We were all sworn to secrecy."

"I know." Ariel threw her head over the railing to get a whiff of pine scented air. Sergeant Lotus was not messing around when he said he did not want Ariel involved. "Jason told me everything. It's not your fault. I mean, it sucks but what can I do about it? Usually, I'll bitch and whine or make Jason bitch and whine for me, but this time, I decided to not argue. Getting in trouble almost every day gets annoying."

"You really think Cyclamen was telling the truth? About this so-called New World War in Seoul?" Bodhi asked.

"I don't know. I don't care."

"Oh, Ariel. Today, we're going to find out," a third voice chimed in.

Both Bodhi and Ariel perked up and saw Jason walking up the bleachers.

"Are you referring to me?" Ariel asked.

"You? Hell yeah."

She pointed at herself, checking to see if he wasn't referring to Bodhi.

"Yes, Ariel, I'm sure."

"Didn't you take him in for questioning last night?" Bodhi asked Jason.

"Yeah. Why the hell do you need me?" Ariel felt eyes staring at her. She glanced past Jason and noticed the pretty lady she'd been checking out was grinning her way. Ariel smirked back.

Jason looked over his shoulder, noticing his best friend's distraction.

"Focus!" Jason snapped his fingers together.

Ariel brushed him off and sent a playful wink to the pretty lady.

"I am focused." Ariel geared her attention toward her captain. "Chill out."

"Cyclamen gave us zilch. I need you to talk to him." Jason hurried, refusing to waste any time.

One thing for certain: Ariel hated Cyclamen and wanted him dead, but she found it pointless if she was unable to choke him to death. Therefore, Jason's plan was not in her favor.

"What makes you think he'll say shit when I'm there?" Ariel wondered.

Jason snorted. "You're kidding me, right?"

Ariel shrugged. She looked at Bodhi but he was opposed to getting in between the best friends, who also happened to be a man and woman he exceedingly looked up to.

Jason carried on. "He had no problem admitting something fishy is going on in Seoul. Why? Because he saw you. If you weren't there, I doubt he would have said anything at all. He would've happily died right then and there."

"Dead. Hmmph...." Ariel rested her elbows on the bleachers behind her. "He oughta be."

"But," Jason continued, "as soon as he saw your pretty face, he snitched. I get it. You want him buried six feet under. So do I. But right now, he's a valuable asset. We need to find out what information he's locking up in that psychotic, homicidal brain of his. A strong, fantastic Death Dealer like yourself would help greatly with that. You are coming with me right now. Get it? Got it? Great!" Jason marched away.

After Jason removed himself from the bleachers, he noticed there were no footsteps trailing behind. He turned around to see Ariel hunched over her knees, looking at the snow below her feet.

"Are you coming?" Jason nudged, waltzing back over to Ariel's location.

'What am I supposed to do, exactly?' Ariel asked as she interlocked her fingers and twirled her thumbs around.

"You are going to find out what he is hiding. Contacts. Secret codes. The possibility of Black Plague II Infections rising. The works." Jason took a quick peek at the Training Grounds. "She is hot, Little Velvet."

"Fuck off," Ariel jokingly threatened. "I saw her first."

They smiled and exchanged small laughter.

Finally, Ariel conceded. "Let's get this over with."

After bidding Bodhi an adieu, she tightened her boot laces then followed Jason inside the guardhouse tower.

They walked three floors down to the Interrogation Room, where it was dark and empty—only a bored security guard sat in front of the one-way mirror in the Observation Room. Jason asked Ariel to take a few moments to prep herself before joining.

Ariel eyed Cyclamen's every move. Before Ariel made her surprise appearance, Jason offered Cyclamen a coffee and pastry as she prepared herself to visit the man she loathed most and wanted to send into the depths of Malum.

"You can do this." Ariel stretched her arms and cracked both sides of her neck to shake off any radiating tension. "Whatever you do, just talk to him. Do not reach over that table and rip his heart out." She inhaled heavily. "Alright." Then abruptly exhaled. "Terrorist talk. Let's go."

Ariel swallowed her pride as she opened the door.

Cyclamen sat on the far side of the room, smiling the instant Ariel stepped foot inside. Immediately, his eyes caught onto her breast as she unzipped her moss green coat. They were graciously poking out from her lilac sweater.

"Please, join us. Why don't you have a seat?" Jason gestured politely. He cautioned for any signs of tension. "We're just going to have a small chat. No one will die today."

Ariel let the door shut itself behind her. She whistled as she walked slowly over to a chair next to her captain. Alexander denied the coffee and bagel but instead enjoyed the grittiness of a cheap cigarette. No fancy cigars were allowed in that hell hole.

Ariel asked, "How are you coping with cheap nicotine?"

Cyclamen hoarsely chuckled, causing a violent cough to storm out of his esophagus. He gurgled, forming a cloud of saliva inside his atrocious mouth. He spat out a bubble of mouth fluid onto the floor next to Jason's shoes. Without losing focus, Jason simply adjusted his feet.

Ariel held back from reaching over the table and plowing the sunburnt man's head into the floor. She wanted to bang his skull into the hard concrete until she coated the entire room in Cyclamen blood.

"I can't complain, my beauty," Cyclamen coughed. "Thanks for caring."

"Don't think I care," Ariel snickered.

"Alright then." Jason felt he was handling two angry teenagers. "I am going to leave the room and allow Ms. Rose to take over this interview."

Ariel grabbed Jason's arm. In his ear, she whispered, "What are you doing? Don't leave."

"Come on now, my sweet," Cyclamen cooed. "I think that's a terrific idea. About time you and I had some privacy."

"Ugh...You can't be serious," Ariel snarled.

Jason looked her in the eye. "I trust you. Don't do anything rash." He glared over at Cyclamen. The old man had a twinkle in his eye that even made the captain cringe. "Or at least try to not do anything rash. I will be in the next room. Call me if you need anything."

Ariel's best friend headed out the door.

Slam! Jason was now gone and Ariel was left alone with a man who was fumigating the room with smoke and had the worst tan and countless age spots.

On top of the table was an electronic notepad and pen. Ariel turned it on and the first window to pop up listed pre-typed questions.

Obviously, this was well planned. Thanks, Jason.

"Are you ready or what?" Ariel sniggered.

Cyclamen put out his cigarette on top of the bare table, gawking at the beauty across from him.

"Well?" Ariel spat.

"I'm ready whenever you are, baby."

"Enough with the pet names, alright?" Ariel fired back.

Cyclamen gave a thumbs-up.

"First question: How long have you known about the New World War?"

"Not long."

Not really an answer, Ariel thought. "How long, exactly?"

"Not long."

"Can you give me a damn number?"

Cyclamen kept his lips sealed.

"I need you to cooperate. Answer the questions," Ariel demanded.

"I am," Cyclamen assured. "I'm bad with numbers, my sweet. But I do know it hasn't been that long."

"Seriously, shut the fuck up with the pet names." Ariel scrolled to the next question. "How did you hear about the New World War? When will this event happen?"

"Depends," Cyclamen shrugged.

"On?" Ariel needed more information.

"A number of things."

Ariel waited for some more color to be added to the bland description, but again he offered nothing.

"Look, you think I want to be here? I'd rather see you as a corpse but I'm being forced to talk to your ugly face." Ariel drummed her pen on the notepad's screen and shook her leg simultaneously.

"Oh, I'm aware," Cyclamen admitted, unashamed. "However, I'd rather talk to you alone."

"We are alone," Ariel sassed.

Cyclamen looked over at the one-way mirror. "I mean really alone." His eyes bounced at the corner cameras. "No technology. Not another set of eyes. Just you and me."

Ariel was miffed but thought about cooperating. "You promise to answer all my questions, truthfully?" Cyclamen nodded.

Ariel pondered, carefully. Chains cuffed Cyclamen's arms and legs so it'd be difficult for him to touch her. If this was a way to get him to talk then so be it. "Jason, shut the cameras off and wait for me outside."

Jason forced the security guard out of his way and grabbed the intercom. "Unfortunately, I will not negotiate with his terms. I promised the sergeant I would keep you safe."

Ariel understood Jason's concern but he had asked for her help. "Just do it!"

Jason punched the control panel below him. The DDAG guard sitting next to him jumped out of his seat.

"Get out of here," Jason told the boy. "Now!"

The guard sprinted out of the Observation Room.

Jason cursed under his breath, "This motherfucker better not hurt her. If something happens to her, I swear I'm chopping your head off, Cyclamen!!!"

Before unwillingly complying with Cyclamen's terms, Jason fixed his cap and spoke diligently over the microphone. "I'm turning off all devices including cameras and voice recorders. I will leave the room but my walkie stays on. This is for Ariel's protection. Honor this and I will do as you request." Cyclamen agreed. "If you hurt her, I will go in there and kill you." Jason's fist choked the mike stand. "Ariel, you've got five minutes."

As promised, Jason turned off all technological devices and bolted outside, fuming at Cyclamen's request to be alone with his best friend. As soon as he heard the crunch of the snow floor, he screamed in fury. *ARGH!!!*

Ariel and Cyclamen were now alone.

Ariel looked over the questions in the notepad and thought most of them useless. She threw it aside.

"Alright then," Ariel began. "Let's get down to business. Why did you mention Seoul, Korea? How did you know that's where I grew up? I know that's the only reason why you named my hometown to begin with."

"Calm yourself," Cyclamen grumbled. "I knew you grew up in Seoul, Korea, because I admit, I had Roger do a background check on you. That's because I've never laid my eyes on anyone so lovely and…perfect. For me, it was love at first sight. I had to know everything about you."

"You stalked me?" Ariel's eyes widened.

"Sweetie, you stalked me too, did you not? But I only wanted to know important things about you. Where you were born. Your favorite food. Favorite color. What those magnificent tits look like underneath your tight Death Dealer garb."

Ariel growled. Her nails dug into the plastic table and she had to resist the temptation to slaughter Cyclamen.

"The war happening in Seoul is pure coincidence."

"Tell me what you know. What war?"

Cyclamen lit another cigarette. "After the New World War, evolution will commence."

Evolution? Why did that sound familiar? Ariel retraced her steps from last night. *Evolution begins in Seoul.* That's it! The memo she read on the cell phone last night mentioned evolution.

"What about evolution?" Ariel asked, scoping for an important piece of the puzzle. "Is the human population at risk again? Has someone recreated the Black Plague II Infection? What? What does evolution mean?"

Cyclamen took a big hit of his cigarette and stared into Ariel's violet irises. He adored her eyes and could get lost in their world repeatedly.

"Look for a man named Ki. Personally, I have never met the guy, but I heard he has been bringing together many of the terrorist gangs around the New World. These gangs are flocking from all over, including District Australia and District South America. Supposedly, he's building an army."

"What kind of army?" Ariel was invested and yearned for more.

Alexander snorted. "Babe, I'm only a local criminal. A pawn in a game of chess. My gang was practically a joke. Someone as important as Ki would not want anything to do with me or my men. I don't blame him. He wants fearsome killers, not amateurs. My gang was not filled with the strongest, like your team proved last night. Ki has an army. Why? I do not know. I'm not sure if he's succeeded at bringing back the Black Plague II but I wouldn't be surprised if he did. There are rumors."

Who was Ki? Ariel had never heard that name. "Where do we find Ki? In Seoul, I'm assuming."

"Yes, but where in Seoul is a blur. I'd look anywhere and everywhere if I were you, but be wary. He is *that* important, so many men and women will be guarding him. Do not underestimate him. Do not trust even the most innocent-looking child. They could be one of Ki's spies. You'll only lose if you ask the questions to the wrong people."

"That's it? You can't give me anything else?" Ariel was outraged at the minimal amount of information provided to her.

"Sorry, babe. If I knew more, I'd tell you," Cyclamen said.

"Why are you telling me all this? Why not the others?"

"I don't like Death Dealers." Cyclamen stuck his tongue out. "Bleh! These men and women think they're superior just because they've been trained to believe they rise above the rest. It's sick."

Ariel shyly agreed. She too felt that way at times.

"You, though." Cyclamen chuckled. "There's just something about you I like. And it's not just your pretty face, fabulous tits and great ass. You rebel with good reason. I respect that very much. It's like you complete me."

"I hate you," Ariel hissed.

"I know," Cyclamen smiled. "Either way, that's all I have for you."

"Fine!" Ariel shot up and hurried for the door. She looked back at him one more time.

"Good luck, my sweet," Cyclamen purred.

Jason stood outside drinking the denied cup of coffee for Cyclamen as he waited for Ariel. She pulled up beside him and hurriedly gave him all the details.

"Ki? I wonder if the sergeant knows about him," Jason said curiously.

"I doubt it," Ariel said. "Take the information I gave you and let everyone know. However, there's something else."

"What's that?" Jason asked.

"There's more he's not telling me."

Jason paused. "I thought he told you that was everything he knew."

"No," Ariel sighed. "He's a liar. He'll do anything to see me again. For now, I have to play dumb. If you need me to question him further, let me know."

Could Jason let her know? Sergeant Lotus was clear on her not being involved after today.

"Will do," Jason breathed, unsure if this was a possibility. "I gotta go get ready for the meeting. We'll talk later?"

"Yeah!" Ariel exclaimed. "Let me know what happens."

Unfortunately, she cannot know.

The noon meeting began and Lotus passed out confidential folders to each member of his guild. The Death Dealers opened them and inside were documents of suspicious activities happening throughout the city of Seoul, Korea.

"All of these incidents have one thing in common: disappearance. People are being kidnapped, taken away from their families and possibly murdered." Lotus turned to Jason. "Can you show us the video of Cyclamen during the interrogation?"

"We were experiencing technical difficulties, sir." *Do not put me on the spot,* Jason muttered in his head. Lotus scrunched his face and Jason quickly took over the session. He provided them with details given from Ariel about Cyclamen.

"So, instead of hundreds of little terrorist gangs running around, there's going to be one massive army?" Seraphina was unclear about upcoming events.

"We're unsure." Jason knew as much as the rest of his guild.

Zaire listed the main points aloud. "Army. Suspicious activity. Black Plague II Infections. Is this Ki building an army for world domination? Because evolution….The virus killed millions and millions of people. There's no way an evolution can occur with an outbreak like that. None of this makes sense."

"It does not," Lotus agreed. He asked everyone to turn to page five. "Here we have a picture of a figure prowling the empty streets of Seoul. Most people believe this person is infected and could be passing the virus to others."

"The Black Plague II was never transmitted through human contact before," Seraphina weighed in.

"Not that we know of, no." Lotus stepped back to view his entire faction. "However, things, including diseases and viruses, do evolve over time. Mostly it's nature adapting to newly created environments or people. Sometimes it's due to scientific intervention." Bodhi raised his hand. "You may speak, Mr. Tigerlilly."

"What are we supposed to do exactly?"

"Your job is to connect the dots and find out what is going on," Sergeant Lotus instructed while his team looked over their folders. Some were highlighting key points and taking notes. "All of you must take extra precautions during this mission. If anyone screws up, our faction will be terminated from the site and another team will take our place. Look over your folders and pack up. Meet at the portal gate right before sunrise."

Zaire wondered, "What about Ariel?"

Seraphina gagged. "What about her?"

"She should be with us," Zaire fought back.

Lotus fixed his collar. "Exactly, Ms. Jasmine," he said, ignoring Zaire's words entirely. "There's no need to concern yourself with Ms. Rose, Mr. Iris." Zaire tucked himself into his chair, upset with the sergeant's crude response.

"Now, if there are no more questions I'd like to close this meeting short."

Silence.

"Good. Now, get some sleep everyone. You all have a long journey ahead of you."

Jason tried storming out of the room but Lotus called after him.

"Jason, hold on a moment."

Jason froze and placed his arms behind his back. Slowly, he turned around and with respect, faced Sergeant Lotus.

"You know what I find hilarious?"

Jason knew where this conversation was heading. "No, sir."

Lotus pulled out his phone and pointed at his laptop. "During all my years as a Death Dealer and sergeant in the DDAG, not once has any piece of equipment gone faulty. Yet today, during an important interview between your best pal and one of the world's crummiest terrorists, the cameras and voice recorders just decided not to work. Now, how can that be, Captain Lilly?"

Jason couldn't lie to his sergeant. Not speaking the truth was unethical. "Cyclamen requested it."

"And you said yes because…?"

"He refused to talk unless he was completely alone with Ariel," Jason said angrily, remembering how outraged he was at Cyclamen's negotiations. "Time was short and I figured it was best to give him what he wanted. The faster he spat out information, the better."

Sergeant Lotus clicked his tongue as he thought to himself. He placed his phone back in his blazer pocket.

"Figures," Lotus sighed. "We got him to talk and that's all that matters."

"Glad, to see you understand." Jason was relieved.

"Before you head out, there's been a change of plans."

Jason was confused. "Oh?"

Kurtis handed over Ariel's probation papers.

"Why are you showing me these?" Jason flipped through them.

"Her records have been updated," Kurtis began. "After you left my office earlier this afternoon, I spoke with the king and queen. During our discussion, I informed them of your promising theory about Cyclamen opening up to Ms. Rose. If this would prove true, we would allow her placement on the Seoul case in District Asia. Since everything has gone according to plan, it's obvious Ariel is valuable and should indeed join you and the others on this mission."

Jason was ecstatic. "That's great, sir, but why didn't you tell the team the news?"

Kurtis shrugged. "They'll find out tomorrow."

Jason wanted to hurry and let Ariel know. "She'll be thrilled."

"Ah…shh, shh, shh…." Kurtis wasn't done. "Do not get too excited. She is going. However, there are restrictions."

"Understandable." Jason reined his excitement.

"She must be under your supervision at all times," Kurtis urged, intensely. "Ariel is only allowed off Faction Abyss grounds when the situation pertains to Death Dealer duties."

"Got it," Jason agreed.

"This means any social outings will be off-limits. No parties. No bars. She will be under headquarters arrest." Jason felt like his best friend was being punished like a child who refused to eat their vegetables. "Ariel can visit a local Lord of Life monastery—if she pleases—any day of the week, but only once a week." Was he through? What more could he possibly add to choke Ariel's freedom?

"Then there's one more thing."

Save the worst for last. Jason assumed this had to be the cherry on top of a horrendous cake.

"If Ariel Rose disobeys me or you in any way, not only is she out, you too will be terminated from your position as a DDAG captain."

What?!! Jason wanted to scream. How was this fair?

"Also, if you mess up and the connection is with Ariel, both of you are out of a job." Lotus' secretary, Mina—a sweet assistant and one of Ariel's past girlfriends—informed him he had an important phone call. He grabbed his briefcase.

Lotus held out his hand. "This is for the safety of our faction. Understand that. I cannot continue to have an undisciplined assassin. Just do as you're told and everything will be okay. Good luck." Jason concealed his understanding with a firm shake.

With that, Lotus exited the conference room, leaving the door open behind him.

Jason didn't know if he should feel joyous. He wanted to fast-forward to the future. Will he still be captain of Faction Divide? Will Ariel ruin everything? Or worse, will he, himself, ruin all that was good? For now, he had to live life day-by-day. It was his responsibility to make sure the mission ran smoothly.

Later that night, Jason updated Ariel on Kurtis' change of heart. She felt good—real good, despite the fun she won't be having. Alas, she would be venturing out with her fellow comrades on a hardcore quest. It was nice to know she wouldn't be relegated to office work while they embarked on their biggest mission yet. Wholeheartedly, she felt blessed.

Before putting himself to bed, Jason set up two white candles and filled a bowl with sprigs of lavender and thyme. He swirled orange blood incense around his altar then kneeled on both knees. He closed his eyes and prayed to the Lord of Life.

"I swear by the Lord of Life, I will do my best to keep Ariel in line. I beg you, my Lord, to help me along the way. Allow me to keep my position as captain. In all of the seven districts, there is no other faction better than Divide. I'll do anything to keep my place. Just please, guide me through it all."

With a soft blow, both fires from the candles faded away and turned into smoke.

Tomorrow was a new day and the real adventure would begin. He was ready. Cautious, but ready.

"Ariel," Jason said aloud. "You better not fuck this up."

WELCOME TO SEOUL

Torches lit and sparked high on the towers of the DDAG headquarters in District North America. Others were paving the way along the cemented bricks throughout the entirety of the structure. It was almost sunrise and most of the innocents in District North America were still fast asleep in their beds while the Death Dealers in Faction Divide were gathering in front of a portal gate, located in the back gardens beyond the upper bailey.

The portal gates: They were the fastest and most convenient way to travel throughout all seven districts in the New World. Not one portal was the same. At Faction Divide's castle, the portal was made out of oak branches that circled around a thick whirling flame that glowed bright blue. With its extravagant stature, it proudly overshadowed everyone beneath it.

The Death Dealers were carrying quiet conversations amongst themselves as they waited for their captain to emerge.

It had been almost two years since Ariel had traveled outside of District North America. She was lucky Sergeant Lotus granted her permission to travel outside Faction Divide's walls; if he forbade it, she would've suffered alone, training incompetent novices about the ways of the professional Death Dealer. Either way, she was more than appreciative and brought a fashionable sense of order and calm demeanor with her. At least temporarily.

The moon was descending its ebony stage, making way for the New World's brightest star, the sun.

Zaire surveyed the area silently with his hazel eyes and waited patiently for his captain to arrive.

Bodhi merrily whistled to himself alongside Zaire.

Seraphina stood alone and her back felt strained. She stretched her arms way, way up then bent forward, feeling a solid *pop*. Mason watched pervertedly as he gnawed on a handful of almonds.

"She's so hot," Mason croaked to a blonde-haired Death Dealer named Lance, as broken pieces of nuts spat out of his mouth.

Suddenly, an eager, deep brown-skinned man marched down the gardens with pride as his trustworthy guild looked at him proudly. Quickly, they parted like the red sea to clear Jason's pathway. Once he was between the portal and his army, his honey brown eyes looked upon them with fierceness.

"Tonight, we begin another mission. Together, we must venture to District Asia and help our fellow DDAG members during this dark time." Jason's guild circled around him. Their ears were wide open as their encouraging leader spoke confidently. "We do not know what may happen, but what I do know, with all certainty, is this: I have the best goddamn guild out of all the seven districts in the New World."

Each assassin cheered: some rose hands with their captain and others drew out their weapons, displaying them with great satisfaction.

"If any guild is to bring true justice to the New World it is Faction Divide. Am I, right?"

They cried out in unison, "Yeah!"

"Am I, right?!" Jason asked again, more proud, more loud.

As high as they could go, the guild roared, "Yeah!!"

Ariel smiled wide as her best friend did what he did best: lead.

"Alright, then," Jason yelled. "Let's fight!"

Jason turned to the portal gate and gently pressed his palm onto one of its stocky branches. The flames heightened at the sight of his touch.

Jason spoke into the blue fire, "District Asia headquarters, please." Slowly, a transparent image of Faction Abyss' castle emerged from the flames. He released his hand and anticipated what's next.

Captain Lilly stepped into the blaze and it devoured his entire body.

One by one, the rest of the guild followed, trooping to the next destination.

The sun was rising behind them but before its rays could kiss their flesh, the assassins landed on the opposite side of the portal, in the gardens of the DDAG headquarters in District Asia. Welcome to Seoul, Korea.

While everyone else retracted to their feet, Ariel remained in crouch position with locked eyes and was terrified to open them. This was the first time she had been home in over a decade. Conflicting emotions—excitement and sadness—rummaged through her. What if Seoul looked completely different? Would she recognize her own hometown?

Immediately, Ariel's nostrils flared. The air...it was fresh and clean and the smell of garbage no longer took over the senses.

You can do this, Ariel thought to herself. *Get up.* Slowly, she released her hands from the cold ground, feeling pigments of snow dribble off her knuckles—she had failed to wear gloves. Once she stood, she realized there was no turning back. It was time to face reality and look upon the place she was born and raised. It was time to see Seoul once again. *Come on...one...two....* Ariel flapped her eyes open. "Three."

Unfortunately, Ariel's first view of Seoul was a few blurred city lights and a white wall girded the castle. She wanted to overlook the city but the giant rock panel blocked her sight.

Ariel switched-over her position, merely disappointed. Her eyes locked onto one of the castle's rectangular towers. As she followed the structure north, for the first time she realized it wasn't enormous at all. In District North America, the pinnacles easily surpassed the clouds and almost touched the sun. In District Asia, there were banks taller than its headquarters.

When Ariel was in second level school, her class took a fieldtrip to District Asia's headquarters, and she felt puny as she entered the castle. She felt she had entered the New World's biggest playground. There were so many closed doors that could lead to unknown places and she was desperate to open them and see what's inside: travel long journeys and go on exciting adventures. However, her teacher, Mrs. Sunflower, kept a strong watch on her.

Jason had his guild crowd center. A short man with messy black hair and a clean-shaven face was walking toward the group. He carried an angelic smile as he approached his North American allies.

"Jason," the man called out. He and Jason hugged briefly. "It is an honor to see you again, my friend."

"Likewise, Sying," Jason responded. "How have you been?"

"I'm doing very well. Thank you. May I?" It was considered disrespectful if a DDAG captain refused to ask permission to speak to another captain's guild. Jason approved.

Sying brought himself forward and warmly welcomed the newly arrived assassins.

"I am Sying Orchid, Faction Abyss' DDAG captain. I am honored to have you all here tonight." Sying observed the fierce group of warriors and basked in all the glory that came with the Death Dealer Alliance Guild. "My faction needs your assistance for what is currently happening in Seoul, Korea. For too long we have been working on our own, hoping and praying we would be able to solve this case solely. However, we were wrong. Due to us wasting time, we are now further behind than we've ever been. I am grateful to be working with the New World's finest DDAG faction. My guild, including myself, cannot express our gratitude enough."

Sying swayed his arms to the east. "First, each of you will be escorted to your rooms to unpack your belongings and get comfortable with your temporary home. Once situated, please, join us in our banquet hall. I had our chefs prepare endless amounts of food and drinks. This is District Asia's welcome gift to you. Once again, we thank you, Captain Lilly, and your team for helping during this rough time. Now, let's feast!"

Everyone cheered excitedly whilst scrambling to get inside. Most of their stomachs growled at the idea of delicious eats.

"Hell yeah! I'm starving," Bodhi cheered. Ariel snorted and followed behind.

The dance hall—although smaller than District North America's—was intimate and inviting. Each eight-foot section had either steel blue or ebony wallpaper: the official DDAG colors of Faction Abyss. On the ceiling was a swivel of golden lights that glittered over your skin. There were four long tables on the outskirts of the dance floor with smaller square tables in the center. Each table was covered in a black tablecloth with a steel blue runner. On top were lit tea light candles and fancy boxes with golden chopsticks placed at an angle, over the lids.

Toward the back of the dance hall was an entire section dedicated to stylishly presented cuisine. There were mounds of different almond cheeses and grapes and rice and noodle dishes. For Ariel, this brought back fond memories of her childhood when she would indulge in jade noodles daily, and sometimes add a side of rice. Something about the striking color of the mint green noodles brought a young Ariel joy. Maybe it was because the noodles looked like gooey candy. Ariel was unsure.

"How are you feeling?" Jason surprised Ariel from behind as she was packing a plate full of regret.

"Well, what can I say?" Ariel plopped down a spoonful of balsamic mixed vegetables on top of her already maxed out plate. "Last time I was here, my aunt had to drag me to the portal gate because I was crying that I was leaving Seoul. Finally, I get to come back and the first thing I see is a white border. I know we'll see the city tomorrow but I want to see what it looks now. I mean, the air alone smells so different. I wonder what else has changed." Jason hugged her shoulder with his hand. "But you know me. I don't bullshit. I am happy to be here. If I had the luxury to revisit familiar sites, by myself or with you, I wouldn't be here right now. Either way, it's good to be home."

Jason knew his best friend would have future troubles while living in Seoul. Ariel was already becoming an emotional wreck. However, masking emotions was one of her many talents. She fooled everyone: except Jason.

The night was fun and eventful with engaging conversations and endless laughter, bringing everyone together. Jason let loose after a few glasses of wheat ale. He sprinted his way to the dance floor and busted out his moves to the tunes of the jazz band as if no one was watching. He tried to persuade Ariel into being his partner but failed. She'd rather watch from afar.

Bodhi was maybe the most gleeful of the bunch. He ravaged his way through four servings of sweet mashed potatoes and green bean/coconut milk casserole.

Even Seraphina managed to handle herself like a lady, only mocking a few people at a time.

Late in the evening, Ariel sat at the bar and grabbed the attention of a sexy Death Dealer named Ivy. Ariel sensed the attraction and connected eyes with the fawn-haired vixen.

Ivy headed in Ariel's direction. Sensual invigoration led Ariel to wonder if things would mature as the night grew older.

Drinking the rest of her wine, Ariel stared aimlessly across a cherry wooden shelf holding bottles of alcohol, pretending to not notice the pretty creature approaching. A suave-looking male was the bartender, and he was busy cleaning the dirty counter from an assassin that was too plastered to clean up his own spill.

Ivy's thick body was embellished in an orange dress that cascaded the cool honey brown color of her skin. A rose gold necklace hung a snowflake in between her plump breasts. Her hair was fixed in a neat bun and a French-braid wrapped around her hair tie, hiding it well.

Ivy was insanely gorgeous and carried a crystalline energy within her. With her velvety bronzed legs, she cat-walked her way to Ariel, swaying her wide hips.

"Hi," Ivy greeted, kitten-like. "You have beautiful eyes."

"As do you." Ariel admired the bright green sparkle in her narrow-shaped eyes.

"What are you up to?" Ivy asked. Ariel noticed a cute mole above the right side of her lip as Ivy half-smiled.

Ariel requested two specific drinks from the bartender. "Currently, getting you a glass of white wine to drink with me. Please, sit." White wine was not too heavy and the ladies loved it.

As Ivy happily slid into the stool next to Ariel, she purposely brushed her chest against Ariel's back. "There's no escaping now, is there?" Ivy crossed her legs, capturing Ariel's gaze.

The bartender placed the lady's drinks on top of two white napkins. "You can try to run away,"—Ariel raised a glass—"but I'm just going to run after you." Ivy refused to lose sight of the gorgeous redhead she'd been eyeing all night. It was satisfying to know Ariel's feelings were parallel. "To us on this night."

"To us," Ivy repeated softly. They clanked the tall glasses and soaked in the sweet vintage beverage.

Ariel and Ivy sipped on their wine as the night carried on. The room abounded with amazing and brave Death Dealers having the time of their lives. Tonight, assassin duties were forgotten. For once, dozens of professional assassins were allowed to lose control and be…normal.

Ariel's heart pounded with anticipation as she led Ivy to her dormitory.

"Are you sure you don't want to go back to my place? You know, somewhere more cozy. I'll even bring you coffee in the morning." Ivy giggled, bringing her arms around Ariel's waist.

Ariel was embarrassed to admit she was on probation.

"Nah!" Ariel made sure to sound playful. "Don't worry your pretty little head about me. Besides, I'm a big girl. I can get my own coffee," she concluded with a wink and a snap of her tongue.

Ivy wanted to pull Ariel by the arm and whisk her away to her apartment. However, she was a woman with an appetite: an appetite for love and a sexy redhead.

"After you," said Ariel, courteously.

Once Ivy strolled inside, her mouth hung open. She was shocked at the blandness of the room. Since she resided in Seoul, Korea, she never needed to visit the dormitories at her own headquarters. However, she didn't expect them to be so boring. The walls were plain white: no paintings, no décor or even ugly wallpaper. The room completely lacked character. The interior decorators could've at least picked out a pop of color for the curtains but even they were drab with their unflattering tea-stained color. Both of Ariel's suitcases sat on the floor unopened. There was a drawer for Ariel's clothes, a lamp, a desk, and one bed: a good-sized bed, at least. It was a queen with white sheets, a white comforter, a tea-stained bed skirt, and tea-stained pillows. Oddly, there was also one breakfast pillow that was gold— as if that'd help the attractiveness of the sorrowful room.

Ariel closed the door behind her and asked, "You alright?"

"I'm great," Ivy assured. "I just can't believe this room. With the all the money that goes into the DDAG, you would think they'd put more effort for the people who visit the headquarters. Not make them feel like prisoners."

"Yeah…." Ariel was halfway paying attention. She didn't want to talk anymore. She wanted Ivy.

Ariel pulled Ivy by the waist and pinned her against a wall. It took only a single look for Ariel to figure out what Ivy craved. She leaned in and embraced her in a passionate kiss. Ivy could taste the residue of white wine on Ariel's lips—making them sweet—and it made her clitoris throb immensely.

Ariel held onto Ivy's ribs, feeling the motion of her body pressing against hers. Gently, Ariel caressed her fingers forward and slid them up to cup her perky breasts and squeeze them softly. Ariel wanted to feel every crevice, every inch of her body.

As they continued to make out, Ariel grabbed Ivy's arms and placed them over her head. Ariel lifted Ivy's dress and her thumbs felt lace panties, making Ariel gush. Ariel brought up her leg and rubbed her thigh against Ivy's crotch, harder and harder with each pulsating movement. Ivy moaned deep inside Ariel's ear, turning her on exponentially. There was something about Ivy that made Ariel want to do things she never would've imagined.

Slowly, Ariel pried herself away but kept her eyes locked on Ivy as she tore off her black t-shirt.

Ivy licked her lips and resisted the temptation to turn into an animal on the prowl.

"Come here," Ariel nodded, heading to the bed.

Ivy followed and let her long and wavy, fawn-colored hair loose. She could smell the sweet vanilla aroma from Ariel's perfume as she kicked off her gold stilettos to get more comfortable.

Ariel laid down and Ivy cat crawled over her. Ivy pressed her lips hard against hers. When their mouths opened, Ariel twirled her tongue inside Ivy's small mouth.

Once Ivy bit Ariel's lip, Ariel unzipped Ivy's dress and pulled it down until it exposed her full breasts.

"Steady now," Ivy chuckled, pecking Ariel's bottom lip. "No need to rush. I'm coming at you until you tell me to stop."

Ariel asked Ivy to stand. Her violet eyes concentrated on every intricate detail of Ivy's curves. Ivy began slipping off her dress, exposing a black-lace bra with matching bottoms and a garter belt meant for holding stockings.

Quickly, Ariel took off her pants and turned to lie on her stomach, showing off her ample ass. "I can do whatever you want. Come try me," she moaned as she peered over her shoulder.

Ivy hovered on top, massaging her breasts all over Ariel's backside. Ariel dug her hands deep into the sheets as she jerked her lower half up. She loved the idea of Ivy watching her from behind and couldn't wait to feel Ivy's thick and soft fingers inside her.

Ivy's lips trailed from Ariel's hip up to her shoulder blades. She paused, noticing red lines over Ariel's back.

"Wings?" Ivy asked, curiously caressing the detailed tattoo. "They're beautiful."

"They're angel wings," Ariel breathed, picking up her top half and resting on her elbows. "When I was training in District Europe, I was taking a jog when—out of nowhere—I tripped over something on the ground. It was a little black book with gold-lined pages, covered in leaves. I picked it up and as I started skimming through it, I noticed there were a bunch of little stories written inside. I brought it back to my dorm and each night, I'd sit on my bed with a hot cup of tea and just enjoy solitude—it was just me and my book. One story really caught my attention. It was about an archangel. He was a fierce and mighty warrior. I can't remember his name but I hope to be just as strong and brave as him one day. He led an army of angels for his god, defeating a betrayer, who was sent to the depths of hell: their version of our Malum. The passion and bravery he must have had to carry during his god's reign must have been so difficult. But it's something to admire."

Ariel was silent for a moment.

"You know, I don't even know what happened to that book. Either someone stole it or I accidentally left it behind. Sadly, I never finished it." Ariel began to wonder what may have happened to that little black book. She had an inevitable attachment to it. *Where did I leave that damn book?* she thought. *Hmmm....* She shook herself back to reality. "Either way, it has a special place in my heart, forever."

Ivy caught Ariel's saddened face and caressed the side of her delicate cheek. Ivy placed her head on top of Ariel's lean back, holding her close.

"Come on," Ivy whispered. "Come with me far, far, away to a better place."

Ariel couldn't deny her. "Yes, ma'am!" She spun around.

No, this place wasn't far, far away but it'd be far away from the sadness, evil and ugliness of their world.

They exploded into one other inside that bland room and escaped into their own fantasy.

Ariel was more than happy to be accompanied by one of the most beautiful women she had ever laid her bright purple eyes on. As soon as their final pieces of garments came off, Ivy leaned back and gazed upon Ariel's athletic body. With the tips of her fingers, she pinched Ariel's nipples until they hardened.

"Hmmm…." Ivy hummed, admiring the beauty in between her legs. "You are so beautiful. I can't think of anyone I'd rather be with right now."

"Neither can I," added Ariel.

With her wet tongue, Ivy licked her two pointer fingers then slid them inside Ariel's warm pussy. They moaned heavily and continued to make love until the trickling of dawn.

The following evening, both factions gathered in the auditorium, located in the middle of District Asia's chapel tower. Jason stood on stage above everyone else and started searching for someone in particular.

"Seraphina?" Jason called out. She poked her head out from the crowd. "Come here!"

Seraphina ran up the steps and walked over to her captain with the utmost confidence in her stride. A cocky smile beaconed over her pretty face as she examined both factions below her. Proudly, she stood alongside Jason and enjoyed having all eyes on her; it gave her intense satisfaction.

"Listen up," Jason yelled, killing the noise in the room.

"Now, before Captain Orchid joins us, I have one quick thing to say." Jason asked Seraphina to come forward. "This is Seraphina, my second-in-command. She is here to make sure none of you—this includes Faction Divide—do anything out-of-line, insubordinate, or straight-up stupid. She will be my second pair of eyes."

"I'd love for her to eye me all day," a short man from District Asia whispered to his fellow DDAG member. Both of them chuckled. Zaire rolled his hazel eyes at the pair of adolescent boys who had nothing better to do than comment on every girl from Faction Divide that passed by. He refrained himself from shutting them up with his hardcore punches by focusing on his superiors.

"We are here to do our job as Death Dealers. We do what is best for the innocent people of the New World. With that being said, there should be no bickering, no fighting, no bullshitting with anyone who is an ally. Not only does this distract from the mission at hand, it wastes time from the real issue. And what is the real issue? People are disappearing. We do not know why and we do not know if they're alive or dead. This may or may not be because of the Black Plague II Infections. We must find out what is happening to our people and do what is best for the New World. Be safe, be cautious, be ready to sacrifice yourself for the greater good."

An echo came from the other end of the room. Sying finally arrived to the party. Jason waved at him, "Captain Orchid!"

With eagerness, Sying paced his way over to the stage to join his marvelous companion, Jason.

The captains shook hands and Jason moved aside to give Sying the spotlight.

Sying held his hands together. "Good evening DDAG members! I managed to hear most of what Captain Lilly had to say. I'm not worried. I believe we all will be on our best behavior."

Seraphina grunted. "Heh.…You've obviously never heard of Ariel."

Jason shoved her. "Shut up," he hissed under his breath. Sying looked over at them, confused and asked if they were okay. Jason cleared his throat. "Yes. My apologies. Please, go on."

"As I was saying," Sying continued, "I only ask the Lord of Life to grant us nothing but success during this mission. I believe, from the depth of my heart, we will bring justice for those who have disappeared within the past year."

Ivy realized she was four people away from Ariel and wanted to say hello. Ariel, on the other hand wanted distance. She preferred to separate work life from personal life.

As Sying continued with his inspiring speech about banning together and fighting for what's right, Ivy continuously peeked over at Ariel. However, Ariel never even glanced at her. With heavy sadness, Ivy sighed and gave up. She tuned back into her captain's calming voice and threw away the passionate memories they'd shared just the night before.

"I'd like to inform everyone that we will begin our investigation on Cheongdam-dong Street in 5th Avenue." Sying pulled out his 3-D map and enlarged it for the entire audience to see. 3-D maps could display an entire city street-by-street. Sying zoomed in on a specific spot. "This section is also known as Gangnam District."

Immediately, Ariel recognized the area. She used to spend a lot of time there as a kid studying the rich architecture of the vacant designer shops and eateries.

"Apparently, most of the people have disappeared in and around this area. So, for those of you in Faction Divide—if you are wondering—it is safe to assume that no one goes and takes a light stroll there, anymore." Sying depleted the map and tucked it back in his pocket.

"I'd like to head over there, search the area within a ten-mile radius and see if anyone can come across any clues that may help. To be honest, no one in my faction has found anything. Not even anything circumstantial. We'll scour for a couple of hours, meet back here no later than midnight, and we'll talk to see if anyone has found a lead. The kidnappings usually occur between the hours of one a.m. and four. I rather not chance an unexpected attack."

"Noted!" Jason was ready to go. "Before we head out, was there anything else you would like to add, Captain Orchid?"

"No, Captain Lilly." Sying adjusted his heavy backpack. "That is all."

"Well, that settles it. Let's head out, then." Jason was pumped. "Divide….What do you say?"

"YEAH!" they all screamed, throwing hardened fists in the air.

Sying was taken by surprise. "Excellent!" he cheered, feeling superb. "Faction Abyss, Faction Divide. Let's move!"

This time, everyone cheered and rolled out. The assassins separated into four black vans and were now on their way to Cheondam-dong Street.

In the beginning of their travel, the assassins were driven through bare streets. There were skeletal trees every square meter and soulless light poles along the sidewalks. At every intersection, only the caution bulb of the traffic signals remained lit. Oddly, it was as if the yellow lights froze in time. Where there should have been city noise mostly made up of traffic and busybodies, the machines outlived humans.

In the far distance, the sun disappeared behind unfinished buildings. Each one had a lone crane on the roof. They were practically clones, all built exactly the same: professional, giant, and colorless. Bodhi guessed this could've been either a valley of businesses or a government plaza at one point.

The van passed an old apartment complex with half of its body missing. The rustic empty floors of the kitchens and the patios were in plain sight. There were piles and piles of rubble, stacked on top of each other in the decaying complex. Wrecked and beaten automobiles were abandoned out front, one of them being a truck with its hood open with the engine missing.

As Ariel looked outside, she was taking in both happy and sad memories. For a moment, she nearly reminisced but re-engaged her thoughts on her sole purpose of the evening: investigation and a commitment to justice. Seoul may have been a memory, but right now it was also her mission.

Suddenly, the factions were approaching an unrecognizable scene.

The city at first was practically a graveyard. But then, it changed.

What the...? Ariel's heart thudded against her ribcage.

In the heart of the city, also known as downtown, there were people....Lots and lots of people. Men, women and children were fluttering about like happy little butterflies in a well-kept colony.

There were no run-down buildings, no vacant parking lots or ghost streets. Instead, downtown seemed brand-new. Apartments were rebuilt, looking prime. There were baby trees that would soon grow to be ten times their original size. Rose bushes and gardens of wildflowers were planted in a newly made park that had to be at least 100 yards wide. Smoke was no longer coming from rejected oil refineries but from active restaurants that seemed to be booming in business: mostly noodle restaurants or salad bars.

For miles, merchants set up tents to sell clothes, handmade jewelry, street foods, crystals, and herbs for enchantments or medicine. Each vendor had nothing but inviting smiles on their diverse faces.

A young man in a suit and tie was selling illusion cards.

When someone threw an illusion card into the air, the card would show you whatever your heart desired: whether it be from your imagination or reality. He had an audience of happy children varying in age. An adorable little girl with a thick braid bounced up with her long feet, threw her card high in the air and out sparked an animal with a mane, a tail, and a horn adhered to its forehead.

Looking at this, Ariel remembered studying ancient animals in Earth's history. She noticed its resemblance to either a horse or a pony, but neither of them had a horn.

Hmmm..., Ariel wondered. *What the hell could that be?*

In the center of downtown, was a gorgeous manmade lake. Lights were placed behind some steps throughout the lake, creating a waterfall effect, and as the stream would flow, there would be a dapple of colors. Even though it was bitterly cold outdoors, people ignored the low temperature and seemed to live freely.

Ariel's birthplace was unrecognizable. She wanted to witness Jason's reaction but he was surprisingly paying no mind. Ariel looked back at the happy people and asked herself: Why was there such a high volume of people in Seoul so suddenly? She had been away for twelve years, but no city in all of the New World had experienced such a dramatic change in a small amount of time. At least not that she knew.

"Wow," Bodhi gasped, amazed at what he was viewing. "I've never seen so many people."

"Me either," Ariel agreed, confused by the whole situation.

Ariel felt she traveled back to a time she was unfamiliar with. A period where Seoul had once housed millions of people. Never, in all her years as a Seoul resident, had she'd seen a grand population. Not even the city lights had ever shined so bright before. It was surreal.

Once the assassins passed downtown, Seoul's flamboyant scene faded. Briefly, it blossomed, but then frightfully wilted. Again, the city returned to grey with its beckoning trees and deserted streets.

The vans parked in front of a gorgeous, white-marbled wall next to a glass building with golden poles that flowed down like a majestic waterfall and stopped once they met its doors below. The word *Gucci* was on the left corner in solid gold. Miraculously, the white marble remained serene, however the glass structure was painfully unlucky. Only the golden railings held on for dear life, but the glass exterior was completely obliterated. The assassins have arrived in Gangnam District.

It may have been beautiful once but now it was just another memorial site for what was forgotten during Earth's reign. The majority of the district was packed with manipulative marketing billboards and posters. Ariel noticed a pattern when she first studied Gangnam: The women chosen for the pictures were always flawless, thin, and dressed in the most obnoxious-looking attire. Sometimes, if she'd happen to come across an ancient photo lying on the ground, she'd take it home, add it to her "Earth" collage wall, then study them with her mom. They'd make up fun tales about the women, placing them in the most obnoxious scenarios. Once, Ariel imagined a beautiful blonde in a spiked dress and rabbit ears, as queen of the New World, who would demand carrots for dinner every night. Ariel never understood the centuries-old fashion but she hated it. Nowadays, Queen Kora Amaryllis, wouldn't dare dress in crow's feathers or oversized shirts or jackets with loud patterns on them. But the amount of advertising displayed throughout Gangnam was so enormous it had to be popular with the wealthiest people imaginable. Ariel questioned its fame but preferred to remain clueless.

The sun was at rest when the Death Dealers jumped out of the packed vehicles. They gathered in front of the broken *Gucci* building and Sying took position in front, asking if anyone had any questions.

Ariel raised her hand.

"Yes?" Sying asked, politely.

"Do you know anything about a man named Ki? Where he may be hiding?"

"Sergeant Lotus did inform Sergeant Tulip, then informed me, however, I'm afraid nobody knows anything about this man. But I promise you, I have my best informants digging deep in our database to hopefully gain more knowledge about this. 'Ki,' unfortunately, is not much to go on."

Damn! Ariel thought, blowing hair out of her face.

Sying moved on and Ariel scarfed down a Vitality pill. She rose her hand again, wanting to ask about the oddity occurring in downtown. However, she changed her mind but kept a mental note for the future.

Jason separated everyone into four groups. They were designated to go north, south, east or west. Ariel was with her usual pack—Seraphina, Bodhi and Zaire—along with four other DDAG officials from District Asia: Hyuna Peony, Charles Lilac, Daoka Sunflower, and Migackt Aster.

Jason sent the groups out but his mind fluttered busily. Ariel shook him out of it with a simple tap on his forearm.

"What's up?" Jason asked, distracted as he scribbled away on his notepad.

"Hey," Ariel said. "Did you notice anything weird while we were heading over here?"

Jason glanced at Ariel, but instantly returned to his work.

"What?" Jason asked before mumbling to himself.

"Focus!" Ariel snatched his notepad and shoved it in his coat pocket. "Eyes and ears on me."

"You know, you could ask if I'm doing anything important before you grab my stuff like that," Jason mocked.

Ariel rolled her eyes. "Whatever. Hear me out."

They began walking together, heading south.

"Did you notice something...I don't know...strange, downtown?" Ariel lingered on the word *strange*, hoping Jason would notice the emphasis.

"Was I supposed to?"

"For fuck's sake, did you not see all the people back there?" Ariel grunted. "Aunt Faith told me Seoul was turning into a ghost town, so we moved. Back there was a shit-ton of people. When someone says 'ghost town,' I picture two hundred people, max. Not five hundred or a thousand."

Ariel and Jason thought of Seoul very differently. He loved his hometown, and enjoyed the great outdoors by playing catch or picking up an ice cream cone at the local shop, a street away from his old neighborhood.

When they drove through downtown, Jason did notice the swarm of people but he wasn't concerned or confused. He was thrilled to see his hometown become alive again.

"Ariel, can't you see this as a positive thing? Seoul is growing." Jason sang.

"Jason," Ariel snickered. "Seoul is now full of men and women roaming around the city as if it's the hottest place in the New World. More people are moving to Seoul willingly. Not forcefully."

"That's a good thing!" Jason said, defending his city. "It means the economy is growing successfully. Plus, people relocate all the time. It's not uncommon."

Ariel laughed bitterly. "Are you blind? You are a DDAG captain, right? Remember to think like one."

Here we go again..., Jason sighed. *She's going to rattle on and on and—*

"Put the pieces together!"

And it begins.... Jason tried to not look pestered. "Yes, dear!"

"Drop the attitude!" Ariel shoved a finger into his chest.

Jason smacked her hand away. "Trying to."

"Anyway, our faction was brought here to uncover a case in Seoul, correct?"

"Correct."

"The case is people disappearing. Why, IN THE HELL, would people move to a place where PEOPLE are MISSING?!"

"I hate when you talk like that." Jason couldn't help it. He wanted to pay attention, really.

"Focus, man!" Ariel punched Jason's arm. "Listen to me!"

"Ah! Okay. Sorry. What did you say again?"

Before saying anything remotely condescending, Ariel took a moment to gather her thoughts, settle down, and ease her way back into the conversation maturely.

"We were brought here to solve one giant missing persons case. Why would anyone want to move to a city where people are disappearing daily? It doesn't make sense." Ariel and Jason reached their target location. "Right?"

"Maybe." Jason wished he had answers but his focus was on the present. "You may have a point, but I don't know. Faith may have overreacted about Seoul. She was very protective of you, so that's all it could be. But my version of Seoul is completely different than yours, you know that. My parents never mentioned decreasing populations or anything like that, so I can't judge Faith's word. My family and I moved because your aunt begged us to. Of course, I was ecstatic because I was going to see my best friend again, even though I was going to miss the hell out of Seoul. Seoul to me means home. It was a good place, growing up. Seeing more people here makes me happy, despite the bad shit happening. You, on the other hand, see this place as a bubble of bad memories."

Ariel kept quiet and looked at the other assassins scattering about, beginning their investigation. Jason may be right. She could be overthinking the situation. It was just that everything she passed on the way to Gangnam District seemed to be off-balance. Maybe this was a good thing. Seeing so many joyful faces was okay. It wasn't not bad for others to enjoy their life, so why overjudge it?

"I'll drop it for now." Ariel unwillingly caved. "Don't think I won't ask about it later."

"I'd be surprised if you didn't," Jason said.

Ariel released all lingering anger and proceeded with her Death Dealer duties.

Jason felt guilty but he knew it would benefit Ariel more if he remained positive and tried to get her to focus on tasks. Ariel worried less when her mind was distracted with DDAG work.

The streets and sidewalks of Seoul were overwhelmed with bushels of dying grass while a few flowers held on for dear life in these long and cold winter months. During the summer, the grass would grow for miles, creating a path to the Outerwoods: the home of the Rural Outsiders who took comfort in living within a tribe that grew their own food, made their own clothes and crafted their own magic.

In District North America, it was roughly between fifty and sixty degrees. In Seoul, the temperatures could run as low as ten degrees between the months of November and March. Luckily, the assassins were out on a night where the temperature was running in the forty range.

Empty buildings faced each other on either side of the street. The taller ones leaned at awkward angles. They should've timbered years ago, but somehow they'd managed to remain sturdy.

Seoul was known for its distinct patterns. They were all over on street signs, restaurants and Earth-classic billboards. The patterns were made up of simple lines drawn horizontally, vertically or in swivels, and were arranged in various combinations. Circles were sometimes added for balance. These geometric patterns were apparently important at one time.

Growing up, Jason and Ariel were taught that Seoul was a magical place for adventure, respect, traditions and values. It was designed to be admired, especially with its futuristic persona. Much of Seoul's olden advertisements had the word *future* slapped on somewhere. The city used to be enamored with technological advancement.

Sadly, that was centuries before the Black Plague II virus spread. With only a brief summary of the city's history, who knows how accurate the assumptions were. However, the two friends loved believing that the history of their city was rich and fulfilling.

Ariel glowered all over the once-lively District, searching for…well, anything. She walked down a street, skimming the walls for any peculiar chippings or cricks.

Daoka carefully turned a wide corner. When all was clear, she skipped inside an old candy store and searched for the possibility of blood or bodily fluids on the walls, floors, countertops or plastic tubes that once held gummy bears and licorice squares.

Bodhi didn't know where to begin so he followed Zaire into a creepy looking toy store. They held their breath as they tip toed inside, keeping their eyes wide open.

Bodhi noticed a cloud of webbing caught onto his pants. He tried to smack it off but once he turned around, he let out a wild scream. "Aaaahhh!!! What the fuck?" There was a shelf full of dolls ripped out of their boxes with missing eyes and naked bodies. Some even had their hair ripped off. He knocked on their heads and realized their skin was made of porcelain.

Zaire laughed so hard, his stomach hurt. "You alright, dude?"

"Pssshhh….Of, course!" Bodhi lied. "Can you believe kids actually played with these ugly things?" He looked back at them, cringing at every broken smile on their cracked faces.

Zaire picked up a plastic jump rope. "I believe children like what they like because they're innocent. Adults are responsible for tainting their minds."

"Huh?" Bodhi was hardly around children so it was difficult for him to understand their innocence.

Bodhi forgot the dolls were still behind him. He turned around. "Argh! Fuck!"

Outside, the rest of the team still scampered around the crud-infested district.

"Most people were taken between the hours of one and four a.m.," Hyuna chimed in as she flashed a green light at the ground; it was supposed to display lost footprints or fingerprints.

Jason gave her a funny look. "Yes, we were told."

"Were we told a specific location?" Charles slid on his radar goggles to scan through walls.

"Not really," Doaka answered as she twirled out from the candy store. She had two pigtail buns on either side of her chubby head. Her face was youthful with a high-pitched voice to match.

"There has to be some sort of pattern. Even the smartest criminal has unintentional behavioral patterns," Seraphina added.

Under her breath, Seraphina chanted a premonition spell:

Lord of Life, give me the power
To chime into the past
For the next lively hour.

Seraphina cupped her hands together, and waited for them to glow. Once a white light pricked in between her fingers, she separated her hands and began to investigate. Temporarily, she could touch anything and trigger a vision of past events for clues.

Ariel marched through alleyways and searched inside several buildings. Since she was terrible with magic, she had to search for clues by relying on gut instinct versus a magical one—and of course she had the DDAG's best equipment.

Jason and Sying would sporadically check in with each other over their walkie-talkies, updating status as needed.

Zaire created dozens of ultra-flare potions that he brought along with him in his backpack. After tossing a vial, it would spark once the glass shattered—*BAM!!!*—followed by a cloud of smoke. This created an infrared light that would reveal layers upon layers of fingerprints, bodily fluids, graffiti, paint, etc…anything and everything placed on a flat surface from the past five years. An official Death Dealer would then have to analyze each layer, then slowly erase any unwanted or unnecessary fragments.

Migackt strolled around the area with headphones that alerted him to suspicious sounds or activity.

Hours flew by but no one found a thing. Jason checked his watch. He hated how the time continued to pass yet still not a clue was found.

"How late is it?" Ariel asked him, fed up, wanting the first night of investigation to be over.

"We have about an hour," Jason huffed. "So, we almost have to start getting ready to head back. Seraphina, what level of premonition did you use?"

Seraphina squinted her eyes and nose and scratched her head, contemplating what may have gone wrong. Her perfect fishtail braids dangled as fingers scurried through her black hair. "It was a level three, so the highest one. However, I feel someone may be using some kind of defense magic."

"Defense magic?" Hyuna asked, taken by complete surprise. "If you think it's defense magic then they're using it against technology, too, because we cannot find anything."

"Exactly," Bodhi blurted out. "Whoever is behind this has got to know what the Death Dealer Alliance Guild is all about."

"Yeah, so?" Daoka asked, with hands on her hips.

"So, are you proposing this is an inside job? With the DDAG?" Ariel was perplexed by his claim.

"Not necessarily," Bodhi continued. "There may be a possibility that this whole scheme is an inside job...but I'd like to refrain from making that accusation."

"Fair enough!" Jason was satisfied Bodhi didn't presume to accuse a fellow DDAG member of betrayal.

"What I'm piecing together is this: What if Ki or someone appointed by Ki studied all that we do in the DDAG? Everything from spells, chants, physical training, technological training, weapon training, the whole nine yards. I don't think this is defense magic. I bet this is something more severe: black magic."

While the others invested themselves into Bodhi's hypothesis, Ariel remained in detective mode, still examining through every cracked window or broken door.

Finding clues for the Seoul case was tricky. It was not as smooth as other cases and it was hard to concentrate on a case that held no solid structure. More and more, the assassins felt helpless, but no matter what, this case had to be solved. The continued peace of the Lord of Life's children depended on them.

"Black magic?" Migackt knew black magic was forbidden in the New World. Even the most evil terrorists hardly messed with it. Black magic was complex. "That's absurd."

"Is it?" Bodhi tested.

Bodhi and Migackt continued to bicker but Ariel kept focus on the job. She had to find something soon. She placed a hand on the side of a chipped metal statue then suddenly she felt…unusual. A bitter chill entered her body, making her shiver. She felt someone was watching her. She feared looking back. Was someone behind her?

Hello…, someone whispered.

Ariel looked over her shoulder, but no one was there. "Jason?" she called out. He was still with the rest of the group listening to Bodhi speak.

"Ugh!" Ariel groaned. "I need sleep."

Ariel followed the path of several boutiques and came across a white, mosaic-tiled exterior known as the Chungha building, once used as a collection of brand-named stores. Up close the walls looked bubbly, but from afar they looked as smooth as coconut milk. The windows varied in size: some short and horizontal, some long and vertical. There were some windows with four panes while others had double. It looked like art for the future: just like she and Jason were told when they were little. At least during its prime.

Ariel paused and read a banner: it said *Louis Quatorze*. Behind it was the logo. The "l" and "q" were intertwined and it looked tacky and messy.

She stood back, admiring the white haven.

Get out…, a voice trailed off.

Ariel turned around but no one was behind her. She scratched her ear, trying to get rid of the tingling sensation on her left lobe.

Ariel rarely felt frightened, but at that moment she wanted to get out of Gangnam District. She knew she heard something. Was someone messing with her?

Don't come back here….

"What?" Ariel asked, spinning around. She searched over her shoulder and above her head but there was nothing and no one. What was going on?

Leave Seoul….

"No," Ariel cried.

Get out….

"Why?" Ariel raised, terrified.

"No," Ariel breathed. "It's all in your head," she said, trying to convince herself.

This time, the voice pierced through her ears like nails on a chalkboard.

People are dying….

"Stop!" Ariel cried.

Ariel's hands trembled but she wanted to cover her ears. She was desperate to phase out the horrific screeching. She shut her eyes, attempting to control herself.

Jason heard a faint squeal.

"Ariel?" Jason called out, unsure of what was happening.

Ariel fell to her knees. She cradled herself, feeling helpless: trapped. The harder she rocked, the closer her head almost hit the ground.

More people will die….

The voice! She recognized it. It was the same one from the bombing at The Golden Throne Room. "WHO ARE YOU?!" Ariel screamed so loud she nearly choked.

"Ariel!!!" Jason yelled, running in the direction of his best friend, who writhed horrifically on the ground.

You cannot save them all..., the voice continued.

"The people of the New World will not be victimized! The DDAG won't allow it!!" Ariel raged, passionately. "Whoever you are, do you hear me?!"

Evolution begins in Seoul..., the voice slithered with a scratchy sneer.

"NO!!!" Ariel howled, fearing for human lives and yearning to save them all. "Who are you? Get out of my head!"

"Ariel!!" Jason was almost there.

As soon as he reached Ariel, Jason threw himself on the floor next to her. Ariel knelt there with unrecognizable anxiety. Jason panicked and feared touching her. What was he to do? He had never seen her so frightened and lost. He wondered how to ease her pain.

Jason was about to wrap his arms around her. As soon as Ariel felt the brush of his sleeve, she fought back, unknowingly shoving Jason out of the way.

Oomph! A heavy palm pounded against his chest.

Ariel wailed out, "GET OUT OF MY—"

"Hey," Jason cried, crawling back to her. "It's me. Follow my voice."

Ariel could only hear the evil consuming her mind. She wanted it gone. Blood dripped out of her ears, causing Jason to panic. Quickly, he lifted her face in front of his.

"Ariel! Come back to me," Jason yelled. He was scared he could lose his best friend at that moment. "Ariel Rose!"

Suddenly, Ariel snapped out of it. "Aaahh!"

The horror had ended but her body remained frozen. Jason placed her head over his chest and focused on her breathing by placing two fingers under her chin. Luckily, her pulse was slowing down and would soon be back to normal. Jason was relieved. He swiped her hair out of the way and noticed her face was covered in tears and sweat and blood.

"Hey," Jason whispered, happy to see his friend coming back around but sad to see her crying with spots of blood. "Come on, sister," he told her. "You're okay. You almost gave me a heart attack."

"What?!" Ariel had forgotten where she was. "What happened?"

"I uh… don't know," Jason admitted.

"Are you alright?" Bodhi asked, running up to them. "Is she okay?" he asked Jason, swiftly. "Well?"

Jason ordered him to remain calm. "Shhh…I don't know what happened."

Ariel released herself from Jason's arms. "I'm fine," she exclaimed, desperate for some air. "Give me a moment."

"Here," Bodhi said, handing her a revival potion to drink to heal her bleeding ears.

"Thanks," Ariel huffed, taking a quick shot of the turquoise liquid. It tasted like an unorthodox mixture of mint, rosemary and aged garlic. Within seconds, the blood that once flowed had dried out. No more pain. No future scarring. If only the revival potion could fix major injuries, it would be the best potion, ever. Sadly, it only healed minor wounds.

Zaire and the rest of the group met up at Ariel's side. They circled around her, speechless.

Jason checked his watch. It was closing in on midnight. "We have to go," he said reluctantly. He rubbed Ariel's head. "Let's get out of here."

"Someone spoke to me," Ariel fumed, still frightened and shaky. "It was a man's voice. Scratchy in the throat. Sounded older: maybe middle-aged. He…he sounded demonic."

"She's tripping," Seraphina remarked sarcastically.

Daoka smacked Seraphina's arm. "That's rude!"

"Little girl, I ought to kick your ass!"

"Seraphina, shut your fucking trap!" Jason roared. "Daoka, you too."

The ladies hushed but Daoka still stuck her tongue out.

"Do you know who it was?" Jason asked her. Ariel shook her head. "I'm glad you're okay. We all are." Everyone except Seraphina nodded and agreed.

"Come on, Little Velvet," Zaire said, grateful to see his comrade regaining self-control. "Let's go."

Ariel was finally comfortable enough to stand and was relieved to be heading back to headquarters.

But before leaving the site, that *unusual* feeling trickled back. This time, however, Ariel knew she was being watched.

She told everyone to move ahead.

"Are you sure?" Jason asked, concerned for her safety.

"Yes," Ariel convinced him. "I'll be right behind you."

Jason walked away but took his time heading back to the vans.

From the corner of her eye, Ariel noticed a blurred figure. She stood transfixed with fear, eyes protruding.

Who's there? she thought. She told herself, "Don't look back," but did the exact opposite. She turned around.

Ariel gasped. "What the fuck?" A tall shadow person, with their head leaned on their right shoulder, was staring right at her. If her heart were to race any faster, Ariel felt that it would thrust out of her chest at any moment. Her breath shortened and her nerves escalated.

The black figure stood in between the shadows of two buildings. Ariel couldn't figure out if the person was a man or woman: they were a great distance away. Curiosity got the best of her and she slowly paced forward.

Two steps later and the shadow glided away, disappearing into the night.

"What?" Ariel whispered to herself. "Where—"

"Hey," Jason called, softly tugging at the hood of her coat. "Sorry. Had to check up on you. You okay?"

Ariel's eyes fluttered. *You were seeing things.*

"Just tired," Ariel answered, completely unconvincing. Jason gave her a questionable look.

"I'm fine," Ariel said. "I promise."

"Alright," Jason smiled. "Let's get out of here, yeah?"

"Hell yeah, I'm done with this place," Ariel joked, trying to seem normal.

As the best friends packed themselves back into the vans, the figure looked down at the assassins with a mischievous grin. It knelt over a high roof of a dirty old mall tower. When the Death Dealers were gone, the figure stood up and looked over at another shadow behind it. It walked up to meet the other. They held hands, then peered over at the city lights downtown, indulging in all the laughter and music from the cheery people below.

They held one another close and together they chanted, "Evolution begins in Seoul!!"

SYMBOLISM

A riel awoke to the sounds of her own screams. As soon as she opened her eyes, she remembered little of her nightmare.

"Fuck," Ariel groaned as she flung the sheets off her hot body, full of sticky sweat. The last thing she remembered was someone sprinting up and plunging their fingers into her cheeks. *That face.* It was so familiar yet so unfamiliar. Ariel rubbed her heavy eyes and ran into the bathroom for a cold shower.

After cooling herself off, Ariel towel-dried her body and put on some comfy clothes—an overgrown pink sweatshirt and black yoga pants. She was no longer restless and wanted to head over to the library, situated next to the great hall.

As Ariel headed to her destination, she noticed a lovely face coming from the opposite end of the hallway—it was Ivy.

Ivy grew giddy at the sight of Ariel. She wanted to haul ass and squeeze the shit out of her. However, Ivy thought that would make things between them uncomfortable or painfully odd. Instead, Ivy went for a calm approach. "Hey."

"Hey," Ariel repeated with a soft grin. She was also unsure of how to react in this situation. "How are you doing, beautiful?"

Ivy flung up two books she held in her hand.

"When I can't sleep, I tend to look for some good reading material to help me relax. Sometimes it helps me doze off," Ivy blushed.

"Funny coincidence," Ariel smiled. "I am actually on my way to the library." Ariel noticed Ivy's taste in books and her attraction to Ivy grew ten times over. "You read about architecture in your spare time?"

"Um....Yeah," said Ivy, quickly hiding the books behind her back, and messing with her wavy hair. "I know it's weird and uncommon but—"

"I love architecture," Ariel interrupted.

"Oh?" Ivy said, shocked.

"It's an obsession of mine." Ariel beamed. "Before the DDAG, I used to visit abandoned buildings all the time. Some of them were beautiful beyond belief while others not so much. Either way, I wish I knew more about the manmade landmarks that were built before the Black Plague II Infections. Especially castles: I. Love. Castles!"

Ivy couldn't believe what she was hearing. Ariel didn't seem like the type to care about ancient homes or forgotten cities. Ivy assumed Ariel's interests would be strictly DDAG.

"I would do anything to travel the world and get paid to study castles. The old ones and the new ones. The history of Earth is so unknown and that intrigues me. I want to learn as much as possible about our ancestors."

"Wow!" Ivy was impressed and at a loss for words. "I never would've imagined Ariel Rose as an aspiring Earth historian."

Ariel laughed. "If I were you, I'd be just as surprised as you are about me."

The lady assassins smiled and shared a parade of giggles. After some time, the laughter faded away. Ariel looked down at the blue carpet while Ivy eyed a vending machine. Ivy wanted to stay but should she should go? Ariel on the other hand, wanted to get to the library.

Ivy curled her fingers inside the sleeves of her honey-gold turtleneck sweater. She gripped at the soft fabric, hoping her nerves would magically go away by digging her long nails through the layer of cotton.

After a long period of wordless conversation, Ivy spoke.

"Well, I should get going." Ivy didn't want to leave but it was getting late and she had to attend training in the morning. To her dismay, she must leave her crush behind and hope to speak to her another day. *Wait!* Ivy thought of something sneaky. "Unless…you need help finding books about some castles, I could be of service." Her heart flushed with hope. What was the hold Ariel had over her? Ivy didn't know. Was it her mysterious persona? Or was it strictly physical?

"I'm fine, thanks," Ariel assured.

Ivy's heart crumbled into tiny bits. "Oh…well….Alright," she sighed, forging a smile. "I guess I will see you around?"

"Of course, you will," Ariel said. "Goodnight."

Ivy pecked her on the cheek. "Goodnight."

As Ivy walked away, Ariel turned around to watch her disappear into the dimly lit hallway. Ariel closed her eyes and relived the night she shared with the coppered goddess. *Mmhmm….* She re-opened them and Ivy was out of sight. Ariel got horny. "Fuck me," she whispered, knowing there was nothing she could do about it except maybe have some special alone time. She pondered for a moment. *Hmmm….* "Nope," she spat then proceeded on to the library.

Once entering the grand library, Ariel was amazed at the sight of it. "Wow!!"

Compared to District North America, Asia's library was more modern and sleek. In New York, the library was only one floor, but it had a richly ornate design. It overlooked the gardens beyond the upper bailey through large bay windows that never opened. The entire room was lined with dark oak and the ceilings were low. A study unit to the east had three round tables with four thick cushioned lounge chairs, each. In the center room were more small square tables for a single person, extravagant golden couches and one long table adorned with black lamps with golden-colored shades. Lining the walls were the books, shelved and organized in careful order. In between the blocks of books were oil paintings dating from 1500 B.P. (Before Plague) to 2500 A.P. (After Plague), each framed in pristine gold.

In Seoul, it was entirely different. First, the decadent library overlooked the training area in the middle bailey of the castle. The bottom floor was paved in white marble while the study tables were checkered with black and white marble. Near the entrance to the right, there were cherry wooden blocks on the floor with peculiar statues on top. One was a smiling fat man, sitting crisscrossed with his pointer and middle finger up and separated in a V shape. On a slightly-taller block was a cute cat, wearing a colorful robe and waist-tie, with a single paw raised up right next to its adorable grinning face.

Moving on up, three steps to the left then five steps to the right, you would reach the second floor, again paved in white marble, but here there was a table piled with official DDAG books. Ariel excitedly picked up several of them and speedily read their back covers, only isolating what was most interesting. There was *The Birth of Practical Magic in the*

New World by Tonya Chamomile—a recently passed Death Dealer from Faction Cosmic in District South America—and *The New World vs. The Old World: Debatable?* by retired Sergeant Johnny Zinger from Faction Afterglow in District Australia.

"Don't mind if I do!!" Ariel exclaimed to herself. Now, she moved on to the third floor—ten steps forward, circle right, then just five more steps up—and instantly noticed the mountain of books lining the mahogany walls in six-shelved bookcases. The books were categorized by genre, varying from children's to romance novels to terrorist psychology. Luckily, there were a couple of spots to sit on the third floor, so there was no need to worry about climbing back down the zig-zag trail.

Ariel set down the two books she picked up on a brightly glossed cherry oak bench. She stared at either side of the room, deciding on where to begin. The thing to do now was research.

"Let's get started."

Hours had passed before Ariel realized there was light in the room. She turned her wrist and checked her watch: *9:34 a.m.* The sun had been out for hours! Where did the time go?

Ariel heard music coming from inside her bra. She pulled out her phone to see who was calling: Zaire.

"Hello?" Zaire was calling to check up on Ariel. "I'm doing okay," she said, after slurping up gallons of dark roast coffee. There were many books circling around her like the portal gate in District North America. At one point, she had to run back to her dorm, collect all necessary supplies—

notepad (electronic and manual), pen, phone, noise-cancelling headphones, and rubies (not necessary but very important to Ariel's sweet-tooth diet). "I couldn't sleep so I decided to do some research."

"Fun. What are you studying?" Zaire asked as he was getting ready to grab breakfast in the dining hall. "Hold on for a sec." He placed his phone down to pull his hair back. Afterwards, he grabbed the clothes nearest to him—a grey thermal and dark blue denim—got back on the phone then headed out the door. "Sorry. So, what are you studying?"

"Magic!" Ariel finished the last of her coffee. The caffeine hit her hard. Her body was jittery but she felt ready for anything.

"Magic? You hate magic. Well, I don't know if you hate it but you're not very good with magic," Zaire nonchalantly rambled.

An employee of the library passed by: a simple guy with black hair and bold-framed glasses.

"Excuse me?" Ariel called to him.

"Well, you're not," Zaire said bluntly.

Ariel closed her eyes, a bit peeved. "Not you! Sir," Ariel called to him again. He looked around, confused then pointed to himself. "Yes, you!" The man slowly walked over to her. "Could you bring me some coffee, pretty please?" She held out her thermos for him to take.

"Uhhh… sure?" the employee was bewildered but he took the thermos anyway, even though it wasn't in his job description to refill coffee.

"Thanks. You're a doll!" The young man began his journey to the nearest drink station but not before Ariel shouted, "Dark roast only!" She hated anything below a robust level.

"Do you get off on telling people what to do?" Zaire mocked.

"Only to those I love." Ariel flipped through pages of a beaten old book.

Zaire laughed and wanted to know more about Ariel's random studies. "So, are you going to tell me what magic you're so curious about?" He turned a corner to a hallway that headed straight to the dining hall. Already he could smell the pumpkin steaming from the pot of chili they were serving for breakfast.

"Black magic," Ariel mumbled, jotting down some notes on her electronic notepad.

"The type Bodhi mentioned last night?"

"Precisely," Ariel answered. "Also, I am looking up defense magic. They may go hand-in-hand, but I'm not sure yet."

Zaire noticed Seraphina a few feet away. He yelled for her to wait for him.

"Tell that bitch I said hello, darling," Ariel scoffed.

Zaire curled his small lip and stared at the ceiling but found the two of them humorous.

Seraphina noticed his eyeroll. "What's wrong?"

"Ariel says hello," Zaire said, with a hoaxed smile, trying to portray Ariel's sarcasm through the phone.

"You forgot to add the word 'bitch,'" Ariel persisted.

"I have a feeling there was so much more emotion involved," Seraphina added.

Ariel raised her voice, hoping Seraphina could hear. "She's right!"

"Anyway," Zaire interrupted, "Are you sure you want to study that stuff? I mean, you've always had a difficult time understanding magic."

"I don't appreciate you underestimating me, Mr. Ponytail man." Ariel tried to make light of his unnecessary comment.

"I meant, are you sure you want to study by yourself? Why don't you ask Bodhi to help you?" Speaking of Bodhi, he was waving to his friends from inside the dining hall. He already sat at a table with a bowl of pumpkin chili and a tomato pesto sandwich. When it came to food, Bodhi was satisfied. Zaire waved back to him. "After all, it is his theory."

Seraphina wanted Zaire to get off the line with Ariel. The thought of her voice alone made her cringe.

"At least Bodhi has an idea of what he's talking about." Zaire continued. "He's not stupid."

The coffee hero returned with the thermos of conscientious. Ariel was tremendously thankful. She lit up as soon as she could smell the dark, liquefied coffee beans. The man was surprised with a bear hug.

"You are the best!" Ariel squealed. She pouted her lips and pecked both of his chubby cheeks. He flushed red as he walked away with a twinkle in his eye.

"Why thank you," Zaire gloated, feeling confident.

"Again, not you." Ariel opened the lid from her thermos and a cloud of steam smoked out from the hot beverage. She blew over the top, trying to cool it down and inhaled the sweetened dark aroma.

Zaire cleared his throat, feeling silly. "So, what do you say? As a matter of fact, Bodhi is waiting for Seraphina and me to eat with him. I'll casually mention what you're doing and I'll have him get back to you."

"Sure," Ariel agreed. "Listen, I gotta go. I'll see you tonight when we meet at the auditorium."

"Okay, Little Velvet. Good luck!" Zaire cheered.

"Bye!"

Ariel was exhausted. Even her eyes strained from the non-stop reading since the previous night. She hadn't been fully honest with Zaire. She was physically okay. Mentally, she was a complete wreck. The figure that was staring right at her yesterday….Who was it? A man or woman? Did this shadow speak to her telepathically? Telepathy was uncommon but not unrealistic. Also, did this unknown specimen have anything to do with black magic? Did it somehow build a wall of invisibility, hiding evidence of all the kidnappings? If this were true, it's the reason the Death Dealers had not been able to gather an ounce of evidence about the missing person cases in Seoul. There were many questions—all unanswered, with little time left to solve them. Ariel was on a mission to figure out what was happening. She was going to find answers, even if it killed her.

Ariel sipped her coffee and looked out the window. Jason was outside showing off his fighting skills to Daoka. She was teeny compared to Jason's tall and buff build. Standing next to him, she attempted to mimic his infamous roundhouse kick. As Ariel watched her best friend from afar, she took a moment to feel grateful. Jason was her savior and thanks to him she was still living her dream as an official Death Dealer. She loved her work whole-heartedly and was willing to die for it at any time, any day.

Daoka looked impressed with Jason's sleek and smooth technique. He moved gracefully but fought brutally. Ariel couldn't blame the adorable little Death Dealer. Jason was a badass. Always had been.

Ariel looked back over at her pile of mess and wondered if she was heading in the right direction. There was no time for fallback. She knew if she didn't find something soon, more men, women and children would disappear, or even die. *Back to it*, she thought, so tired, yet enduringly active in her research. This was not about her. It's about the innocent lives in the New World. She placed the thermos in her lap, hunched over the books and continued where she left off.

"Looks like you've made a mess." A voice was coming from above Ariel's busy body. Bodhi stood over her with a cute smirk over his gentle face. With his thick pullover and matching sweats, he was super cozy. "What are we going to do with you?"

"What time is it?" Ariel rubbed her pulsing eyes.

"It's five o'clock. We've got a couple of hours before our DDAG meeting." Bodhi scooted over a pile of books to sit in front of her. He noticed both of her notepads were filled with scribble-scrabble. "I brought coffee."

Ariel chuckled in disgust. She couldn't bear the scent of coffee any longer. "No more for me, thanks. I don't think my bladder can handle anymore liquids for the rest of the night. Plus, I have a low caffeine tolerance. Earlier, I was so hyped up I was actually being friendly. It was horrifying."

"I cannot imagine that. Ew!" Bodhi joked. "So, have you come across anything or is there something I can help you with?"

"Yes," Ariel began as she re-adjusted herself. "First of all, you and I both know that black magic is rarely used. Finding solid information about it has been a fucked-up ride."

"Agreed." Bodhi took off his maroon pullover and Ariel caught a whiff of his clean-scented cologne. Not only did it revive her exhaustion, it helped her forget the nauseating smell of coffee altogether. "That's because DDAG employees are the only people in all of the New

World who can legally use advanced magic. This includes Death Dealers, sorcerers, witches, alchemists, and everyone else in between. Black magic is rare, but not unreal. The plausibility of someone using intermediate magic outside of the DDAG is pretty low, let alone something more complex like the art of defenses or black magic."

Bodhi and Ariel being on the same page was a great start.

"Since DDAG members are allowed to use top-of-the-line spells and chants and alchemy, well, how did we learn it?" Ariel stretched her fingers. "Through various magic classes at certified DDAG academies. This is the only way professional magic is taught and learned."

"Precisely," Bodhi concurred. "I've narrowed down the suspects: a DDAG employee like an informant or secretary, an official Death Dealer, or even a magic teacher. Ki, that man Cyclamen mentioned, has to have connections to the DDAG. Someone is his eyes and may be part of our affiliation."

"What about a dropout or someone who was kicked out of DDAG School?" Ariel tested.

Bodhi shook his head. "No. When a situation like that happens, their memory is immediately erased of all they've learned at the DDAG, including training sessions and DDAG verbiage."

Ariel started scrambling through the piles of books. Bodhi grabbed her electronic notepad and scrolled through the tabs, examining her notes. One tab aroused minor worry.

"What's this?" Bodhi turned the notepad around for Ariel to see.

"What?" Ariel asked, plunging her nose in another book.

Bodhi looked back at the screen. "Telepathy? Mind control?" He looked at her, remembering the night before. "Is this because of what happened yesterday? Are you alright?"

Furious, Ariel swiped the notepad out of Bodhi's hands. "Why are you looking through my shit?"

Bodhi didn't want a confrontation with Ariel. "I'm just asking because I'm worried. After last night—"

"I don't want to talk about yesterday," Ariel blurted, tossing the notepad behind her.

"Talking about it may help." Bodhi hoped Ariel would speak up. Even if she cried or yelled or got physical, he wanted her to let the anger loose so she could feel better. "I understand you are scared."

With wide eyes, Ariel shot Bodhi a killer stare. She roared "I'm not scared!!" She was lying and Bodhi knew it. Immediately, guilt ran through her and she looked upon his sorrowful face. It wasn't Bodhi's fault.

"I'm sorry," Ariel breathed. "I do *not* want to talk about it right now. Okay?"

Bodhi nodded and switched topics. It killed him to see his role model unstable, living in fear. What could he do? Either way, he'd be there when the time called for it. "Going back to why I'm here, have you come across anything useful?"

Ariel plopped a thick book on Bodhi's lap entitled *Safe Magic*. "I don't get it," Bodhi said, picking it up.

"Safe magic? What do we use it for?" Ariel asked.

"To keep us safe?" Was this a trick question?

Ariel stood up and stretched out her toned body. It ached after being hunched in the same position for hours. Her body was tense and her lower back felt heavy. She raised both arms up, placed her right hand over her waist, and used the left to pull it over her head.

"Spells, enchantments, potions and power are all used from energy within. Safe magic, for whatever reason, doesn't use as much energy as a teleportation spell or something with firepower." Ariel pulled herself back upright, bringing both arms back to center and then stretched her opposite side.

Bodhi was lost. He skimmed through the pages. Everything written between the covers of the book, he knew. "So?"

Ariel exhaled, stretched out her left leg behind her, grabbed the sole of her foot and pulled straight up. With the opposite leg, she slightly bent at the knee. The feeling of her muscles releasing tension was painfully good.

"Sooo…since safe magic uses minimal energy, what if someone were to reverse safe magic, turn it into black magic, then use it against us? All it would require is insanity and more energy." Slowly, Ariel dropped her leg to its prior position, then moved on to the opposite side.

Bodhi tapped on the book's back cover. "Black magic is illegal, but how is that black magic?"

"People do illegal things all the time." After a worthy stretch, Ariel grabbed another hardback and displayed it in between her palms. "*Black Magic: A Myth?* by Jett Poppy. He explains everything." She flipped through it, searching for a particular page. "Here," she handed the book to Bodhi.

A picture of a pale man with no hair and black eyes was drawn out. He had both hands over his face and was screaming. Above his head was a collage—a crying child, fire, guns, money, and other pictures—embodied by a grey cloud.

"That drawing is just an example, but Jett is illustrating what happens when someone uses black magic. Black magic is identified as this: It is forbidden in all seven districts of the New World. It is also known as evil magic. Primarily, it is used for personal gain with the intent to harm others or hide evildoing."

Bodhi's heart skipped a beat. Ariel was on to something. "Hiding evidence. People disappearing— possibly killed. Blood. Footprints. Fingerprints. Hiding all of this is personal gain." Bodhi beamed.

"Exactly!" Ariel exclaimed. "And whoever is working for Ki is illegally using black magic. What I'm thinking is this: why don't we reverse it when we go back to Gangnam District tonight?"

"And how do we do that?" Bodhi asked, rapt and hyped.

"All we need is a spell and one pot of potion: enough to fill a couple of vials." Ariel felt proud. If she was right, the Death Dealers may be able to find clues in a matter of hours!

"That's it?" Bodhi asked, let down by the anticlimactic.

"Yes!" Ariel retorted, not letting Bodhi kick her off her high horse. "I need you to help me write the spell. Once we're done, I will ask Seraphina to help us brew up a potion down in the alchemy lab since she's the best at it." Suddenly, Ariel's throat clogged. The words that just came out of her mouth were revolting. She wanted to vomit.

After clearing her throat, Ariel opened up a fresh page on the manual notepad then handed it over to Bodhi.

"Well, start writing."

Evening had sprung and all the Death Dealers had once again gathered round in the auditorium. No speech was given from either DDAG captain. However, Ariel asked to speak. Prior to all this, Ariel secretly forced Seraphina and Bodhi to join her on stage.

"I can't believe I'm doing this," Seraphina groaned.

"Oh, shut up." Ariel grabbed Seraphina's arm and began pulling her from behind.

Ariel was now standing in front of dozens of assassins. She worried her idea may not be taken seriously. After taking a quick glance at Bodhi for comfort, she began her speech.

"After more than twelve hours of research, I may have come up with a solution to our main problem." Ariel noticed most of the crowd looked either bored or impatient: some slightly interested.

"We cannot find evidence because we are not thinking outside the box. According to my fellow DDAG comrade, Bodhi Tigerlilly, he thought maybe black magic was involved. Well, he was on to something."

Ariel updated the crowd with her research and the hypothesis of black magic. Now, it was time to explain the best part: the solution.

"I asked our second-in-command, Seraphina Jasmine, to cook up a viable potion that may be the key to unlocking what we need to know so we can save the people of the New World." Seraphina pulled out a tiny diamond-shaped vial filled with a lilac liquid that was sealed with a cork. "We decided to call this concoction the Truth. The only step is to throw it at whatever's in front of you."

The auditorium rippled with hushed voices. There were many remarks Ariel could pick up. Some people mocked her, others exchanged questions, and a few were won over. Seraphina walked to Ariel's side. Beyond the voices was Jason, quietly waiting for his team against the back wall. Daoka was cheering solo while Hyuna, Charles and Migackt stood motionless.

Ariel took a breath and hurried to finish talking.

"Since we did not have time to make enough vials for every Death Dealer on this mission, we decided to have a test run tonight with our group. Once we get back, we'll inform you all of the progress of our experiment. With the approval of both DDAG captains, we will begin our first trial tonight in Gangnam District. Thank you."

Jason and Sying made their way toward the front of the room while their guilds remained in their places.

Jason took the floor. "Honestly, I never would've come up with that theory on my own," he cheered, looking at his dominant three with pride. "With that being said, I am not only impressed but very proud of you all. I hope to see nothing but positive results."

Jason could see his best friend holding back a smile. Instead, Ariel's cat-eyes were narrowly intact and she hid all signs of excitement.

Sying was motivated by Jason's amazing trio. "I'm speechless. To be honest, I feel like this idea is thinking too much outside the box. After all, black magic is highly uncommon. Yet, I hope to be proven wrong. Yes, you have my blessing."

The trio onstage sent a single nod to their superior officers as a thank you.

"I am ready to get the hell out of here. Are you?" Sying asked Jason.

"You bet your ass I am," Jason hailed. "With that being said, let's move! To Gangnam District!"

The assassins escorted themselves out of DDAG's headquarters and into the black vans. Ariel, still in shock over what happened, held Mercury close and thought of the possible outcomes of her plan. Ariel swiped a smooth, polishing cloth over Mercury's quillion—to make the emerald really shine.

Bodhi's mind raced with the same implications as Ariel, as well as the farfetched possibility that his theory would prove to be true.

Seraphina was biting her lips to hold back any sarcasm or plain-bitchy remarks. It had taken a lot of convincing from Bodhi for her to finally agree to take part in this experiment. She loathed the thought of helping Ariel but she would never turn away when it came to helping the innocents of the New World.

Straight ahead was the serene *Gucci* building. Soon, Ariel would find out if her idea could vanquish all black magic—if this was even due to black magic in the first place.

Once Ariel stepped foot outside of the van, that fear crept in. Was someone watching her? She slowly perked her head up and examined the rooftops. Luckily, there was no one in sight.

Okay...relax, Ariel thought to herself. *Quit being scared and get over yourself.*

"Same teams, different locations," Sying announced. He called out to Ariel and the other seven. "You all will travel south. There are many different outlets within one building. However, I felt this specific area may help you prove your theory." With a quick flick, he pulled out his 3-D map. Buildings piled like mountains appeared over his palm. "Head over here to the corner of Evisu and Nylon. Begin your research there then work down the street. Enter as many buildings as you want for as long as you want. Well, until midnight."

"We can do that," Seraphina rushed before taking her Vitality pill. She wanted to head out already.

Ariel, Hyuna, and Migackt had forgotten to take their pills earlier so they did the same.

Sying closed the map and placed it back in his pocket. "Please, update Jason and myself if you find anything."

Ariel was confused. "Is Jason not grouping with us?"

Jason walked up. "Sying and I will be monitoring groups today. We'll rotate and regularly check the status of each group."

Ariel huffed. "Fine."

"Don't worry." Jason cupped her shoulder. "You will see me throughout the night."

"You are free to go!" Sying called the next group over.

Zaire pulled out his crossbow.

"Do you really need to pull that out right now? Nothing's happening," Daoka miffed.

Zaire couldn't help but smile at the tiny Death Dealer. "She makes me feel safe."

Daoka zoomed in on the weapon. "She?"

"I named her 'Jewel,'" Zaire revered with the utmost sincerity.

Daoka grimaced. "Well, alright. Jewel needs to go into hiding, though." With her ballerina feet, she skipped ahead of everyone else.

They reached the corner of Evisu and Nylon. Different businesses piled up on top of each other. There was no formal organization. In one building, there was a noodle shop underneath a massage parlor, which was underneath an entertainment store—the entertainment store was called DVD: The Finest Collection of Film. In another building, something called a Japanese steakhouse filled the top layer of a jewelry and furniture store called Quake.

Everyone took in the emptiness of the scene. Centuries ago, this area must've been filled with people happily trotting up and the down the streets. Ariel could only imagine how wild the economy must've been during her ancestors' era. Did they enjoy the overwhelming options of hundreds of businesses kneeling at their feet? What the hell was a film and why was it so damn popular? Film, film, film....There was not one city without the word *film* mentioned more than a thousand times. Was there a connection between a film and entertainment? Ariel felt they had to be one and the same.

The assassins paired up: Migackt with Charles (who didn't talk much), Zaire with Daoka, Bodhi with Hyuna and Seraphina with Ariel. Bodhi handed everyone a pouch filled with six vials.

"Please, use them wisely," Bodhi begged. "We did not brew up enough potion to last us the whole night. If anyone needs assistance, please ask me, Seraphina or Ariel. We'll help you out." Everyone tied their pack to their waist then split up to begin the investigation.

Ariel and Seraphina checked out a few empty stores, one dedicated to men's suits and another being an electronic store. They lit the flashlights attached to their coats to illuminate their paths down abandoned aisles full of cobwebs and rust. Mold even took over parts of the wall. They put on their mouthpieces for safety.

"What do you suppose this is?" Seraphina asked, pointing to a small, black, square device.

Ariel walked over and picked up the questionable aged piece of technology. "Who knows? What I'm more curious about is this: Why is there an apple on the back and why does it look like there's a bite taken out of it?"

They laughed. "Looks like shit to me," Seraphina added. Ariel tossed the black brick to the side and it crashed into a glass cabinet.

They continued searching the area but nothing was out of the ordinary.

"Should we chance throwing a vial in here?" Ariel asked.

"Fuck if I know," Seraphina muttered, looking around. She picked up white wires that split down the middle. On each end were two round sponges: one with an *R* and one with an *L*. "Is this a weird necklace?"

Ariel stared at it, remembering something she read. "From what I remember, they're called earphones. Apparently, you could listen to music through them." She examined them closely. "Come to think of it, they kinda look like our noise-cancelling headphones."

"No, they don't," Seraphina argued. "How do you listen to music through these wires, anyway?"

"Not sure, but I think they plugged into something and music would play." Ariel walked over to an ancient cash register and tried to swipe away the clinging dust. Inside were orange, blue and green papers, each with a different face but the same geometric patterns seen throughout Seoul. "Ancient money," Ariel said, picking up the pointless bundles of paper. "Too bad they're worthless now."

"Alright," Seraphina shouted, throwing the earphones away. "I'm tossing a vial." She flipped one in the air, then caught it perfectly in her hand. Ariel grabbed her wrist before she got rid of it.

"Be careful with our inventory," Ariel reminded her. "We can't afford to be wasteful."

Seraphina shoved Ariel's hand away. "First of all, do not touch me. Ever." Ariel's eyes fell into the back of her head. "Second, we have zilch to go on. We need to start somewhere. Sooo… I'm going to throw the fucking bottle. If you would, please fuck off."

Ariel slowly backed away to avoid pissing her off more.

With a quick arm, Seraphina tossed the vial high. Once it hit the ceiling, the glass shattered into a million pieces and a fat puff of lilac smoke sprouted out. Both of them waited and hoped clues would appear from beyond the purple cloud. A minute passed, which felt like an hour, but sadly there was nothing.

"Let's go try the bookstore upstairs," Ariel proposed.

"Whatever," Seraphina hissed, storming off. Ariel refrained from cursing at Seraphina. She had to stay with the DDAG and could not afford another suspension. If her plan was fruitful, she'd be able to redeem herself in an institution that viewed her as an invaluable asset.

Unfortunately, there was no evidence in the bookstore either. In fact, there was no evidence in a sushi restaurant, a salon, a craft store, or in a department store that carried one-too-many handbags, called *Louis Vuitton*. Ariel admired the simplicity of their logo, which was nothing more than a *V* intertwined with an *L*. The assassins stood in the deserted department store, feeling horribly lost.

Ariel looked at the empty handbags to keep her hands busy while Seraphina eyed a soiled little black dress.

"You know, if this wasn't so old and gross, I'd wear the shit out of this."

Ariel looked over to see what Seraphina was referring to. She eyed the mannequin, and smirked. It may have sparkled profusely once. However, the diamonds that showered the dress became faded, scratched and worn-out.

"I hate to admit it, but even if you wore that piece of crap now, you'd still look sexy," Ariel admitted.

"Yeah." Seraphina placed her hands inside her jacket's front pockets. "You wish you could see me in something small like that."

"Again?" No one had a clue but Ariel and Seraphina had one eventful night together a few years ago. It was a lavish evening of drinks, Vitality, and mind-blowing sex. Seraphina may have wanted to erase it out of her memory, but Ariel enjoyed every second. Did she have any regrets? Absolutely not. "Oh wait... I'm supposed to forget about that night," Ariel mocked. "What are we talking about again?"

Seraphina flipped her the bird then walked over to the window. She noticed Zaire and Daoka on the street scouring around a broken-down automobile.

"Why don't we check outside?" Seraphina suggested but didn't wait for an answer. "Let's go."

Ariel grunted then followed close behind her.

Zaire noticed the ladies approaching. Seraphina asked if he found anything. "Nothing. We've wasted a good amount of vials, too."

"You've been checking outside though, right?" Ariel asked.

Daoka shook her head. "No. We came outside about ten minutes ago. We were just about to pick a spot for vial tossing. Maybe this deranged car, but we're afraid of wasting more potion."

"Vial tossing?" Seraphina thought for a moment. "Cute."

"Thanks!" Daoka grinned.

Ariel walked up the street and noticed a building called *The Coffee Bean* around the corner. "Hey, I'm going to try over here."

"Why?" Seraphina asked, curiously.

"Because I like coffee." Ariel was being totally honest. It was not enough to go by, but then again, they were headed nowhere.

Seraphina stopped Ariel before she could throw a vial. "What if we throw a vial at the same time?"

Zaire and Daoka were paddling behind to join them.

"Why?" Ariel asked.

"I don't know. Just do it!" Seraphina jeered.

"Okay?" Both ladies got their aim ready. "On three," Ariel began. "One. Two. Three."

The vials cracked violently against the brown brick wall. The beautiful lilac color puffed out once again, creating a cloud of smoke twice as big. All four assassins waited patiently.

Suddenly, smears began to appear, then footprints, all in a hazy green color. The smears looked like bodily fluid. It could be saliva, urine, or even sperm. It was difficult to tell.

"Holy shit!" Zaire was stunned looking at the footprints that collided into each other. It was hard to dictate how many people they belonged to.

"Get out your green light," Ariel said to anyone who would listen.

Daoka reached inside her bag and handed hers to Ariel. It was small and round. Ariel inserted her fingers underneath the Velcro and turned on the light, pointing it to another spot.

"What the hell are you doing?" Seraphina barked.

Ariel didn't answer. Instead, she bent down to her knees and whispered. "No marks."

"What are you doing?" Seraphina hissed, losing patience. "Zaire, what the fuck is she doing?"

"Our green light should've been able to show us this evidence last night," Zaire replied. "But it didn't."

"Black magic," Ariel whispered. "Someone, throw one vial in front of me."

Daoka jumped at the opportunity. "I got it!" She counted to three and daintily tossed the vial. It hit the ground and created that light purple fog but nothing appeared.

"Now, throw two at the same time, same spot," Ariel hurried. She was on to something, she could feel it. Her heart raced. The Truth potion could be the answer the DDAG needed.

"Do it with me," Daoka begged Seraphina.

"You're a hyper little thing." Seraphina eyed her cautiously. It was nice to see someone so carefree, but at the same time it terrified Seraphina. How could someone be so hyper during all this...hell? "Ready?"

"Mmhmm..." Daoka sang, rocking her head. They counted to three then tossed.

This time, thick droplets appeared on the cold sidewalk. Blood, maybe. At first, the droplets were sporadically spaced, then they began to form a cluster the closer they were to a wall just across the street from *The Coffee Bean*. It was evidence! Finally!

"We just need to make a stronger potion!!" Ariel cheered. "Oh, my god!" Ariel's jaw dropped.

"We—we did it!" Seraphina got out her walkie and called Bodhi over to their location.

"I can't believe it. This is what we needed." Ariel did a little happy dance.

Bodhi sprinted down the street. "What's going on?!" He noticed the evidence appearing from the scene. "Fuck yeah!" he praised. "We fucking did it!"

"Call the rest of the group over here," Ariel told Bodhi. "Someone else tell Jason and Sying what's happening. They have to see this."

Once the remaining Death Dealers arrived, Seraphina quickly instructed them on how to work the vials. Immediately, people separated and began choosing other spots. Vials were booming.

Within minutes, a huge chunk of Gangnam District was covered in lilac. Everyone began taking notes, scraping up evidence, recording video or taking photos.

As Ariel investigated the streets, she realized most of the smearing in the area was blood. Ariel passed a snack shop and noticed 진화 was drawn in blood across the front door. "Weird," she told herself as she glued her eyes to the strange pattern. She was uncomfortably drawn to it. She looked back over to her team, wondering if anyone else seemed to have been pointing out anything in particular, but everyone was still surveying the area. She looked back at it and placed her hand on top of the green wooden door. With a smooth touch, she traced over the pattern.

A groggy noise crept next to her ear, tickling her lobe.

Ariel looked over her shoulder. Only a dangling broken street sign was behind her. It creaked as it swung against the soft wind, but it wasn't the noise she heard.

Ariel stared at the pattern once more then moved on. A garbage can with a missing lid had been knocked over to the ground. The 진화 appeared on its medal body. In an alleyway, it was drawn between a stairway and a door. She found it on a small car and a worn-out electricity box. It was everywhere.

Ariel grabbed her camera and took a photo of the symbol on a broken window. She opened the camera's gallery and enlarged the photo, drilling the image into her brain.

"What the fuck is that?" Ariel asked herself.

A menacing cry reverberated from behind. Goosebumps trickled all over Ariel's neck. The cry was saying something but the language she did not know. She carefully searched the area. No one seemed to be around except her DDAG team. The wailing, however, swirled all around her, ghostlike.

Suddenly, a rattling noise echoed from the electronic store Ariel and Seraphina were once in. Ariel tiptoed her way over to the building. It was empty. "Hello?" she called out. No one responded. She looked outside, checking off the members of her group. They were all busily racking up as much evidence as they could before the Truth potions wore off.

Rapid footsteps were stampeding across the second floor. Ariel shot up at the ceiling. She focused on a series of snake-like lightbulbs. They didn't seem to move, but as soon as she squinted for a clearer view, she noticed the bulbs were subtly moving.

Fuck! Ariel thought, as she raced outside. *Enemies have found us.*

"Guys!!" Ariel screamed. Everyone was so distracted, they hardly paid attention. A creepy feeling mingled inside her body and the beating of her heart raced furiously.

Evolution begins in Seoul. That voice from the night before. It returned.

Ariel snatched Mercury out of her sheath and gripped her emerald quillion tightly. Quickly Ariel spun, and hastily looked around, fearing that the shadow man or woman was back to haunt her—or, worse: kill her.

Go away! the screechy voice groveled. She overlooked the premises, but no one was there. Why was this happening? She felt like she turned crazy. What was she going to do if she lost control again? What would happen to her?

"I know you're there!" Ariel muttered. "Where are you?" She spun north, and at that moment there it was: the shadow.

The shadow stood high and mighty over the edge of a tall building, gazing down at the assassins below. It had on an overcoat that softly danced against the cold wind.

Ariel wanted to scream and disappear, but she was a Death Dealer, and a Death Dealer never runs away. A Death Dealer kills terrorists and that shadow is a new kind of terrorist.

Ariel took a breath and studied her surroundings. What could be useful? How could she get to it? The building the shadow stood upon was incredibly high, but it was night and she could use the shadows for an advantage. All she had to do was race across the street, leap on the wall, grip a rail or windowsill, cat-crawl up the building, sneak up behind the shadow person and plunge Mercury straight through its heart. Ariel was about to prepare herself to climb. But then, they were ambushed.

"We're being attacked," Migackt yelled. "Spread out!!"

Everyone ran. Ariel flew over a broken car and dropped into a crouched position to stay hidden.

Seraphina flew inside *The Coffee Bean* and swooped underneath a counter.

Hyuna was about to enter a book shop until a loud *crash* came from the second floor. A man came swarming down at quick speed. He landed on his feet with his back to her. Hyuna took a couple of steps away and pulled out her two handguns. They were ready and loaded. With both thumbs, she unlocked the safeties. The man contorted his bald head around strangely. "Get back!" Hyuna warned. He was now facing her.

He was a man but not a man. The paleness of his skin rivaled the coldest winter snow but his eyes…those eyes defied description. They were silver like moonlit mercury: almost a metallic dark grey but a color Hyuna had never seen in human eyes. He looked human, but was he?

He took the same number of steps forward as Hyuna took back. He let out a vile smirk, making Hyuna cringe. "Stop it," she ordered him. "I'm not playing around!"

He lifted his head and howled, baring all his teeth. They weren't normal teeth, but more beastly. A mouthful of sharp, pointed fangs.

"Don't come any closer," Hyuna growled. He took a step. Hyuna aimed the gun right at his head. "Listen to me," she blared with a final warning.

Argh!!! the pale demon screeched! He was about to dart at Hyuna but she fired her gun. *BAM!* The bullet hit him between the eyes. His face flinched back but he failed to fall.

How is he still standing? Hyuna thought. The pale demon cackled in Hyuna's face. He stood proudly, even when the bullet in his head drowned him in blood. He forced two fingers inside the wound and forcefully pulled out the bullet. Oddly, the wound closed up right before Hyuna's eyes. The trace of a bullet was no longer there.

How is there no wound? Hyuna was astonished. She looked at her weapons, checking to see if something was the matter, but she'd been dealing with guns for so long, she knew everything was perfect. It was not her weapons. The man was unnatural: not of this world.

The pale demon flung his mouth open then roared at the top of his lungs. *Aaaahhhh!!!* Hyuna sprinted away, fearing for her life. The man stayed close and kept right on her toes.

Jason and Sying arrived during the middle of the rumble. They saw white monsters flying all around, scrambling from wall to wall between the high-rises. One of those *things* picked up his hand and dug his long claws into Charles' chest, ripping out his heart. The pale demon growled with each tug and pull.

"We need backup at the corner of Evisu and Nylon! We are being attacked by an unknown group of terrorists!!" Jason screamed over the walkie-talkie. "Move, move, move!!"

Sying noticed one of the enemies prowling from above. Gearing from his hind legs, the cold demon rocketed high in the sky then came flying down three times as fast. Sying grabbed Jason by his shirt and pushed him as far as he could. With the power of Vitality, Jason landed more than ten feet away, back first. Sying flipped over a broken street lamp, landing on the other side.

The pale demon was now heading in Sying's direction. Sying jumped up and clung onto a dead traffic light. The man barely missed Sying's feet. Sying clambered down the pole, pushed himself off, spun twice in the air with his leg out and gifted the man with a harsh kick to the jaw. However, the pale demon only winced. Jason got up to join Sying. It was now two Death Dealers against one terrorist.

The monster let out a solid roar then displayed his long claws, wanting to slash their faces together.

Jason took a deep breath and somersaulted backward while Sying took a leap toward darkness.

As the pale demon charged, Jason landed on his feet, formed two fists, and punched the crap out of the monster, face-forward. He fell back but immediately rebounded. Jason punched him again and again and out of nowhere, the man managed to sneak his sharp nails across Jason's ribs.

"Fuck!!" Jason yelled in agony. He had never felt so much pain during his career in the DDAG. Jason tried to ignore the severe affliction and sent a ferocious uppercut to the monster's chin. *Argh!* The monster screamed as he was sent floating in the air.

Sying reappeared and caught the enemy by his neck. He used so much force it brought the monster down to his knees.

"Hold him down!" Sying ordered Jason. Jason lunged forward and planted both hands over the pale man's shoulders. Jason held him down as Sying wrapped his arm around the monster's neck and began pulling his head up. Sying screamed to muster more energy. Both men worked together and after a time of fighting and wailing, the man's head had completely separated from his body. The head slipped out of Sying's arms, becoming airborne.

Seraphina carried her longsword honorably and was ready to kill. One of the monsters, who was tall and scrawny, surprised her from the side. "Heeyah!" she bellowed with confidence as she consistently darted and jived around to never lose sight of him. "You wanna play?"

He screeched loudly, showing off the sharp daggers on his fingers. "Let's play," Seraphina dared him. He ran. She ran. They both swung but she was faster and lighter on her feet. She struck him diagonally across his face. He groaned but his face wasn't wounded. "Okay," Seraphina baffled. "Come at me again, you albino dickwad!" He charged, she plunged the sword: this time at his heart. It went straight through him. He stood there, paralyzed.

"What's wrong?" Seraphina asked him. "You don't want to play with momma no more?" With both of his frigid hands, he took the hilt of her sword and slowly began pulling it out. She fought back but he continued to slide the sword out of his chest. His hands bled but it wasn't fazing him.

He was as strong as Seraphina: stronger, actually. Seraphina dug her toes on the inside of her combat boots, hoping to grip her position. However, he kept pushing her and the sword away until he was free.

Seraphina stood back and watched as the hole in his skin molded itself back up—no blood, no scar but only a tear in his dark shirt. She cracked both sides of her neck, ready to charge again, but then a noise came from behind her.

Woosh! It was another one of them—this time, a female with long hair and a crooked nose. Seraphina put out her hand, signaling her to stay back. Now they were both in front of her. "Ummm…," she said with a shaky voice and dried throat. "Fuck!!"

She was screwed.

They were closing in. Seraphina thrusted her blade on both sides while both the man and woman lunged at her repeatedly. Their nails sparked as they clanked against the metal of her longsword. The woman struck her hand forward, aiming at Seraphina's throat. Seraphina ducked underneath the sharp claws, twirled around and aimed at the woman's collar bone. It smacked the bone, tearing it in half. Although the woman was momentarily shocked, she gripped the sword and easily ripped it off.

Seraphina never lost sight of her balance and quickly aimed her weapon at the male attacker and pierced it through his gut behind her back. She held him in place as the woman was coming at her from the front. Seraphina smashed the woman's nose with her elbow. She barely moved. Seraphina elbowed her again, but under her chin, then jabbed her throat. The woman lost her footing. Seraphina dominated that moment. As fast as she could, Seraphina, pulled out her sword and sprinted away, dispersing into the black of night.

Meanwhile, Ariel was having problems of her own. She was surrounded by three of those monsters: two male and one female, each varying in height and weight. One of the males was a porker with a bald spot. The other man was hefty with spiked brown hair but the woman: she looked surprisingly young, youthful even.

Ariel held Mercury in position. The woman came darting at her like a loaded machine gun. She swung at Ariel's leg. Ariel fell down but instantaneously jumped up and sliced off the woman's hand. *Aaaahhh!!!* The woman bellowed in pain while blood sprouted out like active lava. Ariel spun then backhanded Mercury's tip straight into the woman's eye. With enough momentum, Ariel constrained the woman to floor. Ariel took a deep breath, and slashed right.

"Hiyah!" While part of the demon woman's face floated with the wind, her sole eye twitched as her body plummeted to the grounds of the New World.

Ariel was ready for her next target!

The fat man came in with his dagger claws and his arms scissoring. He was crazy, messy and moved quickly. Ariel dropped to the ground and shoved Mercury through his foot. *Rawr!!!* The pale porker was now prisoned to the street. He cried as he attempted to lift his foot, but Ariel made sure the dagger held him intact. She got back to her feet and executed a swift kick to his spleen, making him tumble to his side. His fat foot still stuck to Mercury. Before moving on to her next victim, the collapsed porker was dizzied from being knocked over. Ariel retrieved Mercury, turned the fallen man over, then plunged her jeweled weapon straight through his Adam's apple. *Gurgle*....He was dead.

The hefty man—the last of the three—chuckled and took off his overcoat, baring his pale but muscular body. Ariel whistled while yanking Mercury out of the dead demon's throat. She juggled Mercury in the air for a bit of entertainment.

"Not impressed?" Ariel asked him. Once he spread his legs apart, he howled then bolted. Ariel returned to her whistling. *Whoo-hooo-whoo-hooo-hoo. Whoo-hoo-whoo-hoo-hoooooo....*

He was closing in. "Finally! You are so close!" Ariel bent at the knees. Once he was within arm's length, she jumped and circled in the air. The man stopped and looked back confused. He was now on the other side of her.

"Come here, boy," Ariel encouraged him. "Come on!"

To the man's right was a barrel. He quickly picked it up. Ariel eyed his movements. As he pulled his arms back, Ariel did the same. The pale demon ran with the barrel in his hands. He pitched the barrel forward with all his strength, aiming for Ariel's face. At the same time, Ariel released Mercury from her hand. It swiftly cartwheeled its way through the air. Once it reached the wooden exterior, it easily sliced its way through. The barrel collapsed but Mercury continued to spin until it plunged in between the man's eyes. He stopped in his tracks and fell to the ground.

Ariel retrieved Mercury and swiped off the monster blood from her beloved dagger on the side of his cheek.

"Ariel, we need your help," a voice called. It was Jason. He waved at her to meet up with him and Sying.

Immediately, she headed their way. "Are you guys alright?" Ariel asked them.

"We're fine," Jason said, as he was downing shots of revival potion to heal his ribs. "I need your help to save the others. You seem to be the only one able to kill these terrorists. Sying and I were lucky enough to destroy one of them."

Ariel didn't understand. "What do you mean?"

"Mercury has been the only one able to slaughter these fuckers and we need you to help us," Jason said. "Sying and I can hold them off for a while but we need you to kill as many of them as you can in order to help everyone escape. Are you with me?"

Ariel looked over at the chaos. It was a blood bath. Most of the assassins were down and it was difficult to tell who was alive. The multitude of screams killed her heart. She knew what she had to do. She had to save as many people as she could. A Death Dealer never turns their back on their comrades.

Ariel looked at Jason. "Always."

Quickly, Ariel said a common prayer with her eyes shut:

Forgive me Lord of Life, I may sin in your eyes.
Please do not loathe me, as I am only doing what is right.

Ariel reopened her violet eyes then bolted like lightning.

One-by-one the pale demons were falling like gravel. With a solid kick there, a firm punch here and a slice-and-dice there, slowly, more and more Death Dealers were set free.

Ariel noticed Zaire was having trouble. His arrows failed to kill the monsters. The pale demons were easily plucking them out, unaffected. Two of them were about to pick Zaire as their prey. However, Ariel wasn't having it. She hustled her way over to save her fellow assassin. The pale demons were close to jabbing their nails into Zaire's body but Ariel sprung and landed a few feet from them. Being quicker on her toes, she zoomed up from behind the beasts. With an elongated arm, Mercury, sliced her way across. Ariel halted in front of Zaire, blocking him from any future attacks. The Death Dealers cautiously stared at the monsters in front of them. Suddenly, a squishy sound was coming from their necks. Mercury cut the monsters heads off like a knife through butter. Their heads fell one way while their bodies fell another.

"I'll catch up with you," Ariel told Zaire. He initially refused to leave, but she forced him to meet her at the vans. With regret, he obeyed and headed out.

Luckily, Seraphina was almost out of sight—heading to the vans—and Bodhi and Daoka were also on the verge of freedom. They were so close to escaping the death ring but two of the monsters—one man, one woman—were aiming for the kill. Jason swooped in and kicked both of them head on, distracting the monsters, allowing Bodhi, Seraphina, and Daoka enough time to flee.

Jason and Sying tag-teamed. Jason did one of his famous roundhouse kicks to the male's chest, but the monster barley flinched. Sying grabbed the cape of his coat and twirled it around the female's head, blinding her vision. She fought violently and screamed as loud as she could. Jason bounced up and plunged an iron fist straight to her face. Sying uncovered her, spun her to face him, then flipped her up over his head back around, smashing her face onto the hard concrete.

Everyone else was gone, but unfortunately, a few didn't survive. Ariel was about to head over to help the captains until a tall figure appeared from within the shadows of a vacant jewelry store. Ariel positioned herself in a karate—kibi dache—stance until the figure's face emerged from the brink rays of her flashlight.

"No," huffed Ariel, scared out of her mind. She paced backwards, terrified of what was in front of her. The figure smiled. Unlike the others, this creature only had four sharp teeth: two fangs on the right side of the mouth and two on the left.

"This isn't real," Ariel cried. "No," she mumbled. "No!!" She refused to be there a minute longer. She sped off like a cheetah.

"Run!" Ariel shouted to Jason and Sying, who were still fighting. Ariel threw Mercury to the right. It plummeted right through the male monster's throat. She retrieved it, and stabbed the female on the left, through the gut. Both of them fell like the earth had quaked.

"You alright?" Jason asked her. He looked back and noticed what was approaching. "No way," Jason gasped.

Sying wanted to ask questions but it was not the time. "We must go," he told Jason.

The remaining three sped to the vans and immediately hopped inside them. Ariel threw herself in the back seat and replayed what had just happened in her head. Jason sat next to her, worried, and checked for any bodily injuries. "Are you okay???"

Ariel shoved Mercury back in her sheath and tried not to get too anxious or cry. She wanted to concentrate on something else but she couldn't. She tried to pay attention to the rhythm of her breath.

"Ariel, talk to me," Jason begged.

Annoyed, Ariel barked, "Did you not see what just happened?!" Everyone jumped in their seat and looked back at her.

"I...I'm not sure," Jason muttered.

"I know you saw it!" Ariel wailed. She began bawling her eyes out and ended up punching one of the van's windows.

"Hey!" Jason grabbed her hands. "Ariel, talk to me."

Ariel looked up at him, scared at what she was about to say. She wiped her tears away and shrieked, "I think I just saw my father!"

BLOOD

O nce the vans parked on the upper bailey, Ariel rushed to her dormitory. She slammed the door shut with all the enormous rage within her, causing the walls that boxed her inside to tremble. She raced to her phone to call someone of great importance: her aunt, Faith.

Faith was cooking dinner when the phone rang. She was thrilled to see it was Ariel calling her. Very rarely did she get to speak to her niece, but during those few heartfelt conversations, warmth filled her lonely heart.

"Hello?" Faith answered with excitement.

Ariel could feel her soul slowly cracking from all the anxiety. "You need to clear something up for me."

Faith paused. Hearing Ariel's labored breathing on the other end worried her. She put down the spatula and sat on the closest chair next to her. "What's wrong, babe?"

Ariel gritted her teeth. "Seoul is full of people. Lots and lots of people."

"You're in Seoul?" Faith looked at a picture hanging on the wall: herself with her older sister, Symphony, in their childhood home in Seoul. Many years had passed since she even thought about District Asia.

Ariel ignored her completely. She was outraged. Faith may have lied to her. How could she do such a thing? "When I was young, you told me Seoul was dangerous. That it was turning into a ghost town. Oh, and might I add, you said we had no choice but to leave. After these past few shitty days, I find it hard to believe. Why did we leave Seoul, Faith?"

Faith was appalled by Ariel's nauseating attitude. "To protect you."

Lies!! Ariel thought. "From what?!" She screamed. She felt her heart race and her blood boil. She tore away her clothes as soon as her skin fired up.

Smoke infiltrated Faith's nostrils. She hadn't realized her pasta sauce was burning. "Oh no!" She rushed to the stove, immediately turning it off, and moved the pan to a cool spot, saving her home from burning to the ground. She tried fanning away the smoke quickly in order to regain her composure to explain herself. "All I cared about was your happiness. In Seoul—everyone was leaving. You would have had no friends, no family…."

Ariel felt betrayed, lied to. She thought back to the past few days: the happy faces in Seoul—despite the high kidnapping rate—the booming economy, lurking pale monsters, her father….Her father.

"Family?" Ariel barked coldly. "What family? You were all I had. You told me my parents were dead!!"

"They…they are." Teardrops hung on the corner of Faith's eyes. Each time she thought of her sister Symphony, all she could think about was the last words she ever spoke to her: *I don't want to talk about it. Leave me alone!* Faith couldn't remember what the argument was about. She fantasized about the what if for years after her sister's death: What if she actually let go of the anger and told Symphony she loved her? Would that have made her loss less painful? Doubtful. Still, the final words Faith spoke to her would forever gnaw at her heart.

"Hmmm…that's hilarious," Ariel groveled with a menacing laugh. Since her arrival, she had lived in a world of unfamiliarity. Her only goal was to solve the hottest case in the history of the DDAG, and continue the next two to three decades as a well-respected and sought out Death Dealer—Death Dealers usually retired between the ages of 55 and 60. However, there was nothing she could do to prepare herself to see the man who used to proudly call her "princess," living and breathing again after ten years.

Faith needed to get to her niece as soon as possible. She ran upstairs to the bedroom, unzipped two suitcases and began shoving clothes inside. "You are scaring me, girl. Are you still in Seoul?"

"You know, being a Death Dealer is my job and I take it very seriously." Ariel took a quick pause. "Despite me kicking ass or getting my ass kicked, I never quit. I've seen some crazy shit, Faith. Crazy, disgusting, god-awful shit."

Faith continued to bag her belongings in silence, allowing Ariel to continue venting.

"But then I come to Seoul, thinking it was just going to be another day of killing some idiotic kidnappers or deranged killers, but inexplicable things began to happen, and then *BAM!*—guess who I see. You'll never get it right, but take a guess."

Faith descended the stairs and flurried out the door with urgency. "I don't know," Faith said, scrunching her face while locking the door. "John?" John was an ex-boyfriend. Ariel called him a handsome but stupid boy with loser-syndrome: he refused to take life seriously. Despite his undeniable potential as a Death Dealer, he dropped out of the DDAG Academy and chose the lazy path of living off his wealthy parents.

"Of course! Why wouldn't it be John?" Ariel sang, sarcastically. A banging came from the door. "Who is it?"

"Jason," her best friend called out.

Ariel rushed to the door and swung it open. "Not...now!"

"Let me in," Jason urged.

Demoralized by frustration, Ariel slammed the door in his face.

Faith rummaged through her purse, scraping out her car keys. "Ariel, talk to me."

"I did not see John, Faith. BUT... I saw my daddy!" Ariel blurted, laughing hysterically. She felt like she was in the midst of becoming insane. She threw herself on the bed and briefly explained the utter horror that stalked her since day one in Seoul: the shadow, the pale monsters, and her father magically brought back to life.

Faith sped down the road in her small blue car to the nearest portal in Brooklyn, New York, District North America. Hearing the news was too much and seemed more like fantasy than reality, but still, she knew she had to be there for Ariel. Ariel was deeply pained by the loss of her parents, and she prayed to the Lord of Life many times to bring them back, but she never imagined her niece actually seeing her father again.

However, Leon wasn't alive. He couldn't be. It was completely impossible. He had gone missing thirteen years ago. Why suddenly crawl out of the grave now?

"Are you staying in Seoul? I am coming to see you." Faith pulled out her wallet, ready to buy a portal flight ticket. It was more than she could afford, but Ariel had always been her priority, no matter the cost or time.

"No," Ariel groaned. "Don't come here."

"So, you are at their headquarters?" Faith asked, a bit relieved knowing Ariel's whereabouts.

Suddenly, the doorknob began to twist and turn on its own. Jason invited himself in.

"Ariel, we need to talk about what happened earlier."

"Is that Jason?" Faith asked.

Jason overheard the familiar raspy voice.

"No," Ariel lied.

Jason went for Ariel's hand. She moved.

"Give me the phone!" Jason demanded.

Ariel shoved him away. "Fuck you! You saw him! I know you did. Don't lie and make me look stupid!"

Faith's heart was breaking during the tussle. To make things worse, the next portal flight to Seoul wasn't until morning. "Let me talk to Jason," she demanded, well above a raised tone.

Jason yanked the phone out of Ariel's hand. "Faith?"

Faith's head perked up. "Jason?"

"Ariel needs you. Can you make it to District Asia's DDAG headquarters?" Jason asked, hurriedly.

Ariel refused to have Faith see her in an unbalanced emotional state. It was completely unnecessary when she could just as easily speak with her on the phone. Ariel pinned Jason to the ground and fought to retrieve her phone.

"Yes! I'm buying a ticket to Seoul now," said Faith, nodding at the cashier as she spoke. "The next trip isn't for a few hours but I am on my way. I will see you both soon. Jason, take care of her for me."

Ariel won her phone back, however, Faith was no longer on the other end.

"You sonofabitch!" Ariel punched the wall next to her so hard, her fist penetrated the drywall.

"Relax!" Jason pleaded. "You're still on probation. Remember that!" He looked at the partially dismantled wall. *Great,* he thought. *I have to fix this shit before Sying finds out.*

Ariel was still convinced Faith was lying. "She's not telling me something. I can feel it." She was conjuring up a hypothesis. "She told me my parents died in a car crash, right? So, what? Did my mom die and instead of coming home to his only daughter, did my father just think, 'Fuck this!' then run away like a coward? There's no way. Faith knew my parents like the back of her hand. They told her everything. What the hell is she hiding?! Why is my dad here?"

Jason did his best to remain calm. He was uncertain about what he saw. Ariel, on the other hand, was striving for truth but only heard fabrications. Jason drew in close to comfort her, but she was disgusted with the utter filth that frolicked out of her captain's mouth, and denied his consolation.

"What if the man you saw just happened to look like your dad?" Jason debated. "I mean, how uncommon is it for someone to have similar physical features to you, me, your dad, my dad? Bodhi? Anyone?"

"Very," Ariel hissed as she crossed her arms. She paced over to the closed window and latched it open.

She looked out in disbelief, but the cold air was refreshing and it cooled her lukewarm body. She breathed in the gentle wind and focused on some snow frosted cherry blossom trees. *Could this really be happening?* she thought.

Jason sighed. "You are my best friend and I support you through thick and thin. But I am not convinced that who we saw is your father. That man—monster—whatever he was…could've just been someone else with a close resemblance to your dad. That's all. Ariel, it's been over ten years. He wouldn't come back now."

Ariel was silent, but her mind continually flashed with vivid memories of recent events: the monsters, the streets covered in Death Dealer guts, and her father with dead eyes and sharp fangs.

Jason walked across the room and stood behind a rugged Ariel, fearing to draw in any closer. "There's a meeting tomorrow afternoon at three. Please, be there. In the meantime, get some rest."

"Get the fuck out of my room," Ariel cried, taking Jason by surprise. At that moment, Ariel felt truly alone. She knew who she saw, despite Jason's denial. That thing was a new form of her father. He was no longer human. Instead, he was an unrecognizable killing machine. The love that once glistened in his baby blue eyes had been vanquished by the color of moonlit mercury. Even though he should have been hitting fifty, he looked like he hadn't aged a day. He looked exactly the same, just lighter-skinned and corpse-like. That only made Ariel rustle up more questions.

"Don't be mad at me," Jason said, defensively.

Ariel refused to look at him. She rubbed her arms vigorously as the wind began to heighten.

"Just be at the meeting tomorrow." Jason was evacuating her room.

Ariel shot him a haughty look. "Get out!!" she screamed.

"I'm leaving!" Jason shouted back, smacking over a chair as he passed.

As soon as Ariel turned to look back outside, the door behind her slammed shut.

"Asshole!"

After a while, Ariel closed her window and desperately wanted to put her mind to rest. Once her body hit the foam mattress, she lowered her lids and cried herself into a world of dreams.

Ariel stood in front of a rock venue with music blaring from behind the walls.

It was made out of grey marble bricks, black-framed doors, and a shield with the pattern ⊙♮, was carved across the banner. The door swung open and two young women popped out: one with blonde hair and a body that, though thin, was not wanting for curves, and the other, a ginger with robust tits, suffocating under the linen fabric of her hazy green sweater and her short skirt was leaving little to the imagination.

They giggled immensely as the drinks in their hands splashed all over the cracked sidewalk. The ginger helped up the blonde, calling her Stacy, and both women held one another up as they messily walked down the music strip.

Ariel followed their tracks close and quietly. When they reached the peak of a darkened corner, that's when Ariel attacked.

Ariel clawed at the ginger first. Her sharp claws scratched their way across her short neck. The ginger smashed against a pole and knocked out unconscious before collapsing to the floor.

Stacy shrieked at the snapping of her friend's neck. Ariel could feel Stacy's fear, and it hauntingly aroused her. Stacy looked into Ariel's eyes then turned to escape. But before she could disappear, she felt a tug on the back of her red coat. Ariel articulately pulled her back as Stacy landed perfectly between her chest and arm. Ariel held her close, feeling her round ass on her crotch.

Ariel could feel Stacy's warm flesh, scarred arm and strands of hair tickling her nose, as if she were actually there. When Stacy begged to be released, Ariel felt all of her emotions: the desperation, the frustration, the exasperation—it rained through Ariel like an angry thunderstorm.

Before moving any further, Ariel intimately caressed her oval-shaped face, and suddenly, Stacy was inflamed with arousal. She craved for Ariel's pale hands to massage her all over, starting with her perky breasts, down to the warmth of her excited pussy.

Ariel could sense Stacy's hormones as they raged with each touch. She deftly glided her hands up Stacy's legs and, without apology, pulled down her wet panties and massaged her bare lips. They both moaned. Stacy couldn't get enough.

"Fuck me," Stacy whimpered, licking her lips.

Ariel brought her head back to kiss her and placed her hand over her neck. She carefully tilted her head to the side.

With the tip of her nail, Ariel gently punctured a hole below Stacy's ear. Ariel stretched out her neck, opened her mouth wide and then....

"AAAHHH!" Stacy screamed in unsettling agony. Ariel wildly jerked her head about as she sucked out the blood flowing through her veins.

Stacy began to convulse and blood spurted out from her mouth. Harder and deeper Ariel dug her teeth inside her skin. Stacy wanted to fight, but she couldn't. Ariel could feel her dying.

Wake up!! said a voice in the distance. *Ariel, wake up!!*

Ahhh!!! Ariel screamed. She flew out of bed and ran to the bathroom.

Once the water poured out of the faucet, she splashed her face with cold water. After taking a moment to breath, she looked upon her reflection in disbelief. She even looked down at her hands to check for any abnormalities. Luckily, everything looked normal. The same long fingers and light pink palms. Ariel was accustomed to bad dreams and sleepless nights, but no nightmare had ever felt so intimately real. She could feel her feet parading the music strip and she could even smell alcohol lingering from the drunken citizens of Seoul as they passed. Even the taste of Stacy's blood remained in her delicate mouth. Killing the poor ginger felt undeniably real. Was it all just a dream?

Even stranger, pieces of the dream and what she had seen in Gangnam District seemed to oddly connect together, but the puzzle was not near complete. Ariel was troubled with ongoing wonder about the questionable acts playing out since she had stepped foot in Seoul.

What was she trying to tell herself? Was this nightmare a premonition? Had Ariel tasted her future?

Ariel kept her notepad in a drawer by her bed. She withdrew it, remembering important details of her dream. She envisioned the entertainment strip, but most of the names were already forgotten. Ariel drew the outside structure of the rock venue with the "Artbook" option on her pad: grey marble blocks, black-framed doors, two pillars and a shield with the pattern 아, etched across. She stared at it with mounting agitation. "Maybe I am going crazy," she sighed. Momentarily, she felt confident, but quickly, she felt ridiculous. "Whatever," she told herself. She slipped the notepad back in its home then returned to bed, unsatisfied.

However, before getting comfortable, Ariel sat back up. Someone had screamed to wake her. But who? It was a female voice....*Ivy?* Ariel looked around her dorm and realized she appeared to be alone. The room was a cavity. Why wouldn't it be?

Ariel reclined again, certain she was losing her mind.

The next morning, Sying called Ariel to the clerical desk. Faith was standing in the lobby, admiring the high ceiling.

Ariel came from behind the door and was nervous about the presence of her family, whom she hadn't seen in two years. Ariel immediately noticed Faith never strayed far from her usual hairstyle: medium-brown hair with simple layers. Her smile remained adorably sweet with crooked, white teeth. She dressed in a somber sweater and loose jeans. Around her neck hung the necklace her sister, Symphony, gave her on her sixteenth birthday: an amethyst crystal decorated in a silver wiring and suspended by a white gold chain.

Ariel welcomed her aunt with a cold "Hello."

"My goodness, have I missed you!" Faith exclaimed. Immediately, she dashed over to her beautiful niece, grasping her with an immense hug. Ariel patted her briefly and took a wee step back.

"It's nice to see you," Ariel hesitated. She did miss her aunt deeply, but she hated her reasons for being there. A shallow phone call caused Faith to waste money on a portal flight. It was a crude accusation Ariel had publicized with cruel surety that led Faith to Seoul. How could she do that to the woman she loved most?

"I really wished you stayed home. It was pointless for you to come here."

After weeks of not hearing from her niece, Faith hoped for a loving hello and a comforting squeeze. Unfortunately, not all dreams come true: even the little ones.

"Get rid of your damn attitude," Faith grunted. "Even though you are a pain in the ass, when someone seems to be bothering my niece, I can't care less about anything else."

"That's not what I meant," Ariel apologized. "I'm sorry you had to come here because of me."

"Oh, sweetie, don't be sorry," Faith assured. "I'm glad I came. I'm so happy to see you." Ariel took in her sweet embrace.

Jason appeared from the lower bailey doors. Ariel insisted Faith should say hello. Jason opened his arms and embraced Faith in an unyielding hug. They clutched on to one another for a long minute. Ariel stood back and patiently waited for them to part.

"It's so good to see you," Faith rejoiced. "How have you been?"

Jason gifted her with one last hold. "I'm great, auntie." Jason's flamboyant personality amused everyone he met. "The DDAG keeps me busy, but I enjoy it."

"So, what's going on with Ariel?" Faith asked.

Jason decided to escort both ladies to a private room. They sat inside Sying's office and Jason and Ariel chatted up Faith about the past few days, being certain to omit what was still classified.

"So, you really think you saw Leon?" Faith wondered if people could rise from the dead.

Ariel was no longer 100 percent certain, but she clung to a minimal amount of positivity for dear life. "It had to be. I mean, that's what I thought when I first saw him." That horrific night came prancing back in her head. "Now, I...I—"

"It's a blur," Jason interrupted, distracting Faith from Ariel's vulnerability. "I will admit, he looked like a long-lost brother but everything happened so fast, it is unclear."

Faith shifted in her chair, feeling uneasy. "How many people died?"

Jason and Ariel looked at one another. Ariel didn't know the exact number. All she could remember was Gangnam decorated in Death Dealer decay.

"Twenty-seven," Jason revealed.

Ariel murmured in astonishment, "Twenty-seven?! We've never lost that many in a night. How many of them were in our faction?"

"Thirteen," Jason replied, with a disapproving look. He felt responsible for the deaths of so many professional assassins. If only he had arrived to the battle sooner. Would that have made a difference?

"I'm sorry," Faith consoled. "May the Lord of Life protect their souls now."

Time rushed on as the three conducted casual, social affairs: a tour of the castle, a simple lunch, and a couple of hours of catching-up and gossiping.

Jason informed Faith of their afternoon DDAG meeting. Sergeant Aurora Tulip—from District Asia—approved Faith's stay at the DDAG headquarters and personally escorted her to a lavish room.

Jason and Ariel were impressed by the luxury of the suite, especially the king-sized bed, the mind-blowing bay window overlooking the front lawn of the castle, the cherry garnished furniture and the pastel colors lining the four walls.

"How do I get a room like this?" Ariel asked.

Sergeant Tulip glowered Ariel's way. Jason had only spoken with her personally on a handful of occasions, whereas Ariel had only greeted her once. There were stories of her heroic adventures in the New World. Rumor had it, that she had killed three men using only a nail file, however there was no proof to verify the myth. Still, her reputation was deservedly powerful. She was intimidating to look at, mainly due to the roughness of her stern face. And yet, she was beautiful—immensely attractive, even—but she was tough. Tough and dominant. Ariel respected that.

"Only the best get to stay in the king's suite," Sergeant Tulip said with charm.

Faith gasped. "The king?" she asked. "Meaning, the king of the New World?"

Tulip genuinely uplifted her full lips. "That is correct, my lady." She had confidence that shined even through the simplicity of kindness. "When he visits our headquarters, he sleeps in this room while the queen sleeps in the chamber suite. Hers is a tad smaller, but just as exquisite."

Before the Death Dealers exited the room, Faith assured Ariel, she would be fine. She made plans to visit downtown—before dark—and Ariel promised daily lunch dates.

Jason and Ariel hugged Faith goodbye before fleeing to the afternoon meeting.

Today, no one carried the adrenaline that seemed to flow endlessly through an assassin's veins. It was a sorrowful time. Many people had been murdered just over twelve hours earlier. Their lifeless bodies were scattered and molding on the trashed yet empty roads. The DDAG nurses and ambulances ventured to Gangnam District to retrieve their bodies. All twenty-seven of them would be given the honorable burial any Death Dealer truly deserved.

Sying and Jason sat down with their guilds while both Sergeant Tulip and Sergeant Lotus arrived with solemn faces. Tulip peered over everyone with dim brown eyes in a formal, two-piece suit and a silk, steel blue tie. Sergeant Lotus glanced over at Ariel, expressionless. Ariel scratched her forehead and fixed the long sleeves of her teal-colored turtle neck.

"They never come to our meetings," Bodhi whispered in Zaire's ear. "It's kind of nice to know they care."

Zaire appreciated Bodhi's enthusiasm. "I wouldn't go that far."

Usually, DDAG sergeants had two things in mind: solving cases, and tracking terrorist capture and kill statistics. If the percentages were above 70% by the end of a given year, no Death Dealers had to be transferred over to other factions and sergeants were given a nice bonus in their yearly review. So, as far as them caring for their guilds, each assassin had their own personal opinion. Ariel, for one, full-heartedly believed Lotus loved his guild, despite his cold personality. He was a tough coach who taught hard lessons and took no shit from anyone. Ariel loved it.

Lotus offered Tulip to begin.

"Faction Divide and Faction Abyss," Tulip declared, "I stand before you with anger and sadness. It is with deep hardship that I inform you all of our losses: We lost twenty-seven good men and women during an ambush that occurred approximately between the hours of eleven p.m. and twelve a.m. Unfortunately, no one saw this coming, so this battle brought on more questions than answers. Who were those men and women? Where did they come from? Why were they there?

"I refuse to stand here and not focus on what's to come. We must prepare for war. Whoever killed our fellow assassins must be found and they must be punished for what they have done. With all my heart, I trust that the Lord of Life will guide us into finding out what all of this means. Surely, this is not a coincidence. We were on the brink of gaining our first strong clues toward this case thanks to the brilliant minds of Ariel Rose, Bodhi Tigerlilly and Seraphina

Jasmine. Then, in the blink of an eye, we were robbed at the scene of the crimes.

"Because of who we are and what we stand for, we will all come together and find the strength to not only live on but to protect each other and all the innocents of the New World.

"Time and time again, the world has been saved from all terrorists, especially those who dare try to revive the Black Plague II Infections. The hopes and dreams for the people in the New World are for them to one day no longer live in fear, and be free. The Death Dealers will remain until all the scum of the New World is wiped clean.

"Death Dealers, we will not fade away. We shall never forget our soldiers. Remember them, keep them alive in your heart, and remember that they died because they believed in fighting for all that is good in the world. May the Lord of Life grant them endless peace and grant us endless strength and prosperity. Thank you."

Sergeant Lotus stood before them now. He took a second peek at his cufflinks to secure them.

"I have come here to offer my condolences. It's never been easy to lose one of my guild members, let alone thirteen. All families of the fallen have been notified and they will send us information on funeral arrangements as soon as possible. Of course, once our informants have received this information, we will then pass it on to you all. Feel free to say goodbye to whomever you wish and to as many as you like. Lastly, both Sergeant Tulip and I have asked the king and queen to give you all the night off from the field. With generosity, they agreed to allow sabbaticals for tonight and tomorrow. We understand work has to be done, but this is a time of mourning and recuperating. Before moving forward, does anyone have any questions?" Everyone exchanged looks but remained quiet.

"Okay. Jason. Sying. You both have the stage."

Both captains eased their way up. Sying asked about clues and looked forward to hearing any helpful information. Sadly, no one had much to say. Overall, everyone's notes and clues and photos were gaunt. Their first meeting after the massacre would be completely unproductive.

Ariel remembered the symbol, 진화. *The picture!* Why hadn't other people mentioned it? She raised her hand.

"Symbolism," Ariel chimed in. Everyone turned to face her.

She continued: "There was a symbol painted in blood all over the place. I found it on street lights and windows and cars and trash cans, all over the sidewalk and alleyways. Did anyone else see it?"

The crowd was silent.

"That's ridiculous. It was everywhere," Ariel smacked.

Sying asked, "Do you have proof of what you saw?"

"I do," Ariel said. She strolled out of her chair and up to the front to use the projector and computer. "All my photos automatically upload to my memory storage." After rapid clicking on the keyboard, Ariel pulled up her photo gallery. Sure enough, the pictures she took were all uploaded. However, the symbol in question was not. It…disappeared.

Growing anxious, Ariel reset the computer. Again, she opened her gallery but the symbol was not in any of her pictures.

"No, no, no!" Ariel knew what she saw. The 진화 was everywhere. There was no way she missed the shot, especially when she was up-close and personal with them.

All the assassins were debating amongst themselves. They spoke in hush tones and exchanged mimicking looks.

Ariel continued searching, fumbling the keys. Her photos were wiped of all evidence pertaining to her discovery. Normally, Ariel was careless toward those who didn't believe her. But this time was different. That symbol meant something and it was a key to a closed door, just begging to be opened.

"I know what this looks like, but I swear I saw it," Ariel said, defensively.

Jason hurried his way over to her and attempted to reboot the system himself.

Sying eyed Ariel questionably. Seldom did he distrust an employee of the DDAG, but if he was concerned, you could see it in his blinking narrow eyes and one raised eyebrow.

"Ms. Rose," Sying gulped. "Did you happen to take another photo or a maybe even a video?"

"This is bullshit!" Ariel fumed. "It was there! I know it was. Bodhi. Hyuna. Did either of you see it?"

They both shook their heads.

"Seraphina?"

Seraphina hunched slightly over the table, interlocking her fingers. "Sorry, but the only thing I saw was blood, fingerprints and footprints. No symbol."

Ariel rushed over to the whiteboard. She grabbed a red marker and drew out 진화, with stiff fingers. The symbol was fairly easy to remember. After slamming the cap back on, Ariel pointed to her messy drawing.

"This is what I saw," Ariel scoffed. "I don't know what the hell it means, but it's obviously important. I'm telling you all, it was *everywhere*!"

Jason sighed and tried not be judgmental. He accepted Ariel's rebellious, outspoken, and prideful persona, but ever since she stepped foot in Seoul, she hadn't been herself. Instead, she was becoming a person Jason feared. She was no longer the brave and independent Death Dealer he had known since childhood. She became this seemingly fragile, weak, and sensitive child. What happened to the girl he always knew? Never in a million years would the old Ariel claim to be hearing voices or seeing strange images. This wasn't his best friend....This wasn't his best friend at all.

"I'm sorry, but we can't go on what you think you saw," Jason concluded. "We have to move on."

Ariel's shock billowed from the inside-out. She examined the room and noticed an array of eyes scouring her.

"I know what I saw," Ariel barked. "You gotta believe me."

"Sit down." Jason hastened to switch topics.

"This symbol was painted with the blood of the people who probably have been murdered," Ariel added. "Someone is going out of their way to mark their territory with innocent blood. Something big is happening!"

Before Jason could speak to the room, Sergeant Lotus reentered and politely pushed Jason aside.

"Can I speak with you outside, please?" Lotus asked Ariel.

Ariel glared Jason's way. "Sure," she hissed.

"Please, continue," Lotus insisted. "We won't be long."

Ariel followed her chief outside the auditorium and threw herself against the wall. She hadn't seen Lotus for days. She was under strict scrutiny and he had to come at a time when she appeared mentally broken. Days ago, he wanted her out of Seoul's way. Now—after giving her another chance—he may not have anything pleasant to say. Could this day get any worse?

Ariel was sure she'd be ahead of the game by now, but she was far from winning. Lotus walked up to her and admitted he knew about her "recent activity" in Gangnam District.

"Who told you that?" Ariel asked, upset.

"It doesn't matter," Lotus emphasized. "I don't know what's going on with you, Ariel, but I'm afraid you're going to have to step off the field for the next seven days."

"A week?" Ariel jumped from the wall. "Why? Because this person thought I was pretending to hear voices? I wasn't! Whoever was talking to me, talked to me again last night. Right before I saw my father!"

"Your father?" Lotus placed a hand behind his ear.

Shit! Ariel thought. The words sputtered out of her mouth like an uncontrollable disease. "Never mind."

It was clear to Lotus that Ariel could not handle living in Seoul. He was certain that he didn't want her to leave the faction completely; she was a good assassin—a great one, after all. Perhaps she just needed a bit of molding? He often considered taking her out of the Seoul case. She would be back in New York, working with novices and trainees, despite the work being less exciting. She would be the top dog in District North America while Jason was in District Asia.

In the end, Lotus knew she'd be okay. She just needed time to herself to think, adjust, and normalize.

"Take a week off. No excuses," Lotus ordered.

"I am on to something. Not my fault everyone in there can't see what I see." Ariel darted away from Lotus and away from the auditorium.

"I'd appreciate it if you stayed for the meeting," Lotus called out to her as she gained distance in the opposite direction.

"For what? I'm going to be gone for a week, locked in a damn box since I can't leave this fucking building!" Ariel yelled, scraping every ounce of frustration within her and letting it fly. "I might as well act as if I don't know a damn thing!"

Lotus hated when Ariel acted irrational but he willingly permitted her to leave. There was no point in ordering her to stay. He felt divided by his decision but it was too late to turn back now. Plus, a DDAG sergeant never goes back on their word unless they undoubtedly have to. For now, he escorted himself back into the auditorium and quietly sat in the back of the room, listening to the rest of what was sure to be an unproductive meeting.

Later that night, Zaire came knocking on Ariel's door. She allowed him in even though she'd rather be alone.

"How do you feel?" Zaire asked her.

Honestly, she felt like her time with the DDAG was coming to an end.

"I'm fine," Ariel lied, continuing to messily fold a load of laundry that had been lying around for two days.

Zaire examined her room with vast interest and immediately noticed a tower of books. He picked them up one-by-one and realized they were mostly about black magic.

"Still studying, huh?" Zaire asked, flaring out the books like a handful of poker cards.

Ariel's obsession with black magic suddenly felt short-lived. "I don't care anymore."

Instead of mocking or interrogating an already beaten assassin, Zaire casually switched topics. "So, what are your plans for your week vacation?" he asked, playfully.

Ariel froze with a pair of pants folded halfway inward. She shook away the anger and finished folding her khakis. "I plan to do absolutely nothing," she articulated with a slight smacking of her lips.

"You don't know how to do nothing," Zaire retorted, looking at another book in her randomized pile: *The Black Plague II Theory: An Invisible Nuclear Weapon?* by Steven Violet.

"You're right," Ariel agreed, then slogged over to her drawers, inserting her clothes in no particular order. "Maybe I'll just read up on some architecture. The library here is fucking huge and orgasmic."

Zaire laughed, effervescent. "You and your damn books."

The door magically opened.

"I brought drinks!" Bodhi boasted as he carried an ale bottle and three glasses.

Ariel clenched her jaw. "I'm good, you guys," she urged, insinuating that she wanted them out.

"Oh, shut up," Bodhi joked. "Have at least one glass. In the words of one foxy redhead, 'A glass of ale a day, makes the pain go away.'"

Ariel noticed the two men staring at her. It was sweet to know how much her comrades cared for her. When Bodhi poured that glass of red ale, she was reminded that she was not allowed to leave the premises for the next seven days. She gave up and acknowledged the fine beverage and her favorable guests.

After the bottle was empty, Ariel noticed how the room got quiet. She figured they were bored, but that wasn't the case. Zaire pulled out a picture of his family, the same one he carried in his wallet for the past seven years. Bodhi immediately placed his hand on his shoulder, understanding his emotions.

Oddly, Ariel could feel his pain too, but physically. She couldn't figure out why.

"You know, you're alive and your family is safe, everything is going to be alright, man," Bodhi reminded Zaire.

Zaire placed the photo back in his wallet and laid flat across the floor. "I know. I'm thankful the Lord of Darkness hasn't taken me, but it's scary, you know?"

Ariel and Bodhi sat silently, allowing him to feel pain. *It's okay to be sad: it reminds you that you are still alive*, Bodhi thought.

"We lost thirteen people in like ten minutes," Zaire scoffed. "Not a day or a week or year, but in ten minutes. People we went to school with and trained with and fought with are dead!" he hid his face with both palms. Ariel stared at him worriedly. Zaire was the strong one of the group, while Bodhi was sensible, Seraphina was sharp-tongued, Jason followed the rules and Ariel was rebellious. Seeing Zaire fragile was an unusual twist.

"You're right," Bodhi coaxed in. "Even losing Death Dealers we barely knew, hurts. So many people were killed thanks to those…things. I mean, I can't even guess what they are. Can you?" he asked both parties.

"Not sure," Ariel answered, pulling out Mercury from her boot and flipping it around her soft fingers. "Those things were not only strong but smart. We've been ambushed before, but we handled other idiots like champs. These guys, though, were different."

Bodhi trashed the empty ale bottle. "I don't think they were human, but that's crazy." He hushed. "Right?"

Zaire and Ariel were on the same boat, but it was difficult to agree with something so out-of-the-ordinary. Both of them answered with a "Maybe." Zaire and Bodhi got up and readied themselves to leave.

Bodhi went back to Ariel and encircled her in a firm squeeze. Zaire followed his lead.

"Thank you guys for coming," Ariel said. "I hope you all find something during my personal vacation."

Both men chuckled.

"I have no problem updating you," Bodhi reassured with a sweet smile. "By the way, Mercury was the only thing killing off those pale demons..."

"Seems like it," Ariel said.

Bodhi put his thinking cap on and came up with something that may be useful. "What if I do some experiments with moonlit mercury? I have a feeling the pale demons couldn't handle the element. If I'm right, maybe I could convince the royal cabinet to craft us some cool weapons."

Zaire couldn't help but laugh at the idea. "The royal cabinet helping us? Yeah right."

"You never know," Ariel said, defending Bodhi's interesting plan. "I say go for it. That's a great idea."

"Sweet! I'll be in touch," Bodhi winked.

Zaire concluded with, "Me too!"

Both men exited the room. Ariel laid on the carpeted floor, then fell fast asleep.

For the next few nights, Ariel was restless due to the ongoing nightmares. She continued to draw out things that captivated her visually but each night became more fluid and distraught than the last. Ariel soon grew terrified once her eyes got heavy. Especially after one night…

She sat on a park bench and waited for a child to come close. An adorable boy with a bowl cut and brown eyes came up to greet her, offering a sample of rubies. She politely declined but charmed the little boy to follow her to a secret hiding place. He held her hand and trotted along by her side, carrying his faded teddy bear. She could feel the innocent boy's curiosity. His mini-body filled with excitement and ready for adventure.

As they were nearing the edge of the park, a black car quietly pulled up to the curb. The boy blossomed, anticipating the epic journey. He loved Ariel and asked if they could be together…forever.

"Of course," she said.

The boy grinned and that's when Ariel woke up.

Where was she taking him? Why? He was only a child. Thank goodness it was all a dream.

Luckily, Ariel had something to look forward to during the day. She kept her promise to Faith and every day at noon, they'd eat lunch. Sometimes Ariel would convince her to play some card games. Faith was never any good but Ariel had mastered the game of poker, thanks to Zaire. He was addicted to gambling during his years at the DDAG academy but once he met his wife, Wendy, he dropped his addiction altogether and embraced love instead.

Since Ariel was confined to headquarters, Faith would talk her ear off about the latest shops and outdoor events happening in Seoul. Faith even managed to bring Ariel back a souvenir from the Day of Rebirth Festival: On December 9, 2217 B.P., the last known Black Plague II Infection was recorded, and every year, the innocents of the New World would band together for a night of good music, great food and lustrous magic.

Faith bought Ariel a bracelet with the DDAG symbol as its charm. "Well, I'm definitely not wearing this during duty." Ariel placed the white gold bracelet on top of her desk in her room and she'd look upon it every day.

After day five, Ariel noticed a pattern. She was not picking victims in a specific area. They were scattered all over Seoul—mainly downtown. However, if her prey was an adult, the majority of the time they were being snatched and taken away or killed. But, if they were a child, they were never harmed, only persuaded into a mysterious black car and driven away.

When Ariel looked over her drawings, the desire to get out of the castle and find answers began to grow. She thought about the consequences each time she peered out the window, knowing that if she were to get caught, she could lose everything she'd worked hard for. Everything she loved could be confiscated in a snap. However, she was born rebellious. During the sixth night of her prison time, she decided to take matters into her own hands and sneak out of the castle.

Bodhi had informed Ariel that most of the assassins were going out for the evening to enjoy a night of booze and dance. He apologized profusely that she couldn't join but she only pretended to be affected.

Once the majority of Death Dealers exited the headquarters, Ariel seized an opportunity. She swallowed her Vitality pill, grabbed Mercury, put on her coat and tightened her boots. She snuck over to the armory tower and ascended the stairs. Luckily, she brought her heavy jacket. It was shaking cold outside. She peeked out the glassless window and examined the guards in the opposite direction.

They seemed bored, mostly, and barely kept watch over the grounds beneath them. She leaped over the window and carefully mounted her way down. Below her was the gardens, but luckily there was no one entering or exiting. Once her boots crunched on the iced grass, she laid low and bolted, noiseless, to the grey stoned wall. With the boost of Vitality, she jumped over the wall and in an instant, she was on the other side of the world. It was all too simple.

Ariel grimaced at the view behind her. Encouraged by scrutiny over Seoul, she took that passion and flew from rooftop to rooftop, all the way downtown, without a need for rest.

Ariel halted once landing deftly on top of a monastery. She returned to the ground and hid in the limited pockets of shadow within the valley of lights in downtown Seoul. Admittedly, Ariel enjoyed viewing the faces of happy people from afar: dashing smiles amongst friends, meaningless chit-chatter, and various acknowledgements through physical gestures like high-fives or handshakes. Ariel was taken back to a time when she was little, when she used to be happy and social. But things changed.

Anxious to get a swift move on things, Ariel looked for the rock venue she saw when the nightmares began. The streets were painted in fluorescent lights, so it was difficult to hide her body. She slipped behind trees and hid behind people taller than her to get by. She also veiled her head with a hood and only the ends of her red hair casually danced in the mild breeze.

The walk consisted of people mindlessly strolling all over the downtown area but Ariel was prepared for anything. She had on her Death Dealer weaponry but without the uniform. She didn't dare blow her cover.

Finally, after a long search, Ariel saw 야: the rock venue. It was well past ten o' clock but Ariel chose to stay until her arms fell off from the cold. Observing people took work, patience and sharp senses, especially when spying alone.

However, after the club shut its doors, nothing happened.

Ariel moved on to another familiar sight: the park. It was ghostly dead with no sight of intruders. Not wasting time, she walked the lone streets of Seoul, where the innocents of this peculiar, populated city were now safe in their homes and cozied up with their loved ones. Nothing. Not a hint of sound or a single pale monster lurking about.

Frustrated, Ariel sighed and quickly ran all the way back to her dorm. It was just as easy climbing back inside headquarters as it was leaving.

Ariel curled up with a cup of lavender tea and slipped on thick grey stockings. She snuggled up under the warm covers and, for the first time in weeks, she had a decent night's rest.

On the seventh night, Ariel didn't hesitate to leave the castle again, only this time, she wanted to patrol the streets in a more sophisticated fashion.

Before leaving, Ariel picked up the phone to call Bodhi. He never failed to inform her of their progress. Unfortunately, the DDAG had yet to find anything solid. Tonight was no different: the assassins went to Gangnam District, searched another section for hours, found nothing, then called it a night. The only thing Bodhi figured out was downtown Seoul had the best cherry blossom tea. Ariel demanded a cup in the morning.

Now to hit the streets.

Once she hit the fluorescent lights of the city, she blended in with the crowds, using a transformation spell: Temporarily she was able to change her identity to a more robust-looking woman with tight, black curls and cherry red lips. In a form-fitting lace dress, she cat-walked the area nonchalantly, pretending to pay no mind to those around her. For a moment, it felt good to be a civilian.

Ariel rummaged every nook and cranny she could for hours. Then, a vibe or something else intuitive ticked inside her: something was about to happen. She could taste it.

Ariel picked up a sense of urgency to the west. She followed the sense carefully. Suddenly, an image sprang out in front of her. A woman.

"Whoa," Ariel said, surprised, now feeling nauseous.

"I'm okay," she whispered to herself. "Keep going."

She did.

Ariel trailed along until she was smacked again. The woman reappeared and, as she was passing a venue, Ariel recognized it from another dream: Club Gold, a jazz venue. Back to Ariel.

"Ho-holy shit," she muttered, losing some balance. "Breathe," Ariel begged. "Whew…."

Ariel got back up and kept on her toes, even in black stilettos. The clinking of her heels trailed her as she paced on by.

Soon enough, Ariel was getting frustrated. She reached Club Gold, but the woman she saw was no longer there. She tried to come up with a plan.

Then Ariel received another vision, knocking her out of her own view. The woman was now passing by ◌̾. She felt the rush of hormones leveling up inside the woman's body.

Ariel was now punched back to her own current state. This was a good time to rush over to ◌̾.

After recuperating from the temporary dizziness, Ariel sprinted off to the rock club. She looked around, and there she was: the woman in her vision, cruising on by, minding her own business.

Ariel remained on the opposite side of the streets and carefully navigated through the people around her.

The woman ended up circling a trail and marching into a plaza of lonely benches and a broken water fountain.

Remaining cautious, Ariel lingered from behind and pulled out Mercury in the case of an emergency. At this point, the transformation magic wore off and she was suddenly back in her own skin, with her own clothes and weaponry.

The woman sat down with her legs crossed, her hands cupping her right knee. Her long brown hair was softly flowing over her face. She did nothing but smile at the broken water fountain.

Ariel began trembling. She wanted to go over and grab her, save her from the possibility of dying. However, it was better for her to wait.

The woman started humming to herself and slowly began to sing just above a whisper with an angelic voice. She was tearfully singing a lullaby.

Ariel remembered learning that song in beginner school.

Who could the woman be? She had to have been a mother; why else would she cry during a pleasant lullaby? Her face was kind and beautiful, and her hands were dry—proof she was a hardworking mother. Could she have lost a child?

"I love you so. I love you so. Mommy will keep you close."

As the woman was finishing her gentle song, Ariel crept a bit closer, seeing an opportunity.

"I look to the sky and I thank the Lord of Life. He has brought you to me. And I'm the most blessed as I can be."

The woman's last note hung in the air while her soft tears rained over her lap.

Suddenly, a figured flashed before her.

Ariel scanned the perimeter. No one else seemed to be around.

The man was tall and lanky, with wavy brown hair. He also wore a trench coat that looked similar to the shadow man's from the week before.

The woman remained in her seat. She only looked up with her saddened face. With the tips of her fingers, she swept her blouse down over her shoulder and titled her head. The figure caressed her neck and slowly hunched over her. Ariel was unable to see what was happening. She rummaged through her backpack to search for her binoculars.

A pinching sound echoed in the distance and the woman moaned with pure ecstasy.

Ariel's eyes returned to the scene. She noticed the woman's arms fell down and her fingers were slowly twitching. Her moans shortly faded away and her soul left her body.

The figure gently released the fallen mother and turned around to wipe his face. Ariel's eyes widened.

"What the?!" Ariel exclaimed. "It can't be!" She sprinted toward the man at full speed. Once she ran up behind him, she hesitated on what she was about to say.

Ariel straightened her posture and made sure Mercury was one with her arm. With the tip of the blade, she tapped on the man's shoulder.

He lifted his head but remained facing in the opposite direction.

"Hey," Ariel called to him.

The man turned around and her eyes watered as her mouth jittered. The man was foreboding, and he looked down on her like a simpleton. He menacingly grinned as he continued to clean the remains of the woman's blood off his pale face.

Purely devastated, Ariel cried, "Hello, Dad."

LOST

Ariel wanted to scram to save herself, but she couldn't. She shouldn't. The man in front of her was Leon Rose: beloved father to Ariel Rose and dear husband to Symphony Rose. Being in his presence now felt entirely different. Like new, even. She felt as though she was meeting him for the first time.

Either way, Ariel wanted answers. For that reason alone, she didn't run. Why had he been gone so long? What form had he taken? He was no longer human—Ariel knew that for sure. It seemed like the Lord of Darkness had put on a new face and chosen the soul of an honest, loving, and deep-minded man, who was most important to Ariel.

They stared at one another and circled around in miniscule steps. Leon kept an abrasive smile perched above his flat chin. Ariel was expressionless but kept Mercury close.

Finally, Leon parted his cupid's-bow lips and asked, "Dad? My, my…what childish dreams we have."

That's not his voice! Ariel cringed at the croaky, terrifying sound that blazed from his mouth. What happened to the man who would brush her hair gently with a soft comb? He would read her stories before bed to help Ariel fall fast sleep, but that comforting feeling has vanished into the depths of Malum. This new, haunting voice would plague her mind and keep her wide awake at night.

Ariel feared her life would be taken by the hands of her father, but who would know?

"You are my dad!" she snapped. "At least, you used to be. What the hell happened to you?"

Leon paused and surveyed Ariel inch-by-inch while feeling the sharp tips of his left fangs with his lengthy tongue. Ariel grew chills on the back of her neck. Nervously, she perched up the collar of her black trench coat to hide her goosebumps. She hoped he would embrace the truth that Ariel was indeed his daughter.

"How do you feel about evolution?" Leon asked.

Uninterested but desperate for words—any words—from him, Ariel played along. "Never thought about it," she admitted. "What about you?"

Leon chuckled to himself. Ariel stood back and watched as Leon was casually skimming the area with his hands behind his back.

"Maybe," Leon confessed. "You know," he rolled on, "I have seen you before."

Ariel caught sight of his cold eyes. "Of course, you have," she smacked. "You used to see me every day when I was little. But one night you never returned home."

Leon was unaffected by Ariel's childish fantasy. Instead, he protruded over Ariel's small body and gently took hold of a small piece of her hair. He inhaled the vanilla scent from her thick red locks. "Your hair. Your eyes. So pretty. In fact, you are one of the prettiest humans I have ever seen. However, you carry so much desperation and longing in your heart." Leon's mouth watered as he craved the sweet blood that flowed healthily within Ariel's soul case.

How did he know her deepest feelings? Ariel was too scared to ask. She kept focus on Leon's pale form in order for her to have complete control over the situation. If she had no other choice, she would attack and kill him right then and there.

Ariel eyed him unpleasingly. "Why can't you tell me what happened, Dad?" she scoffed. "Are you too much of a pussy to admit you left your daughter behind? And who knows what happened to my mother, also known as your wife."

Leon held his breath. With his twig-like fingers, he massaged her scalp. Ariel hated feeling the coldness of his skin. She fought for him to back off. However, he was mighty strong. He never moved, only smiled at her worthless effort.

"I have a wife," Leon hissed defensively. "I have been with her since the beginning. There was never anyone else. There will never be another."

Ariel wanted to expose his lie but carried no proof. She failed to travel with a picture of her family, as Zaire did.

"Nice to know you're an asshole. You want to forget me? Fine. But why Mom? She was the best thing to happen to both of us."

Tension boiled between them after those last words. Leon had been patient with the redhead. Now he was desperate to feed. However, she was special. He could feel it. He knew it. She was going to make this world a better place. He could end her life if he wanted to, but he was forbidden to do so—at the moment, anyway.

"My dear girl, I don't know who either of your parents are. I'm sure your mother was *special*, but I have someone dear to me and I'd be damned if a Death Dealer brat like yourself will convince me otherwise. My condolences for their passing. You have my sympathies, truly," Leon said, remorsefully unconvincing as he placed his cold hands over his chest.

"For the longest time, my aunt convinced me my parents died in a car crash." Ariel looked deep into his dead, silver eyes. "My mom died. As for my father, well, things just got complicated."

Leon let out a low, menacing snigger. He took some steps back to admire her from afar. A light wind snuck its way into the air. It whistled quietly as it danced through Ariel's velvet hair. With advanced senses, Leon could smell her intoxicating scent, even if he were miles away.

"How did you find out about the Death Dealers?" Ariel asked.

"I know you," Leon said.

"And how is that?" Ariel asked.

Leon walked backward without breaking Ariel's gaze.

"I have seen"—Leon trailed off—"visions of you."

Premonitions? Ariel thought. "Visions?"

"Yes," Leon sighed. "You are very, VERY, special…."

"I don't understand. Please explain," Ariel urged. She inched toward a bench opposite the woman's corpse.

Leon invited her into his world. "I am not like you, Ariel Rose. You were born. I was created—*reborn* actually—into a life of immortality. My name is Akhenaten. I walk in light and darkness. My body does not need rest or water to function and my heart needs no beat. The skeleton beneath my skin is indestructible and my blood is not my own. In fact, it is filled with the blood of men, women, children—short, fat, poor, rich, thin, black, white: humans. All kinds of humans."

"You mean," Ariel choked, slowly glancing over at the lifeless body. "You eat people?"

"Oh dear, no," Leon laughed. "I don't eat people. That'd be cannibalistic. All I need is blood. Not a brain, or liver, or a heart. Just thick, red-luscious, flowing pints of blood."

The disturbing view of her father was one of the first steps to acceptance. She must accept the fact that the man standing before her was no longer Leon Rose, her father. This man, this *thing*, was a monster that goes by the name Akhenaten, and he must be stopped.

"You are a goddamn murderer!" Ariel shouted. "What do you want with these innocent people?!"

Leon floated over to the dead woman, bringing his arms around her sagging shoulders. "You see this lovely woman here?" he asked. "She wanted to die."

"Bullshit!" Ariel roared. "No one asks to die. You kill people just like the terrorists in the New World!"

"On the contrary, my sweet," Leon fought back. "Her name was Mary. Beautiful, wasn't she?"

Ariel dared to not look at Mary, knowing it would make her react inhumanely. Instead, her glaring eyes lingered on Leon and her hands were ready. Mercury was the only weapon strong enough to kill those pale monsters. So, the only way to stop him was to dig Mercury through his non-beating heart or through his brain. Before she could go about slaughtering him, Ariel had to know more.

"She lost someone very special not long ago. A child. A son. A young boy with dreams of becoming an alchemist disappeared in the brim of night and was never seen again. Mary woke up to find her son's bed empty and the front door of her apartment open. After failing to discover his whereabouts, she tried drinking herself to death. She refused to live, childless. So, I offered her a gift—death—promising her it'd be fast and painless. Now, it didn't take much convincing. She obliged almost immediately. After accepting my offer, we agreed to meet here. You saw the rest."

Ariel flooded with anger. Leon used the fragility of a mother's love for his own demented desire. How could he do that? Was this the same boy she had seen in her nightmares not long ago? "Did you kill the boy?!"

Leon gazed over Mary's corpse and cackled. Ariel popped in a second pill of Vitality. It was time for him to die.

"You killed that poor kid, didn't you?" Ariel asked, pacing herself over to Leon. Mercury twirled around her fingers and was ready for a gruesome strike. "You sonofabitch!" She lunged forward.

Leon stretched out his hand in time with her jump. Ariel didn't notice a palm was about to whomp on her chest.

"Ugh!" Ariel grunted. Quickly, she flew back. With remarkable speed, Leon sprinted over to Ariel so lightning-fast that she landed on his bent knee and hand before she clashed with the ground beneath her.

Leon carefully perched up Ariel's head and whispered. "No, I did not kill her child. That I promise you." He helped her up. Her world became blurry and she was suddenly nauseous.

Ariel's head spun like she suffered from a wicked hangover and she tried to shake away the moving images.

Then Leon spoke of his visions once more. "I have seen you, Ariel. I know who you are, I know what you do, what you eat, and where. All of this began before you even stepped foot onto Seoul soil. I see the world through your intriguing purple eyes. That is how I was able to find you in Gangnam District both nights you were there. That explains how you and your pathetic DDAG assassins were ambushed."

"You and your pale monsters killed twenty-seven Death Dealers that night! Thirteen from my faction alone!" Suddenly, Ariel remembered something. "Wait....Before Seoul?! I knew I wasn't crazy," Ariel fumed. "You spoke to me. Back in New York after the Golden Throne Room was bombed, you convinced me to come here. How did you get inside my head? Telepathy?"

"It's power within me," Leon chanted. "I can do things you could only imagine. Your thoughts, your secrets, your pain, your happiness….None of your normal human emotions and physicality are safe with me. I don't know why I am linked to you, Ariel. Killing your comrades was part of the plan…but killing you is not."

"Why?"

"Like I said, you're special. You will live and evolve into something great." Leon gazed at Mary, and brushed her hair away from her face. "But if you push me enough, I will do what I must."

Ariel's jaw throbbed and her throat dried. She would soon regret was she was about to do but it must be done.

"Not if I kill you first," Ariel muttered. "For the justice of my fallen comrades!"

"Oh, I doubt that," Leon said. He widened his mouth and his four fangs were now hugging his bottom lip.

Ariel forced back tears. She took rapid breaths then at the top of her lungs, she jolted out with an "ARGH!!" And a rush of energy fired within her.

"Come to me," Leon sang.

Swiftly, Ariel sprinted her way over to her monstrous father. He charged back after a thunderous howl.

They were participating in a game of chicken. Both of them aimed for the other at great speed. Would they mesh together or would one of them break away?

Suddenly, Ariel thought of a different approach. She froze in her tracks as Leon kept on the prowl. Mercury was now tucked in her back pocket. *Just a little bit closer*, she thought. She counted in her head, *One. Two. Three.* After a quick bend of the knee she stretched out her leg and with a heavy foot she rammed her military boot into Leon's rib.

Leon gasped and slouched over. But he laughed it off and charged again. Ariel spun a one-eighty and, with a light bounce, she roundhouse kicked Leon in the chin. Surprisingly, he flew back.

Crunch. Leon's neck popped. He snapped his head over to the Death Dealer. "You've got some fight in you," he laughed.

"I got more than fight in me," Ariel assured confidently. "I'm a fucking Death Dealer that's pissed-off. No one likes to see me pissed-off."

Leon struck a punch but Ariel took hold of his fist, blocking it from her face. With all her might, she rotated his arm around and his body spun like an electric drill. Before his body could hit the ground, he floated in midair, catching Ariel off-guard.

"What the fuck?" Ariel mumbled.

Leon glided back to his feet and whipped out his sharp claws. Ariel felt his metal-like knuckles pulverize her chin. Her head flew back. As soon as she retreated, he struck again. Her face bent even further. "Ah!!" she screeched with a mouth full of blood. She spat out the fluid from her mouth.

Leon stretched his hands so he could plunge his way through Ariel's spleen but Ariel managed to block him. She twisted his arm around hers, bringing him in close and catwalked her way up his chest and sent a massive kick to his jaw. She cartwheeled backward but landed clumsily on her feet.

Leon got angry. He was not weak, and a puny Death Dealer was not going to break him. His lids and head lowered, creating the world around him to turn black.

Cautiously, Ariel flayed Mercury out of her back pocket. It clinked against her belt as it slid out. She could hear violent chatter echoing from Leon's position.

You're going to die, a voice whispered in Ariel's mind, distracting her from her target. However, this time it was…a woman.

"Get out of my head," Ariel whispered as she scurried around.

Leon spread his arms out. His eyes and lips fluttered crazily. Unknown words were spewing from his mouth. The pronunciations sounded tight and his jaw clenched as he spoke. His mouth barely opened with each word. The language… it was not English.

Your blood will be our blood and our blood is evolution.

"Who is talking to me?" Ariel asked Leon, but he was still possessed in his corner of the plaza.

Ariel was contemplating her next move. Should she stay or should she run?

Run, the voice screeched. *Run away and never come back. Or stay here and die.*

"Stop," Ariel demanded. She was pacing around the area, searching for the woman speaking to her. "Where are you?"

"Right here."

Ariel turned around. "What. The. Fuck…? Mom?!"

She screamed in horror and fell to her knees. Her skin grew more pale and a vein protruded down the side of her neck.

"Mom!!" Ariel bawled with a mix of disgust and sadness.

Memories flashed before her eyes: The smile that used to light up a room. Blue eyes that brightened up even the most terrible, gloomiest day. The smell of her homemade rubies. A woman whom Ariel looked up to. A mother who was strong, loving, proud and independent. A wife who was her husband's rock and queen. A beauty who stood at 5'6" with caramel brown hair, milky skin, and subtle curves…was gone. She was not resting in paradise with the Lord of Life, but instead the Lord of Darkness had trapped an innocent woman into a colorless, soulless, lifeless murder-demon-machine just like her father.

Facing one dead parent was tough, but two?! Ariel felt lost—trapped in a fake world with evil fantasies of all good things turned bad.

"No!" Ariel cried, begging the Lord of Life to take her away from this alternate dimension.

Leon snuck behind Ariel. She now stood in between her two *reborn* parents. Her water-filled eyes ping-ponged back and forth between two lost souls. Her entire body shook.

"Surprise," Symphony hissed with a shrill voice. No longer was she a mother with the once-nurturing, silvery tone that used to tell Ariel stories of ancient kingdoms and mythical creatures.

The heat of pain seared throughout Ariel's body as the sight of her dead parents became more difficult to deal with.

Symphony poised herself with both hands on her hips and a sensual grin crossed her small face.

Ariel managed to get up from the ground, even as her body trembled. Leon popped his knuckles and Symphony sashayed her way to Ariel with swaying hips, tucked-in torso, breasts out and hands loose.

"Why are you calling me your mother, little girl? Have you lost her?" Symphony purred.

Leon tiptoed his fingers over Ariel's shoulder. She spun around and shoved his hand away.

"She thought I was her father," Leon laughed. "Over and over she called me 'Daddy.' How quaint. By the way, this is my love, Nefertiri."

Ariel extended her arm, aiming Mercury's sharp edge below his chin. Leon stretched his neck and dared Ariel to plunge it through his throat.

However, she couldn't do it. Ariel stood in between her parents, transfixed, then dropped the dagger to the ground. Tears flowed like two rippling rivers from her purple eyes. Symphony walked up to her daughter—whom she painfully no longer recognized—and wiped the relentless tears away.

"My dear, sweet child," Symphony whispered. "You are incredibly lost." Gently, she picked up Ariel's chin. "You have no inner peace. You crave acceptance from your fellow assassins and you want nothing but the truth about your past. Why? What do you hope to find?"

Ariel cringed at the sight of Symphony's four pointed teeth. They were as sharp as her perfect insight into Ariel's soul. Ariel wanted to desperately squeeze her mother in a long and warm hug and forget what she had transformed into. If only it were that simple. She missed a mother's touch. Faith was more than a gift in Ariel's life…but she was not her mother. No one could compare to her mother or her father, not even the beastly imitations caressing her here, making sick mockery of the parental love she once had and missed dearly.

After clearing her throat, Ariel answered with a croaked voice, "I—I hope to find out what happened to both of you. All I know is that there was a car crash on Hannam-Dong street, here in Seoul. You were pronounced dead yet here you are. I—I don't know anything more than that but I believe you both are connected to something important."

Ariel pulled out a sheet of folded paper. On it was the 진화 symbol. Both of the parents looked at it questionably.

Leon glared at the peculiar human. "How do you know about this?" he scolded.

"Doesn't matter!" Ariel spat. "What does this symbol mean?"

Ariel's parents eyed one another.

Ariel was impatient. "Well?!" she yelled. "What does it mean? Is it connected to a man named, Ki?"

"It's a language." Leon answered. "An ancient language."

"Language?" Ariel looked over the area. All the street signs and banners and windows were written in a language? Even the fountain had writing on it. "All of this," she began, grazing her hand over the solid structure, "is a language? Well...wha-what does this mean?" She tapped on the paper over and over again, desperate for answers, thirsty for truth. "Tell me, please!"

Symphony's face was calm, her lips parted just so. She gazed upon Ariel's face and indulged in her fear. A trickle of emotion flowed through Symphony, entirely.

"She's weakened by her emotional depravity," Symphony asserted to her one true love. "I feel a whirlwind of confusion coursing through her veins."

Ariel's throat was too dry for her to speak. She swirled her tongue in her mouth. She felt a soft grip around her arm.

"My dear, you are special. Leon and I have been linked to you since the bombing in New York," Symphony admitted.

"Like a magical bond?" Ariel asked.

Symphony felt the pain of Ariel's wounds swell up inside her broken heart.

"Something like that," Symphony continued. "What you see, we see. Finding you is all too simple."

Leon stepped in. "That's what I was trying to explain to her earlier."

"We do not know why, but we believe you are the key to something much, much greater." Symphony paused.

"Evolution." She swiped her thumb over the wrinkled piece of paper.

"Evolution?" Ariel asked. "Is that what this says?"

Suddenly, a sword and an arrow sprung out of nowhere, barely scraping the side of Leon's cheek. The couple disappeared, leaving Ariel to fend for herself.

"Where'd they go?!" Ariel shouted.

"Ariel, get down!" an urgent voice yelled from behind.

There, standing on a rooftop, were Seraphina, Zaire and Bodhi.

Leon and Symphony reappeared behind her. Ariel stood there, conflicted between the two groups. Should she run away and explain later? Or should she fight?

They are not your parents, anymore, she thought to herself. *Your parents died. They*—she looked at her friends—*are your new family.*

Seraphina leaped from the roof to kill the two pale demons below her. Zaire and Bodhi followed her lead. The three Death Dealers glided down in sync.

Ariel, battered by mixed feelings, grabbed Mercury from the ground and stood there looking over Leon and Symphony.

The three assassins landed perfectly in a crouched position, shaking the ground beneath their feet.

"Let's get this over with," Seraphina commanded. Ariel stood motionless. "Come on," Seraphina said to Ariel.

Zaire waited and stood in silence while Bodhi checked up on Ariel.

"Are you okay?" Bodhi asked her.

"Ummm—I—" Ariel's jaw was rattling. She couldn't find the right words to say.

"She won't kill us," Symphony cackled. "She thinks I'm her mommy and Akhenaten is her daddy. Aww...."

"No," Seraphina snapped. She turned to Ariel. "They're fucking with you. Manipulation magic. It has to be. Get it together. Fight."

"Ariel," Bodhi called. "Is it true?"

Ariel stared at them, knowing they were indeed her parents. But what would the DDAG think? "No," she lied.

"What happened earlier?" Leon asked, smacking his lips. "She must be upset because Nefertiri and I cannot live up to her expectations. She is unsure of what she believes. She's conflicted. Sad, isn't it?"

Zaire cocked back his arrow. "I'm sick of talking," he muttered. "Attack!!" He fired his arrow, sending it in Symphony's direction. With one simple swipe, she flicked it away. Furious, Zaire sprinted toward her. Seraphina ran with her sword at hand.

Bodhi stood in front of Leon with a pack full of Elixia and his Fantasia mask. Quickly, he grabbed a handful of sand and blew it into Leon's face. Leon coughed and gagged and flayed about in a circle. Bodhi slipped on the mask and waited, preparing the world he was about to create for the pale demon until….

"I have something to tell you," Leon croaked. "Magic doesn't work on me." After a piercing scream, he attacked Bodhi. With quick wit, he sent three solid punches in a second: one to the head, then to the nose, then a final one to the throat.

Bodhi fumbled back, almost losing balance. Before passing a low kick to Bodhi's ankle, Leon was struck from behind. Ariel sent a flying dagger to Leon's back.

"Ahhh!!!" Leon wailed. Ariel leapt for Mercury and pulled her out quick. Borrowed blood dripped from the side of his spine onto the pavement.

Leon looked back at her and Ariel felt immediate regret. Looking at the red flow running down Leon's side, she nearly wished she could take it back.

Bodhi pulled up next to Ariel. After a sharp *clink* a random spiked chain appeared from underneath Bodhi's coat.

"Since when did you play with that?!" Ariel asked in complete shock. Only during training had Bodhi been seen with a weapon in his hand. Ariel admired his surprising confidence.

"I've been practicing for quite some time," Bodhi acknowledged with delight. It was amazing to see him look tough. Keeping a strong stance and balance, he swiped the chain left, then right.

Ariel noticed the pool of blood on the ground running dry. Leon's skin began to regenerate itself. He grunted as each piece of skin was reconnecting.

"What the hell?" Bodhi said, worried but did not lose his readied posture.

Once Leon fully healed, he sprouted up and his eyes shot open like a beast reborn.

"I thought Mercury was able to kill these fuckers!" Bodhi screamed.

"She did kill these fuckers." Ariel screamed back. "I don't know what the hell is going on!"

A thunderous Leon howled with full might. *Argh!!!* He charged toward Ariel and Bodhi.

They stood together as one. Death Dealers never lost sight of each other, even during the most horrific battles.

Bodhi and Ariel exchanged glances. Bodhi circled his eyes. Ariel understood his signal.

They waited for Leon to come even closer. Leon was now on all fours, digging his way through the cement with his major sharp claws. He dug so deep, he could feel the dirt under his nails. Clusters of dirt clouded the air like smoke behind him.

"One," Bodhi began to count.

"Two," Ariel continued.

They halted.

"Three!!" they shouted together.

Ariel leapt way up, almost touching the roof of the nearest building. Bodhi spun in the air and his spiked chain flew behind him.

Once Bodhi had his eye on Leon, with full force he grunted, "Ahhh!!!" then chucked the spear toward Leon, aiming for the opposite side of his heart.

With his superb vision, Leon immediately noticed the silver dart heading his way. He stopped in his tracks and flipped back. The spear barely missed him. The sharp tip only scratched his throat.

Ariel came flaring down like a fiery lightning bolt. With fists ready and adrenaline high, she pulled her arm all the way back and stormed up to Leon, smashing his face with a ferocious punch. He fell and she landed on him, her knees boxed over his shoulders.

Meanwhile, Seraphina was tossed against the water fountain, back first. After a quick *snap*, Seraphina screamed, "Ahhh! Shit!" The fountain behind her crumbled to the bottom of its base.

Zaire ran for Symphony, who stood still with a smirk on her tiny face. He was only an inch away before he heard a *clap*. Symphony disappeared.

"Where'd she go?" Zaire asked himself.

"Over here," Symphony sang.

Zaire turned around, while placing another arrow into Jewel. Before he could fire her up, Symphony was already a step ahead of him. In the blink of an eye, she was now face-to-face with the long-haired assassin. His crossbow fell and his hands were now in her grasps.

After stretching her head way back, Symphony snapped forward, butting heads with Zaire. He gasped and flung to the side. His view was hazy. Symphony slapped him across the face and he almost lost complete balance. She slapped him again then kicked him in the chest, sending him to crash into a store's front door. His spine hit the glass and it broke into miniscule pieces.

Seraphina was slowly regaining consciousness. But before she could recuperate, Symphony was tugging at her long black hair. With harsh strength, she pulled up Seraphina, who screamed with torture. Desperate, she tried to shove Symphony off, but it was no use. Her strength was far too great to compete with.

Bodhi heard Seraphina's cry. As he looked back at Ariel—who was punching her way through Leon's face—he was sure she'd be okay. For now, he ran to Seraphina's rescue.

"Pride is a bitch," Symphony snapped. "So am I." With an exuberant, grotesque stretch of her jaws, Symphony's four fangs unsheathed from her perfectly white teeth. She tugged Seraphina to one side, tore a chunk of cloth from her sweater and displayed her bare neck.

"Get off her!" Bodhi ordered. He jumped, lassoing his spiked chain over his head.

Symphony took notice of the Death Dealer coming for her.

"Hiya!" Bodhi sent the spiked chain flying through the air. Symphony pulled Seraphina in front of her to shield herself.

Bodhi noticed what was happening. "Uh?! No!" He tried to pull the silver metal back quickly but it was too late. It latched onto Seraphina's upper arm and it dragged her across the pavement, scraping her knees.

"Shit!" Bodhi yelled. "I'm sorry. I'm so sorry!!!" he cried, examining Seraphina's wound. The spike was deep inside her skin. She bawled at the excruciating pain— it was unlike anything she'd felt before.

Symphony noticed Leon being pulverized on the ground.

Quickly, she stormed her way toward Ariel and Leon.

Ariel's world was now turned upside down. Symphony had pushed her off.

In an instant, Ariel fell to her side.

"I'll see you again," Symphony threatened, silver-eyed and ferocious.

Before Ariel could react, Symphony and Leon vanished. They disappeared.

"Where'd they go?" Ariel asked herself. "Shit! Where'd they fucking go?!"

"You have to leave it in," Seraphina yelled, catching Ariel's attention. "I can't lose any more blood." Bodhi sat next to her with a piece of his shirt ripped apart. He bandaged her bleeding arm with the torn cloth.

Ariel looked around one last time. "Fuck!!"

She ran to her comrades and swallowed in air once she saw the disaster on Seraphina's arm. Ariel dropped to the ground, freaking out. "What happened?" she asked. Seraphina's arm was painted completely red. It even dripped down to her pants.

"Long story," Bodhi retorted.

Shuffling footsteps approached Ariel from behind. She shot back with Mercury ready. It was Zaire. His legs wobbled and both his hands were supporting his back. His posture was crooked, but there didn't seem to be any serious injuries.

"Let's get back to headquarters," Zaire growled. "Now!"

Seraphina was sent to the hospital wing in the north tower, in the upper bailey. Zaire, Bodhi and Ariel sat in the cafeteria and waited for any information on her status.

Bodhi kept blaming himself for what happened, but Ariel continued to reassure him that it was not his fault.

"What if she's not able to fight again?" Bodhi asked.

"Seraphina is a tough one," Ariel admitted. "If anyone is going to survive, it's her."

Zaire had hardly spoken a word since their return to the castle. Instead, he mainly looked out the window at the training site.

Several times, Ariel attempted to ask how Zaire was feeling, but he would only give short answers.

"How did you all find me?" Ariel asked, curious and strangely thankful.

Bodhi didn't look her way, only twirled his thumbs around, keeping Seraphina close in thought. "Scrying. I wanted to see how you were doing and when you weren't in your dorm, I began to look for you everywhere, then I got worried. I called Zaire and Seraphina, and Seraphina thought of the scrying spell. We were able to find you with a crystal that lit the way for us. Seraphina wore it around her neck."

Ariel hated herself. If only she had remained in her dorm that night and followed instructions for once, her friends would be safe. She always thought herself as independent or indifferent to control, but at that moment she rather be less of a badass than a danger to everyone she cared about.

Finally, Jason appeared from behind the cafeteria doors.

Ariel ran up to him and wrapped him in a firm—very surprising—hug. However, he barely put one arm around her.

Aunt Faith was also with him. Ariel squeezed her sweet aunt close and kissed her cheek.

"Are you alright?" Faith asked, concerned.

"Yeah," Ariel answered.

"Are both of you gentlemen okay?" Faith asked, just as concerned.

Both assassins answered with a simple, "Yes."

Jason asked everyone to follow him into the conference area, while Faith was sent back to her room. Ariel graced her with one final kiss and hug then proceeded with the group.

Each assassin sat down in no particular order. It was late and quiet. Even the stars were hiding behind the black sky tonight.

"How's Seraphina?" Bodhi asked.

Jason looked over his team with great sadness. "She'll live, but that's all we know so far."

All three Death Dealers were consumed with worry and sadness. Never in a million years did Ariel think she would care this much about Seraphina. Regret contaminated her heart like billows of black poison. If only she didn't use her that one night they shared together. Would it have mattered? Would they have been a couple? *Maybe.* It was hard to imagine falling in love with anyone, yet alone with Seraphina. Ariel feared commitment.

Either way, Ariel's regret was of no importance. Seraphina surviving was the priority.

The door creaked. Sying entered, along with Sergeant Tulip.

Please, not him! Ariel thought to herself, hoping to not see a specific person. *Oh, please, please, please!*

To Ariel's dismay, Sergeant Lotus appeared a moment later.

Fuck! Ariel's lips tightened and her hands tensed up together. She started to nervously pop her knuckles and shake her right leg. *Why does he have to be here? I'm done. So done!*

Sying cleared his throat and began to speak. "Before we get started, I just want to send all of you and your fellow Death Dealer, Seraphina Jasmine, good vibes. May the Lord of Life guide her during this dire situation."

Jason stood before everyone and took over. "What happened?" he asked coldly, eyeing Ariel first.

None of the Death Dealers moved their mouths. Bodhi's eyes were blinking away tears, while Zaire stayed stone-cold and Ariel's body shook like a strong electric current.

Sergeant Lotus insisted that Jason sit down, as he decided to take over. He stepped to the front of the podium.

Ariel's nerves grew impulsively. She wanted to run, to hide from her predicament.

"Ariel," Lotus called, making her skin crawl. "You better talk."

Habits die hard. Ariel defensively snapped. "If I tell you, you won't believe me."

"Try me," Lotus asserted.

Ariel looked around the room. Neither Bodhi nor Zaire looked her way, but the rest of the audience offered a variety of facial expressions. The leaders looked either angry or monotonic. *Just spit it out,* Ariel thought. After placing both her elbows on the table, she rubbed her face and exhaled roughly. It was now or never.

"I left the headquarters," Ariel admitted.

"Why?" Lotus spat instantaneously.

Ariel bit her tongue, reminding herself to not get mad. "I've been having these dreams. They seemed to be creating a pattern, so I started to draw in my journal. Eventually, I left my dorm and headed out, following the clues."

"Clues?" Tulip asked curiously.

"Yes," Ariel hissed.

"Was tonight the only night you snuck out?" Lotus looked down at Ariel with a monstrous glare.

Ariel did not want to answer but she had to. "No. I snuck out several nights. Eventually, I started to have *visions* and…"

"Visions? Like premonitions?" Sying wondered.

"I think it's much more than that," Ariel said. She swiped her hair out of her face. "I, uh…was walking down the music strip in downtown Seoul and I noticed a woman in my vision was suddenly, physically, in front of me. I followed her. A man appeared, killed her and…well, here we are."

"How did following a man who killed an innocent woman, end up injuring one of our own in the middle of the fucking night?!" Lotus barked, punching the table.

"It was not just a man," Zaire interrupted. "There was a woman too. The man said Ariel claimed they are her parents."

"What the hell, Zaire?!" Ariel screamed. Why would he call her out like that? What was going on with this guy? "What the fuck is your problem?"

"Twenty-seven of our own died, Ariel!" Zaire screamed back. "We don't need you going on these stupid suicide missions, all because you *think* you saw your dead parents! We cannot risk the lives of any more people, including your own!"

"Not this shit again," Lotus muttered to himself.

Ariel switched her attention toward Lotus. "You see?" Ariel groaned. "This is why I didn't want to tell you anything. I always believed my mom and dad died in a car accident over ten years ago. I did! But—but I also believe they are undead...reborn into something disgusting and life-threatening. A danger to the New World. I showed them the symbol I had seen the night we had lost many men. And they said it's not a symbol. It's a language! An ancient language."

Lotus had enough. "Your parents are dead, Ariel!" He yelled. "Dead! Visions? Ancient languages? Your resurrected, undead parents just stroll along the streets at night?! None of this makes sense. Do you know what all of this sounds like?"

Jason tried calming his infuriated sergeant. "Sergeant, please, let's be mature about this."

"Captain, I suggest that you sit down. Now is not a time for you to be protecting Ms. Rose, after all the trouble she's caused. You are just as responsible for this pitiful mess as she is."

"Maybe I do sound crazy, but we are missing a huge piece of the puzzle!" Ariel insisted urgently. She jerked from her chair. "My-so-called dreams are not dreams at all. Those visions I had, seeing the woman before actually seeing her in person, are"—she paused—"links. I believe I am connected to my parents. The pale monsters we fought in Gangnam District are not human."

"What do you suspect they are, Ms. Rose?!" Lotus asked, mockingly. "Soul-eaters?"

"I... I don't know what they are," Ariel mumbled. "However, my mom and dad are like them but stronger and deadlier. They feed off of human blood. It sounds ridiculous, I know, but I'm telling you the truth about everything. Plus, they are killing people all over the city. Not just Gangnam District. We need to search more diligently. These pale...things...are making us believe it's all just happening in one area but it's not!"

"Oh? These monsters are falsifying evidence? And your undead parents—who are stronger and deadlier—are drinking human blood to survive? Heh! I don't want to hear anymore about this," Lotus demanded.

"Sergeant, something bigger than terrorist kidnappers is happening. My mom mentioned evolution. We need to follow them and figure out what's going on," Ariel urged.

However, Lotus had enough. "That's it. You're permanently removed from the Seoul case. As far as your titles, I have to speak to the king and queen about this."

Jason looked sharply at Lotus, then Ariel, then back at Lotus. "Sir, you cannot—"

"Stay out of this Captain Lilly," Lotus threatened. "I once spoke of your stability with our Faction. I told you that if she messed up, you both were gone. Unlike Ms. Rose, though, it looks like I need you here to handle things. But I need you away from her. She is a danger to her comrades."

"WHAT?!" Ariel knew this was going to happen, but it hurt. A lot. She protested against him. "Sergeant, the symbol I found, the visions and my parents have got to be pieces to a bigger puzzle than we ever anticipated. I've always been good at ancient linguistics. Let me study this symbol to see what exactly it is we're missing." Lotus was walking away, but Ariel got in the way, stopping him in his tracks. "Both of my parents said they're linked to me, so I'm obviously linked to them—hence, the dreams, the visions. I need to find a way to control the link in order see what they're doing at any given time. I have a gut feeling all of this has to deal with Ki."

"Enough!!" Lotus screamed. "Pack your bags and leave Seoul at once. I don't want to hear another word from you."

"Please, listen to—"

"Get out of my way before I remove you myself!" Lotus howled. Ariel flinched and let him pass. Before exiting, Lotus muttered in her ear, "Now, shut up, pack your bags, and leave Seoul at once!"

With a heavy heart, she obliged. "Yes, sir," she scoffed.

"Ms. Rose," Lotus snickered. "Get out of my sight!!"

IN OR OUT

Ariel wrestled through her drawers, not paying attention to the armfuls she cluttered in her arms. As she catapulted every pair of pants she owned onto her bed, someone tapped on her door. She yelled for them to leave.

"It's Ivy."

Ariel halted for a second. What was she doing here?

"What do you want?" Ariel asked her as she angrily packed her suitcases.

Ivy, muffled behind the door and asked for permission to enter. An annoyed Ariel allowed it. To make things worse, a high-pitched voice followed Ivy.

"Is it true, you're leaving?!" It was Daoka, poking her infuriatingly cute head from around the corner.

Ugh...not this little girl, Ariel thought. If only she could break Daoka's neck. Ariel was in a bad, BAD mood. Daoka's hyperactive personality could easily set anyone off, let alone when they were already angry elsewhere.

Daoka skipped her way inside Ariel's dorm, then noticed her question was answered. "Do you have to leave?"

Ariel turned around and shut her eyes as she clutched a pair of gloves.

"I need to finish packing," Ariel sighed, shoving the leather handwarmers in her suitcase. "What do you two want?"

Ivy looked at her with drooped eyes. "There were rumors about you."

Ariel shrugged it off. This was nothing new. "And?"

"I got worried," Ivy sighed. "I wanted to check up on you. I happened to bump into Zaire in the hallway. After I asked where you were, he sent me here. He didn't seem happy, though. Is he upset you're leaving?"

Ariel huffed as she grabbed a mountain of books. "The fuck if I know."

"We heard you saw your dead parents," Daoka added with an oddly cheerful tone.

"Daoka!" Ivy snapped, covering her mouth. "Be quiet."

Ariel smirked. "Oh, it's alright," she retorted. "No one believes me. Not even my own best friend." Ariel wandered back to the night Jason implied she was crazy. Even though he was her best friend, he questioned whether Leon were really alive. He knew, though. Ariel believed that whole-heartedly. After he stormed out, not once did he come to check up on her or ask if she was okay. Jason obviously wanted his distance. No part of her. "Why would anyone else want to believe a *psycho* and *delusional* Death Dealer?"

Ivy was afraid to ask any questions, but she was desperate to make Ariel happy. "Do you mind telling me what happened? I'll listen."

Ariel concentrated on Ivy's fluorescent green eyes. She could detect her concern. However, she did not want to explain. *What's the point?*

"I wanna know!" Daoka shouted.

Ivy slammed her lids shut and grunted. "Daoka...," Ivy scoffed. "Don't you have somewhere else to go?"

Daoka pulled a handful of mango gummy candy out of her pocket. "No. Jason rescheduled our session."

Immediately, Ariel reacted. "Session? What the hell are you doing with Jason?"

Ivy felt bad tension arising. She decided to sit on the bed, next to the messy molehill, and stay out of Ariel's way.

"He's teaching me how to be a badass like him," Daoka sang. Her eyes widened with a smile. "Hyuna was interested, but…for some reason she changed her mind."

"When does he have time to teach you anything?" Ariel growled.

Ivy reached for her hand but missed as Ariel walked over to her minifridge. Inside were small bottles of pear juice and bowls of dehydrated fruit.

After taking a huge gulp of juice, Ariel looked back at Daoka, feeling resentful. Not once did her best friend pop in to say a simple hello or a heated goodbye. Hell, there was not even a text message sent. During the past seven days, Ariel sat on the floor, drawing up clues, writing down notes until the crack of dawn, but Jason never opened that door to say, *I'm sorry.*

"He's been teaching me some martial arts during the afternoon and sometimes he'll even want to do weapons training during the late hours, after we come back from investigating Seoul. Honestly, I think he gets more antsy at night." Daoka popped another gummy into her small mouth. "He's quiet after investigations."

"I assumed it was a one night gig between you two, not a nightly tradition." *So, that's what he's been doing*, Ariel thought. *That stupid sonofa—*

"Daoka, do you mind grabbing me a cup of tea?" Ivy interrupted.

"Now?" Daoka asked, not wanting to do so.

"Yes," Ivy hissed with her eyes, blaring. "Winter berry, if they have it."

"They were sold out of it yesterday," Daoka chimed in.

"Then, get me…something else!" Even Ivy's patience had worn thin. She could very well join Ariel in physically kicking Daoka out soon.

Daoka was bugged out by Ariel's and Ivy's harshness. She inhaled the last bit of mango gummies. "Alright," she huffed. "I'll be back. Do you want anything, Ariel?"

"No," Ariel blared, wanting her to leave now.

"'Kay!" Daoka chanted. "Don't miss me too much!"

After what felt like hours, Daoka casually walked out the room and didn't fail to blow a kiss before sealing the door behind her.

Ivy was relieved to finally have Ariel to herself, but she had to talk quickly before buns-girl came back.

"Sorry about that," Ivy apologized. "She wanted to see you."

"I don't know why," Ariel muttered, barely listening. She slammed her suitcase shut and tried to zip it closed.

Noticing Ariel's battle with the difficult-sealing luggage, Ivy offered a helping hand with the zipper.

Once it was completely sealed, Ariel and Ivy looked deep at one another. Ariel missed her (mostly). Ivy was beautiful and sweet, but Ariel didn't know her. For that reason, she didn't trust her. Trust didn't come easily to Ariel.

"Well, I gotta go," Ariel said, breaking the silence. "I'm just going to say goodbye to someone real quick, then I'm leaving with my aunt."

"I'm sorry for everything that happened." Ivy was being genuine. She cared for Ariel, even though she couldn't understand why. "If the rumors are true, I believe you. Seeing the dead is not common. But it can happen."

This caught Ariel's attention. "What do you mean?" she hurried. "Tell me."

Ivy signaled for her to relax. She set Ariel's luggage aside and held her hand between her warm palms.

"Magic is a wonderful thing, but it can be used for terrible things. According to magic historians, in the past, people have been brought back to life after being dead for days, weeks, even months." Ariel only ever understood the basics of magic. If she didn't understand something, her interest waned.

"As to how one was able to bring another back to life is debatable, but it has happened many times before. And it can still happen today."

"Those were my parents. I know that for a fact," Ariel thought out loud.

"I believe you," Ivy said.

People being brought back to life seemed plausible, but what about people being brought back to life in another form? "Is it possible for a human to be transformed into something else, even after death?"

Ivy was uncertain. "I've never come across a study where that has happened, but there is a first for everything. If there is a person so big and so powerful with black magic, why wouldn't they transform innocent people into something evil? There's always a purpose."

It's true. Who would go through all this trouble for nothing? Ariel's parents were like the other pale demons, but much stronger and quicker. Someone, possibly Ki, had a disturbing goal.

The only way for Ivy to understand the gist of the whole situation was to let her in. "I'll tell you everything, but keep this to yourself. Not everyone knows the whole story. And almost no one has wanted to hear it."

Ivy gave her the word. "Promise."

"This is how it happened…."

After explaining the shadow man, the symbol that happened to be a relic of an ancient language and seeing her mom and dad alive again, Ivy took a moment to absorb everything in.

"I won't tell a soul. You have my word." Ivy pulled out her phone and asked for Ariel's email address. "I am sending you links to some ancient linguistic books that may help you. All of them were written by a man named Robert Poppy. He believed there were hundreds—maybe even thousands—of languages before English. It's pretty interesting." Ivy hit "SEND" and a ring chimed from Ariel's phone. She opened the message and confirmed she received it. "I hope he is able to help you. From what you've been telling me, I believe this has a lot to do with someone's sadistic idea to eliminate human lives or just evolve them into something ugly."

Evolve.

Ariel was immensely grateful for Ivy's assistance. It was rare when someone actually wanted to help her, not judge her ideas or actions. It felt...nice.

"I don't have a clue what it could be. My parents have got to be connected to Ki, and Ki is probably the brains behind the entire experiment." Ariel looked at the time. It was getting late. Surprisingly, Daoka had not returned. Ariel wanted to leave before seeing her again. She rushed off the bed. "Thank you. Really. Thank you for everything. I have to go, but seriously: you've helped me so much in a short amount of time."

Ariel was about to head out, but not before being chivalrous. "After you," she said, opening the door for Ivy. But Ivy jumped in and shut it.

"I want to add something."

"Alright," Ariel said.

"If you'd like…." Ivy stopped. She rolled her shoulders and drummed her fingers on the molding. "I could update you on what happens here."

"What do you mean?" Ariel asked as she put on her hoodie.

"Let me help you. I'll give you every detail of what happens here in Seoul: the pale demons, status updates, assassin files…anything you need."

Ariel stared at Ivy, wondering if this was a joke or a promise she'd never live up to. She was more than grateful, but this would put Ivy's Death Dealer title on the line. She could lose everything, like Ariel had.

"I can't let you do that," Ariel hesitated. "Too many people are getting hurt because of me as it is. Do not be another nick on my career kill count."

"I hear they have meetings every Wednesday," Ivy laughed, trying to lift Ariel's spirits.

Ariel cupped Ivy's petite face. They locked eyes.

Keep your hands to yourself, girl, Ivy thought. *Gah! She's so beautiful.* Ivy's lips curled back as soon as the temptation to lean in was irresistible. It was not the right time or the place to be rekindling their romance, even though they were alone in the spot where they had shared a bountiful night of ecstasy.

Ariel's hands were Ivy's favorite feature. Not only did they feel soft and supple over her caramel skin, her fingers were long, dainty and somehow flawless, despite her assassin work. Even Ariel's nails were perfect. Naturally mid-length—not too long—thick and plain. No nail polish needed. They were a perfect rose-pink shade with matte white tips. Feeling those soft paws clasps her cheeks again sent an explosion straight to her clitoris. It throbbed slightly….Ariel's thumb massaged the sides of her neck. If only she would slide one of those hands all the way around and grip her neck ever-so tightly.

Ivy hugged Ariel's hands with hers. Still, she fought the hunger for a kiss.

"This is serious," Ariel whispered, pulling Ivy closer. "Do not do anything that will jeopardize your job with the DDAG. I'm not worth it. I swear to you, I'm not."

Even though she understood where Ariel was coming from, it didn't matter. "I still want to help," Ivy insisted. "You are the reason why we even found any sign of evidence in the first place. If it weren't for you, we'd still be lurking about the streets of Gangnam District completely clueless."

And just like that, Ariel stowed away. She grabbed the packed suitcases.

Instantly, Ivy's hormones died down.

Pissed, Ivy inhaled a thick amount of air through her nostrils. She exhaled abruptly, releasing all the frustration she had bestowed upon herself.

"I'm sorry," Ariel apologized. "If anything happened to you, it'd be all my fault."

Relax and let it go, Ivy thought. *Now, back to helping her.*

"What I do is my choice," Ivy declared. "No one is responsible for what I do except me. If they find out, well, it's up to my sergeant and the king and queen of the New World to figure out what my sentence will be. But if they don't find out, you will be in the loop. If you end up being right, you'd get to rub that in everyone's face."

Those words rang in Ariel's ear. "I love being right," she grinned. She looked over at Ivy, contemplating the pros and cons. Could she fully trust this girl? Was this a ploy? A game? Was someone pitting Ivy against her? Maybe, but then again, what more did she have to lose?

"Fine."

"Really?!" Ivy confirmed, and her spirits lifted.

"Yeah," Ariel answered. "You win. Just be careful. Seriously, don't get yourself hurt, or worse: terminated."

"I can't promise you that," Ivy admitted. "But I can promise to be extra careful."

"Thanks," Ariel breathed. "Well, I really have to go. I'll see you soon."

Both ladies exited the dorm. Before going, Ariel comforted Ivy with a genuine hug. "Bye," Ariel whispered.

"Bye," Ivy repeated, and they parted ways, each of them pondering what's to come.

Ariel now had an errand to run. She had to do something she never imagined doing: apologize to Seraphina.

Meanwhile, Bodhi sat on a comfortable brown couch in Seraphina's room in the healing ward. The walls were white and the tile behind Seraphina's bed was smoothed oak wood. The lights were horrendously bright and they strained Bodhi's eyes. The ward was so high up, the room's window had a gorgeous view of Seoul's downtown lights.

Seraphina had been awake for about an hour, but didn't speak. Bodhi repeatedly offered her tea and food and blankets, each of which Seraphina denied.

Bodhi cried relentlessly—he was interrupting Seraphina's quiet time. A beyond-annoyed Seraphina sat tensely on her bed and she kept reliving the event in her mind: She was suckered into another rescue mission for the stubborn redhead who never ceased to make her life a living hell.

"Zaire hasn't returned any of my calls," Bodhi sighed. He placed his phone on the end table next to a bouquet of purple lilies, homed in a white vase. A gift from Jason.

"I fucking hate her," Seraphina mumbled, finally.

Unsure and uneasy, Bodhi asked her to repeat.

"Fuck…Ariel," Seraphina hissed.

"Hey, let's not put blame on any one," Bodhi insisted, mainly to ease his guilt. "She didn't know we were coming to help her."

Help?! That word made Seraphina irate. Her fist curled and shook like an earthquake. "Help?!" she roared, punching the shit out of the mattress. The throbbing pain reminded her how deep the spiked chain pulverized her arm. "I didn't even want to go on this suicide mission!!" She flung the sheets off her legs. The anger inside made her hot. "You dragged me to do this shit! Zaire didn't want to come either, but you were so worried about Ariel—Little Miss fucking Ariel that seems to get away with every little thing she does! She almost got us killed—again! And for what?! Because Velvet Skank thinks she is uncovering truth. Truth to what exactly? Truth to the kidnappings happening in Seoul?"

Bodhi started trembling in his seat. He begged her to stop. He already felt responsible for Seraphina's injury. To be blamed for the entirety of the situation felt even worse. What kind of man does this make him? A failed man, that's what. A failed main with a failed purpose. Why should he even be part of the DDAG?

"Oh, no, no, no…," Seraphina trailed off. "Parents," she emphasized. "This was all about her damn parents. Somehow mommy and daddy magically rose from the grave and have come back to haunt her ass night after night. But wait! It gets better."

Bodhi was already fragile. He didn't want to hear any more. "Please, stop."

"All of a sudden she is magical and has a gift of premonitions. Or, as she calls them, 'visions'—visions that are connected to her dead parents! What a crock of shit!!"

"Enough!" Bodhi begged. "Ariel is already getting kicked off the case. What more do you want?"

Seraphina wanted Ariel gone. Out! She continued to ramble out of spite. "I want that bitch's head on a spike. Ah!! Fuck!" Seraphina's wound pulsated, immensely. Quickly, she grabbed a pill from a bottle on the counter across her bed and tossed it down her throat without needing water.

"You don't mean that," Bodhi said. "Ariel has helped our investigation. We've moved forward, not backward."

"How?" Seraphina tested, pushing Bodhi to the limit. "The only thing she did was unlock some clues using a reversal spell on some black magic—which, by the way, was not all her. She did include you and me—if you don't remember—since she sucks at spells. You and I were the masterminds, not her."

"You're hurt already," Bodhi emphasized. "Get some rest before you send yourself back to the ER."

Seraphina was suddenly aware of the clock ticking on the opposite wall. She became crazed. "AH!!" She grabbed the lily vase, sped over and chucked it out the window. "I'm in here because of her, goddammit! We all almost died because of Ariel! I hate you for fucking dragging me to go save her! I hate you!!"

Bodhi hunched over on the couch and rain trickled down his prominent cheeks. Stuttering, he whispered, "I'm sorry." He came to the conclusion it was all his fault. If only they had stayed at headquarters. But what would've happened to Ariel? Would she have died? It was all a blur, anyway. There was no going back. The only thing to do was pay attention to what was happening now. Seraphina was severely injured—she had almost died of blood loss. Why? All because Bodhi longed to be strong and successful with fierce weaponry, just like his fellow assassins.

For months, Bodhi practiced with a spiked chain—in his room and even his backyard—during the lonely hours at the DDAG in District North America. Ariel and Jason were like perfect instruments in his eyes and he wished to be a warrior as tough as they were. He had finally gained some confidence to show off his skill, but then ruined it all. He ruined everything. All the months of training were completely wasted. He should've stuck with his basic combat skills, Fantasia and Elixia.

"I hate you for making me go save that bitch!" Seraphina was relentless. "I told you I didn't want to go! Zaire even said we shouldn't go, but did you listen?! No! You begged us to go save that…that bitch! That bitch Jason always has to protect, you always have to protect, even Sergeant Lotus has to protect! I'm tired of her!" Usually, she protected her sanity, but not tonight. Tonight, she wanted to claw her nails through Ariel's skin and file away to the bone. Seraphina could feel it: her insanity letting loose. She couldn't control the frustration, the hatred, the stupidity she felt for giving in to Bodhi's demands. She wanted to wake herself up from all the anger that rushed within her. She felt stuck in a prison full of Ariel's baggage. Everywhere she went, everything was about Ariel.

With all her might, Seraphina punched through the wall. Her knuckles coated in blood. "Get out," she muttered at Bodhi.

"I'm so sorry," Bodhi cried. "I'm sorry I hurt you. I'm sorry I made you go. I'm so, so sorry!"

Unwilling to look at Bodhi's pathetic, sad face, Seraphina spoke fifty decibels louder. "GET. OUT."

Unfortunately, Ariel had been in the healing ward hallway and overheard everything coming from Seraphina's room. Ariel rarely felt responsible for other people's actions, but tonight was different. Because her fellow Death Dealers searched for her, they got caught up in a war that was not meant for them. When Ariel wanted to find answers, she always found a way, but never at the sake of another's life. Seraphina got hurt. She could have died. Luckily, the Lord of Life saved her, but it cut much too close.

Ariel wanted to apologize, for once, and say a quick farewell. She even brought Seraphina a single rose she had plucked from the gardens outside. Sadly, after hearing the hurtful words from Seraphina's mouth—words so brutal they could slaughter Ariel where she stood—she had to make a run for it before either one of them could spot her.

With a heavy heart, she crumbled up the flower, threw it down to the floor and stepped over its thick stem and bright orange petals. With the sole of her boot, the flower meshed as one with the floor. And just like that, Ariel was gone.

Bodhi slouched out of the room and continued to bawl. He dropped in the middle of the hallway and curled into a weakened ball. Ariel overheard his sobs. She wanted to check up on him—just turn back around and rescue him from sadness. However, she thought it was better for her to leave. After all, she was the cause of his sadness, and worse, Seraphina may have caused him to hate her just as much as she did.

With regret, Ariel continued stumbling off until Bodhi's cries faded away.

After being back in District North America for a few days, Ariel did nothing but drink and study up on ancient languages. It was tough starting from scratch. There was nothing on weird, geometric-pattern languages. Zilch!

When Ariel needed a break, she'd go visit her aunt Faith. The only good thing about waiting for a meeting with the king and queen: having access to the outside world again.

As always, Faith attempted to brighten up Ariel's mood by baking rubies as often as possible. When that didn't work, they'd take long walks. Sometimes they would visit the wondrous ocean. It was beautiful and peaceful to view. It brought a lot of good memories. Ariel's father used to enjoy summer activities, especially swimming in the clear blue water. Ariel tried to do the same. She didn't care much for getting wet, but she valued the time spent with her father.

One month passed, and the DDAG was finally gathering DNA that matched most of the missing persons in Seoul. As of yet, no one had been found, but it was good to know the exact locations from which they were taken.

Ivy phoned Ariel one morning and brought up something insightful: "I emailed you a book that will help prove your theory about the undead. It's called *Necromancy: Speaking and Summoning the Dead*, by Iliza Azalea. She mentions how the deceased can be brought back to life in many forms. This includes animals and other people. The downfall, however, is her theory has yet to be proven."

Ariel groaned. "Basically, she sounds crazy like me."

"Maybe, but I would keep the book close. You never know where you can find inspiration." Ariel thanked her for her generosity. "My pleasure. I'll talk to you later."

It was now January 23rd, the day Ariel would finally hear her sentence from the king and queen of the New World. Would she be terminated? Or would be she lucky and stay on as a trainer for novices hoping to be part of Faction Divide? Either result was unsatisfying, but only one of the options was tolerable.

It was early morning when Ariel woke up. Firstly, she drank a big cup of coffee and eventually went into her room to get ready for her trial. Ariel dressed in her most formal attire:

She slid on the most formal, white dress shirt with opaque buttons. One-by-one she buttoned them up as she gazed upon herself in a tall mirror, clear-headed. Next, the black vest. Made out of the world's finest silk, she draped it over her white shirt and carefully clamped the two pairs of buttons together. Two on top, the other two on the bottom. Third were the black slacks that happily hugged her curves without being too tight. She placed one leg inside, then the other and felt the soft linen run up her thighs, then gently over her waist. She tucked in her shirt but allowed the vest to drape over the belt loops. Only a thin belt was needed to hold her pants in place.

Ariel walked over to her closet and grabbed a dressy pair of high-heel boots that came just below her knees. With care, she tightened up the laces that zig-zagged their way from the bottom to the top.

She finalized her outfit by putting her hair up in a loose ponytail, but had volume above her crown. To hide the rubber band, she took a random lock of hair and twirled it around the band twice, then bobby-pinned it in place.

Ariel checked herself before walking out the door. Her collar had to be rolled down, but at least the sleeves were perfectly straight and cuffed. Once everything was in check, she stared at her reflection and said, "Good luck."

Ariel grabbed her dandelion-colored double-breasted coat that hung down to her feet. She left the coat open, since the weather was windy but not too cold. The cuffs of her white sleeves peek-a-booed underneath her coat.

After locking up the front door to her apartment, she checked her phone. No missed calls. No missed texts. Jason still hadn't spoken to her. The night after she came back home, she attempted to call him, but it went straight to voicemail. Ariel missed her best friend more than anything. During the course of their friendship, there were spurts of distance of not speaking to one another, but they never lasted more than a week. Once, Jason was angry because Ariel threatened to kill a girl because she was overprotective of her best friend. Jason had the hugest crush on Daniela, but unfortunately, their relationship went nowhere. Another time, Ariel ignored Jason for a week because he had left her behind at a club to go smooch with a gold-digging floozy. She didn't mind being his wing woman but Ariel hated when he left her to go make out with one of the New World's snobbiest rich brats. However, this time broke a new record.

Ariel sighed with disbelief and lost some confidence. She needed to hear Jason say it would all be okay. Her own reassurance only went so far. She never realized how much she depended on him. It kind of irritated her.

After a quick phone call to Faith informing her that she was on her way to headquarters, Ariel jumped inside her car and drove to a familiar, yet nerve-racking destination.

Ariel checked in with Mina—her ex-lover—at the front desk of District North America Headquarters.

"What the hell did you do this time?" Mina mocked, speed-typing on her keyboard.

"You wouldn't believe me if I told you," Ariel said, avoiding the question.

Mina only chuckled. "Nothing you do surprises me, Little Red." A beep came from her computer monitor. "The king and queen will see you now." Mina smiled.

"Thank you."

"You're welcome."

With a single hand, Ariel opened a tall metal door that led to the path of fortune. An empty, long corridor stood before her, sending chills down her spine. It was too quiet.

As she walked, her high-heel boots clanked loudly atop the white floors. On each side of her were rows of golden pillars, all dressed in bouquets of candles. Above her head hung crystal chandeliers, all blooming in a sea of yellow-gold color.

On the left, in between each pillar, were handmade statues of previous Death Dealer sergeants who had passed on to the next life.

There were men and women—all of them good, all of them brave and bold. One day, Sergeant Lotus would have a statue of himself made. After retirement, it was customary for a sergeant to get their statue done. It was a century-old tradition.

On the right, there were enormous rectangle windows that overlooked the castle gates into the city of New York. A beautiful sight, it was. You couldn't see the horror that cascaded the streets, especially at night. Ariel took in the lovely scenery, enjoying the little things—the pointed rooftops of the beautiful but abandoned lofts, the skyscraping business towers, the sea line and the wave of oak trees—before the possibility of hearing some distressing news.

Ariel was now on the other side of the hallway, only a door away from seeing the two people who were about to construct her future in the Death Dealer Alliance Guild. Before going any further, she took a deep breath and hoped, *Everything is going to be okay.*

She strode in confidence and style inside the trial room, and there, in front of her, were the king and queen of the New World, sitting on their royal thrones: King Sebastian Peony and Queen Kora Amaryllis.

They were center stage in their tree-inspired seats. A commoner had to walk up five steps before meeting their height. Behind them hung paintings by the now-passed artist, Chino Maul. He was a naturalist painter, an enthusiast of all things the New World had to offer, including the cragged mountains, moody sky, and majestic rainbows. Throughout his entire life, all he would do was travel and paint, living off the land's provisions all the while. At least once a year, he'd send paintings to the King and Queen of the New World as thank-you gifts, simply for ruling. No one of royal power ever turned a painting down.

Ariel had met them once before, and despite her ruthless antics, they were kind and fair. Now, due to current events, they might not be so gentle.

King Sebastian bore a thick platinum crown that sat comfortably around his ears and descended to the bottom of his chin. The top of the crown spiked up. The spikes mimicked thick branches. Pinnatisect leaves made out of jade and copper were placed intricately in between each branch, creating a gorgeous collaboration of color and natural harmony.

For the queen, the crown had been made differently. Kora's thin branches intertwined and rounded from the back, over her ear, then sloped into a *V* shape, between her blue eyes. Four single branches—two on the left, two on the right—each carried a single and thick jade leaf lined in delicate copper.

Every five years, a new king and queen were elected by popular vote of the citizens of the New World. King Sebastian was the youngest king to be voted in of all of New World's history. He was only four years older than Jason, a year away from thirty. He was a promising king, and had enjoyed a peaceful and eventful reign thus far. Many people were saddened because this was now his final year as king.

As far as looks go, well, many men and women swooned at the sight of the King Sebastian. Unfortunately, he was already betrothed to another: an alchemist named Scott. He was not very tall, but he was incredibly well-built—under those royal vestments, one could picture a firm body with a tight six-pack and plump muscles. He had a striking face to match: his eyes were moss green and his imperial facial hair was always groomed to distinguished perfection. Always he smiled, his pearly white, straight teeth gleamed proudly. His style, however, tended toward bland repetition. Every time he made a public appearance, he wore the same navy blue suit with a ribbed vest, pale blue dress shirt, and blue-plaid tie.

Like most queens before her, Kora was in her mid-forties, and had vast experience with not only the Death Dealer Alliance Guild—she was an informant once—but also with New World Law. She never married, but she had been in a serious relationship with a blacksmith named Bryson Blossom for seventeen years. Within her forty years of being alive, she was known as being amazingly knowledgeable, strong, and a consummate badass!

Also, Kora was insanely beautiful. Even Jason had an undeniable crush on her for a short time. Despite being almost fifty years old, she looked no more than thirty. Her platinum blonde—almost white—hair flowed all the way down to her bottom and was never over-styled. Kora was keen on maintaining her natural waves. She was shorter than Ariel, but her confidence was much higher. Her skin was like the color of almond milk and perfectly smooth. Often, she wore formal dresses that suited her sharp curves but were never revealing. For Ariel's trial, she stuck with a frost-blue, halter-top dress bedazzled with white diamonds around the neck. Ariel had never seen her in the same outfit twice. Oh, to be queen for a day.

Ariel greeted them. "King Sebastian Peony. My queen, Kora Amaryllis." She bowed. "I am honored to be here, despite the circumstances." Even Ariel minded her manners around the king and queen. She stood up straight and kept silent.

Sergeant Lotus was sitting on a side bench. Ariel could feel his cold eyes blaring. It was an uncomfortable feeling, but she did her best to forget he was there.

King Sebastian was the first to speak: "Ariel Rose. I feel we have met before," he remembered.

"We have," Queen Kora chimed in. "She was the one who saved David, the scientist, from becoming a potential Black Plague II victim. You remember? He worked at the Pacific Laboratory a few miles from here."

"Ah! You are right." Sebastian's eyes locked on Ariel as they swayed up and down her.

Sebastian sat there, thinking and twirling his fingers around. Ariel wished that at that moment she could read minds. However, she felt an odd bit of contemplation raying off of Sebastian while Kora felt neutral. It was difficult to explain.

"You saved David by going behind the DDAG's back and doing your own, private investigation," Sebastian continued. "Clearly, that is something to remember."

What do I do? Ariel thought. *Just say something!* "Yeah...sorry. My bad." *What the fuck was that?*

"Don't be," Kora smiled. "You saved an innocent, and for that, we are thankful." Ariel felt good. "However, that is not why we were brought here today."

Now, that feeling was gone.

Sebastian snapped his fingers and Mina rushed over to him with a black folder. Papers flew out as he opened the flaps. He quickly skimmed through the pages. "There is a request from Sergeant Kurtis Lotus to relieve you of all titles from the Death Dealer Alliance Guild due to...'insubordination and unfair treatment of fellow assassins.' How do you plead?"

Not guilty! Was Ariel's immediate thought, but was that all true? "Guilty to a degree, my king."

Sebastian was about to hand the papers over to Kora but she refused them.

"I've read through everything already, my king. Thank you," Kora said. "Is it true that one of your DDAG Death Dealers, Seraphina Jasmine, was injured because of an undivulged investigation that you took upon yourself?"

"Yes," Ariel answered, honestly, feeling guilty.

"Why?" Sebastian asked.

Ariel gulped as she gathered her thoughts. "It's a long story."

Kindly, Sebastian asked, "Is there a way you could possibly give us a short version? For time's sake, you understand?"

Ariel nodded her head, even though she didn't know if she could do as her king asked. "Of course!"

Think, think, think.

"It started off with a voice, a shadow man that ended up looking like my dead father…during the ambush…symbols that are actually an ancient language, and dreams. At first, I believed they were dreams, but they turned out to be visions. Clues. Each night I was having a bad dream, but each one took place in Seoul. I found that weird. Eventually, I snuck out of the DDAG in District Asia, then I would follow the clues. The night Seraphina got hurt is the same night I started understanding my visions…or, rather, premonitions. I saw a woman in my head, then suddenly she was in front of me. I followed her to an empty part of Seoul, where a man showed up and… it was…is…coming to find out, my dad. Later that night, I saw my mom. I don't understand it and I know I sound crazy but—"

Kora put a hand up, stopping Ariel's ramblings. "I read and read over your records and it does sound crazy." Sebastian, brow furrowed, nodded in agreement.

That's it. It's all over. This was the end of her Death Dealer career. Ariel felt she was never going to be taken seriously again.

"But I know crazy," Kora added. Was this supposed to make Ariel feel better?

Sebastian pulled out a sheet of paper then held it up for Ariel to see. "What does this mean?"

진화! The symbol! "That's what I'm trying to figure out, my king. Honestly, since I've been back, I've been studying the works of Robert Poppy, an ancient linguist. I am hoping to someday understand this…language. I also think this language has something to do with a man named Ki. According to Cyclamen, he is important."

"That's the second time you've mentioned language. What makes you think this is a language?" Kora asked, curiously.

Back to the crazy dead-parents story. "I was told by my parents. Mainly, my dad."

"So, as of now, you have yet to find out anything verifiable about this symbol—or language, as you believe?"

"No, my queen."

"What makes you think you saw your parents?" Sebastian asked.

"I know it's them. They're no longer human, but for sure, it's them!" Ariel paced. "I know I haven't seen them for over ten years, but I remember what they look like. The weird part is, they don't look like they've gotten any older. They still look young but dead—"

"Young but dead?"

"I don't know if this is making any sense, but they're dead. Or, as they mentioned, *reborn*. Even their names have changed. It's as if they don't remember their life with me or before me."

A snort came from the side. Sergeant Lotus leaned all the way back in his seat.

"What do you think they are, then?" Kora asked, studying the strange symbol on paper.

"I thought they were just another pair of pale demons, like the ones who ambushed us, but they're fuc—…sorry, a lot stronger than the other ones we fought. I think they may be some type of second-generation pale demon. Like an upgraded version. I don't know, but they've turned into killing machines and that *language* is the key to what they're plotting. Ki has got to be the one using this dead language as some sort of code. I'm not sure, but I would like to figure that out."

The king and queen peered over at one another.

"Would you like to state your opinion first, my king?"

Sebastian nodded. He got up from his throne, put his hands behind his back and stepped down the stairs. Ariel barely had to move her head up when her king got close. "I say, we give you fourteen days to prove you are telling the truth. The language, your parents, Ki—everything." He looked back over at Kora, who remained sitting tall in her cushioned chair. Both of her arms rested on the branched arms. "What do you think?"

For a moment, she was quiet. Kora looked at the 진화, then Sergeant Lotus, then at the king and defendant.

"I think that's fair," Kora agreed.

Ariel was given another shot! She felt both worried and relieved. Fourteen days to prove she wasn't crazy....A full two weeks to keep in touch with Ivy and read loads of books, to gather proof.

Sergeant Lotus was not happy. He hopped from his seat and hissed, "My king, if I may, I would like to speak."

Shit! Ariel feared what her sergeant may say. He was not happy with her in the least. She silently prayed to the Lord of Life: *Please, have him agree with the king and queen! Send me positivity, my Lord of Life.*

With abundance, Sebastian strolled over to Lotus, keeping a sharp eye on him. "You may," he stated.

"With all due respect, I don't think Ariel deserves any more chances," Lotus insisted.

"Why is that?" Kora snapped.

"Ms. Rose has been given chances over and over again. You have no idea how much trouble she's caused in the previous years, not just during her time in Seoul," Lotus ranted, glaring Ariel's way.

"In fact, Sergeant Lotus, I do," Kora boasted, shutting Lotus down. She rose from her throne and glided across the platform. "There is not a single day that goes by where I do not check up on my DDAG factions. Ariel Rose is a familiar name in the papers, I admit. More than once, her name has appeared on important documents. However, she's done most of what she's done because she felt it right to do so. There is no excuse for her rebellious actions, and yet she has saved more innocents than you could possibly imagine. Put that into perspective before judging her."

"But she has broken the rules!" Lotus jarred.

"Do not raise your voice to my queen," Sebastian threatened.

"My apologies, my king."

"Apologize to your queen, not me," Sebastian advised.

Seeing Lotus take orders gave Ariel a cheap thrill.

Lotus bit his tongue, holding back curse words. "My queen, I am sorry. Rules are meant to be followed, not broken."

Kora clicked her tongue repeatedly. "Right you are. However, life is not black and white. There are shades of grey and white and red and black and blue. Life is complicated, not simplistic. Sergeant, you should look around you, not just at what's in front of you."

Sebastian jumped in. "Let me ask you this, Sergeant Lotus: have you given Ms. Rose a chance to explain herself? To prove what she is saying is indeed true?"

"She attempted to show us the symbol she swore she saw all over Gangnam District, but the picture she displayed during the meeting was blank," Lotus noted. "All we saw was a broken window and some garbage on the street."

"Just because you do not see it does not mean it isn't there," Kora implied.

"That's crazy. If she claims she can see a symbol, yet no one in my guild or Aurora Tulip's guild can see it, then she has to be making this up," Lotus besmirched.

"We live in a magical world, do we not?" Kora mocked.

Lotus sighed. "We do."

"So magically, the evidence could've disappeared from the lenses. Or maybe, Ariel is the only one able to view the symbol. We do not know this for sure. Which is why she must prove herself honest and true. What if she is special? Throughout the DDAG's history, there have been plenty of special Death Dealers." Kora looked over Ariel with a soft smile. Ariel grinned back. "Which is why giving her fourteen days to prove herself guilty or not guilty...is fair."

This was it! Then end of round one. Lotus was beneath the king and queen. No longer did he have a say in Ariel's future. The royals had spoken. It was victory! For now....

"Yes, my queen. My king." Lotus shuddered his last words. "As you wish."

Ariel couldn't believe it. She was still an official Death Dealer. Now, she just had to prove her innocence. It was going to be difficult, but she had to do this, not just for her sake but for the future of the New World. Something big was going on—it was just not figured out yet. However, Ariel was going to find out within the next fourteen days. *Bring it on!*

"This is the plan. You will remain here and begin training novices during the day," Sebastian informed, making Ariel cringe. "After class, you are allowed to speak to whomever you wish and study whatever your heart desires. You are allowed access to District Asia in Seoul, but you cannot, and will not, join up with the others during their investigations. If you must step foot outside of the DDAG headquarters, Captain Jason Lilly must accompany you."

This took Ariel by surprise. "Jason? He hates me right now. I haven't even heard from him."

"Even though he's your captain, he must still do as he is told. Jason is a good leader, and a good leader must abide by the rules," Kora explained. "I have read about you two numerous times. You two work wonders together and I'd rather not have you both separated." She snickered over at Lotus. "Ever."

"Yes, my queen," Ariel said, worrying how Jason was going to take the news. They hadn't spoken in over two weeks, but now they were forced to work together—despite current feelings.

"You are dismissed," King Sebastian stated.

Ariel bowed.

"Feel free to let either of us know if there is anything you may need," Kora concluded. "I hope to hear from you soon."

"You will hear from me soon. Good-bye my king. My queen." Without looking over at Lotus, Ariel exited the trial room with her head held high. With determination and pride, she marched forward to her next destination. Already, she was about to begin round two of her fight.

In fourteen days, she would have everything figured out. Ariel would make sure of that. When another day passed, she would be one step closer to finding Ki, knowing what happened to her parents, and reading the mysterious ancient language as fluently as she did English.

Ariel was back outside the castle. Instead of proceeding down the hill to her car, she made a sharp left turn.

There was someone she had to see. Someone who she knew had answers. Someone who needed to talk and explain to her what the hell was going on. Besides, she had a feeling this person missed her. Next stop: Alexander Cyclamen.

COLONY

Ariel marched her way straight to the one-and-despicable, Alexander Cyclamen. She kicked open the door of the Observation Room, shocking the young informant trainee inside right out of his chair. "I need to see Alexander Cyclamen!" Ariel made clear.

Gulp. Nervous, the young man muttered, "I am not a security guard....I am just covering Alex's lunch. I, uh…I believe I need to see an approval form—"

"The king and queen are busy and I need to speak with Alexander Cyclamen, now!" she reiterated.

The glasses-wearing informant scampered off. Ariel waited impatiently behind the two-way mirror.

Ariel's body was getting hot from the pressure of finding out the truth. She peeled away her double-breasted coat and unknotted two buttons from her dress shirt. After she rolled up her sleeves, voices echoed from the other side. She was about to investigate the commotion's whereabouts until she heard the door from beyond the two-way mirror open abruptly.

Cyclamen was being dragged by two prison guards, and the frightened man was nervously juggling with Cyclamen, begging him to sit down.

"Who wants to see me? You can't throw me in here and not tell me who the fuck is demanding my pretty face!" Cyclamen smugged.

"I do-…I don't know who she is bu-…but she was adamant about seeing you." The poor, fragile man was trembling and kept trying to slide his glasses back into place while Cyclamen proceeded to nag.

It was time to crash the party. Ariel rushed her way inside the Interrogation Room. The battle with Cyclamen was about to begin. The men fell silent once she made her loud entry.

"I'll take it from here," Ariel snapped.

Without question, the trainee made himself scarce by fleeing the scene. The prison guards asked Ariel to call them once they were through with their "little meeting."

As soon as the crowd diminished, with only two left remaining, Cyclamen didn't hold back from letting her know his innermost feelings. "Well, I haven't seen my sweet girl in a while. You look hot in a suit, baby," Cyclamen crooned.

Ariel didn't interact. At least momentarily. She flipped a chair over and sat against the top, bringing her arms forward and crossed. Cyclamen eyed her as she threw her coat across the plastic table.

They both stared at one another in the soundless room. Only the clock ticked with each passing second. Cyclamen drooled at the sight of Ariel's breast poking out from her dress shirt. "Are you going to talk to me, baby?"

Ariel reached into her pant pocket, pulled out a white sheet of paper, then slammed it in between them, hiding its contents underneath her palm.

"Is that a love letter? For me?"

"I have something to show you," Ariel began. "Tell me everything you know about the drawing. No beating around the bush or lying. I don't have time to be your eye candy, so just get to the point."

Cyclamen only chuckled. "Baby, I already told you everything I knew. I'm a nobody. What other information could I possibly have?"

Slowly, Ariel unveiled the secret message written on the wrinkled sheet of paper. Cyclamen hunched over to get a better view. His brows perked up and Ariel noticed immediately.

"Tell me what this is," Ariel demanded.

Sheesh, Cyclamen huffed. "To me it looks like a kid's drawing. What's with the circle and the lines?"

"Cyclamen," Ariel scoffed. "This word has to be connected to Ki: the man you mentioned when I last saw you. What does this say? What does it mean? And what is he planning to do?"

"Oh...," Cyclamen fell back in his uncomfortable chair. "That's the dead language they were talking about."

Ariel's eyes dilated. "Do you know this language?!"

Cyclamen *tsk*-ed. "Sorry honey, but I don't. The only thing I know about this is Ki is using it as a secret code: a sort of password, if you will."

"A password for what? Entry to his secret lair?" Ariel mocked.

Cyclamen shrugged. "I wouldn't be able to tell you."

Suddenly, Ariel pounced in her seat. Darkness dominated her view. An electric charge zapped in between her lungs and she felt like she was transporting into another dimension.

Finally, Ariel's world no longer spun like a tornado. However, when her view cleared, Cyclamen was nowhere to be found. Ariel looked around and noticed she landed in an entirely different room.

Before her was a man standing beside a throne as black as crow feathers. It was hand-carved with the most intricate detail on its wooden frame and had a fine, glossy finish. The border was triangular and, at its point, a peculiar shape was engraved: something almost *t*-shaped, but instead of a vertical line on top, its capital curved and formed into an oval. The thick cushion was sewn of black velvet. There was also a matching throne, just smaller in size.

The man was drinking from a stone goblet that he held with his skeletal fingers. His skin was perfect porcelain and his flat hair reached his elbows. As he put the cup down, Ariel noticed the golden hue in his deep-set eyes.

He traced along the tips of the radiant throne and sighed, "Evolution is about to begin."

GASP! Ariel squirmed in her seat. Where had she traveled now? The walls, the boring paint and the atrocious ticking clock: she recognized it all. Thank god! "What the fuck just happened?"

"Woah!" Cyclamen freaked. "You okay, baby?

Ariel was short of breath, her head cocked low. "No."

Carefully, Ariel got up and excused herself from the room. She poured herself a cold cup of water before heading back, in order to recover. Similarly, to the night of Mary's death, Ariel felt nauseated and dehydrated.

Ariel knocked back the cool beverage in one refreshing gulp.

"Excuse me?"

When Ariel turned around, she saw the future informant whom she frightened just moments ago, fixing his collared shirt.

"Yes?" Ariel scoffed.

"I don't mean to impose, but I did zoom in on the picture you were showing Cyclamen."

A vexed Ariel had little time to prove her innocence. Timing was crucial. Every second of every day for the next two weeks was currency.

"Mind your business, kid," Ariel suggested, walking off.

"Wait!" The young man implored Ariel to listen.

Ugh….Ariel held her anger. "Make it quick."

Giddy, the trainee rambled, "I am currently studying ancient linguistics at the DDAG Academy here in New York. I have actually been awarded for the discovery of Latin: one of Earth's oldest languages."

Ariel was impressed and was beginning to think of him as favorable; useful even. "What's your name?"

"Rylan," he cleared his throat and held out his hand. "Rylan Celosia."

Ariel smiled softly and shook his hand with deference. "I'm Ariel."

"I know," Rylan blurted with enthusiasm. "I mean…I pretended to not who you were earlier because I wasn't sure you wanted Cyclamen to know…." *Now, you look like a stalker, you idiot!* "But anway, you're pretty well-known and ummm…."

Oddly, Ariel found Rylan's queer personality endearing. "Is it because I'm a perfectly *bad* example of a Death Dealer?"

"N-no….Well, not quite." Rylan had never forgotten when Sergeant Lotus visited the DDAG Academy. When he entered the auditorium, the entire body of students hushed. Sergeant Lotus appeared, carrying his brawny physique and macho charisma. On the left side of his chest, he wore a silver DDAG logo pin: a longsword wrapped in a bold green vine, slashed down the middle of an OMEGA sign. The pin was given when an individual had saved more than 10,000 innocents in the duration of their DDAG career. Sergeant Lotus had two pins. That deemed respect.

As Sergeant Lotus spoke, you wanted to listen. In his guttural voice, he told stories of war and loss, Faction Divide and the epic rise of Captain Lilly. Death Dealers were practically celebrities in the eyes of future DDAG members.

Jason Lilly was a definite favorite. Not only was he well on his way to earning his first DDAG pin, he was likable and respected.

Ariel Rose was usually the black sheep in Sergeant Lotus' speeches. However, in the beginning, she was highly recognized for her adrenaline and drive to save innocents. She had saved more innocents than Jason, technically, but her missions were undertaken without consent. Those innocents, even though they were saved, were not counted toward her Innocent Lives Saved record. It was the sad truth and Rylan never agreed with it.

Over time, Ariel Rose's name was fading from Sergeant Lotus' speeches. She had been acting out, it seemed. However, Rylan had never forgotten her. In fact, he admired her on paper. Mina had been one of his trainers for a semester and she would casually bring up Ariel's misfortunes with Sergeant Lotus. While Mina saw the blunders as repetitive and idiotic, Rylan applauded Ariel's bravery to save men, women and children all on her own. How brave can one be to attack terrorists alone without needing help? That should prove not only how much of a dedicated Death Dealer Ariel was, but how important the lives of innocents were, even at the risk of medals and titles.

Ariel looked down at Rylan sitting at his desk, blinking up at her, and wondered if he could be useful. She was desperate and could certainly use the help. Finally, she asked, "Would you mind helping me, Rylan Celosia?"

Excited, Rylan jerked up. "Yes! I mean, no! No, I do not mind helping you, Ariel. Ariel Rose."

Ariel smiled. "Alright." She looked over at the mirror and forgot she was keeping Cyclamen waiting. It was time to go back in and hustle. "I would like to start working with you tomorrow, if that's okay. I have a long list of things to do today but we'll start in the morning."

They exchanged numbers.

"I'll call you," Ariel remarked.

"Okay!" Rylan marveled. As Ariel was walking away, he called out, "Have a good day!"

Ariel returned to the Interrogation Room, where Cyclamen was all grin.

"I missed—"

"Shut it," Ariel interrupted. "What do you know about my parents?"

Cyclamen smirked. "They're dead, aren't they?"

"Do you know something about them? Are they connected to Ki?"

Cyclamen got up from his chair and casually walked around the room with both hands cuffed behind his back. He trotted silently, which made Ariel angry. If only she could choke him or cut him—just a little—enough to make him scar, but not fatally. Breaking his arm also sounded like a splendid idea.

Finally, Cyclamen blurted out, "Ki…is raising an army with some very powerful people."

Ariel perked up. "Where is he?"

Still, Cyclamen said he didn't know.

"Quit bullshitting me, Cyclamen," Ariel roared. She darted from her chair, ran up to Cyclamen, then pinned him against a wall and shoved her arms into his throat. "Talk to me, you bastard! Where is he? What has he done to my parents?"

"No—" *Cough!* Cyclamen could barely breathe.

PUNCH! Cyclamen's nostrils immediately bled. "Tell me what you know!" Ariel yelled.

"Ariel!!" A voice came from the PA system.

Jason?! "Fuck you!" Ariel yelled to her so-called friend. He was no friend of hers. Only a backstabber, a betrayer.

"Nowon—" Cyclamen groaned.

Bang! Jason kicked the door open. "Let him go!" he ordered Ariel, but she refused to cooperate.

"Nowon District!"

"What about it?" Ariel screamed, punching him again. "Is that where Ki is?"

"Ye—yes!" Cyclamen crackled. He looked over at Jason. "Can you get her off me?!"

"Let him go!" Jason hissed at her, the volatile mess who was up to no good once again.

"Not until he tells me everything he knows!" Ariel snapped back. "Talk!" She shoved him back against the cemented wall and his spine cracked.

"You are too damn feisty sometimes," groaned Cyclamen. Ariel reared back to punch him again. He had enough of her gruesome attacks so he started talking. Luckily, there was no Vitality in her bloodstream. Otherwise, Cyclamen would've been pulverized. "Ki stays somewhere in Nowon District. I don't know the exact location, but he's there. As far as your parents, he may have had something to do with it."

Desperate and appeased, Ariel let him go. "Explain the details," she instructed.

"Baby, I only know that Ki is located in Seoul, Korea—possibly Nowon District. He's creating an army and the rumors say he's created human weapons."

"Human weapons?" Jason asked, approaching. "With super strength like Vitality? The men and women who ambushed us in Gangnam District were more than human weapons. They were fucking monsters."

"They're meant to be far worse than you Death Dealer punks," Cyclamen scoffed. "Supposedly, he's making normal people powerful. Almost nuclear."

"What does that have to do with the Black Plague II Infections?" Ariel asked.

"I don't know," Cyclamen answered. Afraid, he added, "Seriously, I don't know, so please don't jack up my pretty face, my sweet. I'm done messing with you."

"I gotta go," Ariel hurried. She grabbed her wrinkled sheet of paper and was about to head out the door before Jason caught her by the arm.

"We have to talk," Jason pleaded.

Ariel wasn't in the mood to be *social.* There was too much to figure out. "We'll talk later," she smacked, then sped out the Interrogation Room. Jason ran after her.

Once Ariel stepped foot into the sunlight, Jason managed to take the lead and block her from venturing further. He held his hands up and said, "Sergeant Lotus wants us to work together."

"Wrong!" Ariel cringed at the name of her sergeant. "The king and queen requested for us to work together, not Lotus. And we will…but not now. I have a lot of shit to do."

"I know I haven't been the greatest friend lately, but neither—"

Lately?! This sent Ariel in a frenzy. "You haven't bothered to speak to me in over two weeks! You were too busy fucking Daoka or Hyuna, or both! Fuck you!"

"Fuck me?! Fuck you!! Do you know how much I sacrifice each time I defend your ass? Especially against Lotus?" Jason shouted, yanking off his cap.

"And do you know how much bullshit I have gone through during the last few months? Huh? Instead of helping me, you started being against me! And worst of all, you actually believed I was crazy!" Ariel bawled, barely holding herself back from smacking Jason square across his squarer face. Instead, she wiped her eyes, and pointed to the Interrogation Room. "After what Cyclamen said in there, do you still think I'm fucking crazy?!"

Jason didn't speak, only glared at her. His chest slowly motioned up and down while he breathed deeply.

"That's what I thought!" Ariel sibilated, throwing her coat back on. The air suddenly grew colder. She nudged him as she passed.

Jason sighed heavily. "When do you want to get together?"

Without looking back, Ariel simply stated, "When I fucking tell you."

Rylan and Ariel got together in the headquarter's library the next evening. Ariel sadly had to reschedule their morning appointment due to her new training classes. It wasn't as bad as she thought it would be. In fact, she sort-of had fun training the clueless bots—as she referred to them.

At first, Ariel was clueless on how to conquer a successful class, and she had five classes to run. After taking attendance, Ariel introduced herself—they all knew her immediately—then she had them state their names and career goals, followed by three random facts about themselves. Afterwards, she had them round up their weapons and asked them to display their skills. She scored them on a scale from one to five in three different categories: style, skill, and confidence. Ariel thoroughly enjoyed seeing the student's potential. She spent time with each of them and went over their current levels and how they could improve and conquer their Death Dealer goals. The students wanted to impress her and Ariel loved their determination. Before releasing them, she even referred to them as her little bots.

Tired from training, Ariel dressed in shorts and an oversized shirt and slipped on some black sandals. Rylan dressed in a checkered dress shirt and baggy jeans. With him, he brought a pile of manual notebooks and bundles of boxes with many, many books. Ariel's eyes glistened as she scrambled her way through the mess. There were new books, old books, and books she had never heard of. One caught her eye.

"Jett Poppy's *Black Magic: A Myth?* I used this to create a reversal spell, called the Truth." Ariel remembered how proud she felt about the whole thing. It brought her so much joy, especially when her friends helped her. *Friends*....Bodhi was whom she missed most. *I need to check up on him*, she thought, making a mental note. As she caressed the fine leather of the book's spine, she realized something didn't make sense.

"Why would we need this?" Ariel asked. "How would this help us?"

Rylan loved explaining his research. "Believe it or not, black magic can be used in various languages, even dead ones. Originally, when I discovered Latin, I found it by using elements of deciphering spells. Latin has yet to be used in black magic. If it were ever used in a negative way, I wouldn't have been able to find it with deciphering spells alone. If someone were to mainly use Latin in any type of black magic, the entire language would have been kept hidden from good people. Evil people will do anything to keep their secrets safe. If we can't figure this out with my deciphering spell alone, then we may have to use some black magic."

"Wow," Ariel roused. "That's amazing."

Rylan blushed as he organized the materials he was pulling out.

"Do you think three minds would be better than two?" Ariel had a suggestion, and it dealt with a pretty, sun-kissed lady. "There is another Death Dealer that I'd like to join."

"Of course!" Rylan gasped, stoked to be working with not only one, but two Death Dealers. "When are you going to call him? Her?"

Ariel was already dialing away on her phone. "Now."

Less than thirty minutes passed and Ivy arrived to meetup with her crush—and some other guy. Ariel caught her as soon as the Death Dealers were dismissed for the evening—another night of investigation and another night of not finding a damn thing.

Ivy was ecstatic to see the redhead she adored so much. "Ariel!" she called out, waving at her.

Ariel signaled for her to sit with them by the window. Ivy paced over quickly and embraced Ariel in a bear hug, chest-to-chest. Rylan moved aside, not wanting to intrude.

"This is Rylan," Ariel introduced. "He is going to be helping us with our investigation."

"Right," Ivy remembered. Honestly, she'd rather have Ariel to herself, but if this was going to be the way to spend time with her then she'd take it. "I'm Ivy."

"Ivy Snapdragon, by any chance?" Rylan asked while shaking her small hand.

Ivy felt honored that someone knew of her. "Yes, I am."

"You were the one to take down Knuckles in District Asia using your awesome snake sword!! You saved an entire family in under a minute!" Rylan rambled, trying not to get overly excited. "You're amazing!"

Ariel knew nothing about Ivy beyond her shared fascination with architecture. This was a bit of a turn-on. "An entire family in under a minute, huh? That's cool. And Knuckles...?"

"Yeah," Ivy chuckled. "I didn't understand the nickname either."

Both ladies laughed while Rylan stood in the background, waiting.

Ariel readjusted her focus. "Sorry. Let's start, shall we?"

"Let's!" Rylan cheered.

Only an hour had gone by, but unfortunately, Ivy had to return to Seoul: she was dozing off and needed rest before the morning briefing. Before saying goodbye, Ivy updated her on something important. "There's word about Bodhi's theory on moonlit mercury."

Both Ariel and Rylan shot their heads up. "What's going on?" Ariel hastened.

"The experiments have been effective. The pale demon's blood mixed with mercury dies instantly. Their DNA can't handle the metal: just as Bodhi predicted."

And? Ariel thought. There had to be more. "Is the royal cabinet going to make us moonlit mercury weapons?"

Ivy sighed. "They keep saying maybe but we have yet to see any progress."

"We have to push them to approve our weapons!" Ariel urged.

Rylan weighed in. "If Ki is creating an army with these pale demons, we have to be prepared. Or...you Death Dealers have to be prepared. You know what I mean."

"Right," Ariel nodded. "Do you think Bodhi would be willing to make a petition to hurry the approval?"

"I'll ask him," Ivy assured, placing a hand on her shoulder. "He misses you, you know." she added with a soft curve of her lip. "You mean the world to him."

Shit! Ariel thought. *I was going to call him earlier! I can't now. He'll be asleep.*

"Check up on him," Ivy suggested. "Well, I have to go."

Before Ariel hugged her goodbye, she mentioned Nowon District.

"Jason had mentioned it once before. I'll bring it up again and hopefully we'll get out there soon enough. I'll see you later this week," Ivy concluded.

"Bye."

Rylan grinned with his hooded brown eyes, perking up.

"What?" Ariel asked.

"You two a couple?" Rylan teased. He couldn't help himself.

Ariel shrugged. "It's complicated."

Coincidentally, Rylan expected that response. "Of course, it is," he winked.

Ariel playfully told him to shut up and they continued to study.

After a few hours, Ariel advised Rylan to get some rest. They had handwritten miles of important notes but had found nothing conclusive, yet. Ariel helped Rylan pack his belongings.

"Same time tomorrow?" Rylan asked, before heading back to his apartment.

"Sounds good to me," Ariel insisted.

"Okay. Can't wait!" he exclaimed.

They said goodnight and Ariel drove to Aunt Faith's home.

Ariel didn't want to be alone in her own apartment. She already felt like she was losing the most important people in her life.

Faith never unmade her bedroom. It remained exactly the same as it was years ago, when Ariel was growing up—just after her parents disappeared.

The annoying pine wallpaper with white daises had stayed intact, and her twin bed was still decorated with cupcakes—all over the bedsheets and comforter.

Even though Ariel could no longer stand the dainty decor of her childhood, she loved being home with Faith. It brought comfort and warmth. Ariel looked at the unchanged room and wondered if Faith felt the same of Ariel.

That night, she tucked herself in—but not before eating a small bowl of rubies—then slid under the covers and called it a night.

Ariel shivered in her sleep.

Brr....

Annoyed, Ariel forced herself up to close the window. She stumbled between her canary yellow curtains and slammed the window down.

Brrr...."Fuck me," Ariel rattled, rubbing her arms.

"That's very inappropriate language," a disembodied voice wisecracked.

What the hell? Ariel spun around. There was a man in the room, nestled on her old rocking chair. "Dad?! How did you find me?"

"We're linked, remember? And you still call me Dad. How adorable," Leon breathed, snidely.

"That means she'll probably still call me Mom. We are able to follow wherever you may go." Symphony crept up from the shadows beside her bed. Her hair swooped down over her breasts and she stood in perfect posture.

Leon got up and held Symphony's waist. They both gazed at a defenseless Ariel. She was without Vitality, Mercury was far away and she was completely groggy. What were they doing there? How did they get there?

"What do you want?" Ariel sniveled, still shivering.

Symphony strolled up and whispered, "Evolution is happening in Seoul."

"I still don't know what that means," Ariel cried.

"My dear, evolution is near. We need you," Leon said in a trill voice.

"Why me?" Ariel asked, unable to comprehend what role she could possibly have in this *evolution.* "I have nothing to give."

"But you do," Symphony interjected. Ariel's single tear shined in the moonlight. With a soft touch, Symphony wiped it away.

Symphony's once warm hands were now as cold as death. All her motherly affection had been vanquished and taken over by this wretched monster.

"I'm sorry, my child, but you need to find us soon," whispered Symphony as she brushed Ariel's hair out of her face with her long claws.

"Why don't you just tell me where you are?!"

"Then that'd be too easy," Leon laughed. "If you don't find us, we'll find you over and over again until you can't take it anymore."

"Please, just tell me what is going on!" Ariel cried as she looked into her mother's sadistic eyes.

"You'll figure it out," Symphony said, surely. "You are so close."

"Close to what? Finding Ki? Evolution?"

Symphony avoided the question. "Go back to bed, my dear."

Ariel refused to listen. "No! Tell me what is—"

And just like that, they were gone.

"Damnit!" Ariel yelled. "Sonofabitch! Argh!!!"

Knock, knock, knock! "Ariel, are you okay?" Faith worried. "Can I come in?"

"Fine…," Ariel huffed. "I'm fine."

"Do you need me to bring you anything?"

"No, I'm just going to go back to bed," Ariel lied. She couldn't possibly go back to sleep after this. "I uh… have cramps."

"Oh?" Odd. Usually, Ariel didn't complain about her period. At least, not while growing up. "Okay. Well, goodnight, babe."

"Goodnight," Ariel repeated.

Ariel sat on the floor and looked out the window. She gazed up at the starless sky and wondered what *evolution of Seoul* actually meant. Black Plague II plus pale demon party couldn't add up to anything good. Ariel took out her notepad and read through the pages of notes she had jotted down earlier that evening.

Ariel whispered, "This is going to be a long two weeks."

Over the next few days, Rylan and Ariel met each night at the same spot by the window in the library. They had done tests trying to read the symbol in the alchemy lab using various deciphering spells and enchantments, but nothing ever worked. But despite many failed attempts, Rylan and Ariel never gave up.

Ariel did check up on Bodhi on the fourth night, and she was incredibly happy to hear his voice. Their conversation only lasted for an hour but they managed to catch up with one another. Bodhi seriously missed his friend and wanted her back in Seoul, but he understood why she couldn't just drop in and say hello. Ariel was grateful he didn't hate her, especially after Seraphina's chaotic scene in the healing ward.

Before hanging up, Ariel reminded Bodhi, "I am always here for you, loser." To which he replied, "I know. And so am I."

Ivy managed to steal away from Seoul and join in on most meetups, updating Ariel on anything important she had missed. Ivy mentioned that the guilds began to search Nowon District, but they had yet to find Ki or anything even hinting his whereabouts.

Ariel was yet again, lacking sleep. She feared the night, for it became an enemy. She kept the lamp on, relying on the orange light to keep her safe. She was afraid to see her dead parents lurking inside her room or watching her slumber. Instead, she stayed up as late as possible. It was beginning to show in her sullen eyes and wayward hair.

On the ninth night, Ivy brought up some valuable information.

"So, Bodhi made the petition," Ivy slurred in.

"What?" Ariel puffed, almost choking on her cup of tea. A few drops fell on her green shirt. "When? Are we close? Is the cabinet approving to construct moonlit mercury weapons?"

Ivy licked her thumb then attempted to clean off the tea stain. "Slow down," she said. "We're all working as hard as we can."

"Who's we?" Ariel wondered.

"Me, Bodhi, Daoka, Hyuna, Captain Orchid and Zaire."

"Zaire?" Ariel was surprised. "How's he doing?"

"He's good. Honestly, he's still mad at you…but he's good."

"Figured," Ariel said, honestly. "Anyway, I think I'm on to something."

Rylan pulled out two books: *Black Magic: A Myth?* by Jett Poppy and *Dead Languages: Not Dead After All* by Robert Poppy.

Ivy looked at them with intrigue. "Interesting. They're brothers?"

"Yes!" Rylan chimed in. "Very famous brothers, in fact."

"Nice," Ivy smiled.

"So, here's what Rylan and I have done the past two nights." Ariel picked up a vial of black liquid and handed it over to Ivy. She eyed it intensely. "This is something we made up called The Translator. I managed to mix the elements of black magic while Rylan mixed in some deciphering spells."

Rylan explained his discovery of Latin to Ivy, catching her up with all the details—including evil reviving and claiming a dead language.

Ariel continued. "With that being said, we believe with this mix, we should be able to immediately translate what this symbol, or language, says."

"How do you know what language it is, exactly?" Ivy asked, curiously. "I mean, how did you figure out Latin?"

"Through an old book," Rylan stated. "Eventually, I found books that went over the history and origins of the

Latin language. It's all about connections. If Ariel can find more of this language, she'll be able to connect the dots and figure out the name of what she's reading."

"I'm excited," Ariel emphasized. "You ready?" she asked her small team.

"Yes!" They answered in unison. It was hardly a rousing cheer from a hall stocked with Death Dealers, but at least these two gave her support.

Ariel laid out a poster board with 진 화 written on it in large, bold font. Ariel threw back the dark liquid, making a scrunched face.

"Tasty?" Ivy mocked.

Ariel choked. "Very."

Ariel hunched over the board and concentrated on the drawing. The others leaned over the table with her.

"Anything?" Rylan asked, impatiently. Ivy shushed him.

Slowly, the words began to get cloudy. The letters swirled in a foggy tornado, then suddenly, the words sorted themselves out as if in English: *Evolution.*

"Evolution?" Ariel gasped.

"What?" Ivy asked.

"The word is evolution. The blood of the victims in Gangnam District was spelling out 'evolution." Evolution. Blood. Black Plague II Infections. Where was this leading? "Holy shit."

"What does that mean?" Rylan questioned.

"I don't know," Ariel sighed. "But I need to find out."

Ariel grabbed her phone and began dialing a number. The phone started to ring. "Are you guys investigating tonight?"

"It's Saturday, we have the day off," Ivy uttered, puzzled.

The phone kept ringing and eventually went to voicemail. "Shit!" Ariel spat. She grabbed her jacket. "Rylan, do you mind picking up after me, please?"

"Okay," Rylan answered. "Where are you going?"

"I have to go see someone," Ariel hurried. She advised Ivy to follow her. "I'll see you tomorrow morning," Ariel called out to Rylan.

"Be careful!" Rylan yelled back. He was curious of what was happening but he knew he'd find out soon enough.

Ivy followed Ariel to the portal gate outside the DDAG headquarters. "Where are we going?" she asked.

"Seoul, Korea," Ariel said into the portal.

"Are you allowed there?" Ivy asked, hoping she was not about to get herself in trouble.

Ariel nodded. "The Queen and King said it was okay. As long as I'm not invited to your investigating parties. I am not allowed to have fun, apparently."

"Bummer," Ivy joked.

As soon as the mirror images displayed, they walked through the blue flames.

They were now in the Seoul gardens of District Asia. "Do you happen to know where Jason's dorm is?" Ariel paced inside.

"I do not," Ivy spoke, little more than a murmur. "You don't?!"

"Nope," Ariel admitted. "He hasn't been my favorite person for a long while."

Ariel noticed Captain Orchid in the entryway. "Where does Jason reside, Captain Orchid?"

"He's in dorm 2314," Sying responded, politely. "Is everything alright?"

"Yes," Ariel smiled. "Thank you."

"My pleasure."

Once Ariel reached the dormitories, she rushed through the hallways, scouting for room 2314. Ivy followed her every step of the way.

Finally, Ariel found what she was looking for. There were moans coming from the inside.

"I don't think we should be bothering him," Ivy urged, knowing what event was happening behind closed doors.

"Wait here," Ariel told Ivy. She banged on the door. "Jason!"

The moaning stopped but no one was coming. "Jason!" Nothing. Ariel exhaled deeply. "Alright, I didn't want to have to do this."

"Don't!" Ivy whispered, but it was too late.

BAM! Ariel kicked the door in, slamming it wide open.

"What the fuck?!" Jason screamed, butt-naked. He and Hyuna threw the covers over their bare bodies.

Ariel walked up to them and simply said hello.

"Excuse me?!" Jason retorted. "Can't you see I'm a little busy?"

"Oh yes," Ariel scorned with wide set eyes, looking over the shocked pair of assassins. She picked up his tangled clothes on the floor then threw them at his face. "Get dressed. We have to go."

"Now?" asked Jason, baffled.

"I told you I would let you know when I needed you, and now is the time. So, can I have both of you put on your clothes and get out of bed?!" The couple looked at one another, furious at the careless interruption. "I'll wait."

"Could you give us some privacy?" Hyuna hissed.

"No," Ariel blurted.

Sure enough, the only thing to do was comply with Ariel's demand.

They came out from the covers and dressed in front of Ariel, displaying their naked bodies. Ivy, meanwhile, hid by the doorway. Now that she could see for herself, Ariel found Hyuna attractive, but nowhere near as gorgeous as Ivy. She had droopy breasts and a small torso and her legs were killer-sweet. Jason on the other hand, was more like a brother, so seeing his thick and large penis did nothing for Ariel sexually, but she'd be lying if she said he did not have a magnificent body. No wonder many women flocked to him. Especially with his hard-earned abs and killer muscle tone.

Once they were fully dressed, Ariel advised Jason to gather the usual DDAG equipment. Hyuna left, angry and embarrassed, but Ariel couldn't care less. *She'll get over it.*

While, Jason was packing his things and getting ready to go, Ariel walked over to Ivy.

"I have to go. Stay here, okay?" Ariel told her with sincerity.

Ivy didn't want to leave her side. "Why can't I go with you?"

"I don't want you to get hurt," Ariel declared. "You're too important and you have to be safe. Please, stay here."

Ivy loved knowing that Ariel cared; she just didn't want them apart. She wanted to protect her, make sure she didn't get hurt. However, Ivy gave in. Ariel was stubborn and she knew she wouldn't win. "Call me when you get back, okay?"

"I will," Ariel whispered.

Jason was finally ready. "Can we go now?" he whined.

"Yes," Ariel snapped. She kissed Ivy on the cheek. "I'll check up with you later tonight."

The best—but angry—friends started pacing down the hallway.

Jason couldn't help but ask, "Are you two a couple, or what?!"

"It's complicated."

Ariel and Jason headed straight for Nowon District in one of the black vans. The night was pitch black, even with the city lights blaring in downtown Seoul. Jason had to keep the brights on in order to see more clearly. Minutes into the ride, Ariel attacked Jason for his failure as a best friend.

"Can't we just agree that we both messed up?!" Jason snarled, tightening his fists on the steering wheel.

"You disappeared! In the meantime, you're fucking Daoka, then Hyuna—"

"Whoa, whoa, whoa!" Jason interrupted. "Who told you I had sex with Daoka?"

Ariel rolled her eyes. "It's what she didn't tell me."

Jason shot a haughty look at Ariel. "You mean to tell me, no one told you I'm having sex with someone that has the personality of a twelve-year-old, but instead of asking me, you assumed?"

Ariel crossed her arms and kicked her feet up on the dashboard, looking out into the raven night.

"That's what I thought," Jason hissed.

Ariel kept quiet. For the remainder of the ride, neither of them spoke.

Finally, they reached Nowon District. It was empty, quiet, and beaten. Ariel felt she was in the Lord of Darkness' dimension.

"Scary shit," Ariel muttered.

"Yep!" Jason spat. "Ready to go?"

Ariel released her tightened seatbelt and got out of the car. There was nothing but empty, broken houses. The nature here was oddly robust—shrubs and trees stood taller than the houses and arched over the streets, but still, the quietness of the district was terrifying. Each step they took echoed behind them.

"No one has found anything here?" Ariel asked Jason.

"No leads," Jason answered.

"Well, I brought a couple of Truth vials," Ariel said, passing some over to Jason. "Bodhi managed to create a strong enough dose that we no longer need to throw two."

"When did he manage that?" Jason asked, surprised.

"A few nights ago. He had Ivy give me a boxful."

"Hmmm…," Jason sang. "Good job, Bodhi."

They continued to search around and Ariel was trying to pick a good spot to toss the Truth potion. She noticed they were coming across a forest patch that had swallowed an abandoned house whole.

"Maybe here," Ariel said to herself.

Before she threw a potion, a disturbing howl was coming from within the pine trees.

Ariel took a step back. "What the hell is that?"

Jason shrugged. "Beats the hell out of me."

The two Death Dealers waited for a moment, but then the howling disappeared. "Okay," Ariel said. "Let's try this again." Ariel threw Truth.

Awooooooo….The noise grew louder and sounded close.

Ariel grabbed Mercury from its sheath while Jason pulled out his double-barrel shotgun.

Clink! "I'm ready!"

Awoooooo….

The howl grew significantly until it sounded fairly close. Ariel readied herself, bending at the knee. Jason stood behind her and aimed his shotgun straight forward.

The bushes in front of them shook violently and the leaves were falling out of place.

Ariel and Jason held their positions and were more than ready to attack.

Suddenly, a huge animal jumped out at them.

Woah!! They jolted back.

"What is that?" Jason asked, terrified.

"I, uh…I don't know," Ariel answered.

Gracefully, the creature walked toward them with her long, furry legs. She stood on all fours and met above Ariel's belly button. If she stood up, she would probably be taller than Jason.

Her coat was a thick and beautiful, pearly white with a tail to match. Her paws were gigantic—probably as wide as Jason's hand—and her claws were short, black and blunt.

To their surprise, she didn't attack. Instead, she stared at them, just as curious about them as they were about her. When she walked, she took small and careful steps—cautious of any danger. She had a triangular face and a long snout. Her ears pointed up proudly whenever she tilted her magnificent head. Ariel was intrigued by her upturned eyes. They were like bright yellow gems—beautiful and mystical.

Ariel thought maybe she was looking at a 'dog' for the first time, but it somehow seemed unlikely. She had to get a closer look. The moment was exciting and dangerous.

"Get back here," Jason whispered, grabbing onto Ariel's arm.

"Shut up!" Ariel fought back, slapping Mercury across his hand.

"You don't know what that thing is!" Jason argued.

Ariel focused on the animal's beautiful face. The white-furred beauty walked over to a boulder and proudly stood high above them as if she were queen of the forest.

Slowly and carefully, Ariel put Mercury aside and pulled out her hand. She wanted to feel an animal, know what it's like to touch something with fur. She was probably the most beautiful thing Ariel had ever seen.

Growing up, Ariel found pictures of children with pets. Pets were rare in the New World. It'd be honor to own an alley cat or a crow. There used to be hundreds of different animals, each one perfect in their own way.

Ariel managed to meet at the animal's feet. "Hey," she whispered, bringing her hand up. "You are so gorgeous." She ripped off her glove and placed her hand over its fur.

Oh my god!!! Ariel thought. Her fur was ultra-soft and thick—like how her mother's hair used to be—and she was undoubtedly warm. She pressed her fingers along her side then caressed her all the way down to her tail. Her body only flinched when she touched a few tender spots, but she never fled.

Jason began slowly walking over to them. Ariel stood in front of her face and cupped it in her hand. Her head was so large, it overshadowed her own. With her free hand, she gently caressed the fur in between her jewel-like eyes, then down the middle of her long snout.

Jason wanted to pet her also. Get a glimpse of what Ariel was feeling. He took off a glove and stepped forward, but before he could share the same enjoyment as Ariel, the animal jumped off the boulder. She landed on her strong legs then sprinted off, running straight through the purple smoke from Truth, then disappeared into the forest.

"Fuck you, Jason!" Ariel whined.

"I didn't mean to scare it away!" Jason was disappointed he scared the furry girl somehow.

"Anyway," Ariel groaned. She walked back over to the purple smoke. She took a vial of Translator—her new concoction—out of her coat pocket and drank it in one gulp. "Yuck!" The taste was bitter and tart. "I'm never going to get used to that."

As soon as Ariel looked down, instead of seeing 진화, she now saw the word "evolution," followed by a trail of blood.

"Do you see this?!" Ariel asked Jason.

"Obviously not," Jason jerked.

Ariel took out another Translation vial and had Jason drink it.

"Ew...," Jason winced. "That is disgusting."

Ariel waited for a reaction.

"I still don't see anything."

"Why am I the only one able to see this?!" Ariel grumbled to herself.

"See what?"

Argh! "Just follow me!"

Together, they trailed up the blood path through the haunting forest. Ariel was growing impatient after trotting along for what felt like hours.

"Are we there yet?" Jason griped, yearning for his bed.

Suddenly, Ariel was taken away.

Gasp!

Ariel was no longer with Jason, but back in a familiar spot. Again, she saw two black thrones and the same older man, this time looking out the window.

"Is she here?" he asked, to which someone responded, "Soon." It sounded like Leon.

What the hell is going on?!

In the blink of an eye, Ariel returned to Jason.

"Where'd you go?" Jason was concerned. One minute Ariel was walking normally then randomly, fell over into the dirt and rocks.

"I think we're getting somewhere," Ariel breathed. Immediately, she got back up and ran. Jason ran close behind.

Again, Ariel was kidnapped to another place.

Gasp!

This time, there was a hole in the floor and someone flew straight inside. Underneath the forest floor, was an underground town of some sort. There were no streets, only narrow dirt roads. There were countless stone homes that looked horribly outdated—way older than 2000 A.P. (After Plague)—especially with their cracked, tiled roofs. Ariel could see hundreds of pale demons in gothic scenery. Someone was approaching the castle gates, but before Ariel could take a peek inside, she was sent back to Jason.

"Okay," Jason mumbled, helping Ariel up. "Stay on your feet, soldier."

"A hole!"

"Asshole? Huh?! Who are you calling an asshole?"

There it was! It blended in with the dirt and grass, but thanks to Truth, Ariel spotted it easily. *Evolution* was largely written in blood over the darkened floor.

Jason shook his head. "You want us to dig our own graves or something?"

Ignoring him, Ariel rushed inside.

Jason unwillingly followed. Immediately upon landing, Ariel noticed the dark and horrifying castle in the near distance.

"Where are we?" Jason asked.

"I don't know." Ariel skimmed the city for any familiar sights. "This way."

The town was empty and quiet. Jason and Ariel carefully walked their way over to the castle grounds. Oddly, there was no food or water to be found. Not a trace of vegetables or fruit or even wells to hold clean water. There were locked carts that Ariel was too scared to open due to the foul smell swelling from them, and Jason was freaked by the absence of nature.

"Are we in some kind of ghost town?" Jason wondered.

Ariel shrugged. "Not a damn clue."

The pair eventually made their way to the entryway. Instead of being traditional, Ariel advised that they crawl up one of the towers in order to avoid any potential danger.

Soundlessly, they cat-crawled up one of the stone towers and snuck their way inside through a glassless window.

Ariel landed quietly on top of a cemented paveway and instantly, gravitated down to her knees. Jason followed her lead. They both crawled until they reached the edge of the paveway.

Carefully, Ariel peered her head over.

Oh. My. God!!!

To their astonishment, beneath them was a colony of pale demons. They all crowded the floor, growling loudly. Above a few flights of stairs were the black thrones Ariel had seen before.

They were definitely uncivilized. The rowdy bunch were taking jabs at each other with their razor claws, fighting over the last morsel of some tacky looking food. Jason noticed a small woman pinning a man to the floor and, without shame, began fucking his brains out.

Bleh....Jason rubbed his throat, holding back vomit.

Ariel searched for any children and luckily, there was not a child in sight. The pale demons seemed to be strictly inhumane adults.

"What do you suppose this is?" Jason wondered.

Ariel looked over at the thrones and noticed a familiar face. It was the man she had seen in her visions, and he was looking out the bay window. To the side of him were none other than her parents. They held hands and smiled vividly.

Ariel sighed. "We're looking at an army."

RUNAWAY

"**T**here's so many of them," Jason whispered under his breath as his eyes surveyed the ground beneath him and Ariel. *Wretched*, Jason thought. Disorganized and terrifying creatures. All of them pale, with silver eyes and dagger-like claws. They were squirming about violently, growling and spitting at each other. *What kind of people are they?*

Ariel wanted a better view. Keeping low, she crawled on all fours, moving soundlessly, making sure Jason followed close. Once they turned a corner, Ariel perked her head up and noticed the old man from her visions taking center stage. He stood there with his long black hair and golden eyes in the most pristine black suit. He held out his arms and smiled graciously over the horde of pale demons.

They roared and cheered together at the sight of him, some wailing and jumping around like excited toddlers. A column of a dozen pale demons emerged and climbed up to the podium with poise. The men wore full black capes with red silk undersides secured to black velvet trench coats. Under their coats, they wore sleek black pants and ruffled red shirts. The women had on horned headdresses, each with three golden links draping down the sides of their foreheads and a throne symbol holding each piece together. They covered themselves in off-the-shoulder white dresses that draped down to their feet, each held with golden rope.

Ariel's parents held their positions in the corner of the stage, casually looking over the pale pack with demonizing smirks. The dozen men and women who had ascended the stage lined up behind the older man in the center and stood tall with clenched hands.

Softly, the old man waved his arms as the wind kissed his long hair. The rowdy bunch gradually hushed, and soon enough, all eyes were upon their mighty leader.

"My children," the old man began with a surprisingly smooth and charming voice. He had an accent neither of the assassins had heard before. It was different and sounded intelligent: prim and proper.

"As your king, I stand before you, proud and blessed. Each and every one of you has put in so much effort toward the upcoming war."

There really is a New World War!! Ariel had ignored the truth. Cyclamen had been right since the night of the bombing of the Golden Throne Ballroom. The best friends looked at one another, thinking the same thing: *War is coming....*Quickly, Jason reached for Ariel's hand and simply nodded, letting her know it would all be okay.

"We have put in so much hard work toward our goal and we're getting close. After the next moonrise, we will see our evolution."

Yeah!!! They all screamed loudly and pumped their fists. Hearing their king speak of evolution called for praise and worship.

Carefully, Ariel leaned in to Jason's ear. "Do you understand what their evolution means?"

Jason shook his head. "Whatever it is, we may be screwed."

The old man looked over to Ariel's parents and invited them forward. They kissed his hand and stood on either side of him.

"My two favorite children: Akehanten and Nefertiri, named after Egypt's wisest pharaoh and his queen...."

"*Psst*....What the fuck is a pharaoh?" Jason asked.

Ariel wrinkled her face. "I don't know!"

"Rebirth itself is theirs," the silver-eyed leader sang. "Soon, I promise, you all will also be able to embrace the light, no longer fearing the sun. Come with me, my sons and daughters, to the New World, and there, we shall drink our way through the maggots that roam our world. We will kill them. Slaughter them. Do as we wish, until we've had our fill."

"Drink their way?!" Ariel gasped.

"Why should we allow these ants to take over our world yet again? For centuries, we were in control, until those slimy, homo sapiens began killing us off. No longer will we hide. We will rise again!"

Ariel's pink lips frowned. "What do we do?"

"My youngest children are wiser than I imagined," the old man murmured, looking over Ariel's parents. "They are the key to our future."

Jason tapped Ariel's shoulder and pointed at a closed, wooden door with steel locks on the opposite side of the room. "Those twelve came from there. I think we should sneak our way in."

"How?" Ariel wondered.

Jason fingered his way up and there was an opening, a few feet above the door.

Ariel agreed, and they carefully headed to their destination, crawling back on all fours.

"The council and I have decided to let you all celebrate our victory early." The old man clapped. Ariel froze and quickly looked over the ledge. From below, the grey granite floor opened and out sprouted a cage full of naked men and women, all of them crying out in fear. Their hands and feet were tied together.

Ariel grabbed Jason's leg, and his stomach plopped directly onto the ground.

"Hey!" Jason huffed as Ariel kept pulling him. "What are you—"

Ariel covered his mouth. "Shhh….Look!"

Jason couldn't believe his eyes. He had expected something vile from the pale demons, but nothing as torturous as stringing up people so ghastly.

"We need to get over there!" Ariel urged. She was about to get up, but Jason stopped her mid-stance.

"It's too dangerous, even for you and Mercury."

"Do you not see that those people need our help?!"

"Yes!" Jason said. "But I don't want you running a suicide mission. Got it?"

Ariel didn't want him to be right. She looked back over at the prison cage and witnessed a slew of pale demons tormenting innocents between the rusty bars.

One of the demons clawed at a young brunette, and immediately, half of her face spouted blood from the deep carvings. She howled in agony and tried to cover her face, but another demon lunged at her thin arms, holding on to her firmly and pulling her close. She screamed once she felt his ice-cold skin. He cackled, his mouth wide open, and with his long tongue, he licked the blood off her face.

"For you, my children, feast tonight!" The council stood gracefully with expressionless faces. "Remember, on the next full moon, we will begin our fight! Evolution begins in Seoul!"

Leon and Symphony cheered together, "Evolution begins in Seoul!"

While the pale demons stripped the helpless humans from the cage one-by-one, the council, the king, and Ariel's parents stood by quietly and smiled, anticipating miracles to come.

"Let's get out of here," Jason persisted.

The thought of leaving innocents to die severed Ariel's soul in two. If she only had enough strength to kill all the pale terrorists on her own, she would happily slaughter them all away and burn their bodies and their pathetic castle into soot. However, as she kept looking down on her enemies, she knew she'd have a quick death.

As the chaos grew louder, Jason and Ariel took advantage of the noise and hustled their way over the window, staying vigilant. Jason signaled for Ariel to climb over the window. With a soft leap, she threw herself over the ledge, fell on her feet and then—

"Hello, Ariel."

Slam! Jason landed.

"You alright?" Jason was taken aback at the sight of an enticing woman with a closed-mouth smile and fangs that peeked out over her bottom lip.

Ariel's breath was taken away. She felt immense strength just by standing in the woman's presence. Like the others, she portrayed a human form, yet she was completely different. It was as if the sun burned out, allowing darkness to halt time, making her invincible and ageless through starlight. She was flawless. Like Ariel, her eyes were most captivating. They sparkled in a golden hue—just like the king's. Beautiful. Enticing. Yet incredibly haunting.

Nervously, Ariel shivered as the room suddenly began to feel even colder and the woman was staring right at her, taunting. Ariel stood back but her arms were mere inches away from Mercury, just in case she needed to fight. "Who are you?"

As the woman gazed at both of the assassins, Jason's thoughts skidded into a frenzy. Should they run or stay? Who was that woman? How was she so damn sexy yet scary at the same time? Do the others know they were there? Then, as the woman moved around them in a wary circle, Jason realized that Ariel's visions were not only true, they led them to that place for a reason. They must stay for the sake of innocents.

"I'm Bathory. We've been waiting for you," she moaned.

Ariel spun and kept her eyes focused on Bathory's seductive movements. Jason stood near Ariel, readying himself for anything that may happen.

Bathory moistened her lips as she moaned at the sight of perfection of Ariel and Jason's astounding faces and warm bodies and beating hearts.

"Follow me, please," Bathory said politely as she began swaying away.

Frantically puzzled, Jason and Ariel looked at one another then followed her out of the room. Bathory never checked up on them, only kept moving forward into a hallway lit only by flaming torches. Ariel moved at a safe distance from Bathory, and Jason was only an arm's length away.

Bathory slowly opened up a beaten wooden door and courteously offered them entry. "After you."

They carefully escorted themselves inside the unknown room, keeping a watchful eye on what may lay ahead.

Suddenly, the council, the king and Ariel's parents were sitting before them at a long banquet table.

"Weren't you all in the other room like five seconds ago?!" Jason gawked.

Amused, the king stood up, walked over and threw his arms around the perplexed assassins.

"Welcome to my home," the king sang.

"What kind of home throws such bloodthirsty celebrations?" Ariel quirked her thin eyebrows.

"My dear, we are not cannibals," Bathory cruised in. "You are mistaken."

"What are you, exactly?" Jason asked. "For sure you weirdos aren't human."

A mummified-looking woman with layers of exhausted wrinkles spoke: "Throughout our lifetime, humans have given us so many names."

"Bloodsuckers," a thin man with shiny grey hair chuckled. "Cold ones, ice demons, night stalkers, and—what was the other one? It was rather odd, but incredibly popular for a time."

"Vampires." Bathory chimed in.

"That's it!"

"So, what are you?" Jason asked again.

"We have never called ourselves anything. We were simply brought to life through a god's creation and he made us immortal. However, I personally have a name: Jure," the king informed them. "And I was hoping to see you tonight."

"What for?" Jason growled.

"Not you, my boy," Jure laughed. "Her."

Ariel glared. "Why?"

"We think you are the key to something big. Something revolutionary!"

"The key to what?" Ariel asked. "Does a man named Ki have anything to do with this?"

Jure had never been more thrilled in all of his existence. He eyed her excitedly, hoping she was the one. "I wish I could tell you myself, but I think our sorcerer would prefer to speak with you. He'd explain it better than I."

"Who?" Ariel had spent tiring weeks investigating the Seoul case and yearned to know the ins and outs. She looked over at her parents, who held subtle faces at opposite ends of the table. Looking at their white faces not only hurt her heart but made her want to fight and free them from the wretched hell that overtook their humble souls—even if it meant killing them and allowing their spirits to rest in peace.

"Can we go now?" Ariel hurried.

"My pleasure," Jure grinned. "Come along. Jason, you can come, too."

Ariel's parents followed close behind as they followed Jure and Bathory down a steep set of stairs. The remainder of the council stayed behind. Round and round they went, descending many stairs into the lowest parts of the castle. The place was mostly quiet except for the echoing of their footsteps and the *woosh* coming from the torch flames as they passed.

Jason could also hear the rustling of the pale demons viciously celebrating the coming feast, through ripping and roaring of human flesh. The screams were becoming faint the further they went down.

Finally, they reached the sorcerer's lab.

"You ready?" Bathory asked, one pale hand upon the wooden door.

"Whatever," Ariel groaned.

Jure mentioned, "Be nice." He opened the door and once the assassins stepped into the white light, they couldn't believe their eyes.

"Holy shit!" Ariel exclaimed, then covered her mouth to swallow her screams.

"Oh, my god!" Jason cried.

Before them in the plain white room were people stuffed inside hollow tubes: naked and stripped of all bodily hair.

Their eyes and mouths were intact, closed, but from the neck down, hundreds of pins attached to what looked like floss, sucked out their blood and poured it into large plastic containers. Ariel's eyes widened at the sadistic horror before her. Jason wanted to vomit at the sight of their skin stretching from the pinpoints, so gruesomely that the bodies almost looked flat.

Jure looked back at Ariel with a small smirk. "They're alive. In a way."

Ariel was too shocked to say anything. Jason intervened. "What is this place?"

Bathory walked over to a containment tube and scraped the tips of her nails against the thick glass. Jason and Ariel cringed at the irritating sound.

"A blood bank," Bathory said.

Jason wanted clarification. "What did you say?"

"It's a blood bank," a random voice called out. "Do you like it?"

Ariel and Jason looked to the right to see a short man approaching from the other end of the laboratory. He looked similar to Captain Sying Orchid—slanted eyes, black hair, and light skin—but much older.

Ariel stepped forward. "Now, who the fuck are you?"

The man pulled out his right hand, and smiled. "Ki. Ki Marigold."

Both Jason and Ariel eyed him, steamed up and hardened their fists. A few moments passed before Ariel realized he had on a white coat and a notepad.

"You a scientist?" Ariel asked him.

Ki walked away, laughing. "You are quite the investigator."

Jason watched Ki attentively and readied his hand behind him in case he must pull out the big gun.

"I am," Ki assured. "However, my king and queen would rather call me their sorcerer. They say I have special powers."

"You do," Jure exclaimed. "If it weren't for you, we'd still be stuck with our second generation. They're good, just not"—he gaped at Leon and Symphony, still fascinated by what they'd become—"Great." He couldn't take his eyes off his immortal children.

It was Leon and Symphony who had made Jure's wish a reality, but Ariel didn't understand why they were so-called great. Still, Cyclamen had been right all along, which made Ariel wonder, *What else does that hideous bastard know?*

Ki sat at a desk with a 4-monitor computer: one of the most highly-priced pieces of technology Jason and Ariel had ever seen. Jason was hopelessly jealous—he had a love for computers.

With one press of a button, the tubes full of mutilated humans began descending into the floor beneath them. Once they reach ground zero, the floor was now a squeaky clean, pearly white, marble floor.

"What you just saw was a blood bank. Before you ask any further questions, I will explain." Ki grasped a tablet and brought up old news articles from 2136 After Plague. "Victor Haskoff. Have you heard of him?"

Jason scratched his head, trying to remember where he'd heard the name.

Ariel nodded. "He was that crazed lunatic that wanted to cure the Black Plague II viruses. He swore to the New World he would create an antibody, but he failed."

Jason eyed Ariel, remarking her detailed knowledge of a historical figure.

"Research," she said to him, and he shrugged.

"That's the short version, yes." Ki said, scrolling to the next picture. It was another news article about the New

World finally being rid of the Black Plague II Infection. "Do either of you know why the virus was called the Black Plague II?"

Jason put his foot down. "Come on, man. We don't have time to be quizzed. We want to know what the hell is going on."

However, Ariel wanted to play along. In her mind, it'd be best to do as he says but remain cautious of anything else conspicuous. "It was named after some event that happened in District Europe, or 'Europe,' as it was called before the plague."

Ki eyed Ariel for a moment, enjoying her surprising knowledge. "Good, but not quite right. The Black Plague was called the Black Death. Originally, it began in Central Asia, where flea-infested rodents, like rats, passed on plague disease when they snuck their way onto ships. The rodents then traveled over lands that circled the Mediterranean Sea—what we know now as the Great Heaven Sea—and from there, the Black Death consumed Europe and killed over 100 million of their population during the 1400's Before Plague. When the Black Plague II sprang upon our ancestors, the Earth's population went from over 8 billion people down to 200 million people in the span of 200 years. So, there's a slight similarity between the two plagues insofar as they devastated populations."

Ariel slid a finger under her collar, adjusting her shirt. Hearing about the death of millions irked her. "Okay," she shrugged, trying to be cool.

"That's at least what Earth's history books tell you," Ki rambled.

"Excuse me?" Jason asked.

"Everything I told you was a lie. A glorious lie that was carried on for centuries."

Growing impatient, Ariel growled. "Ugh! So what's the truth?!?"

Bathory spoke. "We killed all those people, my dear."

Bathory only caused more confusion.

We?!? Ariel thought. "You? How?"

Jure added, "My queen and I have been alive for a very, VERY, long time."

"No, you haven't!" Jason protested. "That's impossible."

"Listen to me, boy," Jure smiled. "We have been living for centuries. Believe it or not, we are the first of our kind. Like Akhenaten and Nefertiti, we were created by magical, spiritual and powerful humans. Even on our first day of life, we were the strongest, quickest, and smartest beings on Earth. We didn't need to feed on animals or vegetables or grain. All that we needed was human blood, and our people sacrificed many, many people to us. However, we have never seen the gift of light. Instead, we were night walkers that raided and killed sleeping armies against our creators. We never knew how long we would live, yet here we are. For eons, Bathory and I have survived. It wasn't until the 1200's Before Plague when we wanted to create a rawer, more murder-hungry army to feed our people and expand our population: The second generation was born during the late 1300's Before Plague by a man named Thomas Snow. He was the reason why we were able to kill and rebirth over 100 million people. We are the Black Death."

"All those people, you killed them by the millions," Ariel cried.

Bathory wasn't afraid to emphasize, "More like by the billions, sweet girl."

Jason was speechless…infuriated! His veins pulsed down his arms and his eye were red and bulging. They had killed the New World's ancestors quickly and effectively, with no signs of remorse. "The Black Plague II Infections: that was your plan, too?"

"No," Jure interrupted. The look in his eyes darkened as anger rose in his tone. "We do not know what caused that turmoil." Jure took long steps across the shiny floor and his oxford shoes squeaked. "It killed most of our people!"

"Like how you killed most of ours!" Ariel roared.

Jure swiftly floated across the metallic tile, hovered over Ariel and got as close to her face as possible. She could smell the horrible stench of blood that fumigated his mouth.

Jure grabbed the sides of her face, pushing harsh force into her temples and jawline. Immediately, Jason sprinted to Jure, about to knock him over. However, Bathory stretched out her hand and with a dinosaur-like claw, she lifted her arm up. Without touching him, she pulled Jason up from the ground, held him in midair, then tossed him across the room.

"My people are more important than your pathetic humans! What do you have to live for? You all are greedy, selfish, egotistical maggots that fog up this world. You kill everything you're afraid of. You've allowed differences to be the cause of continuous bloodshed. My people feed on yours to live, but we do not kill because you look, think, or act different. We kill because we have to! The Black Plague II killed my people, too!"

Ariel tried to release herself from his grip but even when she fought to break free, he only gripped her harder. With any more pressure, she was sure her bones would break.

Jure's breath rapidly shortened as he stared at the red-headed Death Dealer. Ki tapped his shoulder. "Let's not get carried away," he insisted.

Blurry, Jason was slowly picking himself up. His back was in terrible pain.

"Let me explain," Ki continued. Jure didn't let Ariel go. Instead, he brought her forward and gripped her by the hands and neck. "The Black Plague II aged people quickly and they died quickly. We do not know how it was transmitted or what caused it, but an infant could turn 30 overnight. A 30-year-old could turn 100 in a day. It varied from case-to-case—which you know by now."

Jure pulled Ariel's head back, nearly snapping her neck. "Argh! Mmhmm…."Ariel hissed.

"With humans dying, their people were dying. Once the infections ceased, Jure and Bathory wanted to bring it back—in a way."

"How the fuck is bringing back a pandemic going to solve their problems?!" Ariel shouted.

"Not only did I bring back the virus," Ki boasted. "I improved it!"

That was music to Bathory's ears. "You have done wonders, Sorcerer."

"What have you done?!" Ariel growled, still fighting with Jure, pulling and swiping, desperate to be let loose.

"Blood is most pure when a man or woman turns 27. It's hard to explain why, but through multiple human testing, our people seem to savor by that blood most. Like fine wine, blood ages gracefully, but only for so long." Ki keyed a couple of letters on his tablet. Out popped a single tube with a woman inside. "All of our subjects are 27 years old. By bringing back the virus, I have managed to perfectly age children and make someone older or younger in only three days. It's wonderful, I assure you. I keep the blood bank in my laboratory. I check their vital fluids and make sure the blood continues to flow serenely."

"How is that wonderful?" Ariel yelled, stiffly. Mercury's quillion was penetrating against her spine and she couldn't shake her off. "You're kidnapping people! Innocent people!! Defenseless children!! That is not something to be proud of."

"Oh, calm yourself," Ki asserted. "One of your losses is another one of their gains. It's survival of the fittest."

"What do you get out of all this?" Ariel tested. "You are obviously not one of them!"

"I will be," Ki sang. "I just prefer real food at this time. I'm not really in the mood for blood—at least not yet. For now, I would like to enjoy the simplicities of a human life. Besides, when I'm reborn, I will be immortal. Just like you."

"What?!" Ariel screamed. "This is bullshit! I'll never become one of you!"

"You will!" Ki said, menacingly. "We hope you are what we need. The psychic bond you have to Akhenaten and Nefertiti proves to be vital. No human has that power, to have linked visions with one of our own. That's stupendous. You may be the successor of the fourth generation of our people. Half-human, half-…what do you call us? Pale demon?"

"Fuck you!" Ariel spat as she began flinging her body about violently.

"Hold her!" Bathory commanded Jure.

"I will kill you all!" Ariel attempted to jump, hoping she'd spin backward and plow Jure in the face, but he was too strong. Even with Vitality in her bloodstream, he was much more powerful. His strength overshadowed Leon's times ten.

Leon and Symphony rushed over to the fighters.

Suddenly…. *AAAAHHH!!!*

Ariel shot a look over at Ki. His mouth was wide open, his head flung back. Behind him was Jason, with his pocket knife stabbed through his back.

"NO!!!" Bathory screamed.

Quickly, Jason pulled the knife out, and rushed to jab Ki's ribs. *Jab! Jab! Jab!* Jason flickered his hand so fast, before Leon and Symphony reversed their direction to head toward Jason, Ki was stabbed over fifteen times.

"Jason!" Ariel yelled. "Look out!"

Jason flung his head up and noticed Ariel's parents sprinting toward him. He ran back.

Growl! They were getting near. Leon lunged forward.

Ha! Jason ran forward, dropped to the ground, then slid underneath Leon's thin body.

Symphony was close to picking Jason up by his feet, but somehow he managed to shoot up and pound with a hardcore *punch!*

POW! Symphony jerked back.

Bathory was attempting to use her magic against Jason by trying to lift him above the ground, but nothing was affecting him. Before she knew it, Jason came at her with an elbow to the nose.

"Ack!" Bathory groaned.

Enraged, Jure pushed Ariel out of his way. She flew over Ki's monitors and banged right into the human tube. *Smack!*

"Fuuuck!"

Jason was now facing the king and queen of the pale demons. They glared at him, not allowing themselves a moment of sympathy for the umber-skinned assassin. They thought of him as another fool, a petty weakling with a feeling of entitlement, deserving none.

Ariel got up, worried that Jason may have been killed during her short fall. Jason was taking out his gun but she had feeling it was a useless weapon.

Relentless, Jason fired. *BANG!* The bullet flew right through Jure's skin without affliction.

Ariel scoured the room to find her parents, but they were gone. *Where did they go?* She panicked. *Backup?!* She refused to stay and find out.

Jason was still firing away, even though the bullets had zero affect. Suddenly, he felt a hand grab his arm.

"Let's get out of here!" Ariel shouted, holding onto her best friend.

Ariel ran for her life while Jason kept shooting. They were pointless, except that each shot bought them another half a second.

This was too dangerous for even the most brutal and experienced Death Dealer. No one in that situation would've been safe.

The assassins headed out the door and zoomed their way back up the stairs. As they ran, Jason spotted a distant window.

"Hey!" Jason shouted. "Look up!"

Ariel noticed the possible exit. She fiercely hurdled over the ledge. For a moment, she held onto it, checking if it was safe to drop. They were too high up.

Ariel scanned the scenery. A few trees were scattered all around. Without much thought, she jumped and landed on a thin branch. She stopped and waited for Jason.

Jason popped out the window and, like Ariel, gripped the ledge just in time.

"Over here!" Ariel screamed.

Jason noticed her post and hurriedly headed in her direction.

Woosh! He landed on the same branch.

"Hurry!" Ariel yelled. "If we jump across a few trees then climb our way down, we can get the hell out of here!"

Jason surveyed the trees, in hopes of finding one with thick, solid limbs. "Follow me!"

Ariel copied all of Jason's moves to refrain from making any fatal mistakes. The moon seemed to follow them as they flew through the bare, skinny trees.

Finally, Jason poled himself down to the ground with Ariel close behind. Once they hit rock bottom, the best friends got the hell out of there. They booked it all the way to the secret entrance without looking back.

Amazingly, they made it to the surface but did not stop there. They rushed over to the van, crumbling the thin twigs and dead leaves underneath their boots, creating a choir of echoes.

Jason unlocked the car from a few feet away.

They threw themselves inside, tightened their seatbelts, then sped off!

"I'm sorry," Jason cried.

Ariel's eyes watered and she covered her face with her hands.

"I'm so fucking sorry," Jason continued. "Those are your parents. You did have visions. Everything you were talking about was the truth, and I'm sorry for not believing you."

Sobbing, Ariel threw herself at Jason and wrapped her arms tightly around his chest. Jason brought an arm over her shoulder and kissed her head.

"Forgive me?" Jason needed forgiveness. He messed up—bad.

For the first time, Ariel did not want to hold a grudge. Not only did she need her best friend, he needed her: they needed one another. Like Queen Kora had said the day of the court hearing, they were at their best when they worked together. Even though Jason had been in the wrong, she loved having him back in her life. And she never wanted to lose him again.

"Always."

LORD OF LIFE, FORGIVE ME

Jason sped all the way back to headquarters. So much was happening and in so little time. Ariel knew it was time for the cabinet to approve the moonlit mercury weapons, and fast! She spoke to her captain about the dilemma both Faction Divide and Abyss would face if they failed to have their special weaponry soon.

"The pale demons said next moonrise they would attack, but after the chaos you and I created, who knows if they'll wait that long." Ariel's heart dropped at the thought of her comrades dying, innocents dying, the whole New World dying. "We can't take any chances. The cabinet needs to hurry up!"

Jason nodded while keeping a close watch for any pedestrians that might pass by. His foot was heavy on the gas pedal, and someone could get hurt if he wasn't careful.

"We must remember to elaborate on what we saw," Jason urged. "Even if they don't believe us, we have to fight our way through them. There's no time for voting or processing. We need those weapons stat." Jason lowered his eyes and sighed. He glanced over at Ariel before setting his eyes back on the road. "I didn't agree with Bodhi's petition because I was mad at you. I wanted nothing to do with you. I was wrong. Personally, as captain, I should've helped. It would've hurried things up. Sorry."

Ariel only looked at the ghostly corrupt buildings that haunted the streets of Seoul. "Well, better late than never, I guess."

Jason failed as a friend but he was going to make it up to her.

As they entered headquarters, Jason swerved into an empty parking spot. As soon as he shut off the engine, Ariel shouted, "Shit!"

Jason slapped a hand to his chest, feeling his heart as he jolted in his seat. "Woah!" he screamed. "What's wrong?!"

Ariel growled as she grabbed both sides of her scalp. "Argh! I didn't ask Ki about evolution! Th...th...the language: what it was, why he chose it and why he's using it." She pounded the glove compartment with her boot. "Gah! I'm such an idiot!"

Ah! Jason snapped his fingers. He glided his hand under his seat and pulled out a seven-inch, three-ring binder. He eyed it confusingly while flipping it side to side.

Ariel asked what it was. Jason said nothing. Only handed over the thick binder.

Ariel opened it up and flipped through the uneven pages. There were piles of notes, pictures, diagrams, formulas and charts that all belonged to Ki. Intrigued, she skimmed through the papers, trying to understand exactly what was between her hands. There were loads of information: the beginning of the blood bank, Doctor Victor Hashkoff's essays, news articles surrounding the Black Plague II Infections and much, much more!

After feeling like Jason handed her a treasure chest, Ariel finally asked, "How did you get your hands on this?"

Jason chuckled and placed his hands behind his back, remembering the harsh *crunch* that seared down his back earlier. Thinking about his spine smashing straight into the hard floor sent him pulses of pain.

"When you all were distracted by each other, I crawled my way over to Ki's desk and grabbed his notebook. I hoped it was important."

"It's kind of obvious, isn't it?" Ariel mocked while examining a detailed picture of a man undergoing the blood bank tube. Approximately 250 .25mm needles are used per person to draw out two pints of blood in sloth-like speed every 112 days.

Wow..., Ariel thought, *Imagine if this was your life.*

Jason pointed to a random word when she flipped to the next page. He tapped abruptly, bouncing the binder on her knees. "What does that say?'

*Ummm....*Ariel's forehead wrinkled up as she hissed, "Tests...?"

With a proud smile, Jason said, "I can't read it. All I see are words written in a secret language that everyone originally thought were neat shapes. You can read it. I can't."

Ariel looked back at Ki's chicken scratch all over different materials of paper. If only she remembered to ask him what language it was.

"I know for a fact that not only will you figure out how to read this without magic but you'll find out the name of the language in no time." Jason hopped out the car and opened Ariel's passenger door. "Don't worry. You got this!"

After a deep breath, Ariel hugged the binder close to her chest.

"Question."

"Yeah?"

Ariel narrowed her eyes and bit her bottom lip. "Bathory used magic on you twice but the second time, nothing happened. How did you manage that?"

Jason flipped out a small bottle filled with a misty grey liquid. "Come on now. This is simple magic. Have you never heard of a magic shield potion?"

Ariel felt ridiculous. That was Magic 101! Even she could figure that out if she put her mind to it.

"Since when do you carry that in your pocket?"

"Always have in case of emergencies."

"Smart."

Jason placed the teeny bottle back in his coat pocket. "Let's get inside."

Most people were either home or asleep inside, but luckily, the best friends noticed an average-looking secretary relieving herself for the evening.

"Excuse me," Jason called out. "Can you give me either Captain Orchid's or Sergeant Tulip's phone number? I need their personal, I only have their business phones. Actually, their addresses would be better. This is an emergency!"

"I'm sorry," she responded, "but I'm tired and I want my bed and I am not allowed to give away any personal information. Good-night!"

The brunette with purple-framed glasses—more violet than Ariel's eyes—tried to stomp her way out the door. Ariel didn't blame her because it was late, however, this was important. She noticed the tag on her right breast. "Megan?"

The girl grimaced, exhausted by her confinement to the same damn room for over ten hours. "Listen, I can't help you two."

Jason intervened. "As captain of Faction Divide, I demand—"

"I know who you are," Megan interrupted. She was too exhausted to care of his importance. "Look," she huffed, pondering at the sight of a door that would lead the way to her freedom, "Captain Orchid gave me strict rules about not giving out his personal information. With all due respect, he did include captains and sergeants. He enjoys his life outside the DDAG in private." She was about to storm out, but not before concluding with, "Oh! Same goes for Sergeant Tulip. Goodnight."

As the sound of Megan's clinking heels trailed off, Ariel snuck over to the tired receptionist's desk while Jason was trying to come up with another plan. "We could try to call Sergeant Lotus but he's probably still too hot-headed right now."

Tap-tap-tap-tap-tap-tap....Jason glanced over his shoulder and noticed Ariel at Megan's computer. Nervously, he sidled over to her but kept his eyes open for anyone who might pass. "What are you doing?" he whispered, bending over the counter, trying to look over the monitor. Ariel typed away as Jason glared at her for not responding. "Are you always this cheerful when you're under stress?"

Ariel was horribly exhausted but she did not sneak into a pale demon lair and almost have her head removed for nothing. Innocents could get slaughtered if she wasted anymore time.

Annoyed, Jason walked over to the opposite side of the desk and concentrated on Ariel's battle with the keyboard. An overwhelming amount of folders were open, but one was well-cited: it was a *Contacts* folder.

"Are you locating Orchid's address?" Jason asked.

"Better," Ariel grinned. "I'm looking up Queen Kora."

Looking up the king and queen's information was far beyond against the law, though Ariel wasn't a virgin to law-breaking. When Jason first learned of his best friend's crude actions, he questioned everything about her: her maturity, her drive, her determination and her career as a professional assassin. Over time, he had learned that was simply who his best friend was and nothing was going to change that. In fact, he could now think, in full confidence, that he wouldn't change a thing about her.

"Why the queen?" Jason wondered. Surely, she had better things to do than see them.

Ah! Ariel found what she needed and quickly printed out a sheet of perfectly useful information. "I don't know how she'll react to us showing up at her home, but I know she'll listen."

Ariel felt like she had already prevailed. Queen Kora would demand her whole force to create the moonlit mercury weapons for the Death Dealers to siege and defeat the pale demons. Ariel felt certain Queen Kora would not deny her or Jason in their time of desperation. Faction Divide and Faction Abyss must battle soon or the human race would become extinct.

Jason and Ariel rushed over to the portal gate. The weather was finally starting to warm up and the fresh green grass grew so tall, it was hugging the hinges of the portal's legs. The flowers would soon bloom.

Ariel looked into the bright blue light and chanted, "District Europe headquarters." As soon as the fire spread out its beckoning flames, the captain and his warrior flew to the other side of the portal gate and were now in the gardens of Faction Masquerade: a district vastly different from Divide.

When Ariel trained in the city of London, she loved every minute of it. It was a *new world* all on its own. District North America, primarily Manhattan, New York, used to be known as "The One District." Innocents from all over the globe would trot their way through that bountiful world of beautiful architecture, live jazz music, tasty sweet treats and entrepreneurship. However, within the last decade, swarms of gangs had migrated into the land of perpetual freedom. Quickly, innocents grew terrified to continue living their simple lives in their once-safe haven. Each gang claimed their territory with spray-painted logos drawn across a series of neighborhoods. Families were forced out of their homes and businesses suffered from constant robberies. If it weren't for Ariel, the crime rate may have doubled or even tripled since the rise of gang migration.

Daily, Ariel would snoop through the auto-denied case files and help those who could not defend themselves. She had saved about a hundred people on her own, including small families. Over time, she had enough of Sergeant Lotus ignoring those who cried for help. Never weakening or giving up, she fought long and hard for auto-denied cases to be taken into account. After a harsh feud pitting Ariel Rose and Jason Lilly versus Sergeant Kurtis Lotus and the royal cabinet, a law had been passed called, "The Innocents Consideration Law." From then on, every single case had to be looked at, cross examined and taken with the utmost seriousness and respect. Even with a new law and support from the New World's hierarchy, a low percentage of cases were still being pushed aside. Because of this, Ariel continued to snoop through ignored files and take on the bad guys one at a time; old habits die hard.

Being in London brought Ariel back satisfying memories. London was now called "The One District," and for good reason. Not only was crime scarce, the entire district was well-populated, wealthy, and economically booming. It was one of the few places in the world that still carried a rich history from before the plague. Europe had preserved many, many books and scripts in their libraries and museums. Ariel gained most of her knowledge of castles in places like Ireland, Scotland, Italy and Greece. Positivity flooded

London and even the vaguest individual couldn't resist the liveliness of the city. Ariel wanted to live in London once, but not if it meant being part of a faction less desirable than her cherished Divide. Maybe one day, after she retired.

Jason brought out his 3-D map and inserted Kora's address. Luckily, she only lived two blocks away from the headquarters' tall clock.

London was five hours ahead of New York and the sun shined through the thick grey clouds. The rain loved Europe. It heavily nourished the district with clean water, making it the greenest and healthiest part of the globe. The air always smelled fresh and inhaling the moisture felt clean.

Jason and Ariel ran through the streets filled with busybodies—most of them grabbing a bite for lunch.

Beep! The map chirped. They had reached their destination.

Ariel was in awe. Even though Kora lived in an apartment, the architecture was exquisite and rich. The complex was built like a miniature castle, but instead of using traditional grey stone blocks, it was kept together by a vanilla exterior. The porches, although small, were closed off by small black balustrades, around which rose vines curled.

"What's her apartment number?" Jason asked while shutting off his map.

Ariel answered, "31C." She was in the fourth apartment on the lower level. Before walking up the small stairs, Jason and Ariel made sure their appearances were decent. Jason tucked in his shirt and put away his gloves while Ariel ran her long fingers through her velvet locks, hoping to get most of the tangles out. "Ready?"

Jason nodded.

"Alright." Ariel lead the way. She inhaled the cool, crisp air and slowly let it all go. *Here we go.*

Knock, knock.

Jason looked around, trying to busy himself.

No one came to the door and Ariel asked if she should knock again, but he only shrugged.

Ariel bit her tongue, pondering for a moment. Before she was able to knock again, the door slowly opened.

Kora answered in a short, white negligee and see-through robe. Even outside the DDAG she looked like a million bucks.

"Ariel? Jason?" Kora was surprised to see two assassins at her doorstep. She rarely had visitors because her life revolved around work, but now having two guests whom she'd never spoken with outside of District North America was randomly odd. "May I help you?"

"I apologize, my queen," Ariel said while bowing. "We wouldn't be here if it weren't an emergency."

"I would ask how you found me, but I have a feeling I know how," Kora said, smiling at Ariel.

When Kora turned to Jason, she caught him ogling at her body. Easily, she could've been offended, but she'd be a liar if she said she wasn't flattered. After all, he was insanely handsome and young. It felt great to have someone fifteen years younger drooling over her. "Captain Lilly."

*Mmmm....*Jason cleared his throat. "My queen!" He bent at the knee and put it his head down. "I also apologize for the inconvenience, but my Death Dealer, Ariel Rose, is telling the truth. We wouldn't be here if it wasn't an emergency."

Kora tied off her robe at the waist then stepped aside. With a kind gesture, she invited them into her home. "Stop saying sorry, and come in."

Before Ariel entered her home, she imagined Kora being a collector of Earth antiques and top-of-the line everything. To her surprise, Kora lived simply.

The color scheme was strictly white and silver, creating an effect of a breezy, open space. In the living room were a couch, a loveseat and a glass coffee table holding a silver tray, on which sat three round candles. No paintings, no books, no extra shelving or side tables.

"Would either of you like some tea or coffee?" Kora asked as they followed behind.

"Allow me to get that for you," Jason insisted.

Kora shooed him away. "Never get in the way when someone is offering you a drink in their home. Now, what do you want to drink?"

"Tea for me, please," Jason said, thankful and eager to satisfy his thirst. Ariel asked for water with lemon instead.

They were led to a small kitchen with a large window and a great view of London's grand Ferris wheel. It had been dismantled a hundred years ago, but it was brought back to life the year Ariel was born, after a petition with over a million signatures begged the king and queen to have it be rebuilt and refurbished.

In the kitchen's corner was an adorable breakfast table with a bowl of fruit in the center and four chairs. The best friends sat down and patiently waited for their queen to join them.

Kora brought over their drinks of choice while she got comfortable with a glass of water with frozen raspberries used as ice cubes.

"So, you've found me." Kora smiled at them. "I am your queen and neither of you are less than worthy to ask of my assistance, even when I am dozed out."

Ariel looked out the window. "My days are opposite of yours," Kora laughed. "I get my rest during the daytime here in order to work the required hours in District North America."

"Do you never see the moon?" Ariel asked, wondering how only seeing the bright star would affect someone's sanity.

"Rarely," Kora frowned. "I miss it, honestly."

Jason asked, "Why don't you move to Manhattan? It would be more of a convenience for you."

Kora shook her head and grabbed an apple from the fruit bowl. "District Europe is my home. Not only was I born and raised here, but so were my mom and dad, and their parents, too. I love my home and I wouldn't want to be anywhere else in the New World. Plus, you're only queen for five years. If sacrificing the moonlight is what I have to do in order to remain in my minimalist home with my friends and family minutes away, then it must be done."

Moonlight! Ariel remembered why she and Jason were there. *Moonlit mercury!* "Forgive me, my queen, but with all due respect, I'd like to quickly catch you up on why Captain Lilly and I are here. Again, I am sorry for—"

Kora put her hand up, mouthing *shhh....* "No. Stop apologizing, and you're not disrespecting me in the least. Please, tell me what is going on."

Jason mainly sat back in silence while Ariel took over story time. She began with the bombing of the Golden Throne Ballroom, all the way up to the pale demon lair. Ariel opened up Ki's notebook and explained the blood bank more thoroughly, using the illustrations as a guide to not forget anything.

"All-in-all, I believe Jure and Bathory want to create a whole new generation of pale demons by having complete control over how humans evolve." Randomly, the image of the young boy being taken away in a black van fell into Ariel's head. Still, it made her cringe to think there was no age limit of the victims those murderers chose. "They don't care about who they kill. Those things were created specifically to ward off enemies. Love was obviously not programmed into their DNA."

Jason added, "The king and queen of the pale demons said they will attack during the next moonrise, but we're afraid we may have sped up their battle plans. We'd love for you and the king to convince the royal cabinet that we need moonlit mercury weapons stat."

Kora sighed. Her heart was heavy and her eyes watered at the sight of men, women and children being shoved into tubes and pricked with endless needles. "I am not a blacksmith, but don't weapons take a decent amount of time to be created? Especially with moonlit mercury?"

"Yes," Ariel rushed. "But the man who made my dagger, Mercury, is a top-of-the-line professional. I'd like to speak to him; he lives in the Outerwoods of District Antarctica. Before he created Mercury, he did mention this: The longer the sorcery takes to craft an enchanted weapon, the more powerful it becomes. He may not be able to create the weapons as strong and solidified as mine; however, they'd be forceful enough to hold off their plans of total world domination. We'd scare them, hopefully. They would have no choice but to fall back and try another day."

Kora got up from her chair and walked over to her wine rack. Carefully, she skimmed through the panels, choosing wisely to satisfy her taste buds. Ariel suggested dry white wine. "That is a grand idea," the beautiful, fairy-like queen agreed. She brought out three tall glasses and filled them up to the rim. Carefully, she watched her step as she carried them all between her petite fingers.

Kora handed a glass to Jason, who graciously accepted—even though he hated wine—and handed one with a purple stem to Ariel. The queen lifted up her glass and the captain and assassin shadowed her movements. "I will speak to the royal cabinet but I am adding a request: After you finish your glass of wine, I'd like for you both to speak to the man who created Mercury directly and ask him to make the weapons as soon as possible. We will not wait for the cabinet to make up their minds. They will waste all the time they can muster and my people are my priority, not them. Do we have a deal?"

Jason and Ariel grinned, raising their glasses even higher. "Deal!"

They clinked their glasses together, and Kora finished her wine in one smooth gulp. "I expect to hear back from you on Monday morning. Good luck!"

Before running away to Antarctica, Ariel and Jason were exhausted and desperate for some shut-eye. They drove to Aunt Faith's home and went no further than her living room. Ariel flung herself to the couch while Jason cuddled up on an accent chair and plopped up his feet on a matching footrest. He dozed off as soon as Faith covered him up in a warm blanket.

After sleeping for a few hours, Ariel changed into some warm clothes for their day trip to McMurdo Station in Antarctica. It was drastically cold there, but Ariel loved it. Almost daily, the world was paved in snow and the city's night lights varied with columns of bright colors throughout every neighborhood. The population was tiny—ranging between one hundred to two hundred Rural Outsiders—but everyone was genuinely happy. Small families colonized together and grew crops with their magical seeds that survived even through the harshest conditions.

Jason drove straight home before going to headquarters, also grabbing his heaviest coat and snow pants. Finally, they ventured off to District Antarctica.

Their headquarters—Faction Aurora—was located in the South Pole and was the smallest of all seven districts. The castle felt more like a small home than a Death Dealer Alliance Guild, but Ariel adored the simplicity of the castle's cozy structure. There was one bailey—the main bailey—and no "real" garden. There was a ginormous carpet of fake grass around the castle walls that added a bit of life to the bland snow-scape, but Ariel wondered if trees and flowers and bushes could have added some character. Inside, the library looked more like a first level classroom and the main entrance had the cramped faux-hominess of a doctor's office. Overall, it was cute.

Outside, only one sniper was guarding the entrance. Ariel asked one of the local Death Dealers how long it'd take them to drive to McMurdo Station.

"It's about 900 miles out," the young assassin averaged.

"Shit," Ariel huffed. "I don't remember it taking that long."

The handsome man laughed, and the snow on his goatee trickled off with each bountiful chuckle. "Yeah, the drive can range up to fifteen hours and the Rural Outsiders don't believe in travel portals. You may as well hurry up, now."

A lightbulb shined in Jason's head. "Do you have a plane?" he asked, hopeful.

The Death Dealer nodded. "We do, but we don't have any pilots out here. At least not today."

Jason grinned. "You do now," he smacked. "May I borrow your plane?" Ariel had forgotten Jason learned how to fly while he was training in District South America. How could she? He bragged about it for weeks.

"Uh…," the man hesitated. "I don't know if that's such a good idea."

"Please, Mr.—"

"Call me Luke," the assassin insisted. "Calling me mister makes me feel like an old man."

"Okay, Luke," Jason said, respectfully. "We have orders from Queen Kora Amaryllis, herself. This is an emergency and it's a matter of life and death. Not just for my guild but for yours, Australia, South America—all of us, and the innocents of the New World. We have to speak to the Rural Outsiders now, and we cannot waste any time. Please, show me your plane and I will speak to your sergeant if you'd like, so you will not get into any trouble."

Astonished, Luke asked, "Queen Kora really sent you?"

"Yes," Ariel answered, hoping he'd hurry.

Luke looked over them both and evidentially gave in. "Alright," he sighed. "Follow me."

Jason and Ariel walked with Luke a few miles up the road—a straight shot from Faction Aurora's headquarters—and ended up at an aircraft hangar. Before them was a midnight blue Twin Otter aircraft, perfect for their travel. Luke escorted them inside and handed over the keys to Jason. "Please, be careful with her, Captain Lilly."

Jason understood completely. "Will do. Thank you, Luke."

"You're welcome. I'll either be here or back at headquarters when you get back."

"Thanks," Ariel said, rushing the conversation. "We'll see you soon. Jason, let's hurry up."

After parting ways, Jason and Ariel hopped into the plane, which was roomy enough for six more passengers, and prepared for takeoff. Jason's adrenaline pumped. It had been years since he'd flown a plane. He inspected the body, checked for any damaged parts or low fluids, and read the gasoline meter. The components worked flawlessly and they were good on gas and emergency supplies. After starting the engine, Jason placed his feet on the rubber pedals and his hands around the yoke in the cockpit. Slowly, he drove the aircraft to the run-up area and ensured his plane was ready to fly safely. Everything was perfect. Jason pushed the fuel knob and advanced the yoke slowly to increase the engine's performance. Once the plane felt ready, Jason sped up gradually down the runway. Luckily, there was no wind to worry about, so he figured the flight should be smooth. Faster and faster the aircraft went and as soon as the plane gently bounced from the ground, Jason pulled back the yoke and lifted Ariel and himself into the cold, crisp air.

"Woohoo!" Ariel screamed, excited to be on a plane for the first time. Slowly, the ground beneath them expanded until the city looked like it was built with children's blocks. For two hours, Ariel looked over the most inspiring atmosphere. The mountains were buried in white, with a few of their tops baring the sedimentary rock beneath the thick blanket. The sea had cracked blocks of snow sprinkling over its still waters like powdered sugar. As they soared through the fluffy clouds, Ariel felt free. It was nice to get away from the noises of the New World. She could get used to the silence and the beauty of District Antarctica. She could certainly retire in London, but perhaps she'd visit here from time to time.

Finally, the neon lights of McMurdo Station appeared. Ariel suggested they make a low-key landing. She did not want to startle the Rural Tribes. They may have been peaceful, but if they felt threatened, they were brutal killers. Almost Death Dealer level—almost.

Jason landed close to a colossal mountain that looked like three conjoined pyramids.

"You ready?" Ariel asked.

"Let's do this!" Jason cheered.

They disembarked from the cockpit and landed on a soft cushion of snow. They trailed down to the Rural Tribe's grounds and casually entered the small city. Ariel looked around, trying to remember the layout of McMurdo.

Jason had never seen a city—or station, rather—so small. It was kind of adorable. However, he found it odd that there was not a vehicle, tree or shrub in sight. Only homes and a few small businesses over layers of snow, including a salad bar, a tea lounge, and a farmer's market. The roads were created with molten lava by a Rural Tribe that lived around two-hundred years ago. After climbing Antarctica's most active volcano, the tribesmen and women used their magic to halt its eruption and gather pounds of lava to create the roads and square houses seen today. Jason had heard that it never snows or rains in Antarctica, so vegetation had to be mostly cared for through magic. Well, that's what he assumed.

Ariel and Jason passed some orange lights on a lamppost.

"We're close. I believe he lives towards the green lights just two blocks up." Ariel bit her tongue. "Yes! I think…."

"You haven't failed me yet," Jason assured. "If you are set in that direction, then let's move on."

"You got it, Captain." Ariel marched forward, her boots crunching deep into the thicket of snow.

While they were approaching the man's home, Ariel stiffened. "What if he doesn't want to help us?" she worried.

Jason shrugged. "Then, we have to piss on the royal cabinet to hurry up. We'll prevail even without the Rural Outsiders. I mean it."

"Thanks, but I'm tired of fighting," Ariel admitted. "We need help. I don't want to be questioned anymore."

"Any help you ask for, you will receive," Jason said. "Let's go in there and see what happens before assuming the worst, okay?"

Ariel nodded and moved forth. She knocked on the man's door and said a silent prayer: *Lord of Life, please make this quick.*

A clamor came from the room when the door opened. A woman in a heavy, black chenille coat and black, faux leather snow boots appeared.

"Dior!" Ariel screeched, fanning out her arms.

"Ariel, my girl, come here!" Dior screamed, gifting her with friendly kisses on the cheek.

Jason stood back, waiting for Ariel to introduce him.

"How are you doing?" Dior asked, happy to see her good friend once again.

"I'm great," Ariel lied. "By the way, this is Jason, also known as Captain Lilly of District North America, Faction Divide."

Dior embraced him with a generous hug. "Nice to meet you. I heard a lot about you when Ariel visited my husband."

"I wish I could say the same." Jason glanced around the room, noticing the merry people dancing and drinking. There were dozens of people—beautiful families that looked grateful for the simple lives they lived, despite their world being 99-percent ice. Dior's home looked more like a hotel, especially with the grand space in the living room alone. Jason could only imagine how big their bedroom must be.

But why would an outsider want to live in such huge space? It didn't make any sense.

Seeing people so carefree made Jason a bit envious. "Who's your husband?" he asked.

"Baptiste," Dior sang with love in her heart. "He created Mercury."

"That's why we're here," Ariel chimed in. "I must speak to him—it is extremely important. Is he busy?"

Dior chuckled. "For you? Never. I'll go grab him. Wait here and enjoy some ale or wine or liquor. If you prefer something non-alcoholic, we have tea and juice. I'll be right back."

As the woman trailed away, Jason muttered. "And you were afraid of what, exactly?"

"Shut up," Ariel groaned.

The room continued on with their pleasant evening. The tribe was so comfortable with their way of life and Ariel adored that. The band was on fire. The sounds of poppy flutes and slapping guitar made the scene cheery and irresistible. In Jason's corner of the room was a small bar where an attractive bartender with teal-colored hair was cleaning the counter.

Jason asked Ariel if he could grab her a drink. "Wheat ale if they have it," she responded.

Jason walked over as the bartender was counting her money from the tip jar.

"Excuse me," Jason called out politely. The beauty gazed at him with her jaded eyes.

"Hello!" she greeted as dimples formed from her cute smile. "What would you like?"

"Do you have wheat ale and red ale in stock?" Jason hoped.

The bartender moved her fingers with ease as she impressively pulled out two bottles from a cabinet, slid them on the countertop and in a second flat, popped off the caps.

Obviously, she was a professional, but something about the way she looked at him filled him with lust. Did she happen to be interested in him? He could only wish.

"That'll be two ichor, please," the lovely lady smiled with a twinkle in her eye.

Jason pulled out two shiny green coins with an omega symbol on one side and the Lord of Life symbol on the other: an infinity symbol with a fiery star in the middle. "You know what," he added, grabbing an extra ichor coin. "Keep the change."

"Big spender, huh?" the bartender teased. She took the money from his hand and introduced herself. "I'm Abigail."

"That's a cute name." Jason kept staring at her exotic face. She had perfect bone structure—high cheekbones, diamond chin—and her eyes were feline-shaped. Her skin was similar to Ivy's, but more of a darker caramel. It was rare to see a woman with electric hair and facial piercings. Seeing an alternative beauty made Jason giddy—the feeling was similar to his first sexual awakening during second level school. Confusing but arousing. "I'm Jason Lilly," he said, then bowed.

When Jason emerged, Abigail was caught laughing. "What's so funny?" Jason asked.

"I don't believe anyone has ever bowed to a bartender before," Abigail recalled. "How adorable."

Jason snorted. "I've been trained to treat a pretty lady with respect. Do you work here, or…?"

Abigail chuckled. "Baptiste hired me to bartend at his hotel."

"What?" Jason asked. "Hotel?! Isn't this his house?"

"Yes." Abigail nodded. "If someone needs a place to stay, he'll offer them a bed, food and water free-of-charge the first night, then fifteen ichor for the following nights. But he also does live here. He and his wife sleep on the top floor. He loves helping people, so he created his home to cater to travelers or husbands thrown out by their wives."

Jason laughed hysterically. "That's a man's man, right there."

Ariel approached Jason. "We have to go," she whispered, squeezing his arm. "He's ready to talk."

Jason stood in between the two gals, hating to leave the teal beauty behind. However, his best friend and Baptiste were waiting for him. "I'll be right there."

Ariel nodded. "Hurry up," she emphasized. "We're going to be outside in the back near the campfire."

As Ariel walked away, Abigail couldn't help but ask who she was. "That's my best friend," Jason sneered before taking a sip of his red beer. "I have to go—business—but it was nice meeting you."

"Same," Abigail praised. "I'll see you around."

"You sure will," Jason gloated. "Bye."

Outside, Ariel, Baptiste and Dior were sitting on a log in front of a roaring fire. The wind picked up some speed, causing the flame to prance around.

Jason quietly joined them, respecting Ariel as she spoke. Jason always thought his best friend was a convincing speaker, but today, ever since their mini trip to London, there was more confidence and certainty in her tone.

"The pale demons said they would move on the next moonrise, which is roughly a month away, but we need to be prepared before that in case they make a surprise attack. Thousands of good people may be butchered sooner than we think. Without the moonlit mercury weapons, we all may become pale demon-fodder. Could you help us?" Ariel's cold hands tightened together as the anticipation coiled inside her ribs.

"What do you say?" Jason asked, handing Ariel her drink.

The wife and husband looked at one another. Without words, they both knew what they were agreeing to.

"Ariel," Baptiste began in a hoarse voice. He was fairly old. His braided hair was a mixture of white and grey and depressed wrinkles had overtaken his skeletal face. Dior had to be around the same age or a little younger. Unlike her husband, she did have some grey strands but the dominating color of her tangled hair was a faded auburn. You could tell she loved to smile due to the fine lines around her small lips. Baptiste held his wife's hand proudly. "The poor people of the New World do not deserve to be preyed upon by the Lord of Darkness' monsters."

"Do you really believe he created them?" Ariel lifted her bottle and drank some ale.

"Yes, I do," Baptiste said. "The Dark Lord works in mysterious, unnatural ways. I have not forgotten my history lessons on the Black Plague II Infections. The Lord of Darkness did that. I wish the Lord of Life had stopped him—killed him off. Sadly, it was out of his control. Now, he's at it again with an army."

With that being said, it was hard to think of him opposing the request. "So, will you help us?" Jason asked, hoping for a good answer.

"Of course," Baptiste consented. His wife clapped ecstatically.

Ariel threw her arms around the happy couple. "Thank you!" she cried. "I'd kiss you but I don't think that's appropriate."

Dior giggled. "My dear, you'd make an old man happy."

Ariel squished his face with a hard kiss on the forehead. "Thank you, thank you!!!"

"Before you get too excited, there are a few cons to your idea," Baptiste said, making Ariel nervous.

"Okay," she said, sitting back down. "Please, explain."

"In order to reach its full potential, your dagger took six months to create." Baptiste extended his arms. Ariel reached over for Mercury and placed her in his aged hands. "That was working over ten hours a day, seven days a week." He felt Mercury's smooth body, remembering the loving craftsmanship he had put into it. Mercury was his favorite piece of art. He never thought he'd see her again. "You need me to create weapons for two guilds before a month's span. This can be done. I have been training my people to do this for years. They're professionals. However, they will not be at their strongest."

"I had a feeling," Ariel acknowledged. "I did inform Queen Kora of this."

Baptiste held Mercury up against the moonlight and watched it glow with power. "The more you allow your dagger to bathe in the moonlight, the more powerful it becomes. It will never stop consuming power, unless you stop it. However, if a weapon is not given enough time to be born and baptized in the light of the moon by a sorcerer, it may break."

No! Ariel thought. *This is not good.* "What are the chances of that happening?!"

Dior shrugged. "We do not know. We've never tested it. What we'll do is pray to the Lord of Life to help us and we'll put all of our energy and magic into these weapons. I promise, all of us will do our best."

Baptiste handed Mercury back to Ariel. "Here, here!" he agreed.

Ariel was grateful. "Thank you." She hugged them again, trying not to lose control. Her tears trickled down into their coats. Jason rubbed Ariel's back.

"We'll kill those fuckers," Jason exclaimed. "If we die, we die together, fighting for the greater good."

Ariel and Jason slammed their fists together, feeling united. "For the greater good."

"The greater good!" Baptiste and Dior cheered. "To the Death Dealers!"

"Woo!" Jason roared.

Together, they all raised their glasses and howled into the dark sky. Jason and Ariel stayed the night drinking with their friends and praying for victory.

It was Monday morning. Time to get back to business. The best friends met up with Queen Kora and King Sebastian Peony in the courtroom.

It was more gloomy than usual and the room was deadly quiet. Everyone put on their best business professional clothing in order to be taken seriously. Ariel felt hot, despite the seventy-two-degree temperature outside. She could hardly tell if it was the stuffiness of the courtroom or her anxiety consuming her body.

The king informed the captain and his assassin of his knowledge about the weapons, thanks to his queen. "We'll be sure to convince the royal cabinet to approve your requests. Do you have any questions before the hearing begins?" Jason and Ariel assured they didn't. "Sit back and relax, and hopefully this will be quick and easy."

All twelve men and women from the cabinet entered the courtroom. They sat in their assigned seats along rows of rounded benches.

Ariel fell into the bench with arms crossed over her chest, her breath ragged.

"This is going to be a long day," Jason muttered.

The door behind them opened and Bodhi entered, followed by a group of DDAG assassins. Together they stomped, echoing through the once-quiet courtroom. The assassins sat as close as possible to the front. Ivy cut her way through the crowd over to Ariel and sat next to her. With a soft smile, Ariel whispered, "I'm glad you're here." Ivy blushed.

The king rose and everyone stood up with him. "Thank you all for taking the time out of your busy schedules to be here. I am King Sebastian Peony and to my left is my beautiful queen, Kora Amaryllis. Today, we are here to discuss the Moonlit Mercury Weapons Petition. Anyone who would like to come to the podium and speak to the royal cabinet will have a chance to before a final decision is made. There are no rules as to how to speak. Just refrain from any vulgar language and speak nothing but the truth. You all may sit." The crowd shuffled back to their seats. "Let's begin."

The royal cabinet had turned the entire petition into a complex situation. For two hours, the cabinet was in stern opposition to the weapons simply because, "It would cost the royal bank too much money."

Ariel took the podium, catching every assassin's eye as she made the long walk up front. She spoke about the Royal Outsiders in District Antarctica, but they refused to work with an outside source. For fun, she asked, "What would you do if I told you they were more than willing to create these weapons for us and they happily accepted? Would you still refuse their donation?"

A man with glasses and a bald spot turned maroon. "That is illegal! We cannot provide weapons to our armies without examining their tactics and work ethics and magic. For your sake, I hope you hadn't done that Ms. Rose."

Ariel flushed, digging her nails on both sides of the podium. "My dagger, Mercury, was made by a Rural Outsider named Baptiste. Not only was his craftsmanship flawless, he gifted me with a weapon that was perfect for me—specifically for me! Just because our government doesn't employ the Rural Outsiders, doesn't mean we cannot trust them."

A snobbish-looking woman groveled. "You shouldn't even be with the Death Dealer Alliance Guild if you do not carry one of our own weapons. Who allowed this?"

Ariel wanted to smack the woman across the face. "Baptiste knew my father, and he made this gift in his memory. My father, Leon Rose, was a blacksmith and he trusted Baptiste with his life. No one allowed this. I just kept Mercury close to me and told everyone it was what the cabinet gave me. No one is at fault but me."

"Then we should have fired your father for insubordination," the balding man barked.

Ariel thought about firing up her plea but that might hold her back from getting results. Instead, she conducted herself to remain calm. "My father was honorable and one of the best at his job. What also made him a great man was his sense of equality. He never believed he was superior to the Rural Outsiders because we are all people. Maybe you all should stop judging those who prefer to live on their own. Some people do not want to be governmentally employed and live in the city. So, what? That's their choice. More than six billion people have died within five centuries. The Death Dealers fight to keep innocents safe, and this includes Rural Tribes. We will continue to fight for their freedom and safety. If they want to repay us with moonlit mercury weapons then they should be allowed to! We need those weapons, quick! Do you want to die?" Ariel paused as the cabinet looked on in horror and reproach. "No? I didn't think so. If you want to live, then understand that we must have those weapons, with or without your consent!"

Ariel stormed away from the podium and didn't look back. When she sat back down, Ivy boasted about her terrific speech. Ariel felt dark inside, eager to stab every cabinet member, but what good would that do? Instead, she held onto Ivy's hand and waited for someone else to speak.

Bodhi stood up and took the podium. He fixed his tie and rolled up his sleeves before speaking into the microphone. Nerves hit his belly as the entire cabinet lured at him. Once he cleared his throat, he began.

"Good morning my king, my queen, and the royal cabinet. For those of you who don't know me, I am Bodhi Tigerlilly." Bodhi dropped his eyes to look over some notes he had prepared. "Before anything else, I'd like to thank all of you for being here and being kind enough to listen to what we have to say."

Ariel huffed. "Yeah… kind, my ass," she mumbled.

"Sh!" Jason spat.

"I have known Ariel for about five or six years, and honestly, I understand why you all think she's unreliable."

Ariel shot a haughty look at Jason. "What is he doing?"

"Just listen," Jason commanded.

"Visions. Dead parents. Seeing things that aren't there. Taking all of this information and shoving it in a box hides what is actually happening." Bodhi pulled out a vial of The

Truth. "This here is something Ariel, Seraphina and I had created. Once we put our minds together, we created a potion that opened a lot of doors for us. However, this would never have been made if it wasn't for"—he pointed at Ariel—"that redhead right there. She was the reason we finally started gathering clues and realized we were working with black magic. Also, she was the only one to defeat pale demons because of Mercury: her moonlit mercury dagger. Thanks to her, many Death Dealers were saved the night of the ambush. Yes, many died, but more importantly, more were saved. Each of us who fought that night saw what moonlit mercury can do to those pale people: It slaughtered them, easily. Our regular 'human' weapons did not stand a chance during the ambush. Now, imagine a full blown war?! None of us Death Dealers are going to survive, but worse, the New World might not survive." Bodhi rolled open the petition form. "There are hundreds of Death Dealer signatures from all seven factions. We are not asking for you to provide weapons for all of us. Yet. But Faction Divide and Faction Abyss must be properly equipped before the next moonrise. Like Ariel said, we will have those weapons with or without your consent. We fight evil every day; do not be part of that statistic."

Ariel was moved by her dear friend's words. She placed her hand over her heart and took a sigh of gratitude. Finally, someone spoke of her work as being important. More importantly, it was Bodhi: a man she could always count on.

Bodhi thanked them for their time and headed back to his seat, then melted.

There was a murmur in the courtroom among the royal cabinet.

Another hour or so passed by and almost everyone had spoken and fought.

Once no one else had anything to add, the royal cabinet escorted themselves out to converse in private.

The Death Dealers sat in the courtroom quietly and waited patiently for the startling conclusion.

Thirty minutes later....

Once the members of the cabinet returned, everyone rose to their feet. The head of the cabinet—Savanah Daisy—announced their verdict.

The tall blonde bowed to the king and queen, then spun to look at the crowd of nervous Death Dealers. Savanah walked up to the bench where Ariel, Jason and Ivy sat. Not a moment too soon, she gave an answer.

"We have come up with a conclusion," Savanah began.

Anxiously, Ariel gripped Ivy's hand as well as Jason's.

"My Death Dealers, I trust you all with the lives of our innocents and it is with great pleasure, I'd like to grant all of you the privilege to have moonlit mercury weaponry."

The guilds cheered and applauded with relief. "However," Savanah continued. "Your weapons will be made by our blacksmiths only. We will not tolerate a Rural Tribe's magic, even if it is donated. I'm sorry, but if it's weapons you all want, then you must abide by our terms. Agreed?"

"Agreed!" The assassins repeated.

Kora gave a wary look to Jason and Ariel.

"Great," Kora exclaimed. "We'll get started immediately. Until then, train, train, train! We wish you all luck in the upcoming war. You're all dismissed."

"Damnit!" Ariel cried, gripping Jason's arm. "What are we going to do?"

"What's going on?" Ivy worried. She continued to mouth off worthless comforts to try to help Ariel remain calm.

Kora walked up to them and asked Jason and Ariel to speak privately.

"I'll talk to you later, okay?" Ariel ensured Ivy.

"Okay," Ivy said. "Call me."

"I will," Ariel hurried.

Jason and Ariel followed Kora to the opposite side of the courtroom and into a corner.

Kora spoke softly. "Did you do what I asked?"

Ariel nodded her head. It was an honorable request and she had no regrets in doing it, but there was one grave thing to fear: getting her queen in trouble. In the New World, the royal cabinet was the highest in the monarchy branch. They outweighed the king and queen in most circumstances. If they ever found out Queen Kora asked for help from the Rural Tribes, she could be thrown in jail for life, easily. Allowing Ariel to get away with most of what she'd done was one thing. But for Kora to work with people "beneath" her in Death Dealer matters could be deemed unacceptable.

"Good," Kora smiled. "I do not intend for them to find out. I will figure out a way for the weapons to be transported here in secret."

Ariel opposed. "No! You've done enough. Let me figure that out, my queen."

"You are very loyal to me," Kora mused, "but please, do not worry. I am able to find my way out of such things. When I was your age, Ariel, I was the same way: rebellious, adventurous, independent and courageous. That side of me has never left, and it will never leave you. I will make sure neither of you nor I will get into trouble."

The king snuck up to them. "I pray for your victory and for the Lord of Life to help guide you all. I will keep quiet. I, too, will make sure my queen is safe. None of you have anything to worry about as long as I'm king."

Ariel stared into the king's gentle eyes and knew he would keep them safe from harm. "Those weapons will never be as good as the Rural Tribe's creations."

"No," Kora blurted. "But they'll be good for backup."

Ariel grinned. "Thank you, my queen, my king…. For everything."

"Our pleasure," King Sebastian smiled.

As Ariel and Jason began stepping out of the courtroom, only one thing came to her mind: her parents.

During the next moonrise, she will have to battle against her reborn, killing-machine parents. The ones who put to her bed and read her stories. The mom and dad who cooked her special breakfasts and spoiled her with endless treasures of Earth. A mother that held the family together and a father who made everything better. The parents, who were no longer her parents, may have to die, and Ariel would be the one to kill them.

The more Ariel thought about it, the more it saddened her.

Forgive me, Lord of Life, she thought. *For I may sin in your eyes.*
Please do not loathe me, as I am only doing what is right.

MOON PHASES

One week had passed and the hollow moon hung strongly against the night sky. Ariel stood in the library with Rylan, studying the damn symbol that agitated her. Almost every night, they would devour themselves into books and brew up endless spells for hours, trying to learn the mysterious language.

"The only thing we know is it may be a form of this other language." Rylan pulled out a stained document with faded ink. "This one." He pointed to a 醬 symbol. "Its structure is similar: the lines move up and down, sideways, and slanted. However, they seem to be more complex than—" he pointed to 진화 written on a piece of paper. "I highly doubt they are the same."

Ariel was displeased as she glared at the atrocious mess they'd built over the past few nights. Instead of them constantly packing and unpacking, they left their materials in a private study in the library. "Are we wasting our time?"

"It may feel that way, but we're not." Rylan rid his hands of ink and paper and rubbed his irritated eyes. "Ki chose this language for a reason and you have every right to know why. Who knows what else the pale demons have planned. If they are using this language, they certainly know how to read and speak it."

Ariel tittered nervously. "When I say, 'New World War,' what comes to your mind?"

Rylan shrugged and threw his glasses on a stack of brown encyclopedias. "We're screwed."

Ariel picked at her lips and wondered if New World War meant something else entirely. "Cyclamen said New World War and Ki mentioned a fourth generation of pale demons: New World War, a new generation of pale idiots, and 'evolution begins in Seoul'….our battle against them is just going to be their warm up. How fast do they plan to consume the innocents of the New World? That same night?! Days, maybe? Months? A decade?! How many people do they plan to change and how many will spend the rest of their lives in a life-sucking tube?"

Forty-eight hours earlier, Ariel sat with Rylan and went over Cyclamen's interrogation and that dreadful night with Ki and the immortals. Those three little words, *you're the key*, became a distortion in her mind. "He wanted to create a fourth generation, but he's dead now, right? There's no reason to worry about a new uprising of pale demons. Ki's no more and you possess his work now, so the science must've died with him."

Ariel wasn't convinced. "When you first helped me, you did mention how evil people will do anything to keep their secrets safe."

"Correct, but science is complicated. Not everyone understands it or can manipulate it."

"True." Ariel abandoned her seat to look out the window. "Language can also be complicated. If bad guys are doing anything to keep their secrets safe—including learning an ancient language—why not force others to learn their science? Or why not have a backup scientist in case anything bad happened to Ki? Am I crazy?"

"Not at all," Rylan assured. "You may have a point, actually. There may be another crazed scientist out there that works for Jure and Bathory. If not, they'll find another. I mean, they found two. Why not three?"

"We need to figure out this language. Whoever understands it is a suspect." Ariel sighed heavily.

"We'll get there," Rylan whispered. "Soon."

"Maybe." Ariel stormed back to the table. "I need to know what it is, so it'll be easier for me to locate." Ariel smacked her knuckles on the table. "I can't keep downing potions to read this shit," she groaned as she shuffled through Ki's notes.

"I don't blame you." Rylan clicked his tongue. "You, um… look stressed. We should call it a night and go to a bar...or something." His face turned red.

"No." Ariel grabbed her sweater. "I'll try to force myself to sleep. Good night."

Rylan sighed at the sight of her walking away. But then, she turned back around and his mouth curved on both sides.

"Can you organize our mess? I wanted to do it tonight but I really just want to go home."

Next time, Rylan thought. "Sure…I mean, of course. Have a good—"

"Thanks!" Ariel interrupted, sprinting home, leaving Rylan alone.

After the royal cabinet failed to work with the Rural Tribes, each sunset grew more disappointing, and Ariel needed to relax. After she sped home, she marched to the kitchen and had a fill of re-heated mushroom tacos and black rice. She was grateful for the food, but as soon as she took in the last bite, she left her dirty dishes on the kitchen counter and jumped into bed.

Aunt Faith hoped her niece would still be sleeping over, but Ariel, temporarily preferred solitude. It was better that way. If Ariel had been around Faith, her anger would've suffocated the happiness Faith held on to so tightly. Aunt

Faith didn't deserve that unfair treatment. Especially when her only fault was a good heart.

Jason checked up on his best friend a few times, but he was so busy in District Asia, they barely had time to carry a decent conversation. Ariel understood. She just didn't like the limitations that wedged them apart. The last time they spoke, it was certainly less–than-cordial.

"Hey!" Jason huffed in an apparent rush. "What's going on?"

"Uh…," Ariel scoffed. "There's something I've been wanting to ask you."

"Alright."

"How is Zaire doing?" Ariel still hadn't heard or seen him. She had attempted to contact him a few times, but he continued to ignore her completely.

"He's fine," Jason answered, knowing where this was going.

"Good," Ariel continued. *Good for him,* she thought. "Does he still hate me?"

"Yeah, he still hates you," Jason snorted. "He supported the moonlit mercury weapon petition, but later, he made clear he was doing it for Bodhi and the innocents."

"At least he's okay," said Ariel. Then that was the end of their conversation.

Once Ariel hit the bed, she pulled out a book she hid under her pillow since childhood—*The Diamond Princess*—and casually read through it. The princess wore a pink dress and a crown made entirely of white diamonds. A smile never left her face and each day she'd give a lucky peasant a small diamond. After some time, each person throughout the kingdom had a small diamond, which they each sold to wealthy merchants for a better lifestyle. Soon, everyone was happy and together they threw a party to thank their princess.

Ariel had promised her mother she'd be like the princess—sharing and caring—and meant it. However, due to the constant struggles of her childhood and the never-ending battles that came with the DDAG, she turned out different.

After returning the book to its hiding place, Ariel turned off her lamp and shut her eyes.

A few hours later....

"A war is coming," someone whispered.

Ariel woke up and checked the time on her cell phone. It was almost four in the morning. "Ugh...." She flung the sheets off herself.

"The fight will begin during the next full moon. Evolution begins in Seoul."

Ariel was more awake now. "I swear, if it's—"

Symphony appeared on her vanity, dangling the rose necklace she gave to Ariel when she was a little girl.

"Put that down," Ariel demanded, eyeing the soulless woman in disgust.

Symphony stared at Ariel with a sly smile. "Why? Is it important?"

Ariel glared at her. The hatred within her was so thick, she wanted to vanquish the venom that had consumed her sweet mother with her bare hands. The moon was invisible and only the stars dimly lit her bedroom. "I mean it," Ariel spat.

Symphony giggled. "Night after night, you grow more angry. I do want to thank you for the wonderful entertainment."

Ariel jerked up from the bed and stormed over to Symphony, swiping the necklace out of her hand. "Don't touch this. Ever!" She wrapped it around her neck. "This item is more valuable than your immortality."

Symphony lingered on the vanity as Ariel turned away. "My dear, you and I will never agree to anything."

Ariel lost patience. "What do you want, Nefertiti?"

Symphony was blown away by her brazen attitude. She was amazed that Ariel no longer seemed frightened by her. "Sweet child, I am only here to warn you about what's to come."

"Haven't I been warned already?" Ariel groaned, sitting back on the firm mattress.

"What your captain did to Ki was…unanticipated." Symphony found his death unsettling, but it was merely a bump in the road that Ariel had yet to travel. *She'll never know*, Symphony thought. *Not until she becomes one of us.* "I am here to let you know our army is aware of what's happened and they're not happy."

"How big is your army?" Ariel asked. "Is it bigger than two Death Dealer factions combined?"

"Maybe," Symphony shifted from the vanity. "Maybe not. You will find out soon. And keep trying to warn your precious human allies, but you're only wasting time."

"Why wait for the next full moon? Why not now?"

Symphony glided along the purple carpet, her feet floating in the air. "You'll see."

In the blink of an eye, Symphony was gone.

Ariel shifted nervously. "Shit."

After just twenty minutes of target sword practice, Ariel sent her training class home early so she could meet up with Ivy and Rylan in the library. But before scampering away,

Gabriella, a young brunette student who never seemed thrilled for class, called out to her. "I have a question...."

If it were a year ago, Ariel would've been impatient and declined to talk, but as of late she insisted her students ask questions. "Is everything alright?"

Gabriella took a deep breath. "Are we going to die?"

Ariel's mouth widened under her lowered violet eyes. "No," she said. "Who told you that?"

Gabriella peered down at her feet and twirled her mahogany hair. "No one," she muffled.

Ariel didn't want to push her, but it was her duty as a teacher to protect her students from such nonsense. "I won't say anything to this person if you don't want me to. No one has the right to shove such stupid shit in your head."

Gabriella shook her head. "No one told me we're going to die. I'm just scared that we are."

Ariel noticed tears streaming from the student's brown eyes. "Don't cry. It'll be okay."

"You don't understand," the trainee winced. "I don't even want to be a Death Dealer. My mom pushed me to do this because she's a sergeant. I told her I wouldn't be good at this, but she forced me to follow her footsteps anyway! Look at me! I'm pathetic. I'll never be as good as my mom! All I want to do is be a photographer, but she is convinced it's not a real job!"

Who would do such a thing? Ariel thought. "Who's your mother?"

Gabriella wiped her tears on her forearm. Ariel gently perked up her head and wiped what was left with the end of her shirt. Gabriella forced herself to get a grip. "Sergeant Tulip in Faction Abyss."

An answer Ariel was not expecting. "She must be a real pain-in-the-ass then."

Gabriella giggled lightly and held up her hair, allowing the soft wind to cool her down. "Yeah, she can be. She's a good mother, but she is so glued to her work she forgets her children have other dreams. My dad wanted to be sergeant, but he remained a captain instead because he loves my mom so much."

"Wow, really?" Ariel was amused. "So, your father is—"

"Captain Sying Orchid? Yeah."

The day was getting better. "Whoa! They are so opposite. I never would've imagined that."

Gabriella's parents were more than she could bear. Their high titles made growing up difficult. People begged to meet her parents, and sometimes people would falsify friendships with her just to get a glimpse at the sergeant and captain of Faction Abyss.

"You and me both," she admitted. "My mom kept her maiden name in honor of my grandfather who died in combat and my sweet dad didn't argue. My mom always gets what she wants. It's pretty annoying, honestly."

Ariel couldn't relate. After all, she got her way most of the time.

"You've got to respect your parents though. They're one-of-a-kind. As for your mom, just talk to her. At first, she may not want to hear it but ask her to listen. You're her daughter and she loves you more than anything. Tell her how important your dream is to being a photographer. Prove her wrong by working hard and showing off what you can do. I have a feeling she may surprise you."

"I guess," Gabriella huffed, releasing her thick hair.

"As for the future, I can't guarantee it'll be easy, but I promise to not let anything bad happen to you or any innocent in the New World." Ariel hardly believed her own promise, but she couldn't allow people to believe there was no chance of survival. "The Death Dealer Alliance Guild will not allow the war to venture out of Seoul. We will fight until there's no more of those pale fuckers left."

Gabriella took Ariel's words seriously. Hearing her promises was a relief. Still, she couldn't help but worry. "Thank you. I'll let you go now. Sorry for bothering you."

"You're fine." Ariel smiled and watched Gabriella stride off the training field, feeling better.

On her way to the library, Ariel texted Ivy to join them. Rylan deserved freedom outside of his training, but she still needed his assistance. Rylan gathered up what they had been studying for the past week while Ariel was setting down her backpack. The rest of the night was going to be committed to studying—again. Ariel read her text with a disapproving look.

"What's wrong?" Rylan asked.

"Ivy can't make it," Ariel muttered.

Rylan stood over the desk, barely glancing over at the beautiful redhead. Oddly, he was satisfied with Ivy's absence. Not because he didn't like her—he did—but because Ariel and he would be alone.

"Are you upset about that? I mean…disappointed or something?"

Ariel shoved the phone into her pants pocket and reeled out a stack of notes and Ki's journal. "No!" she spat.

Rylan smacked his lips. "Why do I not believe you?"

Ariel casted a vertical wrinkle between her eyes and her lips pursed slightly.

Rylan choked on his words. "Sorry."

As the hours passed by, Ariel and Rylan had made little progress. Ariel was rapidly tapping her pen when she gazed out the window to see the waxing moon. "Fuck!" She pulled out her phone.

"Who are you calling?" Rylan asked.

Ariel ignored him as she anxiously waited for the ringing to end.

"Hello?"

"Bodhi!" Ariel checked the time. "I know you are probably barely waking up, but I need to ask you about the cabinet. Have they made any progress?"

Bodhi was breathing into the phone as he forced himself up from the comfort of his bed. He stretched his arms and walked over to his laptop.

"Hello?" Ariel asked, impatient as she flicked underneath her fingernails.

Bodhi waited for his laptop to turn on before answering any questions. "Let me check my email."

Rylan whispered, "Anything?!"

Ariel signaled for him to wait.

Unfortunately, Bodhi had to be the bearer of negative news. "There's been a delay." *Please don't yell at me,* Bodhi thought as he slammed his computer shut.

"A delay? WHAT DELAY?" Ariel screamed, making Rylan jerk out in his position.

"Apparently, there are not enough workers to finish the weapons in time at the amount we need. Sergeant Lotus and Sergeant Tulip have to decide if they want to squash the entire plea or make do with what they can offer us now." Bodhi clumsily walked over to the bathroom and flicked on the lights. *Ahh!* His eyes swallowed the pain that radiated from the bright white bulbs. After gathering back his vision, he wobbled over to the sink.

"And what can they offer us? A butter knife?" Ariel looked back at the moon, loathing its current phase. Soon, its body would grow full and the war would commence. Ariel could hear a running faucet from Bodhi's end. "Are you brushing your teeth?"

Bodhi raised his eyebrows. "Yes." He brushed the bristles vigorously against his teeth, sending ripples of annoyance through the phone.

"How many weapons are they planning to give us?" Ariel asked, to no one in particular.

"Ten. If we're lucky."

"Are they not giving you what you all need?" Rylan asked, concerned. His eyes were heavy, and his body begged for some rest. Plus, he had an ancient linguistics test early in the morning.

"Less than half of what we need." Ariel began, tossing a pen in the air. "But not even that is guaranteed. I have to check in with Baptiste and see if they are able to finish the weapons on their end."

Ugly as that sounded, it brought Rylan slight relief. Ariel generated nothing but positivity since she left District Antarctica, but now her whole plan seemed blocked: the language remained a mystery and now, the weapons were delayed—or worse, voided.

"I'll talk to them again," Bodhi said after spitting out mouthwash. He couldn't allow the royal cabinet to fallback. When he created the petition to create moonlit mercury weapons, people were actually offering support, making him feel important and worthy. The royal cabinet may have been poking their asses, but Bodhi wasn't going to have it. He climbed the ladder of confidence. He may have fallen once before, but he refused to slip again. "They have to come around. Lives are at stake. If we die because they refused Death Dealers strong weapons, it will be all their fault."

"The problem is, if we fail, a million others will die," Ariel huffed. "New World War means exactly that: a world war!!!" Anger sheeted through her with terrible intensity as she began imagining a world populated with pale demon scum. How many innocents would soon be part of a blood bank and how many would become the fourth generation? "Bodhi, everyone is going die!"

"I'm sure they're just trying to scare you," Bodhi coaxed.

"I'm not taking any more threats lightly," Ariel grumbled as she moved to sit next to Rylan. He was jotting down ideas for another translation spell.

"You are a great fighter and your enemies fear you. Relax." Bodhi was frightened underneath his calm exterior, but he did not want Ariel to worry more. She had been through enough.

Ariel refused to relax and was irritated with Bodhi trying to comfort her. Lives were at risk and she hardly understood what was happening. Even though Ki was dead, who had the right to assume he had no successor? The pale demons were smart. Their sorcerer may be a corpse, but how soon would they find another? Or how many men and women would be manipulated into helping them? If a fourth generation of pale demons arose, would their strength surpass her parents'? Ariel did not want to find out. During the next full moon, both DDAG factions would have to slaughter each and every last one of them.

"You do your thing with the royal cabinet and I'll talk to the Rural Tribe," Ariel declared to Bodhi. "For the time being, we must rely on them for our weaponry. We cannot just pray to the Lord of Life for a damn miracle from those royal idiots."

"I will try to persuade them, okay? I'll let you know if anything happens. Plus, Seraphina told me if I needed any help with the royal cabinet, to let her know."

Ariel scraped her fingers along her scalp and bit the inside of her cheek. "Fine." She paused. "Wait…Seraphina wants to help. Really?"

"Don't tell her I told you," Bodhi laughed. "The last thing I need is her twisting my balls or something."

"Same here." Ariel managed to chuckle a bit.

"I'm going to speak to Sergeant Lotus first and I'll go from there. I'll talk to you later."

"Bye." Ariel tossed her phone on top of the table. Rylan noticed her sorrow.

"You know, you are great?" Rylan blushed. Ariel only crossed her arms and looked out across the white flooring. "I mean, you are Ariel Rose! One of the greatest Death Dealers of all time!"

"I am not," Ariel groaned, feeling lost. "I cannot figure out this funky-looking language or convince the dumbass royal cabinet that lives are at stake, and we need pure moonlit mercury weapons—regardless of where we retrieve them. My parents are soulless freaks that kill men, women, AND children. Apparently, I'm the key for a new generation of pale demons—wonderful! Just what I always fucking wanted."

Rylan forced himself to smile to keep Ariel from losing control. He had only known her for a smidge of his life, but he saw her as a woman with the heart of a fierce and dedicated warrior.

Confusion and anger ruled Ariel's mind as she stood up. Rylan tried to console her with sweet remarks, but it was not what she needed; she needed closure.

Rylan stood behind her with bundles of notes she had taken earlier. "I think you should re—"

"Don't fucking tell me to relax!" Ariel shouted, not realizing her tone. "Sorry, but I hated Bodhi telling me to calm down and I'm going to hate you telling me the same thing. I can't just sit here and pretend everything is going to be okay! The world is at the brink of war! Why does no one get that?! Why should I feel calm when soon we could all be dead?!"

Ariel turned and noticed Gabriella at a nearby bookshelf. She stared at Ariel in tears, feeling betrayed.

"Shit!" Ariel muttered to herself

Rylan was uncertain of how to help the velvet assassin. "I mean—well…what I meant to say is…you're exhausted and obviously we're not getting anywhere tonight. We'll try again tomorrow." Rylan smiled softly as he handed her a neat stack of her notes along with some books and her backpack. The redness in her eyes was begging for rest.

"Whatever," Ariel hissed. She stomped her sandals against the metallic floor, sending a violent echo that rattled the windows.

Rylan watched her pass Gabriella without a word and disappear, and all he could do was sigh and scratch his neck. "Who knows if I messed that up."

The next day, Ariel met Rylan again, but it was another session of disappointment. Bodhi did inform her he had spoken with the cabinet, but he didn't refrain from admitting they were not being flexible with their plea.

Two days later, Ariel asked Rylan to meet her in the gardens of the headquarters. She grew tired of seeing the same room with the same stuffy vibe. Maybe studying outdoors would do them some good.

Ariel had been exchanging messages with Bodhi from dawn to dusk, waiting for the news to finally turn around.

Sergeant Lotus and Sergeant Tulip had decided to make do with whatever weapons they had to offer, luckily, but who knew if the cabinet would even push their workers to complete the purity of their weapons?

The wind picked up and Ariel could smell the floral fragrance from the array of daffodils and aster. Her hair fluttered as the premature dandelions danced around her. She pricked one from the healthy grass and made a silly wish— "I wish to have my parents back." She shut her eyes, counted to three, then softly blew against the white petals. Ariel watched them float away and mesh with the half-moon.

It's almost time, Ariel thought, fearfully. Ariel hugged her own legs and rested her chin on her knees.

"How sentimental, my sweet child," a voice sang.

Ariel spun her head back, and there was Leon with his silver, lifeless eyes and his fangs hanging from his half open mouth.

"Can't you two ever leave me the fuck alone?" she groaned.

"We never will," Leon grinned. "We will haunt you until you are finally one of us."

"I will never become one of you," Ariel muttered. She got up from the soft grass and brushed off any dirt that lingered on her green pants and white shirt.

"Yes, you will," Leon fought back.

"That's what you think," Ariel growled as she glared at the man who once carried her in his protective arms. "You and your so-called lover need to get it through your head that I will slaughter the both of you. I promise."

"Why don't you just do yourself a favor and listen to us." Leon drew closer and dug his nail into Ariel's chin. She groaned as he was picking up her head. "Just give it up, girl. We don't want to kill you. However, everyone you love will not be so lucky. Especially, that—who is that woman…Aunt Faith?"

Ariel's eyes widened. "Don't you touch her!"

"I'll do as I please. Besides, she won't be the only one. Bodhi, Seraphina, that best friend of yours…are all going to die. Unless, you give yourself to me and my people. If not, let the games begin."

"Ariel!" someone screamed. It was Rylan slowly walking up.

"Who are you, my dear boy?" Leon licked his fangs as he stared at the boy's thin neck. He could see the beating of his pulse running through his veins. "Don't you look…sweet."

Rylan trembled and his palms became sweaty. His glasses were bouncing away from his face as the fear fueled inside his quivering body. He internally begged for mercy.

"Get the fuck away from him!" Ariel smacked Leon upside the head, making him distracted enough to focus back on her. Ariel could sense her father's urge to taste the innocent student's blood. It was glued to her mind and body. *How am I sensing this?*

Leon chewed his lip as he thought about consuming Rylan as a late-night snack. However, he cut himself away from this temptation and instead leeched onto Ariel's deep fear: losing all those she loved.

"Don't threaten my family, friends, or any other innocents, ever!"

With brute force, Leon grabbed the front of Ariel's shirt and pulled her to meet him eye-to-eye. Usually, Ariel would fight back, but without the dosage of Vitality, she'd only hurt herself.

"He won't die…tonight. But he will be mine. You won't know when and you won't know where, but I will take his life, along with everyone I've mentioned. Watch out, girl. I'll see you on the next full moon. Change your mind by then. If not, prepare to lose." Suddenly, Symphony appeared next to her husband. Leon let Ariel go and met up with his one true love. They kissed. Symphony winked Rylan's way and instantly, they were gone.

"Who was that?" Rylan looked around, terrified they could be anywhere.

"…They're gone." Ariel fixed her shirt and gathered her things. "You've met my parents."

"You…Your…," Rylan shook his head. "That is not natural. They didn't even look alive!"

"They're not." Ariel looked up at the sky. "Follow me."

Yes! Rylan thought. *I will follow you anywhere.* "Okay! Where are going?"

Ariel halted and realized she'll need some heavy clothing. "Do you have a coat?"

"Yes?"

"You're going with me to Antarctica."

After they made a quick stop home to grab some warm attire, Ariel and Rylan rushed back to the gardens and traveled through the portal gate. She guided him the whole way, and even talked the pilot into flying them over to the Rural Tribes. Rylan's breath was taken away at the sight of the white beauty that flooded Antarctica. He was used to the cityscape of New York, where nature was barely regaining its rightful land. In District Antarctica, meanwhile, Mother Nature never seemed to have left. It was the largest snow desert.

Finally, they landed in McMurdo Station, and the first friendly face to approach the two DDAG members was Dior. However, her usual smile was nowhere to be seen, or felt.

"What's the matter?" Ariel asked her as they hugged. Dior looked at Rylan and introduced herself before speaking further.

"My dear, we have an issue."

What else can go wrong?! Ariel shrugged. "What's going on?"

Dior asked them to follow her to Baptiste. He and his tribe were sitting outside around campfires, indulging in another day's work. Most of them looked tired and out-of-breath.

Baptiste invited everyone inside his home. They sat inside a small room with a faux-leather couch and different shapes of carved rock screwed to the wall. Baptiste brought over a thermos filled with hot cider and poured them all a small glass. Ariel didn't care to drink. She wanted to know what was wrong.

"Can you tell me what's happening, please?" Ariel asked Baptiste.

Baptiste frowned before he drank some of the warm beverage. His eyes drooped as he looked at her from the opposite couch. "We are creating the weapons. My people have put in a lot of work, but the moon hasn't been strong enough for the weapons to reach even an average potential."

"That must be why the royal cabinet is stalling," Rylan added.

Ariel huffed, heavily. "This can't be right." She shot from her seat and began pacing in the room. "Why is this happening?"

"To make strong and everlasting moonlit mercury weapons, we add in our own magic: the Lord of Life's touch.

However, the moon has not reflected upon us like it usually does. Our people have barely felt the light." Dior held onto Baptiste's hand. "We're pushing them to try harder, but I'm afraid they'll become weak. The more magic they use, the more of their strength is taken away."

"So, how are the damn weapons now?" Ariel punched the inside of her hand.

"They're mediocre at best." Baptiste pulled out a small knife and handed it to Rylan. "That little girl has full potential, but compare her to the weapons your factions need—it's useless."

"The royal cabinet usually hires amateur alchemists, wizards, and witches, so if your weapons are lacking, theirs will be as good as a children's toy," Ariel sighed.

Dior got up to meet Ariel. She held both of her arms and looked deep into her violet eyes. "We're not giving up, my love. We understand the dangers that await us all. You need those weapons at their best ability and we're hoping to get them there. We just need a bit more time."

"TIME?! There is no time!" Ariel screamed. "We need those weapons! You don't understand!"

"We do," Baptiste urged. "This is a minor setback."

"Minor setback?! MINOR—" Ariel punched the wall. *BOOM!* "FUCKING—" Then punched again. "SETBACK! We can't have setbacks! Tell your people to hurry up and put all their energy into those weapons. 200 million lives are at risk."

"Ariel, maybe you shouldn't—"

"Shouldn't what?" Ariel snapped, interrupting Rylan.

Nervous, Rylan only shook his head.

"The royal cabinet is not helping on their end, so it's up to you all! If those weapons are not done by the time we fight, we will all die and it'll be all your fault!"

Baptiste rose and stormed out of his home in an outrage. Dior looked at Ariel and took control of the room. "First of all, my dear, we love you, but you cannot come over here and bark orders like a Death Dealer lunatic! Settle yourself down or get out of my tribe's way."

Ariel cringed, and wanted to call her *Bitch!* but she held back.

"We are helping you because we loved your father and we'll do anything for his daughter, but we will not work with you under that kind of attitude. My tribe is trying, but they need more time. I will not sacrifice their lives for your arrogance."

Under her breath, Ariel muttered, "Just tell them to hurry up."

"Please leave," Dior requested. "Either come back when you're calm or we'll let you know when the weapons are ready. If they're not completed on time and you're still angry, don't bother calling us."

Dior held the door open and waved an arm for them to exit her home. Ariel stomped out. Rylan thanked Dior for her hospitality then followed Ariel back to the helicopter.

"You should apologize to them," Rylan suggested.

Ariel jumped inside the cockpit. "Shut up."

Without stopping, Ariel and Rylan headed straight back to New York. They didn't speak a word to one another the whole way.

Once they landed back home, Rylan thanked Ariel for saving his life. "Sorry, I didn't mention it earlier, but it's much appreciated."

"I can save the life of a loser, but I can't save the lives of others. How pathetic am I?"

Rylan no longer knew how he felt about Ariel. She seemed so grown and mature before, but now, she was self-loathing and weak. Rylan walked a few feet, then halted and looked back at her.

"I understand why you're angry but quit feeling sorry for yourself. It's not going to get you anywhere."

"Get out of here, you piece of shit!"

Rylan's ego broke into a million pieces, but he refrained from displaying that emotion over his young face. He looked down at his thumbs. "I'm not feeling well, so I won't be able to meet up with you tomorrow. Sorry. Good night."

Ariel closed her eyes and cursed to herself. "I don't fucking need you. I don't need anyone." She knew that wasn't true. She did need him, probably more than anyone else at that moment—even Jason—but she was too prideful to apologize.

On the drive home, Ariel continued to curse to herself, steering with a closed fist and driving recklessly through the streets. Luckily, she made it home safe.

Ariel was fuming for the next several days. She spent most of the time in stale pajamas in her messy bed. She even called out on her training classes, and her phone was ringing off the hook. Jason would leave messages for her to call him back, but she never did.

One afternoon, an unknown number was coming in. Ariel sent it to voicemail and waited to listen once the messenger stopped talking.

Ariel checked the stranger's message: "Ariel, it's Mina. How are you? I have to ask that, but listen: Queen Kora would like to speak with you." Surprised, Ariel accidentally dropped a cookie. "If I were you, I'd consider this important and call back. Okay? Bye!"

Ariel picked up her wasted cookie and immediately returned the phone call.

"District North America headquarters, how may I help you?" Mina said with a high-pitched tone.

"Let me talk to the queen," Ariel hurried.

Mina looked away from her paperwork, surprised to hear Ariel's voice on the other end. "You actually called? Keep up the good work."

"Mina," Ariel whispered as she grabbed another cookie. "I would like to be transferred during this lifetime."

"One day you'll be a nice person. Please hold."

Anxiety consumed Ariel's body when she was placed on hold and the poppy music began. Ariel waited as she sat on her balcony. Finally, Queen Kora's raspy voice came in. "Ariel Rose?"

Ariel perked up her tone. "Yes! You needed to talk to me?"

"Yes, but I'd rather not speak over the phone. Do you mind if I met you at your home? I'd like to see you in private."

Surprise crept in Ariel's chest as those last words were exchanged. "Um…Yeah. If that's what you'd prefer."

"Great! I have your address. I'm on my way." Kora hung up the phone and Ariel looked blankly into the grey concrete between her feet.

Ariel lifted her gaze from the floor and realized, "I need to change!" She ran to her dresser and pulled out a black tank top and denim shorts. With a soft-bristle brush, she combed her hair thoroughly and finished off by simply washing her face.

Twenty minutes later, Kora was at Ariel's front door. Ariel was ecstatic to see her.

After sitting down on a black couch, Ariel asked why she had dropped by. Kora said, "First, I would like to know if you're okay. I've heard you've been quite…upset lately."

Ariel hoped the queen had learned nothing about her recent backlashes. "I see." However, it did not surprise her that the queen knew. News spread faster than intel in the Death Dealer Alliance Guild. "I'm fine, though. Thank you." Kora bowed her head. "So, have you heard anything from the royal cabinet?"

"They're getting somewhere," Kora sighed.

"Really?" Ariel asked, intrigued. "What's going on?"

"Don't worry about them right now," the queen said, politely. Ariel held back her impatience; clearly, they had been the chief reason she was losing hope and sleep. "I come bearing a gift."

"Oh?" Ariel shook her head and blinked her eyes. "I don't deserve any—"

"Don't you dare reject a gift from your queen."

Ariel sighed. "Okay."

"Here." Kora pulled out a diamond vial filled with a bright pink liquid. It twinkled in the sun as its rays shot through Ariel's curtains. She held it in her hand and brought it up to the sun to examine it. The liquid was thick with some bubbles floating in it.

"What is this?" Ariel asked, still turning the smooth glass in her fingers.

"You have done so much for the DDAG—reversing black magic, finding the pale demons, finding and eliminating Ki, urging for strong weaponry—all this and more have made you one valuable and unforgettable Death Dealer. I thank you." *She'll enjoy this*, Kora thought. "No one in the world knows about this magic. Well, scratch that—less than a handful know about this."

Ariel's eyes widened with excitement. *What could this be? An all-language sort of spell? Will I be able to switch bodies with someone?*

It's called Earth Time Travel, and the name says it all."

Ariel gave a whoop of pleasure, making Kora grin. "You mean...I get to go back in time?! Before the Black Plague II Infections?" Today's concerns were pushed aside, momentarily. *This is exactly what I need!*

Kora patted Ariel's back. "Jason informed me you had a love for Earth's history—especially it's ancient architecture. You will be able to go back as far as you wish. Just choose wisely."

Ariel loved the sound of that. "How does it work?!"

"Easily," Kora said to Ariel, smirking. Soon, Ariel would be in another time, in a different world—an old world: Earth. "Think about a time you want to go to. Say the year and place, and boom: You're there. The only downfall is the magic wears out in an hour, so enjoy as thoroughly as you can."

Ariel wanted to see many things during Earth's prime, but what specifically was the tough thing to choose. She jumbled through the choices in her head for a few moments and finally decided where she wanted to go. "When can I use it?"

"Now, if you wish." Kora took the vial and popped the cork. "You cannot tell anyone about this."

"I promise!" Ariel said, her face glowing with excitement.

"As you drink this, your face will pucker because the taste is disgusting." Kora said, making Ariel laugh. "As soon as you are done drinking, say the time and place. You should be at your destination in two seconds."

Ariel nodded and slowly took the vial back. She held it back in the sunlight once more. "Thank you," she told the queen with a full heart.

"You're welcome," Kora said, and stared at Ariel, waiting for her to drink.

Ariel slowly took in the pink potion and tilted her head back graciously. Kora was right—it did taste awful. It had a strong flavor of onion and there were tastes of clove and ginger: a horrible combination.

The vial was now empty and Ariel said, "2017 Before Plague: Seoul, Korea."

Ariel felt her body move like a hurricane. The world around her spun like smoke in a crystal ball. Her vision faded and, for a second, all she could see was black.

Then suddenly, she landed in the middle of an intersection. At the sound of a violent horn, she turned and leapt out of traffic—the busiest traffic she'd ever seen.

Someone was shouting at her, but she couldn't comprehend a word from the angry man. Quickly, she hopped up onto the sidewalk. "Sorry!" Ariel called out. He continued to ramble but he was talking too fast, making it more difficult to understand him. He sped off. Ariel noticed she was now in the middle of a crowded sidewalk. The city was jam-packed with people of all shapes, ages, and sizes.

Ariel gazed up and took in the grand view of Seoul! The ginormous buildings met with the gorgeous purplish-pink sky with thick clouds to match. On the side of a tinted-glass structure was a gigantic poster of some hot guy. He wore all black and had a cross earring on his left lobe. His skin was so smooth, like vanilla frosting, and she had the temptation to dip a ruby into his cheek. He was gripping onto his wavy hair and bit his seductive berry lips. Oddly, Ariel felt aroused. Who gets aroused by a photo of someone they had never met?

"G-Dragon? My, oh my, are you delicious?" Speaking of delicious, Ariel could smell deliciousness in the air.

"Yum. What is that?!" Ariel noticed a food cart full of unusual food. She read the menu but wasn't familiar with any of the items on it. *Bulgogi? Galbi? Kimchi? Altang? What is all this?* As she kept eyeing the unusual menu, she began to notice the energetic sounds in the streets. They were not only coming from innocents but there were noises that sounded like...music. It was so odd. The catchy tunes seemed to come from some kind of blaring speaker. Ariel was unwillingly bobbing her head to a smooth beat.

Ariel danced over to a sweet-looking woman next to a cart full of keychains and snacks. "Excuse me?" She asked the older lady. "Where am I?"

"Myeongdong District," the lady blurted. She began to shout at random people passing by but Ariel couldn't figure out what she was saying.

"Ma'am!" The lady didn't hear. "Ma'am!" Ariel called out louder. The lady looked at her, annoyed. "What are you speaking?"

"Are you not in Korea?" she mocked.

Ariel exasperated. "I'm aware, but what are you speaking?"

"I have no time for jokes!" The lady shooed her away. "I'm very busy. Have a good day!"

"Sorry I asked," Ariel mumbled. She fled and decided to look around.

The people were energetic, like young children in a park. Most of the women wore a high-waisted skirt with an off-the-shoulder top, tucked in. Ariel was used to the rusty and decomposing buildings in Seoul, but looking at them during Earth's time was breath-taking. The stores were completely stocked and packed with customers, while outside there were plenty of things to eat and tid-bits to be sold. Ariel walked inside a store called Laniege and picked up a white box with baby-blue letters. The front side was in English but when she tried to read the back, she noticed the directions were not only in English but in the mysterious language she had been studying, as well as what must have been two other languages. It was unlike anything she'd ever seen. She walked over to whomever was running the cash register. It was a young girl with a bob cut. Over her narrow eyes were turquoise, cat-shaped eyeglasses that coordinated nicely with her heather grey sweater.

"Excuse me?" Ariel asked.

The pretty girl raised her eyes and politely asked, "May I help you?"

Please do! Ariel thought. "I, um…I'm not sure about this language right here." She pointed to the one she'd been eyeing most. "What language is that again?"

The girl let out a small, cute laugh. "You're funny! That's Korean, silly."

Ariel shook her head. "I know we're in Korea but what language is this?!"

"Ko-re-an. It's Korean or Han-guel."

"Han-whatta?" Ariel was lost.

"Han-guel is Korean in Korean." The cashier pulled out a yellow-square paper and a pen and began to write. Ariel watched every direction her hand made.

Once she was finished, the cashier handed Ariel the little square. It was sticky on top. 한글 was written across.

"What does that mean?" Ariel asked.

The girl pointed to each syllable as she spoke. "Han-guel. 한글. That is how we spell Korean in our language."

Ariel wanted to squeal! Korean was the language she had been studying! Korea. Korean. How coincidental! This was it! Finally, everything dark around her brightened up…a smidge.

Trying not to sound anymore idiotic than she did, Ariel gave the girl a subtle thank-you and roamed the streets outside. She checked her watch: about forty-five minutes left.

"What to do?" Ariel asked herself. Suddenly, her stomach growled. "Food it is!"

Forty-five minutes later….

Ariel was transported back to her living room and Kora still sat on the couch, curled up with one of Ariel's good books. She jumped on the couch next to the queen and shouted, "IT'S KOREAN!"

Kora leapt in her seat. "What?!" she asked.

Ariel took out the sticky note she placed inside her shirt and showed it to Kora. "A nice girl wrote this for me. It's 'Korean' in Korean, or 'han-guel.' This is what I've been trying to figure out! I can't believe it."

Kora was impressed by Ariel's findings. "Now, all you have to do is learn it. How good are you at ancient linguistics?"

"I'm good, but that was in a classroom." Ariel became nervous. "I've never taught myself."

Kora wasn't fazed whatsoever. "I'm sure you'll learn quickly. I have faith in you."

"Thank you!" Ariel gave Kora a firm hug, making her lose some breath, but she didn't mind.

This gift was better than I thought, Kora thought. "Tell me, what else did you see?"

Ariel rambled on about the whirlwind of sights, eats, and smells of Seoul, Korea, 2017 Before Plague, that carried her all over the city like a plastic bag. Her favorite thing of all, was the food. "I ordered a bowl of kimchi—to be honest, it smelled funky—but it was delicious! I was told to add that on top of something called bulgogi, and it was to-die-for! I wrapped it in lettuce and I couldn't help but shove it all down my throat."

Kora chuckled. "What the hell is bulgogi?"

"Beats me," Ariel said, shrugging. "Apparently, some kind of meat. It had the taste of mushrooms, but much fattier."

"What about the architecture? Was it everything you dreamed it would be?"

Ariel could still see the wonder of the beautiful city. It was unlike any other. "The buildings were all so tall and beautiful, and not fucked up. I took an elevator to the top floor of some shopping tower and the skyline was insane. Way beyond the city limits was a bridge and I think there was some kind of island on the other end. I'm not sure. There was a mountain with three spikes: two small ones with a red bulb on top and the middle was orange and blue. I don't know what they were for, but it was cool. Oh! And DVDs! I found out what DVDs are!"

Kora never wondered about them, personally but Ariel's excitement was darling. "Yay…. Tell me what they are."

"Movies! People acted out plays—or something like that—and you or me or Jason or whoever can watch these movies in the comfort of our own home, over and over again. The DVDs are placed in a box you control."

"That sounds interesting." Kora was pleased to see Ariel so darn happy.

Ariel briefly mentioned a form of music called K-pop, but before she could explain the control it took over her ears and hips, her phone interrupted them. Bodhi was calling.

Quickly, Ariel answered. "Hello?"

"Hey," Bodhi said, taking a deep breath.

"Is everything, alright?" Ariel asked.

"I have some news. Now, it's not all bad, but it's not good either."

Kora noticed the concern in Ariel's eyes and jerked up from the couch.

Ariel put Bodhi on speaker. "I'm listening."

"According to Sergeant Lotus and Sergeant Tulip, the moonlit mercury weapons have been completed."

Wasn't this good news? "That's great. Isn't it?" Ariel asked.

"Yes and no." Bodhi was next to Seraphina. She signaled for him to blurt it out. "Okay. Well, that's the positive side of it, but as for the flip-side, they're average. The weapons are nowhere near their full potential. If the Rural Tribes aren't done with their half, we may be in a lot of trouble."

Ariel tore away from her seat and was about to jolt upstairs, phone in hand. "I'm heading to Antarctica."

"Jason already headed that way." Bodhi was thankful that Jason was two steps ahead. "Call him."

"I will. Thanks." Ariel hung up and instantly dialed Jason's number.

Jason picked up after a single ring. "Ariel."

"Jason!" Ariel paced around her living room, preparing for the worst. "Can you tell Baptiste and Dior I am so sorry for my inexcusable attitude? I am deeply sorry."

"Tell them yourself," Jason said, passing Dior his phone.

"Hello, sweetheart."

"Dior!" Ariel cried. "I am so, so sorry! Please, forgive me for everything. I was under a shit-ton of stress and I know that is not an excuse but—"

"Don't overwork yourself, child," Dior said, gently. "My husband and I forgive you."

Ariel was relieved, but forgiveness felt unjust. She wouldn't have forgiven Seraphina if it were her. "You're too kind."

"We're human, and we get angry. It's alright," Dior responded. She looked at her husband and smiled. "Would you like to know about the weapons?"

"Yes!" Ariel shouted. "Are they done? How are your people doing?"

"Some need rest, but as far as the weapons…."

This was it. The moment of truth. *Please, be good*, Ariel thought.

"They're not ready."

Ariel fell silent.

"Dear, don't be angry," Dior begged.

Ariel gazed into the eyes of a worrisome queen.

"I'm not angry," Ariel assured. "You've done what you could."

Baptiste grabbed the phone. "We're not giving up!" he declared.

Ariel held back tears. "Thank you for trying. I love you both."

"We love you."

Kora opened the curtain and looked outside. Ariel felt she had already lost the battle that had yet to be fought.

"Hey, are you there?" Jason asked.

Ariel gazed out at the gibbous moon with watery eyes and a nervous-ticking body. "Jason," she cried.

"Yeah?" Jason asked.

"The moon is almost full." Ariel paused. "Prepare for war."

EVOLUTION ENDS HERE

A riel dreamt she was a little girl in Seoul once again, reading fantasy novels alongside her father. They were satisfied with the little things they had. The money was tight and their home was tiny, but despite their miniscule lifestyle, Ariel and her parents lived happily.

"You know I will never do anything to hurt you, right?" Leon asked, as he braided his daughter's soft, velvet hair. He had always wondered where she had gotten such beautiful red locks. Her eyes resembled his mother's, but her hair was a mystery. He secured the French braid with a green ribbon.

Ariel jumped on top of his chest, making him lose a hint of breath as he fell back on the bed. "Of course!" she grinned as she tightened her arms around his neck. "I love you, Daddy!"

"And we love you!" Symphony was at Ariel's bedroom door with a glass bowl filled with red dots.

"Rubies!" Ariel screamed as she ran away from her father to indulge in the sweetness of honey coated cherries.

Leon laughed as he watched his princess light up and sprint her little legs over to a bowl full of goodies. Ariel dunked her hand inside and grabbed as many as she could. She shoved three inside her mouth and smiled after the first crunch. Pieces of the cherries got caught in between her teeth. "Thank you, Mommy!"

Symphony kissed her sweet girl on the lips and told her it was time for bed. Ariel gobbled up the last of the late-night snacks and slid underneath the covers. Leon tucked her in nice and tight then caressed her sweet cheeks. "Goodnight, Princess."

"Goodnight, Daddy. Goodnight, Mommy."

Symphony and Leon held hands as Leon turned the light off. "Sweet dreams," Symphony said. "We love you. Forever and ever."

March 20, 2368 A.P. The sun was setting.

It was late in the afternoon when the guilds gathered in District Asia's headquarters. Most of the Death Dealers were talking amongst themselves, mostly trying to motivate each other for tonight's battle. Bundles of arrows, guns, bullets, swords, spiked weapons and spears were placed on a long table on the stage of the auditorium—enough for each assassin. The moonlit mercury weapons were sully carved—just as Ariel suspected—but the assassins had to fight with what they had.

Jason and Sying had been in a meeting with Sergeant Lotus, Sergeant Tulip and the king and queen since early morning and Ariel hoped they'd be out soon.

Ariel felt a yank on her sleeve. When she turned, she saw Ivy's beautiful face. "Hey." Ariel hadn't spoken to Ivy in weeks. She was too distracted with the war and the lack of powerful weapons designed for their efforts. "Sorry I have been distant. I've been super busy."

Ivy grabbed Ariel's hand, placed something inside her palm, and wrapped her fingers around the mysterious item. "Keep this."

Ariel slowly pried open her hand, and began revealing a rose gold chain. Ivy gifted her with the rose gold, snowflake necklace Ariel had seen on her the first night they met. "Ivy…I…I can't accept—"

"Don't worry," Ivy assured, sweetly. "I know how much you love snow. Plus, you've been working really hard. This is a small thank-you."

Ariel looked at the delicate jewel and, after a moment, she asked Ivy to help her put it on. Ariel lifted her hair and Ivy linked the chain together.

Ariel held the tiny snowflake in between her fingers, feeling the tiny ridges of the design as it tickled against her soft skin. She spun around and embraced Ivy with a passionate kiss.

Daoka was fixing her buns when she caught them mid-kiss. "Whoa." The girls separated. "Are you, like, a couple?"

Ivy laughed. "We're not."

Ariel tucked the necklace inside her shirt. "Not yet." Ivy spun her head so fast, her hair brushed over her arms. She turned a reddish-brown and grinned, widely.

Daoka gazed at them back and forth. "Why not?"

"Ariel," Bodhi called. "Can you come here?"

"Excuse me." Ariel followed Bodhi to a corner. "What's up?"

"Do you think the rural tribes have weapons ready?"

Ariel shook her head. "No. Dior said her people were losing energy because the moon's power was limited. Why?"

"I do not have a blacksmith mentality, but those weapons look…well…shitty."

Ariel couldn't agree more. "I know."

"What are we going to do?" Bodhi huffed.

"There's nothing we can do," a voice chimed in.

Ariel's eyes bugged out. "Zaire?"

Zaire barely glanced her way. Instead, he focused only on his dear friend Bodhi. "We just have to hope for the best."

Peeved, Ariel jumped between them. "Zaire, will you please talk to me?"

Zaire's impatience filled him with a suppressed urge to bolt out of the room but he too had to partake in a New World War, regardless of his hatred toward Ariel. "I'm talking to Bodhi."

"Come on!" Ariel hissed. "You can't keep holding this grudge against me."

"Yes. I can." Zaire muttered under his breath.

"She's right," Seraphina said as she joined the group. "Let the anger go."

Zaire's heartrate increased. "Have you forgotten what she's done?" He grabbed her arm and lifted it up to display the scar that will remain with her for the rest of her years. "Do you not remember going to the hospital? Who's the one that put you there? Huh?"

Seraphina flung her arm back. "I realize that!" She barked. "But some of us may die tonight. Don't you think you should let bygones be bygones?"

"Ha!" Zaire clapped, mockingly. "This coming from the girl who screamed and broke things in her hospital room because of"—he pointed to Ariel's sour face—"that girl right there! You almost died because of her!"

"Enough!!" Bodhi screamed, causing the whole room to freeze up. "First of all, it was my fault Seraphina got hurt. Second, I'm tired of us hating each other. We can't keep doing this. It's not good for our friendship, not good for the DDAG, and definitely not good for the people of the New World." Everyone was shocked by Bodhi's unusual backlash. "Drop the bullshit! We have our people to think about."

Zaire wrinkled his nose as he looked down on Ariel. "We do have our people to think about." He slid on his hat. "Therefore, why should I think about you?"

Zaire walked away.

"Zaire!" Seraphina called out, but he ignored her completely. "Get back here!"

"Let him go," Ariel said, feeling guilty. "He'll come around." However, she had a feeling he wouldn't.

The captains and sergeants of both districts finally arrived. They protruded through the auditorium doors, holstering their weapons close.

Sying and Jason stood back while Sergeant Kurtis Lotus and Sergeant Aurora Tulip took the stage.

"We cannot waste any precious time, so here it goes." Sergeant Tulip slid out her sickle sword and held it across her chest. Its curved body was solid gold and its quillion was made out of fine ruby. "Our only hope of survival is your dedication as merciless fighters. They all must die. Do not— I repeat—do not allow any of those creatures to live. I deny anyone the right to be merciful. Our present castle grounds will become their future graves."

Sergeant Lotus stood up. "Sergeant Tulip is right. I had hoped this was all a conspiracy. That maybe this was all just an illusion." Ariel jerked her head up, and Tulip met her eyes. "However, I was wrong. Ariel Rose, one of Faction Divide's most valuable Death Dealers, had been telling nothing but the truth since the beginning, and I was too prideful to admit she was right. Thanks to Captain Lilly, his second-in-command, Seraphina Jasmine, and Bodhi Tigerlilly, I was convinced of my arrogance."

Kurtis admitting this aloud made Ariel feel more self-assured.

"Pale demons are real and more-than-likely are ready to plunder into our territory. We won't allow it. They can demolish all our castles!" Kurtis whipped out his machine gun and raised it in the air. Everyone grabbed their weapon and roared with him.

"Yeah!"

"They can tear our flags. But one thing they can't do is take away the soul of a Death Dealer. We will rip out their hearts and chop off their heads. The innocents of the New World will not become victims to this ungodly species."

Suddenly, the sun's rays lessened in the distance. Ariel looked outside. The sky was transitioning into a bold purple—almost navy.

"The pale demons are coming tonight," Aurora roared. "Will they win?!"

"No!!!" Everyone shouted.

"Not a fucking chance!" Daoka cheered, as she chewed loudly on a piece of pink bubble gum.

Jason followed Ariel's gaze out the window and, as the sky's color deepened from purple, to plum, to almost-black, he could feel his veins throbbing against his neck.

"Give them a reason to fear us!" Tulip declared, smacking her sickle sword against her palm. "Show them why the Death Dealer Alliance Guild is the protector of the New World!"

"Aye!!!"

Sergeant Lotus and Sergeant Tulip picked up the wooden table between them and the crowd split. They jumped from the stage and slammed it on the floor. "So, grab your weapons and let's get the fuck outside and tear those pale shits apart!" Kurtis grabbed silver bullets for his machine gun and rushed outside, leading the army into war.

The warriors sprinted and picked up a weapon closest to their reach.

Jason walked over to Ariel, who was staring motionless out the window.

Ariel's face was unnaturally pale. "I'm so damn scared."

Jason took out his shotgun and loaded it. "Me, too." He cocked the barrel back, snapping it into place. "You are the most badass person I know, though. I swear, your body is made out of steel and your dedication is savage."

Ariel softly chuckled. "You're a better fighter than I am."

"You're probably right," Jason joked. The best friends exchanged small laughter. "But we got this."

"Yeah." Ariel hugged herself. Jason asked if she was ready to go. "Can I ask you something?"

"Of course," Jason said, as he secured his pocket knife under his pant leg.

Ariel could hear her mother's sweet voice: *We love you. Forever and ever.* "What if I kill my parents?" Ariel asked. Jason looked upon her saddened face. "Will that make me a bad person?"

Jason shook his head. "No," he insisted. "It'll make you a hero."

The best friends hugged while Seoul turned to black and the sky became emblazoned with stars and the moon showcased its full body from behind the grey clouds. Soon, a New World War would begin. It was time: time to stop an evolution.

The Death Dealers stood on top of the castle keep and spread out amongst the towers. Ariel's patience grew tired as she froze, relentless, gazing out at the empty grounds and anticipating any pale demon flesh that should spurt out at any moment.

Jason and Sying guarded the front and back towers, keeping an eye out for any suspicious sounds or squirms from Mother Nature's floor.

"I got this," Bodhi mumbled to himself as he covered his face with Fantasia. He wiggled his pouch of Elixia, making sure it was full and sturdy against his thigh. He had been coaxing Elixia sand infused with mercury, hoping it would work against the undead. There was never a chance for him to test his creation, but hopefully tonight, it would prove itself successful.

"You ready?" Zaire asked as he threw his crossbow over his shoulder. "You need to be."

"I'm good," Bodhi assured, unconvincingly.

Zaire grumbled. "How do we even know they're attacking us here?"

Bodhi scratched his chin. "They declared war. They'll want to attack our home—or headquarters, to be exact."

Zaire looked at the city lights and wondered how many families lived within the bright field, in the very center of Seoul. The pale demons would be attacking soon, but would they slaughter their way through the city first?

Ariel could taste blood in her mouth and throat. It felt unusually similar to the night she woke up screaming from the sadistic nightmare of her murdering Stacy and her friend. *Why am I feeling this?* she thought as she massaged her neck.

Seraphina popped up next to her. "You think they're coming?" She had her longsword in hand and a bluntly carved sai holstered behind her back.

Ariel was quiet. Her ears picked up wind and crows, but there also seemed to be faint footsteps and growls. Her breath shortened as both the quench for blood became stronger and drumming footsteps seemed to grow nearer and clearer. "Do you hear that?" *Where is that coming from?* she thought. She concentrated on nature's movement, trying to capture any forced motion of the leaves, branches, or bushes.

Seraphina looked down at the castle grounds. A figure sprinted across the back gardens. She turned around and marched toward Sergeant Tulip, who was nearby. "I think they're here."

Meanwhile, Leon and Symphony were hiding amidst the darkness, across a small river. Pale demons had spectacular vison. They could clearly spot a child, miles away. Symphony smiled at her beloved and gave him the signal— she bowed her head.

Leon closed his silver eyes and began to mumble in Korean: 항상 절 믿으세요 *(Always believe me).*

Suddenly, Migackt's body stiffened and he turned off his flashlight. Daoka, beside him, asked, "Did you run out of battery or something?"

Migackt didn't answer.

"Hello?" Daoka spat while bouncing her head shoulder-to-shoulder.

Migackt only gazed into the distance. He removed the light from his vest and held it beside him.

"Weirdo," Daoka huffed.

Migackt sauntered from his original post and he casually let the flashlight drop from his relaxed hand, onto the cemented roof. *Crash!* One of Faction Divide's soldiers took notice. Ana eyed him strangely. She tuckered back in her handgun and slowly walked toward him. Oddly, he began removing his armor.

"Are you alright?" Ana asked him.

Migackt had rid himself of his cap, vest, and gloves. Ana called out to him again, but he wasn't listening and he was getting closer to the edge of the castle. He pulled out his entire stock of weapons and tossed them out of sight.

"What are you doing?!" Ana caught the attention of a few Death Dealers around her. They caught a glimpse of what was happening and started throwing questions at each other. He was not stopping. What was happening? "Get back here!"

Ana began rushing toward her comrade. She reached out to grab his arm but then... he jumped!

"NO!!!" Ana screamed as she ran over to the edge. Unfortunately, she wasn't quick enough. She only got a whiff of his hair when she swung her arm over the castle wall. Her eyes and mouth widened as she witnessed Migackt plummeting to his death. There was no way he'd be able to survive the fall, and it was too late to toss him a rope. A mere few seconds passed and his body splattered on the ground.

"Aaahhh!!" Ana screamed. A handful of Death Dealers raced over to her side. They all gasped at the scene of a Death Dealer whose fresh blood smeared along the rocky pathway.

"Oh, my god!" One man mumbled to himself.

"What's going on?" Ariel asked Seraphina.

Seraphina shrugged and immediately they followed the chaos.

Leon trembled his way back to his own body. His eyes opened and he could feel the wind blow north, toward the castle. The battle had begun.

"My love," Leon moaned.

Symphony pulled up her hand for him to kiss. Leon pressed his lips sweetly against her cold skin. "I'll be back." A second later, she was gone.

Woosh! Symphony was behind a short man with a flashlight. Quickly, she snapped his neck.

"Ugh!" He groaned, then died instantly. She vanished and reappeared behind Mason, who was concentrating on the gardens through his 3-D binoculars. After getting tired of the same scenery, he turned around and noticed a pale woman standing before him with an intimidating, sharp smile. He froze at the first sight of her presence.

"Uh…"

Symphony jabbed her long claws inside his stomach and jammed her hand through his back. She reversed her arm—feeling his organs and spine—then vanished again.

Mason stood there woozy.

Jason walked toward him, unaware that one of his own was quietly dying. "I need you to—" He noticed blood oozing from Mason's insides and his intestines drooped to the floor. Jason's throat went dry. "Lotus!" he yelled. "Man down!" Mason fell and Jason caught him in his arms. He gently brought him down but held his head on his lap.

"Sir!" Bodhi called to Jason.

"What?"

"Migackt jumped off the building, another one of ours had his neck snapped, and Hyuna's face got slashed." Bodhi examined the roof. Already, four people had been killed, but no one can catch where the attacks are coming from. "Sir, what do we do?"

"NO!!" someone shouted.

"What the fuck is going on?!" Jason screamed.

"Another person jumped," Sergeant Lotus yelled. "Someone is controlling our people."

Suddenly, a small woman with brown hair from Faction Abyss was half naked and was hauling ass to the edge of the castle.

"Shit!" Bodhi screamed. He sprinted to her, hoping to save her from an unintentional suicide. As he was drawing near, she stopped. Bodhi felt relieved. "Thank god."

But then, a hand appeared from below and grabbed her by her foot.

"No, no, no, no…" Bodhi hurried to get to her. However, she was chucked over the castle gate like a boomerang. "Holy shit!" She flew through the air like a crazed crow until you could see her no more.

Suddenly, a pale demon was flying overhead. Bodhi turned to run away, but the man quickly overshadowed him. Bodhi felt a huge weight topple over his back. Both men fell.

"Ah!" Bodhi screamed. He covered his head, hoping to avoid the pale man's sharpened claws and elongated fangs. "Fuck, fuck, fuck!"

"Get off him!"

The pale demon was shoved off.

Bodhi glanced over and witnessed Ariel stabbing Mercury through his mouth. *Argh!* She kicked him off her dagger.

Bodhi returned to his feet. "Thanks."

"Not now," Ariel scolded. "Fight first. Talk later!" She tossed him a wooden staff with three spiked chains attached. It looked similar to the one he had trained with before.

Dozens of pale demons were now ambushing all sides of the castle. "The wall won't stop them," Bodhi told himself. "But a Death Dealer will." He swung the spears, overcoming his fear of fighting with armaments. He was an assassin and was never prouder.

"Assassins!" Sergeant Lotus shouted. "Kill them all!" The assassins roared, waving their weapons in the air as their loyalty and hearts raised.

Jason looked at Mason's lifeless face. He shut his eyelids and laid him on the floor. He stood up and whipped out his pocket knife. "I'm stabbing all you mother fuckers to death."

Seraphina lifted her sword and sliced at a pale demon's face. He winced but immediately his wounded skin repaired itself. She took out the blunt sai and charged for his neck. It cut him—barely. With all her might, she chucked the moonlit mercury weapon across his throat. He fidgeted but it hardly seemed to cause any damage.

"Zaire!" Seraphina yelled.

The ice-cold man growled and leaned in for a quick attack. Suddenly, an arrow latched onto his eye. *Argh!* He struggled with the pain clinging onto his eye. The little bit of moonlit mercury wasn't enough to kill of the bastard but at least it was stalling his execution. Seraphina snuck over to him and shoved the sai into his back. The man screeched and swung back with the arrow still intact. She ducked. Zaire shot another arrow and it struck him through his cheek.

Seraphina perked up and handed the pale man a hard-earned uppercut. *BAM!* The sai struck his throat and she held onto it for dear life. Zaire ran behind the monster and plunged his body into the sai while Seraphina cut through it. It was a difficult yet successful process. With enough force, the duo managed to kill the pale scum.

"Fuck!" Seraphina scoffed. "These weapons are shit!"

Zaire agreed. "We have to fight our asses off tonight."

Suddenly, a pair of pale ones were charging at them. Seraphina pulled her longsword overhead while Zaire reached for more ammo. Then out of nowhere, Sergeant Lotus jumped in front of them. He aimed his machine-gun right at their white, skeletal faces. "Run!" He ordered. His finger was heavy on the trigger and bullets stormed out. *Bam, bam, bam!* It restricted them from getting a hold of Seraphina and Zaire, and they pursued to escape. Kurtis fired until his round expired. As soon as he heard the final bullet pop, he pulled out his trusty magnum, targeting their face and chest. *Bam, bam, bam!* One of them fell over but the other was pulling through.

Kurtis reloaded his magnum. He got up close to the enemy and shot through his skull. The demon fought viciously, but Lotus kept hurling his way through his brain. The man wailed so loud, it made Kurtis' eardrums want to explode. Once the gun emptied, Kurtis started punching the life out of the pale one. *Jab! Jab!*

Someone surprised him from behind. *Aaahh!* A woman cried. She wrapped her arms around Kurtis' neck and her long hair obscured his vision. He fought to get her off but she held on tight. He slammed his head back, knocking her upside her chin.

When she flew back, Sying came up from behind. He grabbed her by the head and began trying to pry her off his ally. She was strong, despite her tiny form. Sying plunged his elbow into her nose, feeling a solid crack! *Aaahh!* She loosened her grip and Sying was able to drag her across the floor and slide her in between his legs. He placed a foot on top of her palm to hold her in place. He reached over for his longsword, popped his wrist and began sawing through her shoulder. The small woman howled and scratched at his leg but Sying fought through the pain of her dagger-like nails.

Sergeant Tulip appeared and immediately tugged the woman's free arm and stretched it as far as she could. She plunged her sickle sword into her wrist and took control of her position. Sying continued to slice away, even when the blood splattered all over his face. It was tough, but eventually he managed to cut his way through. He kicked away her arm and climbed over her face.

Aurora pulled the sickle sword back. The woman howled in grave pain but she was still managing to put up a fight. Aurora pulled the sword forward, then, back, then, forward, then back, like a charging pendulum across the screeching woman's wrist. "Just. Fucking. DIE!" After a few more strokes, Aurora heard the brash screech of the pavement. She and her husband backed up and, to their surprise, the pale demon was still squirming.

Ariel made a surprise appearance and asked them to move out of the way. She stood above the one-armed demon and, without a second thought, stabbed Mercury inside the woman's torso. She sliced left. *Hi-yah!* Then sliced right. *Ah!* She split the woman's body in two and finally, her life was no more.

"Where's Jason?" Ariel asked them. Neither of them knew. They all started searching for the captain. Luckily, Ariel spotted him but he was fighting a man twice his size "I gotta go!" she told them and hurried over to aid her best friend.

Jason kept combating the giant but he only laughed at Jason's pathetic punches. Jason jumped up and plowed both his feet into the man's hard chest but it only sent Jason falling on his ass.

Haha! The giant lunged for him but Jason pulled out his shot gun and fired at his heart. He swerved back but unnaturally squeezed the bullet out of his body using his pecks. Jason fired, repeatedly. A bullet hit his forearm and neck but each one was magically suckered out—like a strange magnetic repulsion.

Ariel jumped up with Mercury touching the sky. Once she got close enough to the enemy, Mercury decapitated him. He crumbled to the floor and his mutated head landed in between Jason's legs.

Ariel looked at Jason, concerned. "Are you okay?"

"I will be after this man's head is off my dick."

Ariel kicked him over Jason's leg and out of the way. "Sorry."

Suddenly, Ariel and Jason felt hot. They looked to the east and noticed two pale ones holding a tree trunk that had been lit up, like a gigantic match. The friends were afraid to move.

Other assassins were fleeing from the roaring flames. Slowly, Ariel and Jason walked backward, but there were more demons behind them, scrambling about, antagonizing the Death Dealers with terrorizing teeth and ungodly, self-healing skin.

A blink later, Ariel's mother appeared in front of the burning log.

Ariel was enraged and gripped onto Mercury so tight, her skin burned from the pressure. Her teeth clenched like gears and her veins etched along her skin. Jason was more than pissed off and wanted nothing more than to slice that woman's head in two.

"What do we have here?" Symphony smiled.

Ariel watched her closely. "You might as well give up, Nefertiti. You'll only lose."

Symphony laughed and offered a round of applause. "Do you not see what's before you?" She stretched out her arms. "Who's losing, my child?"

Ariel pointed Mercury at Symphony's throat. She looked around and, to her astonishment, she noticed most of the Death Dealers were…dead. Ariel was raised to believe that they would always succeed. But tonight, the castle's roof was covered in Death Dealer flesh.

"Oh, my god," Ariel cried.

Symphony took a step closer to her, feigning pity, but Ariel immediately shoved Mercury in her face. "Look closely, my child," purred Symphony. "Notice what happens when a pale demon touches a petty human in the light of the moon."

Jason shook Ariel's shoulder. "Check it out."

Ariel nervously turned around. Suddenly, the once-dead assassins began to awaken from their slumber. Ariel zoomed in on Hyuna, who was stone-still, facing one of the towers. She called out to her. "Hyuna!"

Hyuna looped her head around and met Ariel's gaze. Like her parents, Hyuna had one distinct feature—silver eyes. Ariel's heart drummed against her chest—almost shooting out—as she witnessed Hyuna's skin lose its healthy complexion and gradually transform into a snowy veil of the dead. *Are they pale demons?!* Ariel thought.

"What have you done?" Jason asked Symphony.

"We've only done what we have to." The reborn assassins rose from the floor. "We must save our people." They cracked their necks, stretched out their fingers, and widened their mouths into ghastly shapes, feeling their newborn souls through the exhalations of their breath. "This…is our evolution."

Symphony disappeared and the fiery tree trunk flew toward Ariel and Jason. Ariel pushed Jason out of the way while she jumped in the opposite direction.

BAM! Zaire was taken down by a burning log.

"Arrrgh!" Zaire howled. "Get this off of me!" The fire was penetrating its way through Zaire's clothes and dancing around his cheeks. If the wind grew stronger, the flames could eat through the layers of his skin.

Ariel felt woozy but forced herself up after hearing Zaire's cry for help. She wobbled her way over to him. "Someone help!" she screamed. "I need a hand!"

Daoka ran up to them. "I got a little something."

"Hurry!" Ariel ordered.

"Hold on!" Daoka yelled back. She closed her eyes and brought her hands together.

"What the fuck are you doing?" Ariel feared for Zaire's life. She refused to let him die, especially when he hated her guts. They were great friends once, and even if he refused to speak to her for the remainder of his life, it was okay, because he could never take the good memoires away. Little Velvet would keep them locked in her heart, forever.

Daoka lifted her hands and the log lifted from Zaire's scorching body and floated in the air. Ariel held back while Daoka was working her magic. Daoka stretched her arms out and the tree trunk obeyed her mental command. "If it's over your head, move! I cannot hold this thing for that much longer!"

Ariel offered a hand to help him up. Zaire, without question, took it. Once he escaped, Daoka released the magic within her and the fiery trunk plopped back down. "Holy moly, that took a lot of energy!"

"That was amazing!" Zaire cheered.

"I know," Daoka smirked, and then skipped away.

Ariel shook her head. "She is so strange."

Zaire screamed, "DUCK!"

Ariel turned around and noticed Hyuna was lunging at her. Ariel fell to the floor and Hyuna unwillingly leaped over her. Quickly, Ariel swooped her leg around, making Hyuna lose balance. Hyuna fell flat but didn't stay down for long. She hopped back on her feet and Zaire smacked her right in the eye with the end of his crossbow.

Ariel tossed Mercury up in the air then threw it straight ahead. It spiraled and sang its way through the air. Zaire dodged in time but Hyuna was unlucky. *Argh!* Mercury landed in between her eye and cheek bone. Zaire paraded up to her, grabbed Mercury's quillion and slashed straight across.

Half of Hyuna's dead skull soared against the wind while the rest of the body slammed forward.

"Oh, my god," Zaire cried. "How could I... I can't believe...Shi—"

Ariel ran to him and held his head. "You did nothing wrong, you got that?" she assured him. "You did what you had to do."

Ariel brought him close to her chest. As she held him in her arms, she was viewing an unfair fight. So many Death Dealers were either dead or revived as pale terrorists. There was no way they could win this battle.

Ariel noticed Jason and Sying taking on two of Faction Abyss' former warriors. Sying looked like he wanted to cry, but he continued to brawl it out. Sergeant Tulip was killing one of Ariel's guild members while Sergeant Lotus was shooting his life away at one of the pale demon originals.

Bodhi was fighting valiantly, but soon enough his spiked weapon was broken into tiny fragments by a former assassin from Faction Divide. Once the moonlit mercury frizzled at the sight of the dead woman's bulging strike, Bodhi whisked out Elixia and blew the grey sand in her direction. The woman roared and swallowed the mercury infused Elixia. She coughed and gagged once the dusty particles hit her throat and the sensation from moonlit mercury burned so bad, she was actually clawing her own eyes out. Once Bodhi noticed this phenomenon, he sprinted over to an original pale one and threw the sand into his silver eyes like a chef seasoning his fried noodles. The man spun around and around, attacking his own windows to the world. He couldn't take the agony. It was too much.

Ivy was holding her own quite well until a tall woman punched her across the face. The hard strike caused her to fall. Bodhi fell on his back and slid over in Ivy's direction.

The cold demon lifted her arm to attack but Bodhi managed to toss Elixia in time. He covered Ivy's body while the woman screamed at the top of her lungs. *Argh!!!* Her trembling fingers dug their way past her corneas. Bodhi held onto Ivy—protecting her at all cost—hoping the howling would soon cease.

The weapons were useless and the pale demon army had grown in a matter of minutes. Is this what the New World would succumb to? A world full of demon trash and blood banks? Suddenly, Ariel's whole life as a Death Dealer felt pointless. What good was it to be a part of the DDAG if you could not save the lives of innocents?

Suddenly, a loud clamor resounded from inside the headquarters.

Ariel looked toward the chapel tower. The door flung open and to her surprise, Baptiste and Dior were standing at the entryway. Her eyes popped out.

"Zaire!" Ariel muttered. She pointed at the tower.

"How did they get here?" Zaire asked, shocked.

"Ariel!" Baptiste called out. He ran to her with Dior by his side.

"What are you doing here?" Ariel asked. "You shouldn't be here!"

Baptiste had a brown satchel with him. He poked around inside and whipped out a nice, firm, and solid moonlit mercury dagger. "This is for you."

Ariel excitedly took it. It was completely identical to Mercury—the same silver body and emerald quillion. It looked just as gorgeous and felt just as strong.

"How did you—"

"We'll answer questions later."

A loud ruckus came from beyond the walls. A whole tribe of Rural Outsiders ran outside, each of them carrying their own moonlit mercury weapons.

Quickly, the tribesmen handed the assassins new weapons. Instead of going back home, the men and women of District Antarctica teamed up with the Death Dealer Alliance Guild and joined in on the fight. A duo of women ran to the fiery branch and wiped out the roaring flames by controlling the movements of the wind.

Ariel and Zaire regained the confidence they needed to slaughter some demon guts.

Now, it was the Death Dealers' time to shine, and thanks to the Rural Outsiders, maybe they had a shot at minimizing the pale army.

One-by-one the demons began to fluster. Originally, they had the advantage of immortality, but now the good guys held moonlit mercury—the pale demons' one weakness, the single core element that may be able destroy their entire species.

Once the Death Dealers held the most pure weapons of all time, the pale ones were suddenly falling….

Ariel killed off two at a time with one dagger for each of their hearts, while Jason's brilliant blade jabbed through a cold demon's flesh like gelatin.

Sying's spear was easy to maneuver. He and his wife, Aurora—with her moonlit mercury scythe—killed off three in less than a minute.

Sergeant Lotus' bullets were now worth every shot. They plowed straight through their brains easily.

The war seemed to finally shift for the better.

Ariel sliced a pale demon in half when she noticed a man standing in a corner. She realized it was Leon. She marched her way over at warp speed but suddenly felt a pulse of pain shoot through her temples and weigh down her body.

Stay back....

"Get out of my head!" Ariel screamed, battling her father's control.

Get down!

Argh! Ariel fell to her knees. "Let me go!"

Ugh! Ariel plopped over once she was released from Leon's horrible manipulation. However, the noisy brawl horrifyingly began to soften into eerie quiet. She nervously perked her head up and saw a swarm of pale terrorists circling around Leon. Symphony stood alongside him with a face brooding pure hatred.

"Hey," a voice called out.

Ivy was calling Ariel. "Huh?"

There was a horrid smile plastered on Ivy's face. Ariel worried she may be under Leon's control.

"You see me, right?" Ivy asked her.

Ariel glared at Leon. "You better not be in her head."

"Remember how you said, we weren't together?" Ivy asked.

Ariel knew this wasn't the real Ivy speaking but there was an undeniable connection to her deepest and truest feelings.

"I know you wanted to be, but you were too afraid of commitment. You need to learn how to love. Maybe you're just too selfish to love." Ivy turned her head slightly.

Is he speaking through her?!

"Let her go," Ariel begged Leon. Symphony softly cackled. "Take me! Please!"

"You're too important," Ivy praised. "You are the key to an evolution. One day, the fourth generation of our people will be born and you will be the reason why."

"Stop!" Ariel bawled. "Let. Her. Go!!"

Ivy pulled out her snake sword.

"What are you doing?!" Ariel trembled. "Ivy, fight this!" She ran for her. She wanted to stop this madness.

Ivy aimed the sword right at her chest.

"No!" Ariel was getting close. All she had to do was reach out and get the weapon away from her.

"Evolution begins in Seoul." In one quick move, Ivy stabbed herself right in the center of her heart. Immediately she dropped to her knees, hunched forward, and slid all the way down the sword's body, painting it in red.

"Aaaahhh!!!" Ariel screamed. "No!" She stumbled to the floor and crawled over to Ivy's dangling corpse. Her hands fidgeted over Ivy's cheeks. She shook her head, as if that would somehow bring her back to life.

"I'm sorry," Ariel cried, holding her close. She kissed her forehead and gritted her teeth. She didn't want to believe this was real. Why did Ivy have to die that way? She was a good person! This was all her fault. "Ivy, come back to me!! You gotta come back!"

Leon and Symphony didn't want to stay a minute longer. *We'll be back....*

They gathered their pack and jumped off the edge of the castle. And just like that, they were all gone. In a single wave, the pale demon army fled from the castle, leaving the war behind.

Jason and the others were speechless. None of them could take in their loss. That day would go down in history as one of the New World's greatest tragedies. It was the first time ever that the Death Dealer Alliance Guild had been so greatly defeated. It would forever be known as the day the DDAG could not stop an evolution.

SPRING IS HERE

The following morning warmed up. It felt twenty degrees hotter than the night of the battle. But even though the sky held a majestic sun and there was not a cloud in sight—only a crisp blue ceiling—the entire world felt sad.

Ariel and a few other Death Dealers survived the night—barely. Ariel managed to gain some battle scars but escaped without any serious injuries. She looked over her fallen comrades, feeling responsible for their deaths. She felt like running away, going back home and hiding underneath the covers forever. However, she had to face harsh reality, the results of the battle between Death Dealers and pale demons. That night would be jotted down as a tragic loss.

Baptiste asked Ariel if she were alright. "I'm alive," she said, while overlooking Hyuna—originally a Death Dealer—a human turned evil—and one whom she and Zaire decapitated.

For years, Ariel dreamt of becoming a professional assassin and purging the New World of the terrorists that roamed within her. However, she'd never imagined slaughtering one of her own. Yes, she may have turned into a pale one unintentionally, but that didn't make killing Hyuna less difficult. Not only was there an Innocent Lives Saved Record at the DDAG, there was also a Terrorists Killed Record. Ariel always looked forward to adding another mark to her tally, but things changed. She didn't mind adding some more pale flesh to her score, but to write down Hyuna's name…was not something she'd like to remember.

Mostly everyone was in the courtyard, saying personal, intimate goodbyes to the fallen soldiers. It was row after row of sadness, with faction-colored sheets covering the corpses of dead assassins lying in the thick, green grass. The king and queen showed up to pay their respects to all who had sacrificed their lives for the good of the New World. Taking their time, they would hover over a hero who died in the heat of battle, close the fallen warrior's eyes, cross their arms over their chests, then softly whisper a Lord of Life Prayer:

May the Lord of Life welcome you and bless you with all his light and love.
Please look down upon us all, and protect us from the sky above.

Kora pressed her soft nude lips over Mason's forehead. Once she returned to her small feet, she noticed Ariel leaning against a full-bodied camphor tree speaking with the Rural Tribe leader.

"I'll be right back," Kora told Sebastian. He insisted for her to take her time. Sebastian heard whimpers coming from behind a rosebush. The king noticed Bodhi crying and he hid his face in between his legs. Sebastian headed over to the weeping warrior while Kora walked over to Ariel and Baptiste.

Baptiste was in awe as he gazed upon Kora's magnificent beauty. He found her to be exceedingly beautiful, but meeting a queen is what triggered his nerves. He never had the privilege to meet someone in royalty. He took off his hat to show respect and bowed to her, sitting on one knee and looking down at the green grass covered in red drops from fallen fighters.

"You may stand, Rural Outsider," Kora insisted softly. Baptiste stood up and nervously clung onto his hat. Dior waltzed over to join them. She bowed. "Are you Baptiste and Dior?"

"Yes," they said together.

Kora looked at them with perpetual gratitude. "I would like to personally thank you both for your hard work on the weapons my guilds desperately needed."

"You're welcome, my queen." Baptiste bowed his flushed head.

"Ariel had told me so much about you both. You and your tribe have got to be the bravest people in the whole world."

Dior gushed. "Well, we're no Death Dealers." She clung onto to her adorable husband's arm.

"You're not," Kora interrupted, making the olden couple feel silly. "But they are trained to save innocents and fight for justice. It's in their soul to right the wrongs, arrest the crummiest criminal, slaughter rapists and fight off those sick fucks who try to bring back the Black Plague II Infections."

Ariel smirked at Kora's bad-assery.

"You all, on the other hand, traveled to another district—which no other tribe has done before. You created powerful weapons and brought them straight to us. And instead of turning back, you all fought alongside professional assassins with everything in you, not realizing what you were up against. That is courageous and honorable. My king and I cannot express enough gratitude."

Kora spread her arms wide and embraced them both in a pleasant hug.

Ariel stood there, silent, allowing her father's friends a moment of glory.

"Thank you again." Kora noticed Ariel biting her tongue and kicking a random stone. "What is it?"

Ariel huffed. "Does the royal cabinet know what happened today?"

Kora looked out into the forest, admiring the Lord of Life's natural gifts. Despite the nastiness of crazed humans and pale demons, the New World managed to remain beautiful. She took off a brown sandal and pressed her toe into the warm lake. "They do…and they're not happy."

Ariel stood beside her queen and embraced the glorious scenery; although it was a hot and mournful day, the view was exquisite. The sky was bright blue like Seoul's ocean and greenery expanded all the way to the outskirts of Seoul. Ariel caught the sound of ripples from the small lake. She looked down and enjoyed the view of a few koi fish merrily catching flies. It would've been a great day for some weapons training and running, but there was nothing to be happy about.

"They're sad because many have died? They should be." Ariel rambled.

"You know what I'm referring to."

Ariel could see Kora staring at her in her periphery, but she refused to look her queen in the eye when she was mad. The stubbornness of the royal cabinet members gritted at her nerves like Cyclamen's gut-wrenching cologne. "They're the ones that fucked us over with pathetic weapons. I've had fruit slicers more deadly than the crap their so-called alchemists and sorcerers made. Even after all we've been through, they are crying that the Rural Outsiders helped us? That's—"

"I know," Kora breathed. She brushed her soft fingers against the back of Ariel's neck. "But we both knew if they found out, there would be consequences."

"So, what do we do?"

Kora sighed as she looked upon someone who resembled her young self—a beautiful young woman who was fearless, prideful and sometimes selfish, but carried a big heart and a passion for saving the weak. "There's nothing we can do except face them."

"Great. They'll probably ban the Rural Tribe from ever stepping foot on DDAG land. And what about me? They'll probably kick me out of the DDAG completely because I got them involved. None of this is their fault. It's mine!"

Dior rushed over to Ariel. "Child, we are not the type to do things without reason. We knew we had to help. Innocent lives were at stake and pure moonlit mercury weapons were the answer for survival. If we never would have come, who knows what could've happened."

Ariel fell silent and imaged the possibilities—including her own death. "Do you know if the royal cabinet has planned anything?" she asked her queen.

"The outsiders will be forced to attend a Royal Cabinet hearing and all twelve members have not failed to admit their rambunctious excitement about my term as queen coming to an end…." Kora trailed off. "But I will defend the outsiders through all costs. I hoped to be their personal attorney on this case. However, that is considered a conflict of interest. So, I'm forced to just to be a witness, but I plan to attend all hearings and make sure they have a fair trial. It's going to be rough, that's certain, but as long as they have support from us all, they'll be okay."

"What happens if they lose?" Ariel asked, concerned. "Will they be locked behind bars?" She paused. "Will you?"

"I don't know," Kora admitted. "The outsiders could be placed in prison for a couple of years, or worse: sentenced to death—but I doubt the sentence would go that far. After all, they intervened to help save lives, not kill them. The cabinet must realize that and they will. As for me, they don't know much. All they know is, I didn't care to stop the outsiders from helping. I plan to admit my involvement, but I do not fear their judgement. Even when I was just a lawyer, the Royal Cabinet never scared me."

Baptiste flayed his arms about. "Well, we'll just worry about all that later," he persisted. "What about Leon's daughter?" Baptiste asked his queen. "What will become of his little girl?"

Little girl, Ariel thought. *I am nobody's little girl anymore.*

"She may get in trouble for insubordination, but she definitely won't get kicked out of the DDAG."

A pensive look crossed Ariel's face. "What makes you say that?"

Kora called Sebastian over. "There will be a small, royal ceremony tomorrow afternoon. Baptiste. Dior. I'd love for you all to join us." Kora assured. "You and your tribe won't have to worry about the tiring travel back home. I insist you all stay the night in our dormitories in District North America."

Dior's soul jumped. "Thank you, my queen."

"I don't understand," said Ariel.

Jason walked up to Ariel as a few Death Dealers murmured goodbyes. "How's it going?" he asked his best friend. He turned around and bowed. "Hello my king. My queen. Thank you for being here."

Sebastian hugged Jason. "Captain Lilly, on behalf of my queen and I, we'd like to thank you for keeping in touch with the Rural Tribes and being their guide."

"You?" Ariel said with gratification. She really had the best, best friend in the world. "Thanks. I didn't know you were helping them get here."

"It's not a big deal," Jason insisted. "I'm just glad they didn't get lost."

"Us too," Dior chimed in.

"I led them over here last night, but didn't tell anyone. I didn't want to get your hopes up. As of yesterday, we were still unsure about the weapons."

Ariel understood.

Once the group fell quiet, Ariel noticed the final body was being carried way in a gurney—his body cloaked in a black-and-red sheet to reflect his faction's colors.

Ariel felt she should be happy for surviving, but she wasn't. Especially now that the link to her demonic parents probably remains. Would they continue to visit her when she slept? Would the gruesome visions of their crimes return? Should she have died during the battle, so the pale colony would lose their "key" to a fourth generation of—whatever they are? She was uncertain, but oddly, for a moment, she regretted being alive. The war didn't feel over and it may be her fault.

"So, what's this ceremony?"

Jason shrugged. "What?"

"You'll find out tomorrow," said Kora as she checked the time. "For now, let's all go home and get some rest. Meet us at District North America's headquarters tomorrow at three. We'll speak then."

Before departing, the king dropped some final words. "My condolences again to all of you. I urge all of you to persevere. It's the only way."

It was the following afternoon and everyone—both DDAG factions and the Rural Tribe—traveled back to District North America and sat quietly in the keep of the headquarters.

Ariel sat hunched over a bench with her hair fallen over her face. Seraphina sat next to her and, briefly, they held hands. Before, it would've been frowned upon, but now, it was comforting and much needed for them both.

Seraphina looked at her with a solemn expression. "I'm sorry about Ivy."

Ivy!! It was painful for Ariel to think of her. It was too soon to hear her name out loud without Ariel's stomach tying in knots.

"Thanks," Ariel muttered. "Who told you about her and me?"

Seraphina nudged her head to the right. Ariel peered over her shoulder and saw Daoka— without the buns—talking to a dark man with black hair. "She's strangely attached to you."

"Yeah, I don't get it. She somehow found my dorm and would force me to chit-chat with her. She even put makeup on me once." Ariel was impressed. "She's a pain in the ass but I kind of like her." Ariel smiled, thankful for Daoka, Seraphina, and everyone else who fought alongside her. It was an oddly warm feeling.

Seraphina busied her eyes by looking around the room. Bodhi sat with Zaire, silently behind the ladies, staring deep into the floor. "I could actually see you two falling in love…or coming close to it. Well, from what I've heard."

Ariel shrugged. "Maybe. She was too good for me, honestly. I planned to maybe date her after the battle was over, but you know how I am with commitment and I probably would've messed it up anyway. Ivy was a sweet girl. And smart and—"

Seraphina noticed Ariel's eyes turning red. Zaire could hear her frigid breaths and he wrapped his arms around her shoulders from behind. Bodhi joined in to console his hero. They all fell silent as Ariel's soft whimpers whirred among them.

Meanwhile, Jason and Sergeant Lotus were walking toward the front of the podium. Sergeant Tulip and her husband, Sying, stood by on one side of the stage, holding each other.

Jason called Ariel up front and asked her to wait for their majesties. He was in tears but held a forced smile across his face. He looked sad—beaten, really. It was understandable, considering his guild had now downsized to less than half.

Ariel brought up her hand to console him. Jason gripped onto it, firmly. "It's alright," she told her best friend with the utmost sincerity. "We'll just have to work a little harder."

Jason locked eyes with his childhood companion, his grip still tight around her petite fingers. Ariel could feel his desperation to not let her go. She stretched her hand to release the tension but he refused to give. He was not hurting her. He just wanted her close.

Ariel could sense so much misery radiating from Jason. Then: "What do you mean you're going to miss me?!"

Jason looked around. "Huh?"

Ariel asked him again, and Jason felt uneasy. "I—I didn't say anything." *What the hell?* he thought.

Suddenly, a door opened and it created a small ruckus in the room. Everyone shot up to their feet with heads bowed as the king and queen strolled down the main aisle. They walked side-by-side with interlocked hands held up to Kora's prominent chin.

Once King Sebastian and Queen Kora reached their rightful thrones, the crowd returned to their seats and Ariel stood before them, motionless.

Then Sergeant Lotus marched forth to Ariel in his typical suit, tie and golden trapezoid belt buckle. He even had his hair trimmed so his presence was even more fresh. For once, when Ariel looked at him, she felt equal and valued instead of useless and problematic.

Lotus skimmed the room with hands behind his back and began to speak with sincerity: "Faction Divide and Faction Abyss, welcome. Today we meet to not only honor and remember the New World's fallen heroes, we are here to give thanks to everyone who was involved during last night's attacks, including the Rural Tribe of District Antarctica. May I have the Rural Outsiders stand."

They rose.

"DDAG, please give these brave men and women a round of applause."

The crowd clapped loudly and slowly there was a wave of standing ovations for the surprise attendance and wondrous bravery of the fearsome tribesmen and women. The outsiders were generously overwhelmed. One tribesman cried out, "Let's give a shout-out to Dior and Baptiste!"

The room roared so loudly, the pictures on the wall shivered. Once the cheering crowds began to hush, everyone sat back down and Lotus continued on. "I hate to be the bearer of more bad news, but unfortunately, the royal cabinet is appalled that we went against their word. However," he looked at his king and queen, "with all due respect, they can kiss our ass." He gazed back into the crowd and they all praised his brute honesty. "Dior and Baptiste, they may try to force you to feel guilty but the DDAG won't give in to their egoism. None of you are terrorists. Only true heroes."

He bounced his focus onto Ariel, who stood splendidly before him. "As for you, Ms. Rose." He brought his arms forward and showcased a bold blue box. He cracked it open to reveal a small, white satin pillow, atop which laid a pure, 48-karat rose gold pin with the official DDAG logo.

Ariel immensely shook her head, but Lotus wasn't allowing her refusal. "No, no, no…," she begged. "I can't. No."

"Ariel Rose," Lotus began. The king and queen stood up and Lotus removed the pin. It was fairly heavy and its polish glared in the sunlight.

Ariel looked back at Seraphina, who didn't seem distraught. *I can't accept this. What about Seraphina???*

"It is with great honor, as your DDAG sergeant, to promote you to second-in-command."

Everyone cheered except Ariel. She did not want this promotion—she didn't deserve this praise.

Lotus enclosed the pin above her left breast, below her collar bone. "You will be second-in-command to Captain Dahlia in District Europe."

What?! Ariel wanted to scream. She never wanted to work with another guild. Not now, not ever. Even when she was a little girl, her goal was to be united with Faction Divide—the greatest guild in New World history. Her friends exchanged looks at each other with mixed emotions.

Bodhi peered at Jason and mouthed, *Why?!*

Jason looked at him with teary eyes and shrugged, helpless.

Ariel's anxiety rose to improbable heights. "I, uh…."

"You deserve this," Sergeant Lotus hailed. He placed his hands over her arms and grinned at his rebellious redheaded assassin: a law-breaking Death Dealer who drove him mad, a woman whom he admired for her fearlessness and unstoppable ability.

Zaire was proud, even though he did not want to see his Little Velvet leave, and Seraphina shockingly admitted to her comrades she would kind of—sort of—miss her.

"Who am I going to bitch at now?" Seraphina huffed.

"You can bitch at me!" Bodhi chimed in, not realizing what spewed out of his mouth. Zaire patted his back and chuckled. Bodhi was confused. "What?"

"I…I don't know what to say." Ariel brushed her fingers over the smooth gold metal of the pin. It was now obvious why Jason felt miserable. They had never been separated before—not like this. Only during their DDAG training. How would they cope without each other?

Kora now spoke. "I know I had mentioned before that I would rather see you and Captain Lilly together. You both are the strongest Death Dealers the DDAG has right now. However, I feel that Ariel needs to grow in the DDAG and she'll reach her fullest potential as second-in-command to a whole new guild."

I guess, Ariel thought, and, *I don't want this.*

"We will go over the details of your training another day. For now, we will applaud you for all you've done."

Ariel tried to understand why Kora granted her a promotion, but it was still something she felt unworthy of. She only ever cared about being part of the Death Dealer Alliance Guild; it was never about fancy titles. It wasn't about making the rules. It was about taking care of innocents. Always had been.

After the king and queen spoke some final words, the small ceremony came to a close. Everyone ventured away, while Jason and Ariel walked to the front of the castle together.

A few people gave Ariel their congratulations and one—Bodhi—gripped onto her, hating to see her go.

"We'll keep in touch, big guy," Ariel giggled. "It's okay."

Seraphina and Zaire also added in a few kind words before saying goodbye.

"I'm going to miss you Little Velvet," Zaire said as he zoomed in on her flashy pin. "Just stay out of trouble."

"Like if that will ever happen," Seraphina sneered. Ariel glared at her. "I'm kidding. But you know it's true."

Ariel scoffed, mildly. "You're probably right."

"You are going to be one amazing commander." Zaire squeezed Ariel so tight, her shoulder blades popped. "Just behave!"

"I'm glad you don't hate me anymore," said Ariel.

Zaire messed with the top of her hair. "Don't piss me off again."

"As long as you don't mess with my hair again!" Ariel joked. She looked at Seraphina, who was standing with her arms crossed. Ariel opened her arms far and wide. "Come here!"

Seraphina rolled her eyes. "Fine."

Bodhi couldn't help but get excited. "Oh! That's so nice."

Ariel smiled. "Get in here!"

The four friends engaged in a long and warm group hug. Before the trio left, they all wished her nothing but luck in London.

After Ariel watched her friends leave the courtyard, she took off the pin for a moment to gaze upon its brilliant craftsmanship. "I'm going to fuck this up."

Ariel did not care for responsibility. Being a temporary trainer was annoying enough. Now, to help take charge of a whole new clan of Death Dealers seemed absurd and dull. There was going to be more paperwork involved. Yuck! *How am I going to pull this off?*

Jason snorted. "You might."

Ariel rolled her eyes.

"I'm joking. You'll be alright." Jason took the pin out of her hand and rubbed the solid gold. It was a pretty little thing, but the meaning behind it was infinitely important. He placed the pin back on her purple shirt. "I am going to miss you. Just remember where you came from."

"How could I forget?" Faction Divide was her home. No other faction could ever replace what Divide had given her. "I'll miss you more, loser."

The best friends heard a peculiar sound. They looked into the sky and noticed a massive bird. "That's not a crow," Ariel said, admiring its golden feathers. "What do you think it is?"

Jason had no clue, but he loved its extravagant stature. As it spread out its majestic wings, he wondered if the bird may be as tall as he was. It soared in the sky freely and carried a beckoning call. It was nature's music captivating the sky.

"I think it's called an 'eagle.'"

Jason scrunched his face. "I read about them. I thought the last one was killed centuries ago."

"Well, the historians may be wrong. They've been proven wrong before." *I wonder....* "What time is it in Seoul?"

Jason looked at his watch. "Close to 9:00 p.m. Why?"

"There's something I need to grab."

Ariel rushed off.

"Where are you going?" Jason called out.

"I'll be back!" Ariel promised. "Don't wait up!" She hurried over to the portal gate and called Rylan.

"Hello?" he answered.

"Meet me in Seoul. I'd like to take you somewhere."

Once she made it to the other side, she waited for Rylan outside of a big, black truck she borrowed from Faction Abyss.

Rylan arrived shortly after Ariel signed some papers to rent the truck for the night. He loved the sight of a pretty girl standing next to a pretty truck.

"That is a classic 2236 A.P. Guardian Vintage Truck! I've always wanted one of those bad boys!"

"Sexy," Ariel giggled.

Was she mocking him?! Rylan felt he had been slapped in the face. "What's so funny?"

"Nothing. I just never imagined a bookworm like you would ever be interested in a truck." Ariel tossed him the keys. "Go ahead and drive."

After she settled in the passenger seat, she pinched Rylan's cheeks and exclaimed, "You like trucks. That's hot."

Rylan blushed. "Thanks! Ummm…Whe-…where are we going?"

"I'll guide you. Don't worry."

Rylan stopped in front of a village of trees and got a little scared of what may be lurking about. "I've never been this far out in Seoul."

"It's dead outside the forest, but inside, it's beautiful. Don't worry. We don't have to move any farther than here." Ariel unlocked her seatbelt and hopped out of the truck with her backpack and a dead bird she had found on the side of the road.

"I still don't get why you grabbed the poor guy."

"I'll be back." Ariel carefully walked up to the boulder Jason and she had seen the night they discovered the pale demon colony. Ariel placed the dead bird on the tippy-top of the gigantic stone then stepped back.

Patiently she waited.

Rylan occasionally asked what was happening, but she would hush him up each time.

Finally, Ariel heard prominent footsteps from beyond the trail of pine trees. Her eyes grew wide with anticipation. Just as she hoped, the white animal appeared before her.

Yes! Ariel thought.

Gracefully, she ascended the boulder and laid down to eat.

Rylan wasn't expecting this. He was terrified of anything he didn't understand. "She better not bring that animal with us!"

Ariel waited silently until the white, furry creature devoured every morsel of its meal. Once she finished her pleasant supper, the gorgeous animal licked her long snout. She stood on her four muscular legs and tilted her head to one side. Slowly and carefully, Ariel tiptoed her way her, making sure to not frighten her by placing her hand out first.

The beauty licked Ariel's hand and wrist.

"You're a wolf," Ariel whispered. "I read about you when I would get tired of trying to figure out Korean." Ariel didn't know if a wolf could comprehend her language, but a sense kicked in that she could. "I didn't tell anyone because you were my little secret. You are so beautiful." She massaged the top of her fluffy head and her fingers bristled through her thick, soft fur. "Why don't you come home with me?"

Surprisingly, the wolf jumped from the boulder and stood next to her, waiting for her command. Ariel had a feeling they were going to be best friends.

Rylan noticed Ariel coming back with the white beast.

Fuck, fuck, fuck!! he thought.

Ariel opened the door, and the wolf jumped inside.

"Shiiiit!" Rylan screamed. "What the hell is that?"

Ariel settled herself in the passenger seat. "She's a wolf," Ariel said, stroking the beauty's strong body. Luckily, the truck was spacious and the three managed to fit comfortably inside. "I'm taking her home with me."

Rylan gulped. "Do—do you think the DDAG will allow her on their property?" His hands became sweaty over the steering wheel.

Ariel didn't care and she made that clear.

"Okay, well, I guess we should go now." His shaky hands turned on the engine.

Ariel smiled at the graceful wolf next to her and she looked deep into her golden eyes. "We shall."

Rylan reversed the truck and turned around back to headquarters.

The road in front of them was pitch-black like Ki's soul.

Rylan asked, "Do you have a name for her?"

Ariel hadn't thought about that. She wondered for a moment, trying to think of something epic. Her eyes gawked at the wolf's shiny white coat. "Wynter," Ariel whispered.

"What?" Rylan asked.

"Wynter," Ariel repeated. "Her fur reminds me of snow and snow happens in winter so Wynter it is. Winter with a 'y'."

Rylan kind of liked that idea. "That's pretty sweet."

Wynter sniffed his face and tickled Rylan's ear. He nervously chuckled. "Oh…ah…She's a curious lady."

Ariel laughed and fixated her eyes on the dark road. Her eyes became droopy from exhaustion and a sudden sense of comfort. Soon enough, she dozed off.

"Take this one to the lab," a man with a mouthpiece said dryly as he leered over Ariel. He had on a white cap and thick glasses, but Ariel couldn't see his face.

Horrific screams jarred out of her mouth and she could feel an unhealthy amount of drugs in her system—her head was woozy and her vision was hazy.

"What about her husband?" another voice asked. This time it was a woman.

Husband?! It wasn't Ariel. Who was she looking at? Whose body was she inhabiting?

The man walked over to another gurney and debated what to do with him.

When the fearful woman looked over, all she could see was the man's forearm.

"He may be useless to me." He called someone over. "Bring me another metamorphosis shot. Mark this as test two; if he fails again, we'll just get rid of him."

The man wailed and begged to be left alone, but no one was listening.

"Leave him alone!!!" the woman bawled. She struggled in her gurney, desperate to be released from its holstering straps. Her wrists felt like they were being lit under a flame the more she fought against the rough rope, but she could not escape. She could feel an indescribable power barricading her body, pressing her back down.

"Shut her up," the man said with a demonic tone.

"Stop! I want to see my baby girl," the woman sobbed. Someone hurried over and shoved a needle inside her neck. It hurt like hell and immediately, she became drowsy. "My little…"—her voice softened—"…girl. *Ariel.*"

"Shall we move them to the transformation ward?" the woman asked.

"Yes," the man said. "Tell Ki that he has one promising donation. As far as the other, we'll see. Has the car accident scene been constructed yet?"

"Yes sir. The falsified bodies have been placed."

The man nodded. "Good. Now, let's begin before Ezo checks up on us."

"Right away, sir."

The woman's eyes blackened until there was nothing left.

"AAAHHH!!" Ariel jumped from her seat, frightening Wynter.

Rylan was opening her door as she woke, but her scream startled him and he fell on his butt. They had just gotten back to headquarters, and luckily, he was no longer driving—or else there may have been an accident. "I—I didn't mean to scare you awake!" Rylan's glasses fogged up. He removed them and cleaned off the lenses.

"Shit!" Ariel spat.

"Are you okay?"

Ariel shook her head. "There was never any accident, and I blamed my father for everything. He did nothing wrong. They never died and came back to life. Ki was not working alone. Oh, my god… the horror they went through. Oh, my god!!"

Rylan slid his glasses back on and brushed off the pebbles imprinted on his black jeans. "What do you mean?"

"Ezo… who the fuck is Ezo?!!" Ariel took a moment to catch her breath.

"What's going on?!"

Ariel looked at Rylan with a frightened gaze. Under her breath, she muttered, "My parents…they never died in a car crash. They were experiments."

Ariel began hyperventilating. Her parents kidnap and death—was it all a ploy to lure her into a pale demon trap and evidentially transform into one of them? She could not stop panting at the possibility. Ariel knew she had to find answers. Even if the rest of her life was devoted to finding out why, she'd die trying to stop an evolution.

ABOUT THE AUTHOR

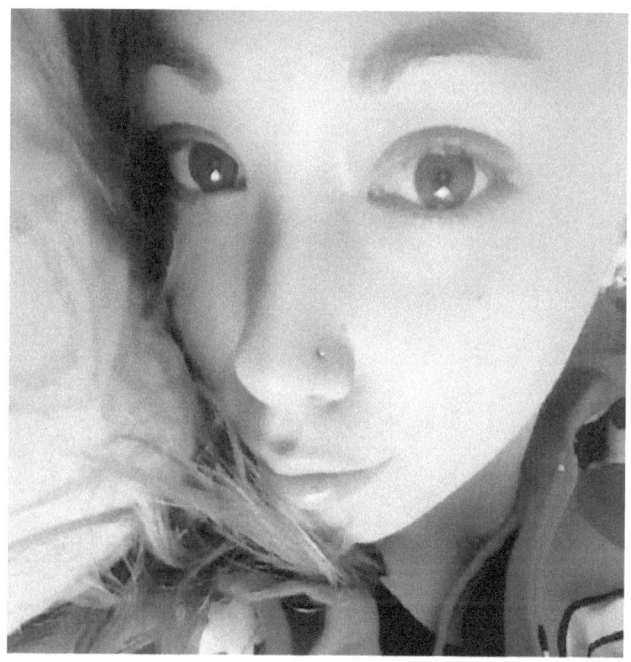

Lara Haughton is the author of the Moonlit Mercury series. This is her first book in a well-anticipated trilogy. She lives with her husband in Austin, TX, and has two spoiled dogs. Outside of writing she can be found munching on Hot Cheetos, sipping wine, or buying video games.

CONNECT WITH LARA AT:
Facebook: www.facebook.com/authorlarahaugton
Twitter: @lara_haughton
Instagram: @larahaughton

LARA HAUGHTON MERCHANDISE:
www.etsy.com/shop/larahaughton